Irish author **Abby G**  career in film and T a lot of standing in t to pursue her love of Mills & Boon with n one, and an author was born. She lives in Dublin, Ireland, and loves any excuse for distraction. Visit abby-green.com or email abbygreenauthor@gmail.com.

USA TODAY bestselling author **Trish Morey** just loves happy endings. Now that her four daughters are—mostly—grown and off her hands, having left the nest, Trish is rapidly working out that a real happy ending is when you downsize, end up alone with the guy you married and realise you still love him. There's a happy-ever-after right there. Or a happy new beginning! Trish loves to hear from her readers—you can email her at trish@trishmorey.com.

Discover more at millsandboon.co.uk.

AWAKENED BY THE SCARRED ITALIAN

ABBY GREEN

PRINCE'S VIRGIN IN VENICE

TRISH MOREY

MILLS & BOON

First Published in Great Britain 2019
by Mills & Boon, an imprint of HarperCollins*Publishers*
1 London Bridge Street, London, SE1 9GF

Awakened by the Scarred Italian © 2019 by Abby Green

Prince's Virgin in Venice © 2019 by Trish Morey

ISBN: 978-0-263-27352-6

MIX
Paper from
responsible sources
FSC
www.fsc.org
FSC® C007454

Printed and bound in Spain
by CPI, Barcelona

AWAKENED BY THE SCARRED ITALIAN

ABBY GREEN

This is for Sharon Kendrick, whose advice
I *should* have taken about two months before I did.

I got there in the end!

Thanks, Sharon!

CHAPTER ONE

LARA TEMPLETON WAS glad of the delicate black lace obscuring her vision and hiding her dry eyes from the sly looks of the crowd around the open grave. They might well suspect that she wasn't grieving the death of her husband, the not so Honourable Henry Winterborne, but she didn't want to give them the satisfaction of confirming it for themselves. So she kept herself hidden. Dressed in sober black from head to toe, as befitting a widow.

A grieving widow who had been left nothing by her husband. Who had, in fact, been little more than an indentured slave for the last three months. A detail this crowd of jackals would no doubt crow over if it ever became public knowledge.

Her husband had had good reason to leave her with nothing. She wouldn't have wanted his money anyway. It wasn't why she'd married him, no matter what people believed. And he hadn't left her anything because she hadn't given him what he wanted. *Herself.* It was her fault he'd ended up injured and in a wheelchair for the duration of their marriage.

No, it wasn't your fault. If he hadn't tried to—

Lara's churning thoughts skittered to a halt when she

realised that people were looking at her expectantly. The back of her neck prickled.

The priest gave a discreet cough and said, *sotto voce*, 'If you'd like to throw some soil on the coffin now, Mrs Winterborne…'

Lara flinched inwardly at the reference to her married name. The marriage had been a farce, and she'd only agreed to it because she'd been blackmailed into it by her uncle. She saw a trowel on the ground near the edge of the grave and, even though it was the last thing she wanted to do, because she felt like a hypocrite, she bent down and scooped up some earth before letting it fall onto the coffin. It made a hollow-sounding *thunk*.

For a moment she had the nonsensical notion that her husband might reach out from the grave and pull her in with him, and she almost stumbled forward into the empty space.

There was a gasp from the crowd and the priest caught her arm to steady her.

Unbelievable, thought the man standing nonchalantly against a tree nearby with his arms crossed over a broad chest. He fixed his gaze on the widow, but she didn't look his way once. She was too busy acting the part— practically throwing herself into the grave.

His mouth firmed, its sensual lines drawing into one hard flat one. He had to hand it to her. She played the part well, dressed in a black form-fitting dress that clung to her willowy graceful frame. Her distinctive blonde hair was tied back in a low bun and a small circular hat sat on her head with a gauzy veil obscuring her face. Oh, he had no doubt she was genuinely grieving…but not for her husband. For the fortune she hadn't been left.

The man's mouth curved up into a cruel smile. That

was the least Lara Winterborne, née Templeton, deserved.

The back of Lara's neck prickled again. But this time it prickled with heat. Awareness. Something she hadn't felt in a long time. She looked up, shaking off the strange sensation, relieved to see that people were moving away from the grave, talking in low tones. It was over.

A movement in the distance caught her eye and she saw the tall figure of a man, broad and powerful, walking away towards the cars. He wore a cap and what looked like a uniform. Just one of the drivers.

But something about his height and those broad shoulders snagged her attention…the way he walked with loose-limbed athleticism. More than her attention. For a fleeting moment she felt dizzy because he reminded her of… *No.* She shut down the thought immediately. It couldn't be him.

Snippets of nearby whispered conversation distracted Lara from the stranger, and as much as she tried to tune it out some words couldn't be unheard.

'Is it really true? She gets nothing?'

'Never should have married her…'

'She was only trying to save her reputation after almost marrying one of the world's most notorious playboys…'

That last comment cut far too close to her painful memories, but Lara had become adept at disregarding snide comments over the past two years. Contrary to what these people believed, she couldn't be more relieved that she'd been left with not a cent of Winterborne's fortune.

She would never have married him in a million years if she hadn't been faced with an impossible situation. A heinous betrayal by her uncle. Nevertheless, she wasn't such a monster that she couldn't feel some emotion for Winterborne's death. But mostly she felt empty. Weary. Tainted by association.

The grief she *did* feel was for something else entirely. Something that had been snatched away from her before it had ever had a chance to live and breathe. *Someone.* Someone she'd loved more than she'd ever thought it possible to love another human being. He'd been hurt and tortured because of her. He'd almost died. She'd had no choice but to do what she had to save him further pain and possibly worse.

Swallowing back the constriction in her throat, Lara finally turned away from the grave and started to walk towards where just a couple of cars remained. She wasn't paying for any of this. She couldn't afford it. As soon as she returned to the exclusive apartment she'd shared with her husband there would be staff waiting with her bags to escort her off the premises. Her husband had wanted to maintain the façade as far as the graveside. But now all bets were off. She was on her own.

She clamped down on the churning panic in her gut. She would deal with what to do and where to go when she had to.

That's in approximately half an hour, Lara!

She ignored the inner voice.

One of the funeral directors was standing by the back door of her car, holding it open. She saw the shadowy figure of the driver in the front seat. Once again she felt that prickle of recognition but she told herself she was being silly, superstitious. She was only thinking of *him* now because she was finally free of the burden that had been thrust upon her. But she couldn't allow her thoughts to go there.

She murmured her thanks as she sat into the back of the luxurious car. It was the last bit of decadence she'd experience for some time. Not that she cared. A long time ago, when she'd lost her parents and her older brother in a tragic accident, she'd learnt the hard way that nothing external mattered once you'd lost the people you loved most.

But clearly it hadn't been enough of a lesson to protect her from falling in love with—

The car started moving and Lara welcomed the distraction.

Not thinking of him now.

No matter how much a random stranger had reminded her of him.

Unable to stop her curiosity, though, she looked at the only part of the driver's face she could see in the rear-view mirror. It was half hidden by aviator-style sunglasses, but she could see a strong aquiline nose and firm top lip. A hard, defined jaw.

Her heart started to beat faster, even though rationally she knew it couldn't possibly be—

At that moment he seemed to sense her regard from the back and she saw his arm move before the privacy window slid up. Cutting her off.

For some reason Lara felt as if he'd put the window up as a rebuke. *Ridiculous.* He was just a driver! He'd probably assumed she wanted some privacy…

Still, the disquieting niggle wouldn't go away.

It got worse when she realised that while they were headed in the right direction, back to the Kensington apartment she'd shared with her husband, they weren't getting closer. They were veering off the main high street onto another street nearby, populated by tall, exclusive townhouses.

Lara had walked down this street nearly every day for two years, and had relished every second she wasn't in the oppressively claustrophobic apartment with her husband. But it wasn't her street. The driver must be mistaken.

As the car drew to a stop outside one of the houses Lara leant forward and tapped the window. For a moment nothing happened. She tapped again, and suddenly it slid down with a mechanical buzz.

The driver was still facing forward, his left hand on the wheel. For some reason Lara felt nervous. Yet she was on a familiar street with people passing by the car.

'Excuse me, we're not in the right place. I'm just around the corner, on Marley Street.'

Lara saw the man's jaw clench, and then he said, 'On the contrary, *cara*. We're in exactly the right place.'

That voice. *His voice.*

Lara's breath stopped in her throat and in the same moment the man took off the cap and removed his sunglasses and turned around to face her.

She wasn't sure how long she sat there, stupefied. In shock. Time ceased to exist as a linear thing.

His words from two years ago were still etched into her mind. *'You will regret this for the rest of your life, Lara. You belong to me.'*

And here he was to crow over her humiliation.

Ciro Sant'Angelo.

The fact that she'd said to him that day, *'I will regret nothing,'* was not a memory she relished. She'd regretted it every second since that day. But she'd been desperate, and she'd had no choice. He'd been brutalised and almost killed. And all because she'd had the temerity to meet him and fall in love, going against the very exacting plans her uncle had orchestrated on her behalf, unbeknownst to her.

If she was honest with herself, she'd dreamed of this moment. That Ciro would come for her. But the reality was almost too much to take in. She wasn't prepared. She would never be prepared for a man like Ciro Sant'Angelo. She hadn't been two years ago and she wasn't now.

Panic surged. She blindly reached for the door handle but it wouldn't open. She tried the other one. *Locked.* Breathless, she looked back at him and said, 'Open the doors, Ciro, this is crazy.'

But nothing happened. He responded with a sardonic twist of his mouth. 'Should I be flattered that you remember me, Lara?'

She might have laughed at that moment if she hadn't been so stunned. Ciro Sant'Angelo was not a man easily forgotten by anyone. Tall, broad and leanly muscular, he oozed charisma and authority. Add to that the stunning symmetry of a face dominated by deep-set dark eyes and a mouth sculpted for sin. A hard jaw and slightly hawkish profile cancelled out any prettiness.

He would have been perfection personified if it wasn't for the jagged white ridge of skin that ran from under his right eye to his jaw. She could only look at it now with sick horror as the knowledge sank into her gut: she was responsible for that brutal scar.

He angled the right side of his face towards her, a hard light in his eyes. 'Does it disgust you?'

She shook her head slowly. It didn't detract from his beauty, it added a savage element. Dangerous.

'Ciro...' Lara said faintly now, as the truth finally sank in, deep in her gut. This wasn't a dream or a mirage...or a nightmare. She shook her head. 'What are you doing here? What do you want?'

I want what's mine.

The words beat through Ciro Sant'Angelo's body like a Klaxon. His blood was up, boiling over.

Lara Templeton—*Winterborne*—was here. Within touching distance. After two long years. Years in which he'd tried and failed to excise her treacherous, beautiful face from his mind.

A face he needed to see now more than he needed to acknowledge her question. 'Take your hat off.'

Her bright blue eyes flashed behind the veil. He could see the slope of her cheek down to that delicate jaw and the mouth that had made him want to sin as soon as he'd laid eyes on it. Full and ripe. A sensual reminder that beneath her elegant and coolly blonde exterior she was all fire.

Her lips compressed for a second and then she lifted a trembling hand—*another nice dramatic touch*—and pulled off the hat and veil.

And even though Ciro had steeled himself to face her once again she took his breath away. She hadn't changed in two years. She was still a classic beauty. Finely etched eyebrows framing huge blue eyes ringed with long dark lashes… High cheekbones and a straight nose… And that mouth… Like a crushed rosebud. Promising decadence even as her eyes sent a message of innocence and naivety.

He'd fallen for it. Badly. Almost fatally.

'Not here,' he said curtly, angry with himself for letting Lara get to him on a level that he'd hoped to have under control. 'We'll talk inside.'

Inside where? Lara was about to ask, but Ciro was already out of the car and striding towards an intimidating townhouse. Her door was opened by a uniformed man—presumably the real driver?—and Lara didn't have much choice but to step out of the back of the car.

As she did, she noticed two or three intimidating-looking men in suits with earpieces. *Security.* Of course. Ciro had always been cavalier about his safety before, but she could imagine that after the kidnapping he'd changed.

The kidnapping.

A cold shiver went down her spine. Ciro Sant'Angelo had been kidnapped and brutally assaulted two years ago. Lara had been kidnapped with him, but she'd been released within hours. Dumped at the side of a road outside Florence. It had been the singularly most terrifying thing they'd ever experienced and *she'd* been the reason it had happened.

For a moment Lara hesitated at the bottom of the steps leading up to a porch and an open front door. She could see black and white tiles in the circular hallway. A grand-looking interior.

'Mr Sant'Angelo is waiting.'

One of the suited men was extending his arm towards the house. He looked civil enough, but she imagined it was a very superficial civility.

She went up the steps and through the door. A sleek-looking middle-aged woman approached her with a polite smile. 'Miss Templeton, welcome. Please let me take your things. Mr Sant'Angelo is waiting for you in the lounge.'

Numbly, Lara handed over her hat and bag, barely even noticing the use of her maiden name. She wore a light cape-style coat over her shift dress and she left it on, even though it was warm. She followed the woman, not liking the sensation that she was walking into the lion's den.

The sensation was only heightened when she saw the tall figure of Ciro, his back to her as he helped himself to a drink from a tray on the far side of the room.

'Would you like tea or coffee, Miss Templeton?'

Lara shook her head at the question from the woman and murmured, 'No, thanks.' The housekeeper left the room.

The muted sounds of London traffic could be heard through the huge windows. It was a palatial lounge, beautifully decorated in classic colours with massive paintings hanging on the walls. The paintings were abstract, and a vivid memory exploded into Lara's head of when Ciro had taken her to an art gallery in Florence, after hours.

They'd only just met a few days previously, and she'd been surprised enough at his choice of gallery to make him say with a mocking smile, 'You expected a rough Sicilian to have no taste?'

She'd blushed, because he'd exposed her for assuming that a very alpha Italian man would veer towards something more...classical, conservative.

She'd turned to him, still shy around him, wondering what on earth he was doing with her, a pale English arts student. 'You're not rough...not at all.'

He'd been like a sleek panther, oozing a very lethal sense of coiled sensual energy.

The gallery had been hushed and reverential. She could still remember the delicious knot of tension deep in her abdomen, and how she'd thought to herself, *How can I not fall in love with this man who opens art galleries especially for me and makes me feel more alive than I've ever felt?*

They hadn't even kissed at that stage...

Ciro's voice broke through her reverie. 'Would you like something stronger, Lara? Perhaps some brandy for the overwhelming grief you must be feeling?'

Lara's nerves were jangling. He'd turned to face her now, and she noticed that he'd taken off the jacket and wore dark trousers and a white shirt open at the throat. Her mouth went dry. She knew how he tasted there. She could still remember how she'd explored that hollow with her tongue—

Stop.

She ignored his question. 'How long have you lived here?' Had he been here all this time? Just seconds away from where she'd been existing so miserably?

Lara thought she saw Ciro's hand tighten on his glass, but put it down to her overwrought imagination. He said, 'I bought it months ago but the renovations have only just been completed.'

So he hadn't been living here. Somehow that thought comforted Lara. She didn't know if she could have borne being married to Winterborne while knowing Ciro was so close. Even the thought of seeing him with another woman coming out of this house made her insides clench. *Crazy.* She had no jurisdiction over this man. She never had. She'd been dreaming. Delusional.

She lifted her chin. 'I don't have time for this, Ciro... whatever it is that you want. I have to be somewhere.'

Evicted. She ignored the fresh spiking of panic.

Ciro lifted his tumbler of golden liquid and downed the lot in one go. For a second Lara wished she'd asked for a drink.

Then he said slowly, 'But that's just it, Lara. You don't have anywhere to go, do you?'

She actually felt the blood drain from her face. How could he possibly...?

'How can I know?'

He read her mind. Speared her with that dark gaze. Maybe she'd spoken out loud. She felt as if she were slipping under water, losing all sense of control.

He lifted a brow. 'The guests at the funeral were a hotbed of gossip, but I also have my contacts, who've informed me that Winterborne left everything to a distant relative and that as soon as you collect your things from the apartment, you're out on the streets. As for your trust fund—apparently you've blown through that too. Poor penniless Lara. You should have stayed with me. I'm worth three times as much as your dead husband and you wouldn't have had to put up with an old man in your bed for the past two years.'

Lara's head hurt to think of how he'd obtained all that information about her trust fund, and her insides churned at the mention of *old man*.

Any money left to her by her parents had been long gone before she'd ever had a chance to lay her hands on it. 'It was never about the money.'

Ciro's mouth tightened. 'No. It was about class.'

No, Lara thought, *it was about blackmail and co-ercion.*

But, yes, it had been about class too. Albeit not for her; she couldn't have cared less about class. She never had. Not that Ciro would ever believe her. Not after the way she'd convinced him otherwise.

She clamped her lips together, resisting the urge to defend herself when she knew it would be futile. She hardly knew this person in front of her, even though at one time she'd felt as if she'd known every atom of his being. He'd disabused her of that romantic notion two years ago. Yet, she couldn't deny the rapid and persistent spike in her pulse-rate ever since Ciro had revealed himself. Her body *knew* him.

Something caught her eye then, and she gasped. His right hand…the one holding the glass…was missing a little finger.

He saw where her gaze had gone. 'Not very pretty, eh?'

Lara felt sick. She remembered Ciro lying in that hospital bed, his head and half his face covered in bandages…his arms… She'd been too distraught to notice much else.

'They did that to you? The kidnappers?' Her voice was a thread.

He nodded. 'It amused them. They got bored, waiting for their orders.'

Lara realised that he was different. Harder. More intimidating. 'Why am I here, Ciro?'

'Because you betrayed me.' He carefully put down the glass on the silver tray. And then he looked at her. 'And I'm here to collect my due.'

My due. The words revolved sickeningly in Lara's head.

'I don't owe you anything.' The words felt cumbersome in her mouth.

Liar, whispered a voice.

'Yes, Lara you do. You walked out on me when I needed you most, leaving me at the mercy of the press, who had a field day reviving all the old stories about my family's links to the Mafia. Not only that, you left me without a bride.'

A spark of anger mixed with her guilt as she recalled the lurid headlines in the aftermath of the kidnapping and her subsequent engagement to Henry Winterborne. She focused on the anger.

'You only wanted to marry me to take advantage of my connections to a society that had refused you access.'

Ciro hadn't loved her. He'd wanted her because at first she'd intrigued him, with her naivety and innocence, and then because of her connections and her name.

Over the last two years, with the benefit of distance and hindsight, Lara had come to acknowledge how refreshing someone like her must have been for someone as jaded as him. She'd been so trusting. *Loving.*

If they had married it never would have lasted. Not beyond the point where her allure would have worn off and he would have become disenchanted with her innocence. Not beyond the point at which her name and connections would have served their purpose for his ambitions. Of that she had no doubt.

Of course he wasn't going to forgive her for taking all that away from him. He was out for revenge.

For a heady moment Lara imagined telling him exactly what had happened. How events had conspired to drive them apart. How her uncle had so cruelly manipulated her. She even opened her mouth—but then she remembered Ciro's caustic words. They resounded in her head as if he'd said them only moments ago.

'Don't delude yourself that I felt anything more for you than you felt for me, Lara. I wanted you, yes, but that was purely physical. More than all of that I wanted you because marrying you would have given me a stamp of respectability that money can't buy.'

Ciro's voice broke through the toxic memory as he said coolly, 'I prefer to think of it as a kind of debt repayment. You said you'd marry me and I'm holding you to that original commitment. I need a wife, and I've no intention of getting into messy emotional entanglements when you're so convenient.'

Lara's blood drained south. 'That's the most ridiculous thing I've ever heard.'

'Is it? Really? People have married for a lot less, Lara.'

She looked at him helplessly, torn between hating him for appearing like a magician to turn her world upside down and desperately wanting to defend herself. But she'd lost that chance when she'd informed him coldly that she'd never had any intention of going through with their marriage because she was already promised to someone else—someone eminently more suitable.

She'd told him that it had amused her to go along with his whirlwind proposal, just to see him make a fool of himself over a woman he could never hope to marry. She'd told him all her breathy words of love had been mere platitudes.

She'd never forget the look of pure loathing that had come over his face after she'd spoken those bilious words. That had been the moment when she'd realised how deluded she'd been. And on some level she'd been glad she was playing a role, that at least she knew how he'd really felt.

He was almost killed because of you.

Lara felt sick again. He hadn't deserved that just for not loving her. And he hadn't deserved her lies. He'd saved her from the kidnappers. He'd offered up his life for hers. And then she'd learned she'd never really been in danger. He didn't know that, though. And right now the thought of him ever finding that out made her break out in a cold sweat. However much he hated her already, he would despise her even more.

Suddenly a ball of emotion swelled inside her chest. Lara couldn't bear it that Ciro thought so badly of her, even if it *was* her fault that she'd convinced him so well. Seeing him again was ripping open a raw wound inside her, and before she knew what she was doing she took a step forward, words tumbling out of her mouth.

'Ciro, I *did* want to marry you—more than anything. But my uncle…he was crazy…he'd lost everything. He didn't want me to marry you—he saw you as unworthy of a Templeton. He forced me to say those awful things… They were all lies.'

Lara stopped abruptly and her words hung in the air. The atmosphere was thick with tension. Taut like a wire. Ciro was expressionless. She could remember a time when he'd used to look at her with such warmth and indulgence. And *love*, or so she'd thought. But it hadn't been love. It had been desire. Physical desire and the desire for success.

He lifted his hands and did a slow and deliberate hand-clap, the sound loud in the room. Lara flinched.

He shook his head. 'You really are something, Lara, you know that? But the victim act doesn't suit you and it's wasted on me. You really expect me to believe you were *coerced* into marrying a man old enough to be your father and rich enough to pay off the national debt of a small country? You forget I've seen your extensive repertoire of guises, and this innocent, earnest one is overdone and totally unnecessary.'

Her belly sank. She'd known it was futile to try. How could she explain how her uncle had manipulated and exploited her for his own gain since the moment he'd taken over her guardianship after her parents had died? The extent of his ruthlessness still shocked her, even now.

And she should recognise ruthlessness by now. She should have known Ciro hadn't been making idle threats two years ago. After all, he was Sicilian through every fibre of his being. He came from a long and bloody tradition of men who meted out revenge and punishment as a way of life, even if they had tried to distance themselves from all that in recent generations.

Ciro had told her once that his ancestors had been Moorish pirates and she could well believe it. She could see that he'd been wounded beyond redemption—not in his heart, because that had never been available to wound, but in his fierce Sicilian pride. Wounded when she'd walked away, and by the ruthless kidnappers when they'd physically altered him for ever and demonstrated that even he wasn't invincible.

She did owe him a debt. But it was a debt she couldn't afford to pay emotionally.

Lara's sense of self-preservation kicked in and she cursed herself for even trying to defend herself. She couldn't bear for him to find out just how vulnerable she really was—how nothing had really moved on for her since she'd known him. How the last two years of her life had been a kind of lonely torture.

She ruthlessly pushed aside all those memories and shrugged one shoulder minutely, affecting an air of boredom. She'd played this part once before—she could do it again.

'Well, it's been interesting to see you again, Ciro. But quite frankly you're even more pathetic now than you were two years ago, if this is how little you've moved on. What would you have done if Henry hadn't died? Kidnapped me? Seduced me away and then meted out your punishment?'

Lara's words fell like stinging barbs onto Ciro's skin.

They cut far too close to the bone. He had been keeping tabs on her. Getting reports on her whereabouts and her activities—which, as far as he could see, had consisted of not much at all. Not even socialising. Her husband had monopolised her attention, kept her all to himself.

Ciro hadn't articulated to himself exactly what he was going to do where Lara was concerned, but he'd known he had reached some kind of nadir when he'd bought this house, sight unseen, because it was around the corner from where she lived. He'd known that he was reaching a place where he simply could not go on without exacting retribution.

Without seeing her again.

He crushed that rogue thought.

In the past few months, as a restless tension had increased inside him, he'd found himself contemplating seducing Lara Winterborne. He'd told himself it would be to prove just how duplicitous she was. But he knew that his motivations were murkier than that. Embedded in a place he'd locked them away two years ago, when she'd morphed into a stranger in front of his very eyes.

When she'd shown him up as a fool who had cast aside his well-worn cynical shell in a fit of blind lust and something even more disturbing. *Emotion.* A yearning for a life he'd never known. For a woman who was pure and who would be faithful. Loving. Loyal. A good mother. Fantasies he'd never indulged in before he'd met Lara and she'd exposed a seam of vulnerability he'd never acknowledged before.

The fact that he'd even considered seducing her away from her husband was galling for a man who had always vowed to conduct his life with more integrity than his mother—never to stoop to her level of betrayal. And yet he'd had to face the unwelcome realisation that his desires were no less base than his weak and adulterous mother's.

Lara watched a series of expressions flicker across Ciro's face. They gradually got darker and darker, until he was glaring at her as if she was the sum of all evil. He started moving towards her then, all coiled lethal masculinity, and Lara took an involuntary step back.

She wasn't scared of his physicality—not even with this tension in the air. She was scared of something far more ambiguous and personal deep inside where she knew he had the ability to destroy her. Where he'd already destroyed her.

He stood in front of her, his scent winding around her like invisible captive threads. He asked with lethal softness, 'Are you suggesting my life has been on hold?'

Before she could respond, a sound halfway between a sneer and a laugh came out of Ciro's mouth.

'Oh, *cara,* my life hasn't been on hold for one second since you decided to take that old man into your bed.'

Lara winced inwardly. She already knew that Ciro's life hadn't been on hold. Far from it. As much as she'd tried to block him out of her consciousness, it had been next to impossible. Since his kidnapping he'd become even more infamous and sought-after. He'd tripled his fortune, extending the wildly successful Sant'Angelo Holdings, which had been mainly focused on real estate, to encompass logistics and shipping worldwide.

And he hadn't been seen with the same woman twice—which was some feat, considering the frequency with which he'd been photographed at every ubiquitous glamorous event on the European and the worldwide circuit.

The gossip about his hectic love-life had quickly eclipsed any rumours about why his wedding to Lara hadn't taken place. Most people had assumed exactly what her uncle had wanted them to assume—that the kidnapping and fresh stories of his links to the Mafia had scared off Lara Templeton, one of Britain's most eligible society heiresses.

If anything the tone of the gossip about her had been as sneering as about Ciro—especially when she'd got married so quickly after the event, to a man more than twice her age. It was as if she'd merely proved her own snobbishness. As if she hadn't been woman enough to handle Ciro Sant'Angelo.

Certainly all the women he had been photographed with since then had run to a type that was a million miles from Lara's cool blonde, blue-eyed looks. Women with flashing dark eyes and glossy hair. With unashamedly sexy and curvaceous bodies and an effortless sensuality that Lara could never hope to embody. She was too self-conscious. Too…inexperienced.

Ciro was shaking his head now, a look of disgust twisting his features and making his scar stand out even more. 'Did you keep up the virginal act with your husband? Or did you fake it right up until—?'

'Stop it!' The sharp cry of Lara's voice surprised even herself. She felt shaky. 'That wasn't an act.'

Ciro made a rude sound, dismissing her words. More proof that she'd been utterly naive to try and defend herself. All she could hope for was that Ciro would get bored and ask her to leave.

'Look, what do you want, Ciro?' Lara's voice had a distinctly desperate tone that she didn't even try to disguise now.

'It's very simple. I want *you*, Lara.' He folded his arms across his formidable chest. 'It's time to pay your debt.'

CHAPTER TWO

LARA'S SENSE OF panic and desperation increased. 'I told—you I don't owe you anything.'

Ciro responded, 'We've been through this and, yes, you do. You owe me a wedding.'

Lara fought to stay calm. To appear unmoved. 'Don't be ridiculous. I'm not going to marry you.'

He shook his head. 'Not ridiculous at all. Very practical, actually. Like I said, I'm in need of a wife, and as you deprived me of one so memorably two years ago, you can step up now and honour the commitment you made when you agreed to marry me in the first place.'

Vainly scrabbling around for something—anything to make sense of Ciro's crazy suggestion, Lara asked, 'Why do you need a wife so badly?'

'The circles I'm moving in… Let's just say things would be better for me if I had an appearance of stability. Settling down. Conforming to societal norms of what people expect of a man my age.'

'An appearance… So this would just be a sham…a fake marriage?'

'Call it a marriage of convenience.'

'But it'll mean nothing.'

Ciro's lip curled. 'As if *that* was a concern in your first marriage… As if you *cared* about Winterborne.'

Lara had to hide her flinch at that.

Ciro continued, 'It'll be a lesson in learning that your actions have consequences.'

She took a step backwards, surprised that her legs were still working. 'This is beyond crazy. If marriage is so important to your image then I'm sure there are many more suitable women who would be happy to become your wife.'

Like any of the hundreds of women she'd seen on his arm over the past twenty-four months, for a start.

'I don't want any of them. I want *you*.'

Ciro was finding it hard to maintain his composure. Lara was right—there were plenty of women he knew who would jump at the opportunity to become his wife. He'd found himself seeking out women who were the antithesis of this woman's cool blonde looks, but none of them had made his blood run hot as she could, just by standing in front of him.

For two years his bed had been lonely and he had been frustrated. Not that the world would believe it. But he hadn't wanted any of them. He wanted Lara. And now, after two years of a kind of purgatory, hating her and wanting her, she was finally within reach again.

He would be the first to admit that his pride had suffered a huge blow when she'd walked away from him and from their marriage commitment. He was, after all, descended from a long line of proud Sicilians.

She'd accused him of only wanting to marry her to further his ambitions for social acceptance and he hadn't been able to deny it. But it hadn't been as much to the forefront of his desire to marry her as he'd let her believe. However, he had to admit that it had always been in the back of his mind…her strategic connections.

But, more than that, he hadn't been done with her.

When she'd told him she was a virgin—most likely a lie—Ciro had been stunned. To think that she was untouched…a rare novelty in his jaded world, had been, surprisingly, and seriously, erotic. The prospect that he would be her first lover had tipped Ciro over the edge of his restraint where Lara was concerned.

He'd always been traditional and Sicilian enough to envisage taking an innocent wife some day, but also cynical and experienced enough to know that it was next to impossible in this modern world. And yet there had been Lara, with her huge innocent blue eyes that had looked at him sometimes as if he was a hungry wolf, and her body with its slender lines and lush curves, telling him that she was this rare thing. An innocent in a world of cynics.

She'd led him a merry dance. Convincing him that she had something he'd never seen before in his life: an intoxicating naivety. But it had all been an act. For her own amusement. Because she'd been bored. Or as jaded as him.

Lara stood in front of him now, tall in her heels, but she'd still only reach his shoulder. For a second something inside him faltered.

Had her eyes always been so blue and so huge? She was pale now, her cheeks and lips almost bloodless. Because she was disgusted by his proposal? Good.

Ciro had to forcibly curb the urge to clamp his hands around her face, angle it up towards him and plunder that mouth until she was flushed and her mouth was throbbing with blood.

No other woman had ever had the same effect on him. Instantaneous. Elemental. He vowed right then that she would never see how easily she pushed him to the edge of his control.

He took a step back. Lara had denied him before but she wouldn't deny him now. She owed him. Owed him her body and the connections a marriage to her would bring him.

'Well, Lara?'

'This is the day of my husband's funeral...have you no sense of decency?'

Ciro could have laughed at her dogged refusal to stop acting. 'Are you telling me you really *cared* about the old man?

The thought that she might actually be grieving for her husband slid into his mind for a second before he brutally quashed it. *Impossible.*

She flushed. With guilt. Ciro didn't like the rush of relief he felt. 'Save your energy, *cara*. Your acting skills are wasted on me.'

'Stop calling me that. I'm not your *cara*.'

Her hands were balled into fists by her sides and her eyes were bright blue.

Ciro uncrossed his arms. 'You never minded it before... If I remember correctly you used to love it.' He mimicked her breathless voice, *"'Ciro, what does it mean...? Am I really your* cara?'"

'That was before.' Lara's cheeks had lost their colour again.

'Yes,' Ciro said harshly, angry that he noticed so much about this woman. Every little tic. 'That was when you were only too happy to court infamy by becoming engaged to me to alleviate your boredom. What I can't quite understand, though, is the virginal act? That was a touch of authenticity that deprived us both of mutual pleasure.'

It was excruciating to Lara that Ciro remembered how ardently she'd loved him. How much she'd wanted him.

Without thinking about it, just needing to wound him as he was wounding her, she let words tumble out of her mouth. 'I never wanted you.'

As soon as she'd said the words she realised her mistake. Colour scored Ciro's cheekbones, making the scar stand out even more lividly. His eyes burned a dark brown, almost black. She was mesmerised by the fierce pride she could see in his expression. He was every inch the bristling Sicilian male now.

'Little liar,' he breathed. 'You wanted me as much as I wanted you. *More.*'

He came towards her, closing the gap. Lara's feet were frozen to the floor. He reached for her, hands wrapping around her waist, pulling her towards him, until she could feel the taut and unforgiving musculature of his body. But not even that could break her out of this dangerous stasis. She was filled with a kind of excitement she'd only ever felt with this man.

She'd thought she'd never feel it again, and something exultant was moving through her, washing aside all her reservations and the sane voices screaming at her to wake up. Pull back.

Ciro's hands tightened on her waist and his head came down, blocking out the room, blocking out everything but *him.* Lara's breath was caught in her throat, nerves tingling as she waited for that firm mouth to touch hers. It was so torturous she made a small sound of pleading…

Ciro heard the tiny sound come from Lara's mouth. He knew this was the moment when he should pull back. He'd already proved his point. She was practically begging him to kiss her… But his body wouldn't follow the dictates of his mind. She was like a quivering flame under his hands. So achingly familiar and yet utterly new.

He could feel the press of her high firm breasts, the flare of her hips, the cradle of her pelvis. He burned for her. He'd been such a fool to believe in her innocence. He'd held back from indulging in her treacherous body. But no longer.

Ciro gave in to the wild pulsing beat of desire in his body and claimed Lara's mouth with his. For a second he couldn't move—the physical sensation of his mouth on hers was too mind-blowing. And then hunger took over. He could feel her breath, sharp and choppy, and he deepened the kiss, taking it from chaste to sexual in seconds.

Lara was wrapped in Ciro's arms, and for a moment she happily gave up any attempt to bring back reality. His touch and his kiss, that masterful way he had of touching her and bringing her alive—she'd dreamed of this so often.

His taste was heady and all-consuming. She barely noticed his hands moving up her body, cupping her face so he could angle it better and take the kiss deeper, make it even more explicit. She craved him. Pressed herself even tighter against him.

The knot at the back of her head loosened and the sensation of her hair falling around her shoulders finally broke through enough for her to falter for a moment. And a moment was all she needed to allow enough air back into her oxygen-starved brain to recall what Ciro had called her. *Little liar.* And she'd just proved him right.

She stiffened and pushed against Ciro. He let her go and stood back, but it was no comfort. Lara already ached for him. The glitter of triumph in his eyes only added salt to the wound she'd opened.

She felt totally dishevelled and unsteady on her feet. Her cheeks were hot and her mouth felt swollen. She'd just humiliated herself spectacularly.

She lifted a shaking hand to her mouth. 'You had no right to—'

'To what?' he said silkily. 'To demonstrate that our chemistry is still very much mutual and alive?'

It wasn't much of a consolation that Ciro didn't look overly thrilled about that fact.

He shook his head, his dark hair gleaming. 'In this at least you can't hide your true nature.'

He started to walk around her and Lara's skin prickled. Her pulse was still pounding. She felt raw.

'How could you do it?' he asked from close behind her. 'How could you take that man into your bed every night and let him—?'

Lara whirled around, bile rising. 'Stop it! I won't discuss my dead husband. Not on the day of his funeral. It's…immoral.'

Ciro emitted a harsh bark of laughter. '*Immoral*, is it? More immoral than promising yourself to a man only to leave him by the wayside as soon as you realise how close you've come to sullying the perfect Templeton family line with a brood of half-Sicilians?'

Lara's heart squeezed painfully. At one time she had fantasised about the children she would have with Ciro, wondering if they'd inherit their father's dark good looks and vital charisma. The fantasy mocked her now. She'd been so deluded.

Her voice trembling slightly, she said, 'You accuse me of being immoral, but you admitted that your motive for marriage was nothing but a cold calculation to improve your social standing.'

Ciro stood back and his dark gaze narrowed on her. She immediately felt exposed.

'There was nothing immoral about seeking out a union that would benefit us both. You really didn't have to go so far as to feign feelings for me, *cara*. It was entertaining, but unnecessary.'

Lara smarted as she recalled yet again how naive she'd been. Because it wasn't as if he'd led her on—he hadn't professed any feelings for *her*. Instead she'd pathetically read too much into every tiny gesture and word, building up a very flimsy belief that he was falling for her too.

Ciro continued. 'Why didn't you try to secure your future by giving Winterborne an heir? Is that why he left you with nothing? Because you didn't fulfil your wifely duty?'

Lara shook her head to negate what he'd said. She couldn't seem to formulate words. Memories were rushing at her in a jangled kaleidoscope of images—Ciro proposing, down on one knee in the middle of a *piazza* in Florence, with everyone looking on and clapping, the pure joy she'd felt in that moment.

And then another memory—the awful dark, dank smell of fear as she'd been jostled in the back of that van with a hood over her head. Ciro's arms had been around her and she'd clung to him with a death grip…

'I don't… I never wanted to marry—'

'Me,' Ciro interjected. 'Yes, I know.'

Lara swallowed. He'd misunderstood her. She'd wanted to marry Ciro so desperately that she was afraid if she opened her mouth now it might all spill out and then he would tear her to shreds.

She couldn't imagine—didn't want to—what he would do if he ever found out that her uncle had been behind the kidnapping in an elaborate bid to show Lara the lengths to which he would go to ensure she married someone 'suitable'.

She had to regain control of this situation and of her fraying emotions. She injected all the *froideur* she could muster into her voice. 'You've proved your point, Ciro. You haven't forgiven me for leaving you. But if it's a wife you need I suggest you look elsewhere. I'm not available.'

She turned away to leave, but before she could take a step her arm was taken by a firm hand. She stopped, every part of her body tense against the inevitable effect Ciro had on her.

He drew her back around to face him. 'Please do tell me what it is you're so busy with now that you're a free woman again?'

He dropped her arm, but the imprint of his fingers lingered. She rubbed it distractedly. She looked at him, but the truth was that she was busy with nothing, because she literally *had* nothing—as he well knew.

She had just enough money in her account to see her through a week, maybe, in an inexpensive hostel. And that was it. She had nowhere to go. No one to go to.

The stark reality of just how isolated she was hit her like a body-blow.

'The fact is you're not busy—isn't that the truth, Lara?'

It was as if Ciro was delving casually into her mind and pulling out her innermost humiliation for inspection.

She tipped up her chin. 'I'll keep myself busy finding a job, somewhere to live.'

Ciro snorted. 'A *job*? You wouldn't know a job if it jumped up and bit you. I doubt an art history degree gets you very far these days. You were bred to fulfil a role in society, Lara. Anything else is beneath you.'

Hurt hit Lara squarely in the chest. She'd once confided in Ciro about wanting to do more than what was expected of her. No doubt he thought she'd been lying.

She lashed out. 'You mean like marrying you? We went through this once before—do you *really* want to be humiliated again, Ciro?'

This was the Lara that Ciro remembered. Showing her true haughty colours. He could recall only too easily how two years ago she'd morphed in front of his eyes into someone distant and calculating. Utterly without remorse.

It had shocked him. And yet it shouldn't have. Because it wasn't as if he hadn't already learnt how beautiful women operated at the hands of his brittle, self-absorbed mother. She'd made a fool of his father over and over again in her bid for desperate validation that she was desired.

His father had put up with it because he'd loved her, and Ciro had believed from an early age that if that was what love meant, he wanted none of its ritual humiliation.

And yet Lara had sneaked under his defences before he'd known what was happening.

His first image of her was still etched into his memory, no matter how much he'd tried to excise it. She'd been standing just a few steps from Ciro on a busy street in Florence, a hand up to her face, shading her eyes, seemingly entranced by an ornate building. She'd been like a vision of a Valkyrie princess against the ancient

Florentine backdrop. Long bright blonde hair falling to the middle of her back… Acres of pale skin…

She'd been oblivious to the attention she was drawing. *Or so Ciro had believed.* But now he knew she must have been aware of exactly what she was doing, with that face of an angel and the body of a siren.

Suddenly someone had jostled her from the pavement and she'd stumbled into the busy road. She would have been hit by a car if not for Ciro grabbing her and pulling her to safety. She'd landed against him, all soft lithe curves. Silky hair under his hands. And her scent… lemon and roses. Huge shocked blue eyes had stared up into his and he'd fallen into instant lust, for the first and only time in his life. Captivated.

But memories were for fools and he would never be such a fool again. He knew who—*what*—Lara was now. He would make use of her and then discard her, exactly as she had done with him when he'd literally been at his lowest point.

'You're really not in a position to bargain, Lara. You have nowhere to go and no one to turn to. You wouldn't survive half an hour outside that door.'

Lara clenched her hands into fists. The only thing stopping her making a vociferous defence was the fact that Ciro was speaking her fears out loud. What skills did she have? What meaningful education? Where would an interesting but useless degree get her in this new digital age? Some menial job in an art gallery if she was lucky? She could probably plan and host a diplomatic function for fifty people, but in reality domestic cleaners were more highly qualified than she was.

Taking advantage of her silence, Ciro said, 'This is what I'm proposing. We will get married in Rome, exactly as we planned two years ago. I think a year of marriage should suffice, but we can review it after six months. During our marriage you will perform social duties as my faithful and loyal wife. You will open doors for me that have remained resolutely shut. And once we agree to a divorce settlement I will make you a very rich woman.'

Lara was incredulous. 'You're serious.'

'Deadly.'

He looked at his watch then, as nonchalantly as if he hadn't just made such a preposterous suggestion. 'My driver will take you back to your apartment, where you will pack up your things, and then you will return here to me. We leave for Rome this evening.'

Lara's head was spinning. Too much had happened in such a short space of time. Her husband dying. Ciro reappearing in her life. His crazy proposal, which made a mockery of his first proposal. The prospect of having to learn how to survive on her own. And now the opportunity for something else entirely.

Something ridiculous. Gargantuan. *Impossible.*

And yet all she could think of to say was, 'Why did you pretend to be a driver?'

Ciro's jaw clenched. 'Because it amused me to see you in action among your peers. Behaving true to your nature. The nature you hid from me when we first met.'

Her chest ached. The woman she'd been when she'd met Ciro—that *had* been her. Infinitely naive and innocent. But she'd learnt many harsh lessons since then, and she had to protect herself around this man or he would annihilate her.

She said, with as much coolness as she could muster, 'This conversation is over, Ciro. You've played your little stunt but I'm not interested.'

He merely lifted a brow. 'We'll see.' He extended his

hand towards the door. 'My driver is ready to take you to the apartment, where he will wait for you outside.'

Without a word Lara turned and walked out. The woman who had shown her into the room was waiting with her things. Lara murmured a distracted thank you and went to the front door, where Ciro's car and driver were indeed waiting. Along with the security men.

Another shiver went down her spine as she recalled that awful moment when Ciro had gathered her in his arms to kiss her on that quiet Florentine side street and all hell had broken loose as they'd been ripped apart and then bundled into the back of a van...

She was tempted to ignore the car and walk around the corner to her apartment, but the driver was waiting with the door open and Lara's innate sense of politeness and a wish to not cause conflict made her get into the back of the vehicle. Also, although she was probably being paranoid, she could imagine Ciro standing at a window, silently commanding her to do as he'd bade.

The journey was short and she got out again only a couple of minutes later. She noticed that Ciro's security detail hadn't followed her to her apartment. *And why would they?* she scolded herself. She was nothing to Ciro except someone he wanted to toy with for his own amusement.

And revenge, whispered a voice.

She hurried inside, needing the time alone. To her relief the apartment was empty of staff. Her few meagre belongings were packed into two suitcases, which were standing neatly in the entrance hall. A reminder to leave as quickly and quietly as possible. But Lara needed time to process everything that had just happened.

She wandered around the apartment that had been like a prison to her in the past two years. She still couldn't quite believe the sequence of events that had led her to this place: marriage to an odious man old enough to be her father.

Of course she hadn't wanted to marry him. When her uncle had suggested it she'd laughed. But then he'd revealed to her that he'd been behind the kidnapping and that he would do worse to Ciro unless she married Henry Winterborne.

Lara sat down blindly on the end of the bed for a moment, overcome with the weight of the past.

Her uncle had been in debt to the tune of millions. His entire fortune gambled away. When she'd told him defiantly she didn't need him, that she had her trust fund, which was due to come to her on her twenty-fifth birthday, he'd told her that that was gone too. He'd had access to it, in order to manage it on her behalf, and he'd gambled it away.

Even then—after his threats and after he'd revealed how far he was willing to go to stop her from marrying Ciro—Lara had still hoped that perhaps if she told Ciro he would be able to protect them. So she'd gone to the hospital where he'd been recuperating and she'd asked him if he loved her—because she'd known that if he loved her then she was willing to do anything to defy her uncle. She'd believed that once Ciro knew about the threat surely he'd be powerful enough to protect himself—and her?

But Ciro had looked at her for a long moment and hesitated. And in that moment she'd known she'd been ridiculously naive.

He must have seen her expression, because he'd said quickly, 'Love? *Cara*, I never promised you love. But I am prepared to commit to you for ever, and I respect you... Isn't that enough? It's a realistic foundation for a life together.'

He hadn't loved her. And so she'd followed the dictates of her uncle in order to protect a man she loved who didn't love her.

Lara had come back to London where she'd been introduced to Henry Winterborne and the marriage had been arranged. Her uncle had made a deal. Henry would bail him out of his debts, restore his reputation, in return for marriage to Lara. A medieval and Machiavellian arrangement.

Lara had been in a fog for days. Lost. Alone. And all the time she was being reminded by her uncle that if she didn't comply he would hurt Ciro.

It had been on their wedding night that Lara had returned to this apartment with her new and very drunk husband and reality had finally broken through the numbing shell in which she'd encased herself.

To this day she had no real memory of the wedding, or saying her vows. It was all a blur. But on that night she'd heard her husband thrashing about the apartment, shouting at the staff to get him drinks. She'd hidden in the bedroom, telling herself that she would leave, escape...send a warning to Ciro somehow... Anything had to be better than this.

And then Henry had come into her room. Crashed through the door.

Lara had tried to get away, but he'd caught her and tried to rip her nightdress. He'd shoved her down on the bed and instinctively Lara had lifted her legs to kick him off. His bulk and his inebriated state had made him fall backwards, and he'd hit his head on the side of a dresser.

The fall and his general bad health had resulted in

him being put into a wheelchair. The shock of the accident, and Lara's uncle's persistent reminders of his threats, had stopped her initial thoughts of trying to escape.

That was when she'd started to see pictures of Ciro, out and about, getting on with his life. The beautiful women on his arm didn't seem to be put off by the livid scar. It only enhanced his charismatic appeal. And seeing Ciro like that... It had broken something inside Lara. Broken any will to try and escape her situation. Any sense of optimism that perhaps she'd been wrong about him not loving her dissipated.

All hope had gone.

With the threat of physical violence from her husband negated, Lara had sunk into a routine of sorts. Days had passed into weeks, and then months, and before she'd known it a year had gone by. Henry Winterborne had got rid of his staff by then, had begun using Lara as an unpaid housekeeper and carer.

When her uncle had died, three months ago, Lara's will to leave her husband had been revived. The threat hanging over Ciro was finally gone. But without any funds of her own she'd been in no position to take legal action.

Before she'd had a chance to assess her options Henry Winterborne had had a stroke, and he'd spent the last two months of his life in hospital. For the first time in two years Lara had had a sense of autonomy again. Albeit within her gilded prison.

She caught sight of her reflection in a mirror on the wall opposite her. She took in her pale and wan features. Why on earth would a man as vital as Ciro Sant'Angelo still be remotely interested in marrying her?

An inner voice answered her: *For revenge.*

And because he had her right where he wanted her. Vulnerable and desperate. Or so he thought.

Lara might have qualms about navigating the world on her own after a lifetime of not being prepared for it, but she'd do it. She'd longed for months just to walk out of this apartment and not look back. To take her chances. But the blackmail her uncle had subjected her to and the guilt of Henry Winterborne's accident had kept her a prisoner.

And there was still guilt. Because the threat to Ciro might be gone, but it had been *her* involvement with him that had led to his kidnap in the first place. If she hadn't ever met Ciro he would never have come to her uncle's attention and would never have been put in danger.

She'd *known* that her uncle had plans for her to marry someone 'suitable'. He'd spoken of little else since she'd left school and gone to university—which he hadn't approved of at all. But Lara had never taken him seriously. It had sounded so medieval in this day and age, and at one time she'd told him so.

He'd reminded her of how much she owed him. Asked her where she would have ended up if he hadn't been there to take her in after his dear brother's tragic death. He'd reminded her of how he'd put his life on hold to make sure she was educated and looked after. He'd reminded her that his brother's death had been a devastating shock for him too, and yet he'd had no time to grieve—he'd been too busy making sure Lara was all right.

Little had she realised how deadly serious he was about marrying her off, and by the time she'd met Ciro, Thomas Templeton had been in dire straits—which had turned Lara into an invaluable commodity. And even though Ciro was a wealthy man, it hadn't been enough for Lara's uncle. He'd needed her to marry a man of *his* choosing, from the *right* side of society.

Lara willed down the nausea that threatened to rise. She needed to focus on the present. Not on the painful past.

She stood up from the bed, immediately agitated. *Ciro.* Back and looking for revenge. And could she even blame him? No. She couldn't. She'd single-handedly brought terror into his life. Forced him to live under the shadow of personal protection. Because he'd been shown to be vulnerable. Something she knew he must *hate*.

She also owed him for the resurgence in the rumours about his family's links to the Mafia, who people believed had been responsible for his kidnapping. Not to mention the humiliation of walking out on him days before they were due to be married under the spotlight of the world's media.

One of the many headlines had read *Sicilian Millionaire to Wed English Society Fiancée!* The article underneath had been less flattering, snidely suggesting that Ciro had been trying to marry far above his station.

The fact that Ciro had managed to ride out the storm of headlines and speculation to thrive and survive only demonstrated the scale of his ambition. But clearly that wasn't enough for him.

Her guts twisted. She'd loved him so desperately once. She would have done anything for him. And she had. Could she sacrifice herself again just to allow him to feel some measure of closure? To allow him the access he craved to a level of society that would bring him even more success and acceptance?

'A year of marriage...review it in six months.'

Ciro's cold proposal was daunting. Could she possibly even contemplate such a thing? Subject herself to Ciro's bid for revenge?

Lara stopped pacing and caught her reflection in the mirror again. Her cheeks were flushed now. Eyes over-bright.

Would it really be a sacrifice when he still stirs up so many powerful emotions and desires? questioned a snide inner voice.

She saw the buildings and the skyline of London behind her, reflected in the mirror through the window. There was a back way out of the apartment. She knew she could leave if she wanted to. Slip away into the millions of anonymous people thronging London's streets. Get on with her life. Try to put all this behind her.

But Ciro would come after her. Just as he'd pursued her once before. Relentlessly. Seductively.

She'd kept refusing his advances at first, intimidated by his charismatic masculinity and his playboy reputation. But in the end he'd won her over, when he'd taken her to that gallery after hours.

She shook her head to dislodge the disturbing memory. All it had been was an elaborate seduction ruse. She'd been different from his other women. Naive, wide-eyed. Except now he thought it had all been an act.

Lara had already been through worse than a marriage of convenience to one of the world's most notorious playboys. Far worse. She'd lost her entire beloved family overnight. She'd been heinously betrayed and exploited by her uncle, her last remaining family member. She'd been belittled and bullied by her husband. And she'd had her heart broken already by Ciro Sant'Angelo, so she had no heart left to break.

Realising that Ciro hadn't ever loved her had made it easier for her to do what she'd had to. To be cruel. To walk away. And yet now she was contemplating walking back to him?

A voice in her head queried her sanity. After everything she'd been through at the hands of her uncle and her deceased husband she should be running a million miles from this scenario. And yet despite everything the pull she felt to go back into Ciro's orbit was strong. Too strong to resist?

Lara knew she had only one choice. She had to do what was best for her and her future, so that she could get on with her life with a clear conscience and leave her past behind once and for all.

CHAPTER THREE

CIRO FELT THE tight knot inside him ease. Disconcertingly, it was the same sensation he'd felt when one of his assistants had informed him of Henry Winterborne's death. Except that had been more acute, and quickly followed by a sense of urgency. Find Lara. Track her down. Bring her to him.

She was his now.

His driver had just rung to say that Lara had asked for help with her bags. Which meant she hadn't tried to run. She was coming back to him.

It irked him that he hadn't been sure, when he was so sure of everything else in his life. Nothing was left to chance. Not since the kidnapping.

His little finger throbbed. The missing finger. They called it phantom pain. Pain even though it wasn't there any more. A cruel irony.

He found most women boringly predictable, but Lara Templeton had never been predictable. Not even now, when she was penniless and homeless. A woman that resourceful and beautiful? He had no doubt that she could slip out of his grasp and then he would encounter her at some future event, with another man old enough to be her father.

So why had he given her the opportunity to run if she

so wanted? Because a perverse part of him wanted to prove to himself how mercenary she was. She wouldn't get a better deal than the one he was offering: a marriage of convenience for a year, maximum. Minimum six months. And when they divorced she would be set for life.

He'd laid it out for her and she'd taken the bait. It was perverse to be feeling…*disappointed*. Especially when he had lived the last two years in some kind of limbo. Unable to move on. To settle.

He'd worked himself to a lather, tripling his fortune. Earning respect. But not the respect he craved. The respect of polite society. The respect of the upper echelons of Europe, who still saw him as little more than a Sicilian hustler with a dubious background. Especially after the kidnapping, which remained a mystery to this day.

His best friend, an ex–French Foreign Legionnaire who worked in security, and who had courageously rescued Ciro with a highly skilled team of mercenaries, had told Ciro that they might never find out who had orchestrated it. But one day Ciro would find out, and whoever was responsible would pay dearly.

At that moment he saw his car pull up in front of the house again. There was a bright blonde head in the back. Ciro's blood grew hot. Lara Templeton would be his. *Finally.* And when he'd had his fill of her, and had achieved what he wanted, he would walk out and leave her behind—exactly as she'd done to him in his weakest moment.

Within hours Lara was sitting on Ciro's private jet, being flown across Europe to Rome. She'd just declined a glass of champagne and now Ciro asked from across the aisle, 'Don't you feel like celebrating, darling?'

She looked at him suspiciously. He was taking a sip of his own champagne and he tipped the glass towards her in a salute. He'd changed into dark grey trousers and a black polo shirt. He looked vital and breathtakingly handsome. From this angle Lara couldn't see the scar on the right-hand side of his face—he looked perfect. But she knew that even the scar didn't mar that perfection; it only made him more compelling.

'Surprisingly enough, not really.'

She'd wanted to sound sharp but she just sounded weary. It had been a long day. She couldn't believe the funeral had been that morning; it felt like a month ago. She'd changed out of her funeral clothes into a pair of long culottes and a silk shirt which now felt ridiculously flimsy.

Ciro responded. 'Your marriage to Winterborne might have left you destitute, but fortunately you still have some currency for me. You must have displeased him very much.'

Lara had a sudden flashback to the suffocating weight of the drunken Henry Winterborne on top of her and the sheer panic that had galvanised her into heaving him off.

She swallowed down the nausea and avoided Ciro's eye. 'Something like that. Maybe I will have that champagne after all…' she said, suddenly craving anything that might soothe the ragged edges of her memory.

Ciro must have made a gesture, because the pristine-looking flight attendant was back immediately with a glass of sparkling wine for Lara. She took a sip, letting it fizz down her throat. She took another sip, and instantly felt slightly less ragged.

'Here's to us, Lara.'

Reluctantly she looked at Ciro again. He was facing

her fully now, and she could see the scar. And his missing finger. And the mocking glint in his eye. He thought he was unnerving her with his scars, and he was—but not because she found them repulsive.

He was holding out his glass towards her. Lara reached out, tipping her glass against his, causing a melodic chiming sound which was incongruously happy amidst the tension.

It was a cruelly ironic echo of another time and place. A tiny bustling restaurant in Florence where they'd toasted their engagement. Lara could recall the incredible sense of love she'd felt, and the feeling of security. For the first time in her life since her parents and her brother had died she'd felt some measure of peace again.

A sense of coming home.

The sparkle of the beautiful ring Ciro had presented her with had kept catching her eye. She'd left that ring in his hospital room when she'd walked out two years ago.

As if privy to her thoughts, Ciro reached for something in his pocket and pulled out a small velvet box. Lara's heart thudded to a stop and her hand gripped the glass of wine too tight.

Ciro shrugged. 'Seems an awful waste to buy a new ring when we can use the old one.'

A million questions collided in Lara's head at once, chief of which was, *How did he still have the ring?* She would have thought he'd thrown it away in disgust after she'd walked out.

He started to open the box, and Lara wanted to tell him to stop, but the words stuck in her throat. And there it was—revealed. The most beautiful ring in the world. A pear-shaped sapphire with two diamonds on either side in a gold setting. Classic, yet unusual.

Lara looked at Ciro. 'I don't want this ring.' She sounded too shrill.

Ciro looked at her. 'I suppose you hate the idea of recycling? Perhaps it's too small?'

'No, it's not that… It's…' She trailed off ineffectually.

It's perfect.

Lara had a flashback to Ciro telling her that the sapphire had reminded him of the colour her eyes went when he kissed her… *That* was why she didn't want it. It brought back too many bittersweet memories that she'd imbued with a romanticism that hadn't been there.

She managed to get out, 'Is this absolutely necessary?'

Oblivious to Lara's turmoil, Ciro plucked the ring out of the box and took her left hand in his, long fingers wrapping around hers as he slid the ring onto her finger, where it sat as snugly as if it had never been taken off.

'Absolutely. I've already issued a press release with the news of our re-engagement and upcoming marriage.'

There was a sharp cracking sound and Lara only realised what had happened when she felt the sting in her finger. She looked down stupidly to see blood dripping onto the cream leather seat, just as Ciro issued a curt order and the flight attendant took the broken glass carefully out of Lara's grip.

She was up on her feet and being propelled to the back of the plane and into a bathroom before she'd even registered that she'd broken her champagne glass. Ciro was crowding into the small space behind her, turning on the cold tap and holding her hand underneath.

The pain of the water hitting the place where she'd

sliced herself on the glass finally made her break out of her shocked stasis. She hissed through her teeth.

'It's a clean cut—not deep.' Ciro's tone was deep and unexpectedly reassuring.

He turned her around to face him and reached for a first aid kit from the cabinet above her head, pulling out a plaster which he placed over the cut on the inside of her finger with an efficiency that might have intrigued Lara if she'd not been so distracted.

He said with a dry tone, 'While I will admit to relishing your discomfort at the prospect of marrying me, Lara, I'd prefer to keep you in one piece for the duration of our union.'

Lara's finger throbbed slightly, and just when she was going to pull her hand back he stopped her, keeping her hands in his. He was frowning, and Lara looked down. He was turning her hands over in his and suddenly she saw what he saw. She tried to pull them back but he wouldn't let her.

The glittering ring only highlighted what he was looking at: careworn hands. Hands that had been doing manual work. Not the soft lily-white hands she used to have. Short, unvarnished nails.

Suddenly he let her hands go and said curtly, 'You've been neglecting yourself. You need a manicure.'

Lara might have laughed if the space hadn't been so tiny and she hadn't been scared to move in case her body came into contact with Ciro's. Panic rose at the thought that Ciro might kiss her. She didn't need her dignity battered again.

She scooted around him and into the relative spaciousness of the plane's bedroom, hiding her hands behind her back. She wasn't unaware of the massive bed in the centre of the room but she ignored it.

'You could have told me you were putting out a press release. This affects me too, you know.'

Ciro looked unrepentant. 'Oh, I'm aware of that. But as soon as you agreed to marry me you set in motion a chain of events which will culminate in our wedding within a week.'

'A week!' Lara wanted to sit down, but she didn't want to look remotely vulnerable. So she stayed standing.

Ciro shrugged. As if this was nothing more to him than discussing the weather. 'Why not? Why drag it out? I've got a busy schedule of events coming up and I'll need you by my side.'

Lara felt cornered and impotent. She'd walked herself into this situation after all. 'Why not, indeed.'

A knock came on the door and a voice from outside. 'We'll be landing shortly, Signor Sant'Angelo.'

Ciro took Lara's arm in his hand, as if to guide her out, but when he didn't move she glanced at him and saw him direct an expressive look from her to the bed.

'Pity,' he said silkily. 'Next time.'

An immediate wave of heat consumed Lara at the mere thought of such a decadent thing, and she pulled her arm free and muttered a caustic, 'As if…'

All she could hear as she walked back up the plane was the dark sound of Ciro's chuckle.

Lara was very aware of the ring on her finger. She turned it absent-mindedly as she looked out of the window at the view of Rome.

She was glad they were here and not in Florence. Florence held too many memories…and nightmares.

It was where she'd met Ciro on a street one day and her world had changed for ever. He'd been in Florence to close a major deal which would convert one of the city's oldest *palazzos* into an exclusive hotel. Something the Sant'Angelo name was famous for.

Not that she'd had any clue who he was at first.

She'd been pushed into the road by another tourist, blind to everything but the beauty of Florence, when someone had grabbed her and pulled her back from the oncoming cars.

She'd looked up to see who was holding her arm with such a firm grip and laid eyes on Ciro Sant'Angelo for the first time. He'd fulfilled every possible cliché of tall, dark and handsome and then some. And, even though Lara had seen plenty of tall, dark, handsome Italian men by then, it had been this one who had stopped her heart for a long second. When it had started beating again it had been to a different rhythm. Faster.

Lara had been excited and terrified in equal measure. Because no one had affected her heart in a long time. She'd locked it away after losing her family. Closed it up tight to protect herself. And yet, in that split second, on that sunny day in Florence, she'd felt it start to crack open again. Totally irrational and crazy. But it had opened and she'd never managed to close it up again.

She'd looked him up on the internet a couple of days after meeting him and absorbed the full extent of his fame and notoriety as a playboy who came from a family steeped in Sicilian Mafia history.

She'd told him that she'd looked him up. His expression had shuttered immediately, and she'd seen him drawing back into himself.

He'd said to her, 'Find anything interesting?'

She'd known instinctively that the moment was huge, and that she trusted him. So she'd said, 'I'm sorry. I just wanted to know more about you, and it was hard to resist, but I should have asked you about yourself face-to-face.'

After a long moment he'd extended a hand and said, 'Ask me now.'

She'd taken his hand and asked him about Sicily, about his business. His deep voice had washed over her and through her, binding her even tighter into the illusion that there was something real, palpable, between them.

Lara turned away from the bird's eye view of the iconic Colosseum, visible in the distance, and looked around the bedroom. When they'd arrived yesterday evening every bone in her body had been aching with fatigue. They'd eaten a light meal of pasta, prepared by Ciro's unsmiling housekeeper, and Lara had been glad that conversation had been kept to a minimum.

It had been an ironic reminder of other meals with Ciro, when they'd been happy just to be near each other. Not speaking.

That had always surprised her about him—that he didn't feel intimidated by silence. It had reminded her of when her brother would tug playfully on her hair and say, 'Earth to Lara—where are you in the world?' because she'd used to get so lost in her daydreams.

She diverted her mind away from the painful memory of her brother. And from daydreams. They were a thing of the past. A vulnerability she couldn't indulge in. She didn't believe in dreams any more. Not after losing her entire family in one fell swoop. Not after being betrayed by her uncle. And certainly not after having her heart broken into a million pieces by Ciro Sant'Angelo.

The bedroom was spacious and luxurious without being ostentatious—much like the rest of the apartment. A pang gripped her. She knew how hard Ciro had worked for this—to show the world that he was different from the Sant'Angelos who'd used to rule and succeed through crime and brute force.

Lara sighed. She hated it that she still cared enough to notice that kind of thing.

She caught her reflection in a full-length mirror and considered herself critically, noting the puffiness under her eyes. She'd had a shower in the en suite bathroom and was dressed in slim-fitting capri pants and a T-shirt. No make-up. Totally boring. Not designed to attract the attention of a playboy like Ciro.

Surely when he saw her in the cold light of morning he'd wonder what on earth he'd done?

After pulling her hair back in a low ponytail and slipping on flat shoes, she went in search of Ciro, vaguely wondering if it had all been a dream and she'd find herself back in London.

Liar, whispered an inner voice, *you don't want it to be a dream.*

She ignored it.

But when she walked into the big living and dining area reality was like a punch to the gut. This was no dream.

Ciro was sitting at the top of a huge table with breakfast laid out before him, reading a newspaper. His legs were stretched out and crossed at the ankle and he was looking as relaxed as if it was totally normal to have whisked your ex-fiancée off to another city straight after the funeral of her husband because you were bent on retribution.

He looked up when she approached the table and Lara immediately felt self-conscious. She wished she had some kind of armour to protect herself from that laser-like brown gaze.

He stood up and pulled out a chair to the right of his. Ever the gentleman. Lara murmured her thanks and sat down. The housekeeper appeared and poured her some coffee. Lara forced a smile and said her thanks in Italian, but the housekeeper barely acknowledged her.

'She's deaf.'

It took a second for Lara to realise that Ciro had spoken. She looked at him. 'What?'

'Sophia…my housekeeper. She's deaf. Which is why it can sometimes feel like she's being rude when she doesn't acknowledge you.'

'Oh.'

'I'm telling you because I don't want you to upset her.'

Affronted, Lara said, 'Why would I upset her?'

'Just don't.'

It struck at Lara somewhere very vulnerable to hear Ciro defend his housekeeper. It struck her even deeper that he would think her capable of being rude to someone with a disability. But then, she'd given him that impression, hadn't she? When she'd convinced him she'd been with him purely for her own entertainment.

'You didn't have much luggage.'

Lara felt a flush working its way up her body. A burn of shame and humiliation. 'I brought what I needed.'

Ciro inclined his head. 'And I guess you're counting on me buying you an entirely new wardrobe of all the latest fashions.'

She hated the smug cynicism in his voice, but she wasn't about to explain that once her husband had become incapacitated, and blamed her, she'd been reduced to being little more than unpaid help. With very little money of her own, and none from her husband, Lara had had to resort to selling her clothes and jewellery online to try and make money when she needed it.

At one point when she'd needed money for something she'd had to sell her mother's wedding dress—a beloved heirloom that she'd always hoped to wear when she married for love, and not because she was being forced into it. The fact that it was gone for ever seemed darkly apt.

Ciro took a sip of coffee. 'You'll need to look the part as my wife. I have standards to maintain.'

Lara realised that she wouldn't survive for a week, let alone months, if she didn't do something to distance herself from Ciro's caustic cynicism and bad opinion of her. She needed to develop a hard shell around her heart. He mustn't know how deeply he affected her or his revenge would be even more cruel.

She shrugged and affected a look of disdain. 'Well, you couldn't very well expect me to wear clothes two seasons out of date, could you?'

Ciro took in Lara's expression. *There she was.* The Lara who had shown her true face in his hospital room two years ago. Making him the biggest fool on the planet. And yet it didn't make him feel triumphant. Because there were those disconcerting moments when for a second she looked—

He shook his head. *This* was Lara Templeton. Spoilt and manipulative. Prepared to marry a man just because he was from the right side of society.

'I've arranged for a stylist to come and take you shopping today. You'll also be fitted for your wedding dress. I've pre-approved the design, so you don't have a choice, Lara. I want to make sure you're suitably attired for this wedding.'

Suddenly the disdain was gone. 'What will people think of me? Marrying again so soon?'

'They'll think you're a woman who has a strong sense of self-preservation. And they'll think you're a woman who knows she made a bad choice and is now rectifying the situation.'

'They'll think I'm nothing but a gold-digger.'

Ciro tensed. 'You walked out on your injured fiancé to marry a man old enough to be your father within weeks of the day our own wedding was due to take place, so don't try to pretend a sudden concern about what people think.'

Lara's cheeks whitened dramatically, but Ciro put it down to anger at the fact that he could see right through her.

He hated it that he was so aware of her with every pulse of blood through his veins. He had no control over it. It hardened his body, made him a slave to his libido.

She wasn't even trying to entice him. He wasn't used to women not preening around him. Or he hadn't been until he'd met Lara and she'd stunned him with her fresh-faced beauty.

She was fresh-faced this morning, with not a scrap of make-up, right down to the slightly puffy eyes. Something about that irritated him intensely. It was as if she was mocking him all over again. As if she knew that she didn't even have to make an effort to have an effect on him.

He gestured towards her with a hand. 'I don't know what you're angling for with this lack of effort in your personal appearance, Lara. But after you've met with the stylist, and once we are married, I'll expect a more... *polished* result.'

Her eyes flashed bright blue at that. And then she lowered them in a parody of being demure. 'Of course.'

That irritated him even more. It was as if there was some subtext going on that he wasn't privy to.

He stood up. 'I have back-to-back meetings all day at my head office. If you need anything, this is my private secretary's number.'

He put a card down on the table in front of her. Lara picked it up. Was it his imagination or was there a slight tremor in her hand?

She still didn't look at him as she said, 'So not even your fiancée gets your personal number?'

He reached down and tipped up her face with a finger under her chin, 'Oh, some people have my personal number, Lara. The people I trust most in the world. I have a business dinner this evening, so don't wait up. The marriage will take place this Saturday, so you'll be kept busy between now and then.'

This Saturday.

Lara jerked her chin away from Ciro's finger. Even that small touch was lighting her insides on fire. Not to mention the nearness of the whipcord strength of his body, evident even though he was dressed in business attire of dark trousers and a white shirt. It was as if mere clothes couldn't contain the man.

'Worried I'll abscond?'

Ciro stepped back and put out his arm. 'You're not a prisoner, Lara. You're free to leave. But we both know that you won't—especially when you see the very generous terms of the pre-nuptial contract. I know the real you now. You don't need to pretend to be something else. This will be a very mutually beneficial arrangement.'

And she knew the real him. The man who wanted her

only for her connections and her class. She was tempted to stand up and walk out with her head held high. Claim back her life. But she'd agreed to this because she knew what had been done to this man was her fault.

He might not have loved her, but he hadn't deserved to be treated the way she had treated him, and he certainly hadn't deserved to be kidnapped and almost killed. She had no choice but to stay. Not if she wanted to live the rest of her life with a clear conscience.

Ciro looked at his watch. 'The stylist will be here at midday and some of my legal team will come before that with the pre-nuptial contract. An assistant will set you up with a mobile and laptop—whatever you need.'

Then he was gone, striding out of the room before she could say anything.

Lara looked at the delicious array of food on the table and her stomach churned. The coffee she'd drunk sat heavily in her stomach.

The housekeeper came back just as Lara was standing up and Lara touched her arm gently. The woman looked at her questioningly and Lara smiled and said *grazie*. The woman smiled widely and nodded, and Lara felt for a second as if she'd scored some kind of tiny victory.

Ciro might think the worst of her but *she* knew who she was. She just needed to remember that.

By the time Lara had walked from the car and up the steps to the porch of the cathedral on Saturday afternoon she was shaking. There were what looked like hundreds of people lining the steps, calling out her name, and the flashes of cameras.

The wedding dress that Ciro had picked out was stunning, but far more extravagant than Lara would have ever chosen for herself. Designed to get as much attention as possible with its long train and elaborate veil. Not unlike the dress she'd worn to marry Henry Winterborne.

Her mother's dress had been simple and graceful. Whimsical and romantic. But then it had been a dress worn for love. Lara was almost glad it was gone now. Hopefully some other woman had married for love in it.

She was not unaware of the irony that for the second time in the space of a couple of weeks she was glad of a veil to hide behind.

The aisle looked about a hundred miles long from where she was standing. And she was going to walk down it alone. She wanted to turn and run. But instead she squared her shoulders, and as the wedding march began she started walking, spine straight, praying that no one would see her bouquet shaking.

The back of Ciro's neck prickled. *She was here.*

He'd heard the cacophony of shouts outside just before a hush rippled through the church. He knew she would be walking down the aisle alone—she hadn't requested any bridesmaids or attendants. She had no family. Something about that lonely image of her caught at his gut but he ignored it.

She was the type of woman who could bury one man one week and marry another a week later. She was not shy or vulnerable.

You offered her little alternative, pointed out the voice of his conscience.

Ciro ignored it. Lara might not like what people thought of her, but she'd soon forget it when she got used to the life of luxury Ciro could offer her.

He fought the desire to turn around, not liking the sense of *déjà vu* washing over him as he thought about how this day should have happened two years ago. And how it hadn't.

In the lead-up to that wedding he'd been uncharacteristically nervous. And excited. Excited at the thought of unveiling his virginal bride. Of being the first man who would touch her, make her convulse with pleasure. And at the thought of the life he would have with her—a different life from the one he'd experienced with his parents.

But she hadn't been that woman.

Suddenly Ciro felt hollow inside. And exposed. As if he was making a monumental fool of himself all over again.

The wedding march grated on his nerves. For a moment he almost felt the urge to shout out, *Stop!* But then Lara's scent reached him, that unique blend of lemon and roses he would always associate with her, and the urge drained away.

He turned to look at her and his breath caught. Even though he'd chosen the dress for its classic yet dramatic lines—a full satin skirt and a bodice which was overlaid with lace that covered her arms and chest up to her throat—he still wasn't prepared.

He'd always known Lara was beautiful, but right now she was...*exquisite*. He could just make out the line of her jaw, the soft pink lips and bright blue eyes behind the veil. Her hair was pulled back into a chignon.

His gaze travelled down over her slender curves to where she held the bouquet. There was an almost imperceptible trembling in her hands, and before he could stop himself Ciro reached out and put a hand over hers. She looked at him, and a constriction in his chest that he hadn't even been aware of eased.

Instead of the triumph he'd expected—*hoped*—to be

feeling right now, the residue of those memories and emotions lingered in his gut. And relief.

It was the relief that made him take his hand off hers and face forward. The scar on his face tingled, as if to remind Ciro why they were there. What she owed him. And any sense of exposure he'd felt dissipated to be replaced by resolve.

The wedding service passed in a blur for Lara. She wasn't even sure how she'd made it down the aisle. The mass was conducted in English, for her benefit, and she dutifully made her vows, feeling as if it was happening to someone else.

Her second wedding to a man who didn't love her. At least she'd never been deluded about Henry Winterborne's feelings for her.

Every time she looked at Ciro she wanted to look away. It was like looking directly at the sun. He was so...*vital*. He wore a dark grey morning suit with a white shirt and tie. His dark hair was gleaming and swept back from his face.

But now she had to face him, and she reluctantly lifted the veil up and over her head. There was nothing to shield her from that dark, penetrating gaze. Hundreds of people thronged the cathedral but suddenly it was just her and him.

Before, she'd imagined this moment so many times... had longed for it. Longed to feel a part of something again. A unit. A unit of love.

And now this was a parody of that longing. A farce.

Suddenly Lara felt like pulling away from Ciro, who had her hands in his. As if sensing her wish to bolt, he tightened his grip on her and tugged her towards him.

'You may kiss the bride...'

One word resounded in Lara's head. *No!*

If Ciro touched her now, when she was feeling so raw— But it was too late. He'd pulled her close, or as close as her voluminous skirts would allow, and his hands were around her face. He was holding her as tenderly as if she really meant something to him. But it was all for show.

Past and present were blurring. Meshing.

Ciro's head came closer and those eyes compelled her to stay where she was. Submit to him. At the last moment, in a tiny act of rebellion, Lara lifted her face to his. She wasn't going to submit. She was an equal partner.

Their mouths met and every muscle in Lara's body seized against the impact of that firm, hot mouth on hers. But it was useless. It was as if a hot serum was being poured into her veins, loosening her, making her pliant. Making her fold against him, letting her head fall back so he could gain deeper access to her mouth.

It was only a vague sound of throat-clearing that made them break apart, and Lara realised with a hot flush of shame just how wantonly she'd reacted. With not one cell in her body rejecting his touch. She pushed back, disgusted with herself, but Ciro caught her elbows, not allowing her to put any distance between them.

'Smile, *mia moglie*, you've just married the man you should have married two years ago.'

Lara dragged her gaze away from Ciro's and looked around. A sea of strangers' faces looked back at her, their expressions ranging from impassive to downright speculative. And there were a couple of murderous-looking beautiful women who had no doubt envisaged themselves becoming Signora Sant'Angelo.

Ciro tucked her arm into his and led her back down

the aisle to a triumphant chorus of Handel's 'The Arrival of the Queen of Sheba'.

Lara somehow fixed a smile to her face as they approached the main doors, where Rome lay bathed in bright warm sunshine—a direct contrast to her swirling stormy emotions. She was Ciro Sant'Angelo's wife now, for better or worse, and the awful thing was Lara knew without a doubt that it was going to be for worse...

CHAPTER FOUR

'WELL, YOU CERTAINLY had us all fooled.'

Lara's fixed-on smile slipped slightly when she saw who was addressing her. Lazaro Sanchez. Probably Ciro's closest friend. She'd met him a few times two years ago, when he would often look at her speculatively and say, 'You're not like Ciro's other women.'

Lara had used to joke with him that he and Ciro had a warped sense of what was normal and what was not, given their astounding good-looks and success in life. Lazaro Sanchez was every bit as gorgeous as Ciro, with messy overlong dark blond hair and piercing green eyes.

Yet in spite of the Spaniard's devastating charm he'd never made her pulse trip like Ciro had. *Did.* She could still feel the imprint of his kiss from the church on her mouth and had to resist the urge to touch it.

Lara decided to ignore his barbed comment. 'Lazaro, it's nice to see you again.'

Lazaro folded his arms. His expression was not charming now. Far from it. 'I'm afraid I can't say the same. You know, two years ago, when you left Ciro in the hospital, I've never seen him so—'

'Filling my wife's head with stories like you used to?'

Lazaro scowled at Ciro, who'd interrupted them and who was now snaking a possessive arm around Lara's waist. She was intrigued to know what Lazaro had been about to say but suspected she never would now.

Then she registered what Ciro had said—*my wife*. With such ease. As if this was all entirely normal.

He turned to Lara. 'We'll be leaving shortly to take our flight to Sicily. You should go and change—there's a stylist waiting for you upstairs.'

The manager of the exclusive Rome hotel that Ciro owned, where Lara had stayed the night before and got ready earlier, escorted her to the suite where the stylist was waiting. Lara welcomed he opportunity to get away from the hundreds of judgemental eyes. Lazaro's in particular.

In the past week, along with the wedding dress, Lara had been fitted for dozens of other outfits. Evening wear, day wear. Night clothes. Underwear. Now, as the woman and her assistant helped Lara out of the elaborate wedding dress and veil, she felt a pang of regret that this wasn't a normal wedding or marriage and never would be. She'd always fantasised about a small and intimate wedding, and the fantasy had included staying in her wedding dress all night, until her groom lovingly removed it as he took her to bed.

But she had to remind herself that she'd only ever been a means to an end for Ciro. Access into a rarefied world. So she needed to forget about fantasies of small, intimate weddings. If life had taught her anything by now it was that she was on her own and had to depend on herself.

'Bellissima, Signora Sant'Angelo.'

Lara's attention was directed back into the room, where the stylist was standing back and looking her up and down.

The wedding dress was on its hanger again, and Lara

now wore a sleeveless mid-length shirt dress in the softest blush colour. It had a high ruffled neck and was cinched in at the waist with a belt. She wore strappy high-heeled sandals. Her hair was left down, to tumble over her shoulders, and a make-up artist touched up her make-up.

For a hysterical moment she felt like an actress, about to take her cue to go on stage.

Ciro was waiting outside when she emerged. His dark gaze swept her up and down. 'You look beautiful.'

The immediate flush of warmth that bloomed inside Lara felt like a betrayal. She didn't want his words to have any effect on her. They weren't infused with emotion. They were purely an objective assessment. She was a commodity. Just as she'd always been.

He'd changed into a dark grey suit and white shirt, open at the neck. Elegantly casual. They complemented each other. He extended his arm and she took a breath before putting her arm in his, so he could lead her down the stairs to the main foyer, where people were waiting.

The crowd parted to let them through, and a few people clapped Ciro on the shoulder as they passed. Lara caught Lazaro's eye. He still had that grim expression on his face. She felt like pulling free from Ciro, so she could go over and tell him that he had it all wrong. Ciro had hurt *her*, not the other way around...

And then she glanced up and saw Ciro's scar, standing out so lividly, and fresh guilt for her responsibility in that made her keep her eyes forward until they were outside and in the back of a sleek SUV. Lazaro Sanchez was right to look at her the way he did.

'Try to smile, hmm...*cara*? You've just married the man of your dreams and you will never have to lift a finger again if you are wise with your divorce settlement when it comes.'

Lara's rattled emotions bubbled over. She turned to Ciro as the vehicle pulled into the traffic. 'I couldn't care less about the money, Ciro. You, on the other hand, are obsessed by it. I pity you—because if it all went tomorrow, what would you have?'

Stupid question, Lara.

She realised that as soon as the words were out of her mouth. He'd have the towering Sicilian pride and immense self-belief that had brought him to where he was today.

But he merely shrugged lightly and said, 'I'd start again and be even more successful.'

That stopped anything further coming out of Lara's mouth.

Ciro conducted some phone calls in Italian while they were en route, and soon they were pulling into a private part of the airport where a small silver jet was waiting.

The pilot and staff welcomed them on board and Lara accepted a glass of champagne when they were airborne. Below them Rome was bathed in a magical golden sunset.

She sneaked a look across the aisle to see Ciro holding his own glass of champagne, which didn't look at all ridiculous in his big hand. Her belly fluttered with nerves and awareness. Would he expect her to sleep with him tonight? Take it as his due? Would he force her?

She shivered. He wouldn't have to. Not like her first husband. She diverted her mind from that bilious memory.

As if sensing her regard, Ciro turned and looked at

her. She cast around for something to say—anything but what was on her mind. 'All those people at the wedding and afterwards...do you know them?'

Ciro's mouth twitched slightly. 'Of course not. They're mostly peers...business acquaintances. A small number of friends and staff whom I trust.'

Whom I trust.

Lara smarted at that. Even though he'd married her, he didn't trust *her*. She thought of the pre-nuptial agreement and how it had specified that no children were expected from the union.

They hadn't really discussed children before. Lara had just assumed Ciro would want them, as he was the last in the Sant'Angelo line.

However, for her it had been more complicated. The memory of losing her own parents and her brother had been so painful she'd always believed she couldn't have borne that kind of loss again, or inflicted it on anyone else... And yet after meeting Ciro, she'd found herself yearning to be part of a family again. He'd made her want to risk it for the first time.

Ciro was still looking at her, as if he could probe right into her brain and read her thoughts. Terrified in case he might ask her what she'd been thinking about, she scrabbled around for the first thing she could think of.

'Where are we going in Sicily?'

'My family's *palazzo*. Directly south from Palermo—on the coast.'

'Does anyone live there?'

He shook his head. 'Not since my grandfather passed away a few years ago. It was his property and he left it to me because he was afraid my mother would persuade my father to sell it or turn it into a resort. She never liked Sicily.' Ciro's jaw clenched. 'As you might have noticed from her absence at the wedding, we're not really in contact.'

Lara said nothing. He'd told her before of his mother's serial philandering, and the way his father had devoted himself to her regardless of the humiliation. How his mother had persuaded his father to move to Rome, away from his homeland of Sicily. But Ciro had spent a lot of time there with his grandfather.

Lara had always believed that his experience at the hands of his mother had explained the ease with which Ciro had believed in Lara's duplicity and betrayal. He had told her once that when he was very small she'd used to make him collude with her in hiding the evidence of her infidelity from his father. Making him an accomplice. Lara could understand how her own betrayal must have been a huge blow to his pride, and more.

But while knowing all that was very well, it didn't really do much to help her now. Ciro's beliefs were entrenched, and what she had done had merely confirmed for him that women were not to be trusted.

Lara was quiet. Unnervingly so. Ciro remembered the way she'd used to chatter when they'd first met. She'd ask him so many questions that he'd resort to kissing her to stop them. And yet there'd been those moments when no conversation had been required and she hadn't filled the silence with nonsense. She'd been just as happy not to talk. Something he'd found refreshing.

This time around he was under no illusions.

He thought of the moment just a few hours before, when he'd emerged from the cathedral with Lara on his arm. When the paparazzi's cameras had exploded into life he'd felt her flinch ever so slightly on his arm, and the sense of triumph which had been so elusive had finally oozed through his veins.

He'd envisaged that moment—the beauty marrying the beast. And yet when he'd looked down at her she hadn't had a look of revulsion on her face at being photographed with Ciro and his livid scar—she'd looked haunted by something else entirely and he hadn't liked that...

In fact, since they'd met again he'd never got a sense from her that she considered him some sort of monster—which was how he felt sometimes, when people looked at him with horror or fascination. In her eyes there was something else...something almost like... sympathy. Or guilt. Which made no sense at all.

Ciro looked over Lara's form broodingly. Her head was turned away, as if the shape of the clouds outside the window was utterly fascinating. The silk of her dress clung to her slim curves in a way that made his hands itch to uncover her inch by inch and see the bounty he had denied himself before...

He'd been such a fool. Lust had clouded his judgement the first time around. Of *course* a woman as beautiful as Lara couldn't have been a virgin. Or if she had been she wasn't one now.

No matter. Tonight she would be his in every way— wife and lover. Tonight he would slake the hunger he'd felt since the moment he'd laid eyes on her. Tonight he might finally feel some measure of peace again.

The late summer dusk was tipping into night as they made the journey up a long and winding driveway to Ciro's Sicilian *palazzo*. All Lara could see was the wide open lavender sky full of bright stars and acres and acres of land rolling down to the sea. It was quiet.

They climbed an incline, and when they reached the top she sucked in a breath.

The *palazzo* seemed to rise out of nowhere and cling to a cliff-edge in the distance; a soaring cluster of buildings with a tower that looked like something from a movie. As they got closer she could see just how massive it was. Lights shone from high windows, and they drove into a huge courtyard with a fountain in the middle. Wide steps led up to a huge open door where light spilled out. It looked incongruously welcoming in spite of the intimidating grandeur of the building.

'You said once that you spent a lot of time here growing up?' Lara said as Ciro drew the SUV to a stop at the bottom of the steps.

He cut the car's engine and put both hands on the steering wheel. Lara was conscious of the missing little finger on his right hand. It made her chest ache. She looked away.

'Yes. We were mainly in Rome, after my parents moved there, but I spent most holidays here with my grandparents. My *nonna* died when I was small, but my grandfather was alive until not long ago.'

'Were your mother's parents alive?'

His mouth compressed. 'They lived in Rome and they didn't approve of her choice of husband. They had nothing to do with me or my father—even though my father moved to Rome to keep my mother happy.'

'That was harsh.'

She'd never really realised how lonely Ciro must have been as an only child. Or how it must have looked to a young boy to see his father giving up his own heritage to keep his selfish mother happy.

Just then a young woman in jeans and a white shirt appeared at the top of the steps. Ciro saw her and uncurled his large frame from the SUV, calling out a greeting in Italian.

The young woman flew down the steps and hurled herself at Ciro, who chuckled, wrapping her in his arms. Lara's breath stopped as something very sharp pierced her heart. She hadn't seen Ciro so relaxed and easy since they'd met again. He'd been like that with her, once...

She got out of the car slowly, and as she came around to where Ciro was extricating himself from the woman's embrace Lara could see that she was a girl of about eighteen, extraordinarily pretty with long dark hair and dark eyes. She was looking up at Ciro as if he was God.

Then she saw Lara and stepped back, clapping a hand to her mouth. Her eyes were sparkling and she took her hand down, smiling so widely and infectiously that Lara couldn't help but respond.

Lara held her hand out, but the girl ignored it and embraced her warmly too. When she pulled back she said, *'Scusi...'* and then she rattled off some words in Italian that Lara had no hope of understanding.

Ciro said something and the girl stopped talking, looking embarrassed.

'Lara, I'd like you to meet Isabella. She grew up here on the estate with her family, who have cared for the *palazzo* for generations.'

Lara smiled. 'It's nice to meet you.'

Isabella smiled again. 'And you, Signora Sant'Angelo. Please excuse me. I do speak English but I forget when I am excited.'

The obvious warmth flowing between Ciro and this young woman was as unexpected as it was heartening. Lara had never seen him look so relaxed.

Isabella took Lara's arm. 'Roberto will come and

get the bags—he's my twin brother. Let me show you around!'

Lara didn't think she had much choice, so she let herself be led up the steps and into the *palazzo* on a wave of Isabella's exuberance. In all honesty she was glad of a moment's respite—glad to get away from Ciro and stop overthinking everything that was to come that night.

Their wedding night.

About half an hour later Lara was led out onto an open terrace, overlooking the sea below. She could see another terrace further down, set precipitously right over the cliff. All was calm now, but she could imagine how dramatic it must be in a storm.

The rest of the *palazzo* was seriously impressive. Apparently it had undergone a major renovation in recent years, and now it was a byword for elegant sophistication and comfort.

It had an opulent cinema room, and a gym with an indoor pool. There was an outdoor pool set into its landscaped grounds. Too many bedrooms to count. Formal and informal dining rooms. A kitchen to die for. And there was even a quaint old church on the property.

Isabella had confided in Lara that Ciro was sponsoring her and her twin brother to go to university in Rome in the autumn. This was a side to Ciro that Lara hadn't seen before—philanthropic.

Isabella said now, 'I'll show you up to your suite. Ciro has asked that dinner be served here on the terrace in half an hour, but I'm sure you'd like to freshen up first?'

Lara nodded gratefully. She couldn't believe that the wedding had been earlier that same day. It felt like a lifetime ago.

She followed Isabella up the main staircase to the

first floor, where the bedrooms were situated. At the end of a plushly carpeted corridor she opened a door on the right and led Lara into an exquisitely decorated bedroom suite, complete with walk-in wardrobe and en suite bathroom. There was even a balcony through a set of French doors, overlooking the sea. It was sumptuous.

Isabella left her alone and Lara slipped off the light jacket she'd been wearing over her dress and took off her shoes, sighing with relief as her bare feet sank into the carpet.

She padded over to the balcony and looked out, drawing in a lungful of fragrant warm air from the Mediterranean Sea. Dozens of different scents tickled her nostrils…lemons…bergamot? The salty air from the sea. It was paradise, and in spite of everything Lara could feel something inside her loosen and untangle.

'Surprised that the uncouth Sicilian has some taste after all?'

Lara jumped nearly a foot in the air and slapped a hand over her racing heart. Ciro was standing on a similar balcony she hadn't noticed, just a few feet away. He'd lost his jacket too, and the sleeves of his shirt were rolled up, revealing strong muscled forearms.

Lara struggled to process his words. 'No…not at all.' She was irritated that she was so skittish around him. 'I always knew you had taste. I never called you uncouth.'

Or had she?

In those awful moments two years ago in the hospital… She'd been so desperate to get out of there before he'd seen what a fraud she was…

Ciro made a noise. 'Maybe not, but as good as.'

It was impossible not to notice how right Ciro looked against the dramatic backdrop of *palazzo* and cliffs and sea. As if he'd been hewn out of the very rock beneath them.

He straightened up from where he'd been leaning against the door. 'I'll take you down to dinner.'

He disappeared, and Lara was confused until she heard a door opening back in her suite and went in to see Ciro standing in an adjoining doorway. An interconnected but separate suite. She could see his bed in the background.

All at once she felt a conflicting and humiliating mixture of relief and disappointment. She knew she wasn't ready to share such an intimate space with Ciro yet. If ever. But she had expected him to want to project a united front. Ever mindful of people's opinion.

'Won't people expect us to…?'

'Be cohabiting?'

Lara shrugged, embarrassed. Maybe this was new etiquette and she was being incredibly unsophisticated to assume that all couples were like her parents, who had shared a bedroom. After all, her first experience of marriage had hardly been conventional.

'I have every intention of this being a marriage in all senses of the word, but we don't need to share a bedroom for that.'

Lara felt that like a slap in the face. Ciro would sleep with her but not *sleep* with her.

He came into the room. 'Dinner will be ready—shall we?'

Lara was about to follow him out of the room when she saw her shoes and slipped them on again, wincing slightly as they pinched after the long day. She also pulled her jacket over her shoulders, feeling a little exposed in the silk dress.

When they went out onto the terrace Lara couldn't

stop an involuntary gasp of pleasure and surprise from leaving her mouth. There were candles flickering in little jars all along the wall and fairy lights strung into the leaves and branches that clung to the *palazzo*'s ancient walls.

With the moon shining on the sea in the distance and exotic scents infusing the air, it was magical. The thought that Ciro might have gone out of his way to—

'Don't get any ideas. This is all Isabella's idea. She's a romantic.'

Lara's heart sank and she berated herself. What was *wrong* with her? Throw a little candlelight on the situation and she was prepared to forget that this was a marriage of convenience built on her sense of guilt and responsibility. Built on Ciro's need for retribution.

A table had been set for two with a white tablecloth and silverware. A champagne bottle rested in a bucket of ice. Out of nowhere a handsome young man appeared to open the champagne. Ciro introduced him as Roberto, Isabella's twin brother.

Ciro lifted his glass to Lara when they were sitting down. It was a mockery against the flickering lights of all the candles. 'Here's to us, and to a short but beneficial marriage.'

Lara longed to put down her glass and make her excuses, but Isabella was back with the first course, and she looked so happy to be serving them that Lara didn't have the heart to cause a scene.

When she'd left them alone, Lara leaned forward. 'You didn't have to marry someone you despise, you know. There are plenty of women who I'm sure would have loved to be in my position.'

Ciro took a drink. 'Ah, but they weren't you, *cara*,

with your unique qualities. You've been a thorn in my side for two years. I need to exorcise you to move on.'

'You mean take your revenge and in the process exploit my connections as much as possible?' She added, 'I hate to break it to you, but I don't wield half the influence my father and uncle did.'

Ciro appeared totally unperturbed by that. He flicked open his napkin. 'You wield influence just by being a Templeton. Marriage to you has automatically given me access to an inner circle that no one admits exists.'

Lara knew he was right on some level. As much as she hated to admit such hierarchical snobbishness existed. Impulsively she asked, 'Why does it matter so much to you?'

Ciro sat back, not liking his sense of claustrophobia at her question. But then he considered it. Why *shouldn't* he tell her? It wouldn't change anything. It wouldn't give anything away. It might actually show her just how determined he was to make this work. And how clinically he viewed this marriage. Even if his thrumming pulse told another story that was a lot *less* clinical.

'My father had a bad experience in England. He went to talk business with a number of potential partners. One by one they smiled to his face but refused to do business with him. He heard later that they had decided to close ranks against him. It wasn't just that he was new money—it was the rumours of where that money had come from. Had it been laundered? Did it come from the money made out of violence and crime by previous generations? He was humiliated. Angry. He made me promise to do better. To get myself a seat at the table so that the Sant'Angelo name could finally be free of negative associations.'

'Was your father the first one to try and break away?'

Ciro shook his head. 'It was his father. My grandfather desperately wanted to remove the stain of infamy from our name. He knew the world was moving on and he had ambitious plans for the Sant'Angelos. To go beyond these small shores, and Italy. He was sick of how our name engendered shock and derision. No respect. Not *real* respect. He wanted us to be accepted outside our narrow parameters. He craved the ultimate acceptance from a world that had always shunned us. But to do that we had to change our ways completely.'

Lara's eyes were wide. 'Where did he get his drive from? Presumably it would have been easier to keep things as they were?'

Ciro had been about to bring this line of conversation to an end—he'd said enough already—but some rogue urge compelled him to keep going, as if to impress upon Lara how determined he was.

'My grandfather's mother had wanted to marry a man she'd fallen in love with but he wasn't from the right family—in other words a family that the Mafia approved of. Her family threatened to kill him if she eloped with him. So, she stayed and married the man chosen for her—my great-grandfather. They had nine children and a perfectly cordial marriage, but she never forgave her family for doing that to her. She hated all the violence and oppression. She rebelled by passing on a new message to her own children—to my grandfather. A message to do things differently.'

Lara had stopped breathing. Ciro's ancestors had threatened to kill a man because they didn't sanction the relationship. History had repeated itself right here and the parallel was too cruelly ironic.

A little shakily she asked, 'What happened to the man she loved?'

Ciro waved a dismissive hand, as if it was of no importance. 'He left—emigrated to America. Does it matter?'

Lara curbed her urge to shout *Yes, of course it matters!* 'Not now, I guess, no.' She avoided Ciro's eye, not wanting him to see how this was affecting her.

'That's why it matters to me,' Ciro said. 'The Sant'Angelo name no longer has anything to do with those old and lurid tales of violence and organised crime, but the stain of infamy is still there. That kind of infamy only disappears completely with acceptance—true acceptance—in a very visible and public way. By association, you will bring a new kind of respect to the Sant'Angelo name that we've never had.'

Lara recalled how sick she'd felt when she'd seen the headlines after the kidnapping: *Mafia Heir Kidnapped and Held for Ransom... Sant'Angelo Kidnapping Proof He's Still Target for Criminals... Sant'Angelo Stocks Plummet After Kidnapping!*

She had brought that infamy into his life. And she hated to admit it but he was right, even though status meant nothing to her. She had to recognise that she'd been born into privilege—what did she know of his family's struggles to prove that they'd moved on from a violent world?

She had made the decision to do this—to make some redress for what had happened to Ciro, for what she had done. It was too late to turn back now.

He gestured to her plate. 'Eat up. Isabella's mother Rosa is a sublime cook.'

Lara saw the delicious-looking pasta starter on her plate but her appetite had fled. She forced herself to eat, not wanting to upset Isabella or her mother.

They conducted the rest of their meal in relative civility, sticking to neutral topics. When the plates for dessert had been cleared away Ciro got up with his coffee cup and went over to the wall of the terrace. Lara couldn't help drinking in his tall, powerful form. The broad shoulders and narrow hips. His easy graceful athleticism. The thought of going to bed with him...of seeing him naked...was overwhelming.

She realised she wasn't remotely prepared for such an intimate encounter with Ciro. What would he do when he discovered she was still a virgin?

A spark of panic propelled her from the chair to stand. 'I think I'll go to bed, actually. I'm quite tired.'

She winced. Her voice was too high and tight. She sounded so prim. A world away from the kind of woman who would undoubtedly be twining herself around Ciro right now, whispering seductive things in his ear.

He turned and leant back against the wall. Supremely nonchalant. He put down the coffee cup and looked at her. 'Come here, Lara.'

There was a sensual quality in his voice that impacted directly on her pulse, making it go faster. Afraid to open her mouth again, in case she sounded even more panicked, Lara reluctantly went towards Ciro. Her jacket had fallen off her shoulders and she shivered slightly in the night breeze.

'Cold?'

She rubbed her arms. 'No, I'm fine.'

I'm not fine.

Lara's hip bumped against the terrace wall. Ciro reached out and caught a strand of her hair, tugging her a little closer. The air between them grew taut. Expectant.

He looked at her hair as it slipped through his fingers, and then he said musingly, 'I don't despise you,

Lara. I will admit that I felt humiliated by you for some time, but then I had to acknowledge that it was my own fault for having believed the façade you'd projected when I should have known better. No woman had ever managed to fool me before you.'

Lara's heart squeezed. It hadn't been his fault at all. 'Ciro, I didn't—'

He put a finger to her mouth. 'I don't care about that any more. All I care about is that I've wanted you since the moment I saw you and I should never have denied myself this...'

'This' was Ciro putting his hands to Lara's waist and urging her towards him. Unsteady in her heels, and taken by surprise, Lara fell into him, landing flush against his body.

The effect was instantaneous. From the moment this man had first touched her, kissed her, two years ago, it had been like this. She cleaved to Ciro like a magnet drawn to its true north. His mouth touched hers and she gripped his shirt to stay standing. When she felt the slide of his tongue against the seam of her mouth she opened it instinctively, allowing him access.

Sicily and this place, even in such a short space of time, had touched something raw inside her. She could no more deny herself or Ciro this than she could stop breathing.

He gathered her closer and she could feel every ridge and muscle of his chest against hers, through the thin silk of her dress. And, down further, the press of his arousal against her belly. Desire pulsed between her legs. She wanted this man with a ferocity that might have scared her if she'd been thinking rationally for a moment. It was as if she was embracing the carnal to avoid thinking about anything rational.

Ciro's whole body was taut with the effort it was taking him not to swing Lara up into his arms and take her to the nearest horizontal surface, so he could lay her down and banish the demons that had been stalking him for two long years.

She felt like liquid fire in his arms. The soft contours of her body melted into his as if they'd been made especially for him. A ridiculously romantic notion that he didn't even have the wherewithal to reject right now, because he was so consumed with desire and need.

She tasted of sparkling wine and something much sweeter. And she exuded a kind of blind trust in Ciro, following and mimicking his movements. Darting out her tongue to touch his, as if she was afraid of what might happen if she was bolder. It ratcheted up his levels of arousal to a point where he had to bite back a groan. It reminded him of how she'd been before...which *had* to be his fevered imagination...

Her effect on him was as explosive as it always had been. Even though he now knew who she was and what she was capable of. It was as if that knowledge had added a darker edge to his desire. Because she was no longer an innocent—if she ever had been.

His hands couldn't rest on her waist. He had to explore her or die. Tracing over the curve of her hip, and up, he felt the silk of her dress slide over her body under his hand.

Ciro held his breath for a moment when he found and cupped her breast, felt its lush weight filling his hand, the press of her nipple against his palm. He wanted to taste her there, explore the hard nub with his tongue and teeth, make her squirm with pleasure. Make her moan...

Lara was drowning in heat and sensation. She'd never felt so many things at once. It was overwhelming, but utterly addictive. The rough stroke of Ciro's tongue on hers made her yearn to know what his tongue would feel like on her breast. He squeezed her there and her body vibrated with pleasure. It was too much. It wasn't enough.

Lara knew that she should pull back, put a stop to this, but some vital part of her resolve was dissolving in Ciro's arms and a fatal lethargy was taking over. A strong desire to put herself in the hands of this man. To capitulate to his every command.

'I've wanted you from the moment I saw you.'

She'd wanted him too—even though it had terrified her. And two years of purgatory had only made that wanting stronger. It was one of her big regrets that Ciro had never made love to her. That she'd had no palpable memory to comfort her in the long and lonely nights of her marriage.

It was also one of the reasons she'd found that superhuman strength to push her husband off her on their wedding night. The thought of any man but Ciro touching her had been utterly repulsive.

And now she was here in Ciro's arms. And she wanted him to touch her so desperately that she blocked out all the inner voices whispering warnings.

But a tiny sliver of oxygen got to her brain and she pulled back with an effort, struggling to open her eyes and calm her thundering heart.

Ciro's eyes were so dark they were fathomless. 'Lara...'

Her tongue felt heavy in her mouth as she said, 'Is this really a good idea?'

CHAPTER FIVE

A COOL BREEZE skated over Ciro's skin and he felt a prickle of exposure. Lara looked utterly wanton with her tousled hair and flushed cheeks. Her too-big eyes. Her plump and swollen mouth.

'Yes. We are consummating this marriage. You want me, Lara. You can't deny it.'

She looked down for a moment and it incensed Ciro. He had seen the way she'd morphed into another person in front of him once before. He tipped her chin back up, expecting to see some measure of triumph or satisfaction because she knew he couldn't hide how much he wanted her, but there was nothing in those huge blue eyes except an emotion he couldn't define. An emotion that caught at his chest, making it tight.

'Say it, Lara. Admit it.'

She bit her lip and looked at him searchingly, as if trying to find the answer to some riddle. Ciro was so used to women jumping into his arms at the slightest invitation that this was a wholly new experience.

Except it wasn't. Lara had been like this before. Hesitant. Shy. *Lying.*

'I do want you, Ciro. I always have.'

Ciro couldn't keep the bitterness from his voice when

he replied. 'That was *one* thing that was honest between us at least.'

Lara didn't want to be reminded of the past. She wanted to stay in this moment. *This* moment, when she could almost pretend the previous two years hadn't happened.

A sense of urgency gripped her and she pressed against Ciro, spreading her hands on his chest. 'Please, make love to me.'

Ciro looked down at her for such a long moment that Lara instinctively started to pull back, suspecting that perhaps this was all part of his plan to humiliate her when she was at her most vulnerable, but then he made a small rough sound and grabbed her hand, entwining his fingers with hers to lead her back into the *palazzo*.

Her heart was thundering so loudly she was sure he must be able to hear it. There wasn't any sign of Isabella or Roberto and Lara was glad. This moment was too raw to be witnessed. This was no benign wedding night consummation.

Lara's hand felt tiny in Ciro's and he instinctively tightened his grip, even as he rejected the notion that she was somehow vulnerable.

Disconcertingly, it reminded him of how fragile and delicate she'd felt during the kidnapping. How he'd been afraid he'd hurt her because he was holding her so tight. But they'd ripped her out of his arms anyway, and in that moment Ciro had known—

He shut his rogue thoughts down right there. *Not now.* Never would he think of that again.

He pushed open his bedroom door and looked at Lara. She met his gaze and there was something indecipherable in her expression. Determined.

She took her hand out of his and walked into the room

and over to the bed, kicking off her sandals as she went. She had her back to him and he could see her hands move. The silk dress started to loosen around her body.

She made a movement and he watched her shrug the dress from her shoulders so that it landed in a silken ripple by her feet. He was frozen to the spot, taking in the naked contours of her body covered only by the tiniest wisps of lace across her back and bottom. Nothing—no amount of anticipation—could have prepared him for this moment.

Ciro was glad she was facing away from him because he was convulsed with need and desire. Once again she was reaching inside him and turning his guts inside out—except this time he would slay the dragon, and once he'd had her she would lose the hold she'd had over him since they'd met.

Lara was practically naked, dressed only in her panties and a flimsy lace bra. She could sense Ciro behind her. Looking at her. She wasn't sure what had possessed her. A moment ago she'd been filled with a sense of bravado, but now little tremors were going through her body at the thought of facing Ciro like this.

And then she heard a rough-sounding, 'Lara…'

Swallowing her fear, she slowly turned around and Ciro filled her vision. She could see the tension in his body, making him loom even larger than he normally did. Suddenly self-conscious, she crossed one arm over her breasts and covered herself between her legs with the other hand.

Ciro shook his head. 'No…let me see you. I've waited for this for so long.'

After a moment Lara did as he asked, dropping her hands to her sides, clenching them into fists. In the dim light of the room she couldn't see where Ciro's dark gaze touched her. But she could feel it. On her breasts, her belly, waist, thighs...between her legs.

Her skin broke into goosebumps.

Ciro walked towards her, his usual grace absent. When he stood in front of her she could see the stark expression of pure need on his face. His eyes were blazing.

'You are more beautiful than I ever imagined.'

Lara ducked her head, overwhelmed by what she saw in his eyes. 'I'm not...truly...'

He tipped up her chin and there was something else on his face now, an expression she couldn't decipher. Something like frustration.

'Yes, you are. You really don't have to put on this act, Lara. It's just us here now.'

He thought she was acting coy. She was stripped bare, save for some scraps of material. She'd never been more exposed. And he couldn't see it.

She realised she couldn't entirely blame him. After all, she'd done her best to convince him she was someone else. Someone who cared more for prestige and social standing than anything else.

'Lara.'

She looked at him and her whirling thoughts stopped. She sucked in a breath.

'I need to hear you say it again.'

Lara's heart squeezed. There was no going back. She needed this as much as he did.

She stepped closer, until they were touching and his clothes caused friction against her naked skin. She went up on her tiptoes and pressed her mouth to his neck. 'Please...' she said.

She trailed her mouth along his jaw, up to where she could feel the rough edges of his scar on the right side of his face. He tensed, and then he put his hands on her arms, hauling her up and closer, before his mouth found hers and the whole world burst into flame.

Lara sensed Ciro shedding his clothes, but while his mouth was on hers she couldn't focus on anything except his intoxicating scent and the dark sensuality of his kiss. Deep and drugging.

When his hot bare skin met hers she stopped and drew back, dizzy from the kiss, and even dizzier when she saw that Ciro was completely naked. The breath left her body as she feasted unashamedly on his perfect form.

She'd never seen him fully naked. Broad shoulders, a wide, powerful chest with a dusting of dark hair that dissected his abdominals in a tantalising line all the way down to where his arousal jutted proudly between his legs. Her gaze stopped there, heat rising inside her at this very potent evidence of his desire for her.

'*Cara mia*…if you keep looking at me like that we won't make it to the bed.'

With difficulty, Lara raised her gaze to Ciro's again.

He took her hand and led her over to the bed. 'Lie down,' he instructed.

Lara lay down on the bed, hoping that he hadn't noticed the tremor in her limbs. Ciro stood for a long moment, his dark gaze moving up and down her body. Then he sat on the bed and lifted a hand, tracing the shape of her jaw and her mouth, which was still swollen from his kisses.

He trailed his hand down, dipping his fingers into the hollow at the base of her throat, and then over her chest to her breasts. Her nipples were two hard points, pressing against the delicate lace of her bra.

Ciro tortured her slowly, trailing his fingers between her breasts, under one and then the other, before covering one breast with his palm, its heat and weight making Lara bite her lip. She could feel the point of her nipple stabbing Ciro's palm, and instinctively she arched her back to push herself into his hand.

His mouth quirked. With an expertise that spoke of his experience he undid the front clasp of her bra and peeled the lace squares back, baring her to his gaze. He squeezed her breast gently and Lara's breath hitched. She was unprepared for the spiking of pleasure deep down in her core. Then he took his hand away and placed both hands either side of her body, so he could lower his head and...

Lara nearly jack-knifed off the bed when she felt the potent drugging sensation of Ciro's hot mouth closing over first one nipple and then the other.

He put a hand on her belly, as if to calm her. She was breathing so fast it hurt—but not nearly as much as the exquisite torture of his mouth on her flesh...the hot, wet heat, teeth tugging gently at her sensitised flesh.

Lara's whole body was on fire now, as the bed dipped and Ciro moved to lie alongside her. The hand on her belly moved down until it rested at the juncture of her legs. With the same expert economical touch he dispensed with her panties, throwing them to the floor. He touched her thigh.

'Open for me, *bella*.'

Lara opened her legs and Ciro's hand slid down to explore where she was so aroused. It was excruciating. It was exquisite. She'd never known anything like it before.

Ciro had been a model of restraint two years before, when he'd discovered she was a virgin. So much so that she'd begun to feel seriously insecure. She'd ached with wanting him but he'd always seemed so in control.

Not any more.

Lara's nails scored her palms as Ciro massaged her throbbing flesh with his fingers before sliding one deep inside her. The sensation was electrifying. Lara instinctively reached for his wrist but he was remorseless.

'Trust me, *cara mia.*'

In the midst of this sensual onslaught Lara felt a dangerous bubble of emotion rise up. She *did* trust Ciro. Perhaps not with her heart any more, but in a very deep and fundamental way. She'd never expected to see him again, be with him again. Certainly not like this. But she'd fantasised about it in her lonely bed so many times...

Shocked and aghast at the welling of emotion—she shouldn't be feeling *emotion* right now!—she almost cried out with relief when Ciro took his hand away and replaced it with his body, settling between her legs as if it was the most natural thing in the world. As if they'd done this dance a million times before.

His weight was heavy and she revelled in it, widening her legs so that he came into closer contact with the cradle of her femininity, where every nerve-ending was pulsating with need.

Ciro had to take a breath and resist the urge to drive deep into Lara's willing body. He could feel the pulse of her desire against him, and the way she was opening like a flower under his body. He couldn't remember ever wanting a woman like this. Lovemaking for him had always held a certain amount of detachment. But here, right now, he was...*consumed.*

But then he'd always known instinctively that Lara had a different kind of hold over him. Something he hadn't encountered before. Something that made him nervous. But right now nerves were gone.

Ciro reached for and found protection, miraculously thinking of it at the last second, rolling it on with uncharacteristic clumsiness.

He positioned himself at the juncture of Lara's legs and looked down into her eyes. It was another thing he usually avoided with lovers, but with Lara he couldn't seem to move unless his gaze was locked onto hers.

Her expression was soft, unfocused. Her cheeks were flushed. Damp strands of her hair clung to her forehead. She was biting her lip.

'Ciro...please.'

In this there was no *other Lara*. He had undone her, exposed her.

He felt her move beneath him and couldn't hold on. He plunged deep inside her, feeling every muscle in his body spasming with pleasure at the sheer sensation of his body moving deep into the clasp of hers.

The very *tight* clasp...

It took a second for him to register in his overheated brain that Lara had tensed, and now she looked anything but unfocused. There was an expression of shock on her face. Awe. And...*pain*?

Ciro moved slightly and she sucked in a breath. His brain didn't seem to be working properly. He knew he was big but he'd thought she'd be experienced enough...

'Lara, am I hurting you?'

'It's okay...don't stop now. Please don't stop.'

She sounded breathless.

She put her hands on his hips, and even as a very uncomfortable truth made itself graphically known to him Ciro could no more deny his primal urge to move than he could stop breathing.

Lara consciously relaxed her muscles, and for a second she almost cried out because the sensation was so intense. But as Ciro started to move again she could feel the pain easing, her body adapting to his, softening around him. And then, pleasure became the dominant sensation as the steady, rhythmic glide of Ciro's body in and out of hers led to a rising excitement, a sense of urgency and desperation that made her reach around to clasp his firm muscular buttocks, silently pleading with him to go deeper, faster...

Lara wasn't prepared for the sudden rush of intense pleasure. It was so unexpected and overwhelming that it was all she could do to cling on to Ciro as his body bucked into hers, again and again, as he too was torn apart and lost all control, finally slumping against her, his head buried in her neck, his ragged breath warm against her damp skin.

For those few moments while they were still intimately joined, their pulses racing, Lara knew complete contentment. Something she hadn't experienced in a very long time. But then Ciro moved, and she winced slightly as he extricated himself from her embrace. Her muscles were tender.

Ciro wasn't looking at her. He sat on the edge of the bed, his back to her, head downbent. His breathing was still uneven. Lara felt a chill skate across her bare flesh and instinctively reached for a sheet to cover herself.

After a moment he got up without a word and went into the bathroom. Lara heard the hiss of the shower. She lay in bed with the sheet pulled up over her chest, totally unsure of herself and not knowing how to behave.

Should she join Ciro in the shower? It seemed like the kind of thing a sophisticated lover would do... But he hadn't said anything and perhaps he wanted to be alone.

He suddenly emerged from the bathroom, taking Lara by surprise. He had a towel slung around his waist and his skin glistened with moisture. For a second she was breathless at the mere thought that moments ago they'd been joined as intimately as it was possible to be joined with another person.

He said, 'I've run you a bath. You'll be sore. Then we need to talk.'

Lara swallowed. Had it been that obvious? Had he noticed she was—*had been*—a virgin?

Feeling totally exposed, and far too vulnerable after what had just happened, Lara got up from the bed as elegantly as she could and went into the bathroom, trailing the sheet behind her.

After the bath, which soothed her tender muscles and her skin, Lara got out and dried herself perfunctorily. She pulled on the voluminous terrycloth robe hanging on the back of the door and steeled herself before going into the bedroom.

But it was empty.

She went out through the door and took a deep, shaky breath before going in search of her husband.

Lara had been a virgin. Innocent. Untouched.

Ciro was feeling such a conflicting mass of emotions and sensations that he couldn't quite pin down what was most prominent: anger, confusion…or, worst of all, a humiliating level of relief at knowing that *he* had been Lara's first lover and not that old man.

With that relief came more confusion and anger, and in the midst of it all was a residual heavy feeling of sexual satisfaction on a level he'd never experienced.

Before, it had been a fleeting thing. Soon forgotten. Much like the women he'd slept with, *before*. But this satisfaction felt as if it was seared into his bones and as his hunger grew for her again. Already. Insatiably.

There had been a moment out on the terrace, after Lara had said, *'Please make love to me...'* when for a split second Ciro had been tempted to reject her. As she'd rejected him. And yet even though he might have fantasised about such a moment in the previous two years, when it had been there, right in front of him, he'd been aware of how petty it was.

And also that he didn't have the strength to reject her. Not when his mouth had been full of her taste and his hands imprinted with the shape of her body.

Madre di Dio.

He heard a noise at that moment.

Lara.

Ciro's whole body tensed against the inevitable re-action his new bride would precipitate. His new *virgin* bride.

Lara tracked Ciro down to a room she hadn't yet been in. A state-of-the-art modern study with humming computers and shelves full of books and periodicals.

He was standing at a window which looked out over the sea. He'd dressed in low-slung faded jeans and a T-shirt. Bare feet. Messy damp hair. She could see his face reflected in the window. The long white line of his scar. His hands were shoved deep in his pockets, which pulled the material of his jeans taut across the perfect globes of his bottom.

Her heart thumped. 'Ciro...look...'

He turned around and she saw the full extent of his anger on his face. '*Dio,* Lara. How the *hell* were you still a virgin?'

'How did you know?'

Even as she asked the question she wanted to kick herself for being so stupid. A man as experienced as Ciro? Of *course* he'd known. He wasn't some boorish bully like her first husband had been.

He emitted a harsh-sounding laugh. 'How did I *know*? I felt it in your body and there was blood on the sheets.'

A hot wash of humiliation rushed up under Lara's skin. She hadn't even noticed the blood. She felt utterly gauche. She pulled the robe around her, tightening it.

Ciro sent her a dark look. 'It's a bit late for that.'

Lara noticed a drinks cabinet in the corner of the room. 'Can I have a drink, please?' She needed something if this was going to be the tone of their conversation.

Ciro went over and asked tightly, 'Brandy?'

Lara shook her head. 'No—anything but that.'

He poured something into a glass, then came and handed it to her. 'It's whisky. What do you have against brandy?'

Lara took the glass, relieved that Ciro was distracted from his inevitable questions for a moment. 'Brandy reminds me of funerals. When my parents and brother died my uncle made me drink some. He said it was for the shock but it made me sick.'

She took a sip of the whisky, wincing at the tart, acrid taste. It slid down her throat and landed in her stomach, sending out a glow of warmth. But she knew it was just illusory and wouldn't last.

'How old were you?'

Lara glanced at Ciro warily. 'Thirteen.'

'You were close as a family?'

Lara nodded, her hand clasping the glass. 'The closest. My parents loved each other and they loved me and Alex. We were a very happy family.'

Ciro surprised her by saying, 'You were lucky to have had that, even if only for a short while. My father loved my mother, but it was a suffocating love and she wasn't happy to be adored by just one man. After he died she remarried within a month. She's now on husband number three—or four. I've lost count.'

The careless tone in Ciro's voice didn't fool Lara. He couldn't be immune to the fact that his mother had failed to be the kind of mother every child deserved. No wonder he was so cynical.

Ciro sat back against his desk, and folded his arms. The reprieve was over. 'So. Are you going to explain to me how you were married but still a virgin?'

Lara took another fortifying sip of whisky and sat down on a chair behind her. Her legs didn't feel steady all of a sudden. She looked up at Ciro and then away. She didn't want to see his expression.

'On our wedding night Henry came into my bedroom expecting to—' She stopped.

'Go on.'

Lara felt sick. She looked at him. 'Do we really have to discuss this now?'

Ciro nodded. Grim.

He stood up and pulled over a chair so that he was opposite Lara, sat down. She knew he wouldn't budge until she'd told him the ugly truth.

'On our wedding night he came into my bedroom... He...we'd agreed that we wouldn't share a room. I some-how...obviously naively...assumed that would mean he wouldn't try to...' She faltered and stopped.

'Try to...*what*? Sleep with his new *wife*? A natural expectation, I would have thought.'

Lara hated Ciro's faintly scathing tone. It scraped along all the raw edges of the memories crowding her head. She stood up and went over to where he'd been standing, at the window. She could see dark clouds massing over the sea and the white edges of rough waves. There was a storm approaching.

It was easier to talk when Ciro wasn't looking at her. 'He came into the bedroom. He'd been drinking all day so he was very drunk. He grabbed my nightdress and ripped it. Before I could stop him he'd pushed me backwards onto the bed. I was in shock... I couldn't move for a moment... He was so heavy and I couldn't breathe...'

Lara didn't even hear Ciro move. He caught her arm and turned her around to face him. She'd never seen that expression on his face before—disgust mixed with pure anger.

'He tried to rape you?'

Lara nodded. 'I thought we had an agreement...that he was just marrying me for appearances. He was old... I didn't think...' She trailed off, humiliated by her naivety all over again.

Ciro was grim. 'Old men's libidos can be voracious.' Then he shook his head. 'Did you really think he wouldn't demand sex from you?'

Lara pulled her arm free and moved away. Some liquid slopped out of her glass and she looked at the carpet in dismay.

'Leave it—it's nothing.'

Ciro took the glass and put it down. Lara flinched minutely at the clatter against the silver tray.

'But he didn't rape you?'

Lara looked at Ciro, remembering how thinking of him had given her the strength to deal with Henry Winterborne. 'No. I managed to kick him off me...somehow.

He was unsteady from the drink. He fell backwards. He injured himself badly in the fall…and he was in a wheelchair for the rest of our marriage. Eventually he had a stroke—that's how he died.'

Lara couldn't excise the memory of Henry Winterborne's bitter words from her head. *'You little bitch— you'll pay for this. Your only currency is your beauty and innocence. Why the hell do you think I paid so much for you?'*

Fresh humiliation washed over her in a sickening wave. She hadn't even known until then the full extent of her uncle's machinations—that he'd actually sold her like a slave girl. Ciro didn't know the half of it.

Ciro was reeling. All he could see in his mind's eye was that paunchy old man shoving Lara down onto a bed and then climbing on top of her like a rutting bull. Anger bubbled in his blood. No, worse—a ferocious fury that she had put herself in harm's way like that.

'Was the prospect of marrying me really so repulsive that you would choose a man capable of rape over me? *Dio,* Lara…'

He turned around and speared a hand through his hair, not wanting her to see the emotions he couldn't control. He'd thought he'd underestimated her before. This put a whole new perspective on her ambition.

She stayed silent. Not responding.

Ciro steeled himself before turning. Wild dishevelled blonde hair trailed over her shoulders. The robe had fallen apart slightly, to reveal the plump globes of her high firm breasts. Breasts he could still feel in his hands and on his tongue…

Her eyes were huge and he hated her ability still to look so…*innocent*. Even when he'd just taken that innocence in a conflagration that had left him feeling hollowed out and yet hungry for more.

He felt the need to push her away. Gain some distance. He couldn't think when she was so close. When she was telling him things...putting images into his mind that made him want to go out and put a fist through the face of a man who was already dead.

Her silence grated on his nerves. It was as if there was something she was withholding.

'Was it that important to you? Status?'

Her eyes flashed. 'You have some nerve when you've admitted you only wanted to marry me for one thing—my connections.'

Ciro's gut was a mass of tangled emotions he really didn't want to investigate. But this woman had always touched more than just his body. A minute ago he'd wanted to put push her away and now he needed to touch her. *Damn her.*

He closed the distance between them, noting with satisfaction how a line of pink scored each of her cheeks. She couldn't hide her reaction. It was the only honest thing between them.

He slid a hand around the back of her neck, felt the silky fall of her hair brushing his hand. 'Not just for your connections, *cara mia*, but also because I wanted *you*. Your social connections and impeccable breeding were a bonus.'

Ciro's words dropped like the poisoned barbs they were into Lara's heart. And yet could she blame him when she'd convinced him that she'd never intended to marry him?

She pulled away, hating the way her body was reacting to his proximity. Excitement was building already, heat melting her core. She was still so sensitised she was afraid that if he even kissed her it would be enough to send her over the edge.

'Well, you've had me now. I'm sure the novelty is already waning.'

Ciro easily closed the distance between them again, and this time he took Lara's elbows in his hands, tugging her towards him. All she could see was that wicked sculpted mouth, and all she could think about was how it had felt on her body. Against her skin.

'Waning? I've wanted you since the moment I laid eyes on you, *cara*, and you've haunted me for two years. Believe me, once is nowhere near enough to sate my appetite.'

His mouth was on hers and Lara couldn't formulate another word. All she knew was that for a while at least there would be no more cruel words. Her heart was pounding, blood flowing to every tender part of her...

Ciro swung Lara up into his arms as if she weighed no more than a bag of flour. She knew she should protest, try to reclaim some minute modicum of dignity, but as he carried her back upstairs she couldn't help but think of how she'd endured two barren years of regretting the fact that she hadn't slept with Ciro.

So she wasn't going to regret a single moment now. No matter how much Ciro might resent her for this inconvenient desire he felt. It would burn out, sooner or later, and this time, when Lara walked away, she would have no regrets.

When Lara woke the following morning she was in her own bed. Naked. The French doors were open and the white drapes were moving gently in a warm breeze. She grabbed for a sheet, pulling it up over her chest even though she was alone.

She had a very vague memory of Ciro carrying her into this room as dawn had been breaking over the horizon, the storm clouds of the previous night banished.

Silly to feel bereft when he'd told her he didn't think it necessary for them to share a room. After all, he wasn't interested in morning-after intimacy. In a way, Lara should be grateful that this time around all the romantic illusions she'd harboured were well and truly shattered.

She tried to absorb everything that had happened in the space of twenty-four hours but it was overwhelming. This time yesterday she'd still been a single woman, on her way to get married.

She'd still been a virgin.

And now…she felt transformed.

She didn't want to admit that Ciro's touch had had some kind of mystical effect on her—but it was true. In spite of the way he felt about her, his touch had soothed something inside her—the lonely place she'd retreated to for the past two years in a bid to survive an impossible situation.

She heard a familiar low rumble and got out of bed to investigate, pulling on a robe as she did so. She went over to the French doors that led out to the balcony, knotting the robe around her.

Hesitantly she peeked over the railings, to see Ciro standing on the terrace below. He was dressed in those faded jeans and another T-shirt and Lara's mouth dried. He reminded her too painfully of when they'd first met in Florence and he'd been casually dressed. When she'd fallen in love with him.

At that moment Ciro turned around and looked up. Lara stepped back hastily, her heart spasming. *Love.* Did she still *love* him?

No. The rejection of such a disturbing thought was swift and brutal.

How could she still love a man who had betrayed her as much as he believed she'd betrayed him? After years of protecting herself from the pain of loss Ciro had come along and smashed aside her petty defences. Leaving her vulnerable all over again. She'd never forgive him for that.

Enduring all the things she had, had made her strong. Strong enough to withstand this marriage so she could finally move on with her life, her conscience salved. But the little whispers of that conscience told her that as much as she might try to justify why she was doing this, she wouldn't be here unless deeper motives were involved. Far more personal motives.

After all, if she'd really wanted to she could have told Ciro the full truth from the start. Or even last night, when she'd had a chance. But she hadn't. *Why?*

She knew the answer. Because however much he disliked her now—resented her, even, for this desire that burned between them—he would truly despise her if he knew about her uncle and his involvement in the kidnapping and ruination of their wedding. In the very public humiliation Ciro had gone through.

Lara knew that after eroding Ciro's trust in her so effectively he would never believe she hadn't had a part in it… She also knew it would be another huge blow to his pride to find out that she'd known who was behind the attack. He'd never forgive her for that.

There was a peremptory knock at her door and Lara whirled around, expecting to see Isabella. But it was Ciro. Immediately her belly clenched at the memory of how he'd felt between her legs, surging into her body over and over again.

'Buon giorno, mia moglie.'

There was something so palpably satisfied about his tone that Lara injected as much coolness into her voice as she could when she answered. 'Good morning.'

'I've decided that we're leaving today. We've been invited to an event in London tonight.'

Feeling prickly at how cool he appeared to be after a night in which her world had been seismically altered, she said, 'You mean *you've* been invited.'

Ciro leant against the doorframe and folded his arms. 'No, *we've* been invited. To the Royal Opening of the Summer Exhibition at the Longleat Gallery.'

Lara was impressed. Henry Winterborne had been incandescent with rage last year when he hadn't received an invitation to the opening. He'd blamed *her*, of course.

Ciro straightened up. 'Isabella is on her way up with a breakfast tray. We'll leave in an hour. I've arranged for a stylist to deliver some clothes to the townhouse in London, so you don't need to pack.'

He walked away and Lara breathed out slowly, her pounding pulse mocking her attempts to affect the same coolness as Ciro exuded so effortlessly. But then what had she expected? Morning-after cuddles and tender enquires as to how she might be feeling?

Lara turned around to the view again. She would be sorry to leave Sicily so soon, but at the same time she was a little relieved. It had been a cataclysmic twenty-four hours and it would surely be easier to deal with Ciro and try to maintain some emotional distance from him in a busy city surrounded by people, than here, in this effortlessly seductive and intimate environment.

CHAPTER SIX

CIRO WAS AWARE that he should be feeling more satisfied than he was. And that irritated the hell out of him.

Lara was standing a few feet away, a vision in a long yellow evening dress. She effortlessly stood out from the crowd. The dress was one-shouldered, revealing the alluring curve of her bare shoulder and the top of her back. A decorative jewel held the dress over her other shoulder. All it needed was a flick of his fingers and it would be undone, letting the dress fall down to expose her beautiful breasts—

Basta! Ciro cursed his overheated imagination.

Her hair was smoothed back and tied low at the nape of her neck in a loose bun. Long diamond earrings glittered from her ears. She wore minimal make-up. She epitomised cool elegance, and yet all he could think about was the fire that lay under her pale skin. The ardent passion with which she'd made love to him last night. It was hard to believe she'd been a novice...but she *had* been. And that bugged him like a thorn under his skin.

How had he missed it? He who considered himself a connoisseur of women?

He didn't like getting things wrong. Underestimating people. He'd learnt a harsh and brutal lesson at the hands of those kidnappers. The kidnappers who'd yet to be caught and whom he was still investigating—with not much luck.

Until that day he would have been the first to admit that life had always come easily to him. Blessed with good looks, a keen intellect and a sizeable family fortune, he'd lacked for nothing. But since those days at the hands of violent thugs Ciro had learnt not to be so complacent. And since the day Lara had informed him she'd never had any intention of marrying him he'd learnt not to underestimate anyone.

His cynicism had become even more pronounced. Any kind of easy charm he'd displayed before had become something much darker.

Unbidden, a memory resurfaced at that moment. Lara, not long after they'd met, admitting to him sheepishly that she'd looked him up on the internet. He'd immediately felt betrayed. And disappointed. She was like everyone else. Assessing his worth. Looking for the salacious details of his family history.

And then she'd stunned him with an apparently sincere apology, saying that she should have asked him face to face. Normally he abhorred women trying to get him to reveal personal details, but within seconds he'd been saying to Lara, 'Ask me now.'

That was the night she'd confided in him about her family and their history. How she had a trust fund worth millions. For the first time in his life someone had surprised Ciro. And it had only added to her allure.

Until she'd pulled the rug out from under his feet.

For the first time in a long time he wanted to know *why* she'd done it. Created that persona. But something held him back. Some sense of self-preservation.

A feeling that he'd be exposing himself if he asked the question.

As if sensing his brooding regard, she turned and looked at him, and for a second Ciro couldn't breathe. She was so beautiful. And the memory was so vivid. He could almost imagine that the previous two years hadn't happened.

But they had.

He cast aside memories and nebulous dangerous thoughts. She was here by his side. *His*. That was all that was important.

He lifted his hand and crooked a finger, silently commanding her to come to him. He saw the way her eyes flashed, the subtle tensing of her shoulders. The resistance to his decree. But then she came. Because she was here in her own milieu and of course she wouldn't cause a scene.

It was time to remember why he had spent two years keeping tabs on her and why he'd married her at the first opportunity. For revenge, yes, but so much more. He caught Lara's hand in his, very aware of the absence of his little finger. The reminder firmed his resolve to stop thinking of the past.

He bent his head close to hers, inhaled her scent drifting up to tantalise his nostrils and threatening to dissolve that resolve. He directed Lara to look across the lawn to where heads of state, royalty and A-list celebrities sipped champagne and mingled. 'Do you see Lord Andrew Montlake over there?'

Lara nodded.

'He was a friend of your father's, yes?'

Lara nodded again. 'Yes—a good friend.'

Ciro smiled. 'Good, then introduce me. I've been trying to get a meeting with him for months, to discuss the chateau he's selling outside Paris.'

* * *

A few hours later Lara's feet were aching almost as much as her facial muscles ached from smiling and pretending that it was totally normal to be back in London society with a new husband just over a week after burying her previous husband. She'd felt every searing look and heard every not so discreet whisper and had held her head high with a smile fixed in place.

They were in the back of Ciro's car now, and she looked out of the window at the streets of London bathed in late summer sunshine. Young couples stood hand in hand outside pubs, drinking and laughing. Carefree.

She'd never had the chance for a life like that. As soon as her uncle had taken over his role as guardian he'd had his nefarious plan mapped out for Lara and she'd been totally unaware of it.

Pushing down the uncharacteristic welling of self-pity, Lara thought of the event they'd just been to. As much as *she'd* been the centre of attention, so had Ciro. Lara had noticed the looks and whispers directed his way too, the way people's eyes had widened on his scarred features. It had made her want to stand in front of him and stare them down. Shame them for their morbid fascination.

She'd seen the masterful way he'd operated, winning people around, charming them into submission. He might have needed someone like her for access into this rarefied world, but it wouldn't be long before he became an indelible part of it. And then her role would be obsolete.

Ciro turned to look at her then, as if aware of her regard. The back of the luxury car suddenly felt tiny. All evening Lara had been acutely aware of Ciro, of his every movement as he'd taken her hand, or touched her arm, or the small of her back. Her skin felt tight and sensitive. Her body ached with a wholly new kind of yearning. And her lower body tightened with need every time his dark gaze rested on her. Like now.

She didn't feel in control of herself at all any more. If she ever had around this man. And she hated it that he seemed so cool, calm and collected.

If he so much as touched her right now she knew she wouldn't be able to control her reaction, but he surprised her by saying, 'We're going to stay in London for a few days. I have some meetings lined up.'

Lara hid her skittishness and said, 'Fine.'

And then, just when she thought she could gather herself, he reached for her, taking her hand and tugging her across the divide in the seat, closer to him.

'What are you doing?' Lara cast a glance at the driver in front.

Ciro said something in Italian and the privacy window went up, cocooning them in the back of the blacked-out car. The streets outside faded into insignificance as Ciro's hand sneaked around the back of Lara's neck, where with deft fingers he loosened her hair so it tumbled over her shoulders.

Lara's heart rate increased as Ciro's fingers massaged her neck—and then his hand moved to where the dress was held up by the jewel over one shoulder.

Excitement curled low in her abdomen as she protested weakly, 'Ciro…we're in the back of the car…'

He said, 'Do you know how hard it's been for me to keep my hands off you all evening?'

She shook her head, mesmerised by the look on his face. She could see it now—the desire bubbling just under the surface, barely restrained—and she felt it reach out and touch her.

With a flick of his fingers the dress opened and loosened around her breasts. She gasped and put a hand up, but Ciro caught her hand and said roughly, 'Leave it.'

Ciro peeled her dress down, uncovering her breasts. Lara shivered with a mixture of arousal and illicit excitement, aware of the people outside the car on the pavement, where they were stopped at some lights. Only the blacked-out windows and some steel and glass separated her from them and their eyes.

Ciro looked at her and cupped her naked breasts, thumbs moving back and forth over her nipples. 'So beautiful,' he breathed.

'Ciro...' Lara was almost panting. She stopped talking, afraid of exposing herself even more.

His dark head bent towards her, and when his mouth closed around one tight tingling nipple the spiking pleasure was so intense she speared her hands in his hair. She quickly got lost in the maelstrom Ciro had unleashed in her body, knowing that she was showing her weakness but unable to do anything about it...

Ciro looked at himself in the mirror of his bathroom and took in his glittering eyes and the still hectic colour on his cheekbones. When they'd returned to the townhouse a short while before Lara had all but fled up the stairs, holding up the top of her dress with one hand, her hair in a tangle.

Ciro had let her go, even though he'd wanted to carry her straight to his bedroom and to his bed. The only thing that had stopped him was the awful suspicion that he'd just exposed himself spectacularly.

Just an hour before he'd been talking with one of

Europe's heads of state, and within minutes of getting into a car with Lara he'd been all over her like a hormone-fuelled teenager.

He splashed cold water on his face, as if that might dilute the heat raging in his body. After a moment he went into his bedroom, restless and edgy. He looked at the interconnecting door between his and Lara's rooms for a long moment before going over and opening it quietly.

She was in bed. Curled up on one side in a curiously childlike pose, her hair spread out on the pillow. Her breaths were deep and even.

Something about the fact that she could find the equilibrium of sleep so easily made him feel even more exposed.

He went back into his bedroom and closed the door. And then he did the only thing he could do to try and dilute the sexual frustration in his body. He headed for the gym.

As soon as Lara was sure that Ciro had left her room she turned on her back and sucked in a deep, shuddering breath. She looked up at the ceiling.

She was in her underwear under the covers. She'd heard Ciro moving about next door, and after coming so spectacularly undone in the back of his car had felt far too raw to be able to deal with seeing him again. So she'd dived under the covers and feigned sleep even as her body had mocked her, aching for Ciro's touch. For him to finish what he'd started.

This evening had been a salutary lesson in the reality of how this marriage would work. Ciro had used her with a ruthless and clinical precision to seek out meetings with the various people he was interested in talking to. She had to remember that was the focal point of the marriage—her desire to make amends to Ciro for what her uncle had done to him.

What she *had done to him.*

And the other stuff? The physical chemistry? The aching desire he'd awoken in her body?

A man of his extensive experience would surely lose interest soon. Wouldn't he? And when he did she'd have to live with that. She'd lived with far worse, so she would cope. She'd have to.

The following days brought a reprieve of sorts for Lara. Ciro was out at meetings all day, and each evening he had a business dinner to attend, where she wasn't required.

Like a coward, she'd taken the opportunity to make sure she was in bed by the time Ciro came home, pretending to be asleep if he came into her room.

She'd got used to her surroundings—just a stone's throw from the old apartment she'd shared with Henry Winterborne—but she deliberately made sure to avoid that street if she was out of the house, and she knew the security men must think she was mad, taking such a long way round to go to the shops.

Ciro had issued her with a credit card, and Lara had swallowed her pride and taken it. After two years of feeling trapped, due to her lack of personal finances, she was embarrassed at being beholden to someone else. More than ever she wanted to make her own money. Be independent.

And yet there was something about Ciro handing her some economic freedom that made her feel emotional. A man who had a lot less reason to trust her than her previous husband was trusting her with this.

She'd also got to know the staff who worked in the house: the housekeeper was called Dominique, and there was a groundsman/handyman called Nigel. Dominique hired in staff as and when it was required for entertaining or cleaning, she'd told Lara. But as yet Ciro hadn't actually ever entertained in the house.

Fleetingly Lara wondered again at the coincidence that had Ciro's new house right around the corner from where she'd been living.

One evening it was Dominique's night off—she lived close by, so didn't stay over at the townhouse—and Lara went into the kitchen, feeling restless.

She'd always loved to cook, so when Henry Winterborne had maliciously turned her from wife into housekeeper she'd welcomed it, far preferring to be in the kitchen than to share space in his presence.

She'd learnt to cook in the first instance from her parents' housekeeper—a lovely warm woman called Margaret, who had been more like a member of the family than staff. And then over the years she'd continued to cook...usually surreptitiously, because her uncle hadn't approved of her doing such a menial thing.

'You were not born to cook and serve, Lara,' he'd said sharply.

No, she thought bitterly, she'd been born so he could exploit her for his own ends.

She shook her head to get rid of the memory and looked around the gleaming kitchen, instinctively pulling out ingredients from the well-stocked cupboards and shelves.

As she cooked from memory she felt a peace she hadn't experienced in weeks descend over her. She tuned the radio to a pop station and hummed along tunelessly.

In a brief moment of optimism she thought that if things continued as they were going, and if she could maintain her distance from Ciro, she might actually survive this marriage...

Ciro had returned home early, to change for a dinner event. He was irritable and frustrated—which had a lot to do with the workload he'd taken on and the fact that he'd barely seen Lara since that first night in London.

Somehow she was always conveniently in bed when he got home, and he was not about to reveal how much he wanted her by waking her up like some kind of rabid animal to demand his conjugal rights.

He wasn't sure what he'd expected to see on his arrival this afternoon, but it involved an image along the lines of Lara being ready and waiting for him to take her to his bed when he got in.

He set down his briefcase in the hall and loosened his tie. For the first time in his life a woman wasn't throwing herself at Ciro.

He scowled. *The second time in his life.*

The first time had also been with Lara. She'd been like a skittish foal around him when they'd first met. It had taken him weeks of seducing her on a level that he hadn't had to employ for years. If ever.

After she'd revealed herself so spectacularly, and walked out of his hospital room, he'd put it down to being part of her act, but now he had to acknowledge that she *had* been a virgin. She hadn't lied about that. At least.

He was about to head up the stairs when a smell caught at his nostrils. A very distinctive smell. Delicious. Mouth-watering. Evocative of his childhood.

He went towards the kitchen, expecting to find Dominique cooking, but when he opened the door it took a second for his eyes to take in the scene.

Lara was bent down at the open oven door, taking something out. She was dressed in jeans and a loose shirt. Bare feet. Her hair was up in a messy knot, and as she turned around with the dish in her hands he saw how the buttons of the shirt were fastened low enough to give a tantalising glimpse of cleavage.

Tendrils of hair framed her face and flushed cheeks. He heard the music. Some silly pop tune. Then realised that Lara was smiling, bending down to sniff the food in the dish. Lasagne, he guessed. It reminded him of the famous lasagne his *nonna* used to make when he was small, hurtling him back in time.

Ciro was rendered mute and frozen, because he couldn't deny the appeal of the scene, nor that it had already existed in the deepest recesses of his psyche, even as he would have denied ever wanting such a domestic scenario in his life. At least until he'd met Lara that first time around and suddenly his perspective had shifted to allow such things to exist.

She'd cooked for him one evening; a spaghetti *vongole*. So mouthwatering that he could still recall how it had tasted, and the look of uncertainty on her face until he'd declared it delicious.

He'd totally forgotten about that until now.

At that second she looked up at him, catching him in a moment between past and present. Between who this woman was and who she wasn't.

Ciro felt as if there was a spotlight on his head, exposing every flaw—and not just the very physical ones. His scar felt itchy now, compounding his sense of dislocation and exposure. The scar that didn't seem to bother her in the slightest.

'What do you think you're doing?'

Lara looked as frozen as he felt. 'Cooking.'

'For who? Your imaginary friends?'

Ciro didn't have to see the rush of colour into Lara's cheeks to know he was being a bastard, but this whole scenario was unacceptable to him on a level that he really didn't want to investigate too closely.

Lara cursed herself for having given in to this urge to do something so domestic, but she refused to let Ciro's palpable disapproval intimidate her. She wouldn't let another man tell her she couldn't cook.

'It's lasagne, Ciro, not some subversive act.'

A suspicious look came over his face as he advanced into the kitchen. 'Why are you doing it, then? Angling to forge a more permanent position in my life by show-casing your domestic skills? As if they might hide your true nature?'

Lara pushed the dish away from the edge of the is-land, curbing the urge to lift it up and throw it at Ciro's cynical head. She said through gritted teeth, 'I really hadn't thought about it too much. I merely wanted to cook. It's Dominique's night off—how else am I going to feed myself?'

Ciro was so close now that Lara could see his long eyelashes casting shadows on his cheeks. They should have diminished his extreme masculinity. They didn't.

Feeling exasperated now, as well as jittery that Ciro was so close, Lara said, 'You've been out for dinner every night, Ciro. Did you really expect that I'd be sit-ting here pining away for your company?'

He flushed as if she'd hit a nerve. 'Clearly I made a mistake in not taking you along to those dinners with me.'

Lara started backing away around the kitchen island,

her jitteriness increasing as Ciro advanced. 'No, it's fine—honestly. I know those things are work-related... not interesting. I'd only cramp your style.'

Then, as if she hadn't spoken, Ciro said almost musingly, 'I had no idea you liked going to bed so early. I seem to remember you telling me that you loved the night-time—after midnight, when everyone else is asleep and the world is finally quiet and at peace.'

Now Lara flushed. He'd remembered that romantic stroll when he'd taken her through deserted Florentine squares under the moonlight? She'd been such a sap, believing he wanted to hear all her silly chattering about everything and anything.

He waved a hand. 'None of that's important. There's only one thing I'm interested in right now, and that's repairing an area of our marriage that seems to have become neglected, thanks to my workload and your proclivity for early nights.'

Lara could see the explicit gleam in his eye and felt herself responding as if she literally had no agency over her own body.

'Actually, I think this week is a good example of how this marriage will succeed,' she blurted out with a sense of desperation. 'You know, if you want to take a mistress then please go right ahead. It might be better, actually, if we're to keep things clear and separate. After all, my worth is only really in helping you to network.'

Ciro barked out a laugh and shook his head. 'Take a mistress and give you grounds for divorce? I don't think so, *cara mia.* And you do yourself down. Your worth isn't only for your social standing and connections—it's also in the place where I want you right now.'

Lara stopped moving, feeling a sense of inevitability

washing over her that, treacherously, she didn't fight. 'Where's that?'

Ciro came and stood in front of her. 'My bed...under me.'

The lasagne growing cool on the island was forgotten. Everything was distilled down to this moment and the way Ciro was looking at her.

He reached out and she felt air caress her skin. He was undoing her shirt and she slapped at his hands. 'Stop! What if someone comes in?'

Ciro was spreading her shirt apart now, his hands spanning her waist. She was finding it hard to focus as he tugged her forward.

'Dominique isn't here and Nigel has gone home. I passed him on my way in.'

Lara knew all that. They were entirely alone in this vast townhouse. She was so close to his body now that she could smell his scent. It reminded her of Sicily, of the sun baking the ground and something far more sensual and musky. *Him.*

She knew he was distracting her, and also punishing her on some level for having had the temerity to bring domesticity into this situation, but all she could think about was how she had denied herself his touch all week.

His head was coming closer, and Lara fought a tiny pathetic internal battle before she gave up and allowed Ciro's mouth to capture hers. He pressed her back against the island but Lara didn't even notice. Nor did she notice when Ciro pulled off her shirt and undid her bra, freeing her breasts into his hands, bringing her nipples to stinging life.

She squirmed against him, instinctively seeking flesh-on-flesh contact. He smiled against her mouth and Lara felt it, just as he broke the kiss and trailed his mouth down over her jaw and her chest to her breasts, tipping up first one and then the other, so that he could feast on them, sucking and licking and biting gently, causing a rush of hot blood to flow between Lara's legs, damp and hot.

Suddenly she was being lifted into Ciro's arms and he was carrying her out of the kitchen and up through the house. Lara's breathing was uneven. She realised she was bare from the waist up, but she could feel no shame, only a sense of rising desperation.

When they got to Ciro's bedroom he shed his clothes with indecent haste. Lara was equally ready, pulling off her jeans and panties, her skin prickling with need as she lay back and took in the sight of Ciro standing proudly by the bed, every muscle bulging and taut as he rolled protection on.

She wanted to weep because she was so ready. It made a mockery of the nights when she'd feigned sleep and believed herself to have scored some kind of victory. It had been a pyrrhic victory. Empty.

Ciro came down on the bed by Lara and she bit her lip. He put a thumb there, tugging her lip free, before claiming her mouth in a drugging, time-altering kiss. Ciro's hands explored every inch of her body until she was incoherent with need, past the point of begging.

But he knew. Of course he knew. Because he was the devil.

He settled his body between her spread legs, and in the same moment that he thrust deep, to the very core of where she ached most, he took her mouth and absorbed her hoarse cry of relief.

It was fast and furious. Lara reached her peak in a blinding rush of pleasure so intense she blacked out for a moment. Ciro's body locked tight a moment after, his huge powerful frame struggling to contain his own climax. It gave Lara some small measure of satisfaction to see his features twisted in an agony of pleasure as deep shudders racked his frame.

One thing was clear in her mind before a satisfaction-induced coma took her over. Ciro had just demonstrated very clearly where the parameters of this marriage lay: in the bedroom and on the social circuit. Not in the kitchen.

When Lara woke the next morning she was back in her own bed. She really hated it that Ciro did that. *What was he afraid of?* she grumbled to herself. Was he afraid he'd wake up and she'd have spun a web around his body, turning him into a prisoner?

The image gave her more than a little dart of satisfaction. The thought of Ciro being totally at her mercy…

She didn't hear any sounds coming from his bedroom and checked the time, realising that Ciro would have gone to the office already.

After showering and dressing she went downstairs to find Dominique in the kitchen. The woman turned around and smiled widely, and it was only at that moment that Lara had a mortifying flashback and saw her shirt and bra neatly folded on a chair near the door.

She grabbed them, her face burning, gabbling an apology, but the older woman put up a hand.

'Don't apologise. It's your home. I might have been married for twenty years, but I do remember what that first heady year was like.'

Lara smiled weakly, welcoming the change in subject when Dominique said, 'The lasagne—did you cook it? It smells delicious. I've put it in the fridge but I can freeze it if you like.'

Lara had been taught a comprehensive and very effective lesson last night in not expecting to see Ciro sitting down to a home-cooked meal any time soon, so she said, 'Actually, do you want to take it home with you this evening for you and your family? I thought we'd have a chance to eat it but we won't.'

Dominique reached for something and handed a folded card to Lara. 'That reminds me—Ciro left this for you. And, yes, I'd love to take the lasagne home if you're sure that's all right? It'll save me cooking!'

Lara smiled and retreated from the kitchen. 'Of course. I hope you enjoy it.'

She looked at the card once she was out of sight. The handwriting was strong and slashing.

Be ready to leave for a function at five this evening. Dress for black tie.

No, she could be under no illusions now as to where her role lay.

On her back and at Ciro's side as his trophy wife.

Ciro's driver came for Lara at five. She checked her appearance in the mirror of the hall one last time. The long sleeveless black dress had a lace bodice and a high collar. She'd pulled her hair back into a sleek ponytail and kept jewellery and make-up to a minimum.

The car made its way through the London traffic to one of the city's most iconic museums. She saw Ciro before he saw her in the car. He was standing by the kerb, where cars were disgorging people in glittering finery.

For a moment Lara just drank him in, in his classic

tuxedo. He must have changed at the office. He was utterly mesmerising. She could see other women doing double-takes.

Then he saw the car and she saw tension come into his form. She felt a pang. They might combust in bed, but he still resented her presence out of it. Even if he did need her.

The car drew to a stop and Lara gathered herself as Ciro opened the door and helped her out. Even her hand in his was enough to cause a seismic reaction in her body. But she felt shy after what had happened last night.

Ciro said, 'You look beautiful.'

She glanced at him, embarrassed. 'Thank you. You look very smart.'

A small smile tipped up his mouth. 'Smart? I don't think I've been called that before.'

Lara felt hot. No... Ciro's lovers would have twined themselves around him and whispered into his ear that he was magnificent. Gorgeous. Sexy.

She felt gauche, but he was taking her elbow in his hand and leading her towards the throng of people entering the huge museum near Kensington Gardens, one of London's most exclusive addresses.

It was only when they were seated that Lara realised it was a banquet dinner to honour three charities. One of which had Ciro Sant'Angelo's name on it.

She read the blurb on the brochure.

The Face Forward Charity. Founded by Ciro Sant'Angelo after a kidnapping ordeal left him facially disfigured.

There was an interview with Ciro in which he explained that after his injury he'd realised that any physical disfigurement, not just facial, was something that affected millions of people. And that a lot of disfigurement came about due to birth defects, injuries of some kind—whether through accident, war or gangs—or domestic violence.

His mission statement was that no one should ever be made to feel 'less' because of their disfigurement. His charity offered a wide range of treatments, ranging from plastic surgery to rehabilitation and counselling, to help people afflicted. To help them move on with their lives.

Lara looked at Ciro. She was seated on his right-hand side and his scar seemed to stand out even more this evening. A statement.

He glanced at her and arched a brow. She felt hurt that he hadn't mentioned this before. 'I didn't know you'd set up a charity.'

He shrugged minutely. 'I didn't think it relevant to tell you.'

Something deeper than hurt bloomed inside Lara then. Something she couldn't even really articulate.

She stood up abruptly, just as they were serving the starters, and almost knocked over the waiter behind her. Apologising, she fled from the room, upset and embarrassed.

Once outside, in the now empty foyer, she stopped. She cursed herself for bolting like that. The last thing Ciro would want was for people's attention to be drawn to them.

She heard heavy footsteps behind her. Ciro caught her arm, swinging her around. 'What the hell, Lara?'

She pulled free, her anger and hurt surging again at the irritated look on his face. 'I know you don't like me very much, Ciro, but we're married now. The least you could have done is tell me what this evening is about. *You're* the one concerned with appearances. How do you think it would look if someone struck up a conversation with me about your charity which I know nothing about?'

Ciro felt a constriction in his chest. Lara was right. But he hadn't neglected to tell her about it in a conscious effort not to include her. He hadn't told her because he didn't find it easy to mention the kidnapping. Even now. Even here, where he was in public and talking about something that had arisen out of that experience.

Lara looked…*hurt*. And then she said, 'I was there too, you know. I didn't experience what you experienced, and I'm so sorry that you went through what you did. But they took me too, Ciro. So I do have some idea of what you went through, even if it's only very superficial. I might not have any physical scars to prove I had that experience, but I had it.'

She turned and went to walk back into the room, but Ciro caught her arm again. For the first time, he felt the balance of power between them shift slightly.

She looked at him, her full mouth set in a line. Her jaw tight.

'You're right,' he said, and the words came easier than he might have expected. 'I should have told you— and, yes, you *were* there too.'

'Thank you.'

Ciro realised in that moment that she had all the regal bearing and grace of royalty, and something inside him was inexplicably humbled. She'd been right to call him out on this. And he wasn't used to being in the wrong. It was not a sensation he'd expected to feel in the presence of Lara.

Lara felt shaky after confronting Ciro, but his apology defused her anger. She realised now that she'd been hurt because she'd felt left out, which was ridiculous when Ciro had set up the charity well before they'd met again.

After the meal people got up to give speeches, and Lara was a little stunned when Ciro was introduced and he got up to go to the podium. He was a commanding presence. The crowd seemed far more hushed when he spoke. And how could she blame them? He stood out.

His scar also stood out, in a white ridged line down the right side of his face. Most people probably wouldn't even notice his missing finger, too transfixed by that scar.

He spoke passionately about the psychological effects of being scarred and how, with pioneering plastic surgery treatments, people could have the option of going on to live scar-free lives. Especially children.

There was a slideshow of images of some of the children and people his charity had helped so far, and Lara had tears in her eyes by the time he was finished.

When he came back to the table Lara felt humbled. She'd seen a new depth to Ciro tonight. Ever since she'd met him he'd always projected a charming, carefree attitude to life. He was someone who'd been graced with good looks, wealth and intellect. Taken for granted—as his due. Not any more. That much was blatantly obvious.

When they had returned to the townhouse Lara said, 'I think what you're doing is amazing. If there's ever anything I can do… I'd like to be involved.'

Ciro turned to face her. 'There is something you can do…right now.'

He took her hand and tugged her towards him.

Instant heat flooded Lara's body at the explicit gleam in his eyes. 'Ciro…' she said weakly.

'Lara…' he said, and then he stopped any more words by fusing his mouth to hers.

It was only much later, when Lara was back in her own bed, her body still tingling in the aftermath of extreme pleasure, that she realised he'd effectively dismissed her desire to help with the charity.

Clearly it was an arena, along with the kitchen, that she wasn't allowed to enter. Which only made Lara determined to do something about it.

CHAPTER SEVEN

'SHE'S *WHERE*?'

Ciro stood up from his chair and stalked over to the window, which took in a view of the Thames snaking through London.

The voice on the other end of the phone sounded nervous, 'Er…she's in one of the Face Forward charity shops, boss. It looks like she's helping with the display in the window.'

Ciro was terse. 'Send me a video and stay with her until she leaves.'

About a minute later there was a *ping* on his phone and he played the video. There was Lara, in jeans and a sweatshirt, hair pulled back, helping to dress and accessorise a mannequin in the window of one of his charity's shops on the King's Road.

She looked about sixteen. He saw her turn and smile broadly at a young staff member. She looked…*happy*. Happier than he'd seen her since they'd met again.

Something dark settled into his chest. A heavy weight. And confusion. Who the hell was she doing this for? What was she up to?

'What do you mean, what was I up to? *Nothing!* I wanted to prove that I was serious about helping with the charity. Or do you expect me to sit around all day waiting for the moment you decide to dress me up and take me out as your trophy wife?'

Ciro had been festering all day and he'd come home in a black mood. Which had got even blacker when he'd found Lara in the kitchen again, cooking.

'I thought I told you that I don't expect you to cook?'

She smiled sweetly at him, which made his blood boil even more, because it only reminded him of the very real smile he'd seen on that video earlier.

'I'm not cooking for you. I'm cooking for me. And Dominique. She can take the leftovers for her and Bill.'

'Bill?'

'Her husband. He's not well.'

'And you know this…*how*?'

Lara looked at him now as if he was a bit dense. 'Because I have conversations with her.'

Ciro was aware that he was being totally irrational and ridiculous. His wife was cooking in the kitchen. Most men would be ecstatic. Especially as it smelt so delicious.

Lara said, 'I know there's nothing on tonight, thanks to the helpful events calendar your assistant installed in the phone you gave me. Unless that's changed?' She suddenly looked less happy.

'No,' Ciro bit out. 'It hasn't changed. The evening is free.'

'Well,' Lara said, sounding eminently reasonable, and far calmer than Ciro felt, 'have you made plans for dinner or would you like to join me? It's *boeuf bourguignon*.'

Ciro forced himself to stop being ridiculous. He had no idea what Lara was up to with this little charade—helping at the charity shop and revealing her domestic goddess side—but he wasn't foolish enough to cut off his nose to spite his face.

'That would be nice, thank you. I'll have a shower and join you.'

Ciro left and Lara took a deep breath. She regretted cooking now. Dominique had left a perfectly service-able stew she could have heated up, but she'd needed the ritual of cooking to centre herself.

She guessed Ciro's security guy would have been on the phone to him earlier, about her going to the charity shop, and she'd expected his suspicious mind to spin it into something nefarious.

She knew he expected her to be like some kind of ice princess, waiting obediently for his instructions, but since they'd begun sleeping together it was harder and harder to maintain that kind of façade. And any emotional distance.

So Ciro could just *be* perplexed and suspicious. He didn't really care who she was, after all. So why not be herself?

The following morning Lara was surprised to see Ciro in the kitchen, chatting to Dominique over a cup of coffee. She felt exposed when she thought of the previous evening, and how Ciro had quickly and efficiently dispensed with dinner so that he could remind Lara of one of her primary functions in this marriage. Being in his bed.

He'd said it to her again as they'd finished eating. 'I really don't expect you to be in the kitchen, Lara.'

She shrugged. 'I know I don't have to do it, but I like it.'

He'd looked at her as if she'd spoken in some kind of riddle and then, when she'd been getting up to clear the plates, he'd pulled her down onto his lap. 'I'm drawing the line here. You do *not* clear up.'

Lara was blushing now because she was thinking of Dominique finding their detritus. Again. But the woman was looking twinkly-eyed. The inevitable effect of Ciro on most people.

She wondered what Dominique thought of their separate beds…

Ciro looked at her then. 'You need to pack. We're leaving for New York this morning. Some business has been moved forward. We'll be there a couple of weeks. Don't worry too much about what to bring—a stylist will stock your wardrobe there. They've been given a list of the functions we're due to attend.'

Ciro walked out the kitchen with his coffee cup and Dominique sighed volubly. 'What I wouldn't give to have my wardrobe stocked for me.'

Lara forced a smile and desisted from saying something trite. She knew she was incredibly lucky. Even if it *did* feel as though she were a bird in a gilded cage.

As she packed her modest suitcase a little later she told herself she was being ridiculous to suspect that Ciro had brought forward the New York trip to keep her in her place, because things were getting a little too domesticated in London.

Ciro seemed to be in a state of permanent frustration around Lara. He watched her broodingly from his side of the private plane as she did a crossword puzzle. A pen was between her teeth and her brow was furrowed. Why wasn't she flicking through a magazine? Or drinking champagne? Or trying to seduce him?

He turned away, angry that he couldn't seem to focus on his own work. And also angry because he'd acted impulsively, deciding to come to New York ahead of schedule purely because the previous night and that dinner had impacted on him somewhere he didn't like to investigate.

He hadn't married Lara so she could be of actual help in any aspect of his life other than in the social arena. And in his bed. Yet she was starting to inhabit more parts of his life than he liked to admit.

Apart from the dinner last night he'd noticed soft touches around the house in London. Flowers. Throws. Shoes left discarded. Unintentional little feminine touches. Not even anything concrete he could point to.

Ciro had never lived with a woman. Lara would have been the first and she was still the first. In spite of what had happened.

Because of what had happened.

He found that as much as it made him feel exposed and discombobulated he couldn't say that he didn't like it. He just hadn't counted on Lara's softness. Her ability to converse with the staff. Her...*niceness*.

She'd been nice before. And then she'd changed. So he wouldn't believe it. He had to believe she was up to something. It was easier.

Lara could feel Ciro's eyes on her. She could almost hear his brain whirring. She knew how he worked. He problem-solved. And she was a problem because she wasn't behaving as he thought she should. As he thought the Lara who had rejected him should.

She felt something well up inside her. The urge to just turn around and let it all spill out. The full truth about her treacherous uncle. About what had happened. She even opened her mouth and turned to Ciro...and then promptly shut it again.

His head was thrown back and his eyes were closed.

She'd never seen him asleep. He looked no less formidable.

The urge to talk drained and faded. It would be self-serving. She might want to be absolved of all her sins in his eyes, but was she really ready to face his disgust? He would get rid of her immediately, of that she had no doubt. As it was, the ties binding them were incredibly fragile.

Ciro was so proud. It would kill him to know that she knew the truth about the kidnapping. That it had been done to him by *her* family. He would blame her. No doubt. *She* blamed herself. Why wouldn't he?

She got up from her chair and pulled a blanket over Ciro's body. Immediately his eyes opened and he caught her, bringing her down onto his lap. She was instantly breathless.

She looked at him accusingly. 'I thought you were asleep.'

'Are you finished pretending to be uninterested?'

She saw something in his eyes then—very fleeting. It almost looked like vulnerability.

Lara might have made some trite comment or pushed herself away from Ciro, fought to keep the distance between them, but instead she said, 'You're not a person who would ever inspire a lack of interest, Ciro.'

'That's more like it.'

He pulled her head down and kissed her.

Lara fought to retain a little bit of resistance, but it was futile. Within minutes Ciro was carrying her through the cabin to the back of the plane, where the bed awaited.

New York felt different from London. Where London felt intimate, New York felt expansive and impersonal.

Ciro had a townhouse there too—which was some feat in a city full of soaring buildings and massive apartment blocks. It was nestled between two huge buildings by Central Park, on the Upper East Side.

His staff there were polite and impersonal. Lara couldn't imagine getting to know them all that well. And from the day they arrived she was sucked into a dizzying round of events and functions.

The days took on a rhythm. Ciro would get up and go to his office downtown. Lara would get up, have breakfast and then go to the park for a run. Invariably she found herself sitting on a bench watching other people—couples, dog-walkers, children and their nannies.

She saw a family one day—father, mother and two children. A boy and a girl. It made her heart ache, and she cursed Ciro for making that pain real again even as she denied to herself that she was still in love with him.

Their evenings were spent either at banquet dinners or less formal functions. Lara had lost count of all the people she'd met. There was no time here for cooking cosy dinners in the kitchen. It was as if Ciro was purposely not letting her have the opportunity.

But even he hadn't been able to complain when they'd been passing a famous pizza place a couple of nights ago and Lara had asked if they could stop. She'd been starving, and so, it turned out, had been Ciro, his driver and his security team. So they'd all stood around the high tables, eating slices of pizza. Ciro in his tuxedo with his bow tie undone and Lara in a glittering strapless silver sheath dress.

It had been a very private personal victory for Lara.

And then the nights...

Ciro would take her to bed in his room, shatter her into a million pieces over and over again and then deposit her back in her own bed. Sometimes Lara was glad, because the intimacy felt too raw. But other times she despised him for the way he seemed to find it so easy to despatch her.

His determination to keep her confined to the box in which he'd kept her since he'd married her was very apparent. She knew it wasn't a real marriage, but their physical intimacy was wearing her down and making it harder and harder to keep her guard up. And she hated him for that. Because he seemed totally impervious to it.

That evening they had yet another function to attend and Ciro knocked on Lara's door.

Feeling incredibly weary, she called out, 'I'm ready.'

He opened the door and came in, his dark gaze sweeping her up and down. It turned hot as he took in her light blue silk evening gown. It was one-shoul-dered, and fell in soft fluid folds around her body—which came to humming life under Ciro's assessing look. *Damn him.*

Her hair was up in a loose chignon and she'd cho-sen dangling diamond earrings. The only other jewel-lery she wore was her engagement and wedding rings.

'Stunning,' Ciro pronounced. And then, 'Let's go. The car is waiting.'

For a second Lara wanted to stamp her feet and re-fuse to follow him, but she swallowed the urge. This wasn't a real marriage. Ciro didn't care if she was feel-ing weary from the constant socialising. He didn't care because this was all about work for him—a means to an end. And essentially she was just an employee. With benefits.

At the function that evening—there had been so many of them that even Ciro felt as if all the faces and places were blurring into one mass of people—he felt disgruntled. When he had no reason to do so.

Lara was at his side, conversing in Spanish with a diplomat. She was fulfilling her role as corporate wife with absolute perfection. She wasn't behaving like a spoilt petulant princess, demanding attention, or moaning because her feet hurt from standing too long.

But he sensed it. Her discomfiture. He saw it when she moved her weight from foot to foot, or when she winced slightly as someone shook her hand too hard. He saw it when she quickly masked a look of boredom. The same boredom he was feeling.

He'd seen it in her eyes earlier—a kind of fatigue along with the slightest of shadows under her eyes. After all, they weren't falling asleep until near dawn most nights.

Ciro had been feeling more and more reluctant to take Lara back to her own bed after making love to her, and was doing it out of sheer bloody-mindedness—so she didn't get ideas and think that their mind-blowing sex was leading to any deeper kind of intimacy.

She'd asked if they could stop on their way home the other night. For pizza. The gratitude on his staff's faces had made Ciro feel guilty about how hard he was working them. Not to mention the almost sexual look of pleasure on Lara's face as she'd bitten into a slice. It had been the best damn pizza he'd ever tasted. And he'd eaten pizza in Naples.

It had been fun. Unexpected. And it had reminded him so much of when he'd known Lara *before* that past and present had blurred painfully.

There were too many of those moments now. Moments that made him doubt his sanity. His memory.

Maybe that was why he'd insisted on such a punishing pace. So as not to give himself a chance to stop and think for a second.

'Do you think we could go now? I'm quite tired.'

Ciro looked around. He hadn't even noticed most of the other guests leaving. Lara looked pale, the shadows under her eyes more pronounced.

A dart of guilt lanced Ciro before he could stop it. 'Of course, let's go.'

They got outside and even he was grateful for the fresh air. He wondered if all this endless networking was really worth it. That would have shocked him if he'd thought it before.

Suddenly his thoughts came to a standstill as Lara stopped beside him and then darted towards a dark alleyway nearby. All he could see was her light blue dress disappearing like an aquamarine jewel into the dark night.

'What the…?'

Ciro flicked a hand to tell his security team that he would get her. As he walked towards the alleyway, though, he felt his insides curdle at the thought that she might be trying to run.

This was it. What she'd been up to.

He'd given her a credit card—maybe she'd just been biding her time. Maybe she'd met a man at one of these functions and devised a plan to escape with someone more charming than him. Someone who would offer her a lifetime of security and not just a year or six months. Someone who didn't have their tangled history…

But at that moment Lara appeared again, in the mouth of the alleyway, and he came to a stop at the same time as his irrational circling thoughts.

He frowned at the sight before him.

She was holding something in her arms against her

chest. Something that was moving. Shaking uncontrollably. She came forward, her eyes huge and filled with compassion. 'It's a puppy… I heard it crying. It needs help. It's been attacked by someone, or another dog. It's bleeding.'

Ciro could see it now—an indeterminate bundle of matted hair and big wounded-looking eyes. Dark blood was running down Lara's dress along with muck and dirt. There was a streak of something dark along her cheek and he could smell the dog from here.

For a second he couldn't compute the scene. Lara, dressed in a couture gown, uncaring of the fact that she was holding a mangy dog covered in blood and filth.

'Please, Ciro, we need to take him to a vet. He'll die.'

A memory blasted Ciro at that moment. He'd been very small. Tiny. Holding his mother's hand as she'd walked along the street. Which had been odd, because generally she hadn't taken him with her anywhere, not liking to take the risk that he would do something to show her up in public.

But on this day he'd been with her, and as they'd passed a side street he'd seen some older boys pelting a cowering dog with stones. He'd stopped dead, eyes wide on the awful scene. He could remember trying to call *Mamma!* but his mouth wouldn't work. Eventually she'd stopped and demanded to know why he wouldn't move.

He had pointed his finger, horrified at what he was witnessing. Such cruelty. He'd looked up at her, tears filling his eyes, willing her to do something. But she had taken one look, then gripped his hand so tightly it had hurt and dragged him away.

The piteous yelps of that dog had stayed with him for a long time. And he'd forgotten about it until this moment.

'Ciro…?'

He moved. 'Of course. Here—let me take him.'

She clutched the animal to her. 'No, it's fine. He's not heavy. There's no point two of us getting dirty.'

Ciro just looked at her. And then he said, 'Fine. We'll find the closest vet.'

Lara got into the back of the car carefully, cradling the bony body of the dog, which was still shaking pitifully. There was no way she could have ignored the distinctive crying once she'd heard it. She adored dogs.

She heard Ciro on the phone, asking someone to find them a vet and send directions immediately. She imagined a minion somewhere jumping to attention.

Ciro's phone rang seconds later and he listened for a second before rattling off an address to the driver.

He said to Lara, 'We'll be at the vet's in ten minutes—they're expecting us.'

'Thank you. I'm sorry, but I couldn't just…'

'It's fine.' Ciro's voice was clipped.

Lara said, 'If you want you can just leave me at the vet with the dog… I can call a taxi to get home.'

Ciro looked at her. She could see the dark pools of his eyes in the gloom of the back of the car.

'Don't be ridiculous. I'll wait.'

After that Lara stayed silent, willing the dog to survive. When they got to the vet Ciro insisted on taking the dog into his arms, and Lara was surprised to hear him crooning softly to it in Italian, evidently not minding about getting dirty himself.

There was a team waiting when they got inside—the power of Ciro's wealth and influence—and the dog was whisked away to be assessed. Lara felt something warm settle around her shoulders and looked up. Ciro had given her his jacket. She realised that it was chilly inside, with the air-conditioning on, and she'd been shivering.

'Coffee?'

She nodded, and watched as Ciro went to the machine provided for clients. He handed her a coffee and took a sip of his own. It was only then that Lara caught a glimpse of herself in the reflection of a window and winced inwardly. Her hair was coming down on one side and she had streaks of dirt all over her face and chest. And her dress was ruined.

She gestured with her free hand. 'I'm sorry... I didn't mean to ruin the dress.'

Ciro looked at her curiously. 'It's not as if you would have worn it again.'

She thought of how much a dress like this might have fetched in an online auction, like when she'd been reduced to selling her clothes while married to Henry Winterborne. She couldn't ever imagine telling Ciro that story. He wouldn't believe her.

She said, 'Of course not,' and sat down on a plastic chair, the adrenalin leaving her system. They were the only people at the vets. The harsh fluorescent lighting barely dented Ciro's intensely gorgeous looks. He caught her eye and she looked away hastily, in case he saw something on her face. She felt exposed after her impetuous action. Less able to try and erect the emotional barriers between her and Ciro.

If she ever had been able to.

'Lara...'

Reluctantly she looked at him.

He shook his head. 'Sometimes you just...confound me. I think I know exactly who you are and then—'

At that moment there was a noise and Ciro stopped

talking. Lara welcomed the distraction, not sure if she wanted to know what Ciro had been about to say.

The vet walked in and looked at them both before saying, 'Well, he is a she and it's lucky you found her when you did. She wouldn't have survived much longer. She's about five months old and as far as we can tell she hasn't been microchipped. She's probably from a stray litter or got dumped.'

Lara said, 'Is she okay?'

The vet nodded. 'She'll be fine—thanks to you for bringing her in. She's obviously been in a scrap, but it's just cuts and bruises. Nothing too serious. She needs some TLC and some food. We can microchip her and keep her in overnight to clean her up, then you can take her home tomorrow, if you like?' He must have seen something on their faces because then he said, 'I'm sorry, I just assumed you'd want to keep her, but I can see I shouldn't have.'

Lara didn't want to look at Ciro, but all of a sudden it seemed of paramount importance that she got to keep the dog. As if something hinged on this very decision.

Without looking at Ciro, she said, 'I'd like to keep her.'

The vet looked at Ciro, who must have nodded or something, because he said, 'That's good. Thank you.' The vet was just turning to leave and then he said, 'You should probably think of a name.'

Lara sneaked a look at Ciro, who was expressionless. But she could see his tight jaw.

'We'll let you know,' he said.

The vet left and Lara said, 'If you don't want to keep her I'll look after her and take her with me when I leave. You won't even know she's there.'

She. Her.

As if they were discussing a person.

Ciro wasn't sure why, but he had an almost visceral urge *not* to take this puppy. A puppy smacked of domesticity. Longevity. Attachment.

'It's fine. You can keep her.'

Ciro told himself that Lara would soon tire of the dog and then he would arrange for it to go to a new home. A home with a family who would appreciate it.

But even as he thought that he felt some resistance inside him. He was losing it. Seeing how Lara had been with the dog had made him feel as if he was standing on shifting sands.

'Thank you.'

'Let's go.'

Lara walked out ahead of Ciro, his jacket dwarfing her slender shoulders. She should have looked ridiculous. Her hair was all over the place and she was smeared in dubious-smelling substances. Not to mention the blood. Yet she seemed oblivious to it.

When they were in the back of the car Lara said, 'Sorry—I know I stink.'

Ciro looked at her in the dim light. Even as dishevelled as she was, she was stunning. More so, if possible. As if this act of humanity had added some quality to her beauty.

'I wouldn't have had you down as a dog-lover.'

Her mouth curved into a small smile. 'My parents got a rescue Labrador puppy when I was just a toddler. We called her Poppy, we were inseparable.'

'What happened to her?'

The smile faded. 'After my parents and brother died my uncle had her put down. She was old… She probably only had another year at the most.'

Ciro absorbed that nugget of information. He could hear the emotion she was trying to hide in her voice.

'Have you thought of a name for this one?'

She turned to look at him and he could see the gratitude in her eyes. He really didn't want it to affect him, but it did. He couldn't imagine another woman looking so pleased about taking on a mongrel of dubious parentage.

'Maybe Hero? I've always liked that name. After the Greek myth.'

The fact that Hero had been a virgin priestess wasn't lost on Ciro, but he only said, 'Fine. Whatever you want. She's your dog.'

When they arrived back at the house Lara made a face and gestured to her clothes. 'I should clean myself up.'

She handed Ciro his jacket. He took it, and there was something vulnerable about the way Lara looked. He had a memory flash of having her ripped out of his arms by the kidnappers and thrown from the van to the side of the road. She'd been dishevelled then too. And the look of terror on her face had matched the terror he'd felt but had been desperate not to show.

'Of course,' he said tersely. 'Go to bed, Lara, it's been a long night.'

Ciro went into the reception room and dropped his jacket on a chair, loosening his bow tie. Except he knew it wasn't the fault of his tie that he felt constricted. It was something far more complicated.

He poured himself a whisky and downed the shot in one go, hoping to burn away the questions buzzing in his head. Along with the unwelcome memories.

He forced his mind away from the past and the image of Lara's terror-stricken face to think of her as she was now—standing under a shower, naked. With rivulets of water streaming down over her curves, her nipples hard and pebbled. The soft curls between her legs would be wet, as wet as she always was when he touched her there—

Dio! He had a wife, willing and hot for him, one floor above his head, and he was down here, torturing himself, when he could be burying himself inside her and forgetting about everything except the release she offered.

Ciro slammed down the glass and went upstairs, taking two stairs at a time. When he got to Lara's bedroom door he stopped, his sense of urgency suddenly diminishing when he thought of how vulnerable she'd looked. What she'd told him about her family dog. Her uncle had had her put down. Just after her family had been taken from her.

Ciro had had his hand lifted, as if to knock on her door, but he curled it into a fist now, and walked away.

CHAPTER EIGHT

IT SEEMED TO take an age for Lara to fall asleep. She could have sworn she heard Ciro outside her bedroom, and even as she'd longed for him to come in she'd known that if he did she wasn't sure she'd be able to maintain the façade that she was as cool and impervious to their intimacy as he was.

So when he didn't appear in her doorway she couldn't help a tiny dart of relief.

She slept fitfully, and when she woke at some point in the night she wasn't sure if she'd been asleep for hours, or had only just fallen asleep.

And then she heard it—the sound that must have woken her. A shout. A guttural shout drawn from the very depths of someone's soul.

Ciro.

The tiny hairs stood up all over Lara's body as he shouted again—something indeterminate. Half English, half Italian. She realised she was getting out of bed before she'd even decided to do so, and she went to the adjoining door to Ciro's room.

And then he unleashed a cry that she did understand.

'No—stop!'

Lara didn't hesitate. She opened the door and flew into Ciro's room, where he was thrashing in the bed.

Naked. A sheet was tangled around his hips and legs, and his hands were balled into fists at his sides. His skin was sheened with sweat. His hair was damp.

Lara went into the bathroom and soaked a cloth with cold water. She brought it back and sat beside Ciro on the bed, pressing the damp cloth to his forehead. She desperately wanted to ease his pain without waking him, if she could help it. She knew he wouldn't thank her for seeing him in such a vulnerable state.

But then one of his hands caught her wrist and suddenly she was looking down into wide open dark eyes. She held her breath. He was breathing as if he'd run a marathon.

'Ciro...?' Lara whispered. 'You were dreaming...'

With a sudden move Ciro had Lara flat on her back and was looming over her, both her wrists caught in his hands. Now *she* was breathing as if she'd been running. She didn't know if he was asleep or awake and he looked crazed. Yet she wasn't scared. She knew he wouldn't hurt her. Even like this.

Ciro was still reeling from the nightmare. So vivid he could still taste it on his tongue. Acrid. He wasn't even sure where he was. All he could see were Lara's huge blue eyes. Soft and full of the same emotion she'd had in them earlier when she'd held the dog. Pity... No, not pity. Compassion.

It impacted Ciro deep inside, and he felt a desperate need to transmute the effects of the nightmare into something much more tangible. He could feel her body against his, all lithe and soft like silk. The press of her breasts...the cradle of her hips.

He was so hard it hurt. Hard and aching. And not just in his body. In his chest, where he felt tight.

He took his hands off her wrists and put them either

side of her head. 'I need you, Lara. Right here, right now, and I can't promise to be gentle. So if you want to go, go now.'

I need this. I need you.

He didn't say the words but they beat so heavily in his brain he wondered if he had said them out loud.

Lara reached up and wound her arms around his neck, bringing her body into close contact with his. 'Take me,' she said, 'I'm yours.'

And in that moment, Lara knew she was done for. She felt Ciro's need as clearly as if it was hers. And all she wanted to do was assuage his pain. She loved him. She still loved him. Had always loved him. Would always love him.

Ciro waited a beat, as if making sure that Lara knew what she was doing, and then with studied deliberation he put his hand to her silky nightgown and ripped it from top to bottom. It fell apart, baring her to his gaze, and Lara found herself revelling in it. She felt the ferocity Ciro felt—it thrummed through her in waves of need, building and building.

Ciro's dark gaze devoured her body and his hands moulded her every curve. His tongue laved her and with big hands he spread her legs so he could taste her there, making her cry out loud when he found and sucked on that little ball of nerves at the centre of her body.

She lifted her head, hardly able to see straight. She was sheened with sweat now too. 'Ciro, I can't wait... please.'

He reached for something and she saw him roll protection onto his length. For the first time Lara wished there could be nothing between them—but this marriage wasn't about that. Procreation. It was just about...

this… She hissed out as Ciro joined their bodies with one cataclysmic thrust.

He was remorseless, using every skill he had to prolong and delay the pinnacle. At one point he withdrew from Lara, and she let out a pitiful-sounding mewl, but he rolled onto his back and urged her to sit astride him, saying roughly, 'I want to see you.'

Lara put her thighs either side of his hips and came up on her knees. She felt Ciro take himself in his hand, and then he guided her down onto his stiff length. She came down slowly, experimentally, savouring the exquisite sensation of Ciro feeding his length into her, and then he put his hands on her hips. 'Take me, *cara mia*…all of me.'

Lara soon found her rhythm, her slick body moving up and down on his, excitement building at her core, making her move faster. The pinnacle was still elusive, though, and she was almost crying with frustration as Ciro clamped his hands on her hips and held her still so that he could pump up into her body.

He pulled her down, finding her breast and sucking her nipple into his mouth as the first wave of the crescendo broke Lara into a million pieces. It went on and on, like waves endlessly crashing against the shore, until she was limp and spent and hollowed out.

In the seconds afterwards it was as if an explosion had just occurred. Her ears were ringing and she wasn't sure if she was still in one piece.

Her body and Ciro's were still intimately joined. She lay on him, exhausted but satisfied, her mouth resting on the hectic pulse-point at the bottom of his neck, and that was all she remembered before she fell into a blissful dark oblivion.

* * *

When Lara woke she realised she was still in Ciro's bed. Dawn was breaking outside. He lay beside her on his back, one arm flung over his head, the other on his chest. Her gaze drifted down over hard pecs to the dark curls where his masculinity was still gloriously impressive, even in sleep.

She knew she should leave because he would soon return her to her room. She wondered with a pang if he'd ever let a woman spend the whole night in his bed.

She was sitting up when Ciro's hand caught her arm. 'Where do you think you're going?'

Lara's heart thumped. 'Back to my own bed.'

'Don't. Stay here.'

Lara looked at Ciro. His eyes were still closed. Maybe he wasn't even awake, so wasn't aware of what he was saying. She lay down carefully and he rolled towards her, trapping her with a leg over hers. She felt him stir against her. He opened his eyes.

A bubble of emotion rose up in her as she took in Ciro's stubbled face and messy hair. Without thinking she reached out and touched his scar gently, running her finger down the ridged length.

'Does it hurt?'

'Only sometimes… It doesn't hurt… It feels tight.'

'You were never tempted to get it removed? Like the people you help with your charity?'

His mouth firmed. 'No. I think it's important for people to see it—to know that if they want to live with their scars, it's okay. And it's a reminder.'

Lara was touched by his sentiment. Then she frowned. 'A reminder of the kidnapping…? Why would you want that?'

'Not that, specifically, but it's a reminder that I'm

not as infallible as I once believed. And it's a reminder not to trust anyone.'

Including me, Lara thought.

Facing him like this in the half-light, with no sounds coming from outside, made her feel otherworldly. As if they were in some sort of cocoon.

'The dream you were having last night…'

Ciro rolled onto his back again. 'It was a nightmare.'

Hesitantly Lara asked, 'About the kidnapping?'

He nodded, clearly uncomfortable. He probably saw it as a sign of weakness.

'I had them too,' Lara said.

Ciro looked at her.

'For months afterwards. The same one, over and over again… The hoods being put over our heads, then taken off. Realising we were in that van with those men. Being ripped out of your arms…left at the side of the road—' She stopped, shivering at the memory.

Ciro reached for her and hauled her into his arms. He said, 'I would never let that happen again—do you hear me?'

Lara looked at him, saw the determination on his face. She nodded. 'I believe you.'

There was something incredibly fragile about the moment. And then Ciro hauled her even closer and kissed her. Their bodies moved together in the dawn as they reached for each other and their breath quickened. This was nothing like the ferocity of last night—it was slow and sensuous, and so tender that Lara had to keep her eyes closed for fear that Ciro would see how close to tears she was.

'Working from home again?'

Ciro looked at Lara and raised a brow, but there was

no edginess to his expression. 'Do I need to ask permission?' he said.

Lara shook her head and helped herself to some of the salad which had been laid out on the terrace at the back of the house by the housekeeper. Ciro had been joining her for lunch the past few days. It had been a week since that tumultuous night, and since then Ciro hadn't taken her back to her own bedroom once. They woke up together, and usually made love again in the morning.

But Lara knew it was dangerous territory to believe anything was changing.

Ciro sat down and helped himself to some salad and bread. The housekeeper came out and poured them some wine.

There was a mewling cry from down below and Lara looked down to see Hero, looking up at her with huge liquid brown eyes. It turned out that she was been a cross between a whippet and something else. Cleaned up, and getting fatter by the day, she wasn't a pretty dog by any means—but she was adorable, mainly white with brown patches. The vet had said that he figured she was crossed with a Jack Russell.

A couple of times Lara had gone searching for her, only to find her curled up at Ciro's feet in his study. He'd pretended not to have noticed her, and when Lara had carried her out she'd whispered into her fur, 'I don't blame you, sweetheart. I know how it feels.'

Hero would lick her face, as if in commiseration for the fact that they were both in thrall to Ciro Sant'Angelo.

Lara absently stroked Hero and she lay down at her feet, curling up trustingly. She said to Ciro, 'Thank you for letting me keep her.'

Ciro shrugged, and then he looked at his watch. 'You wanted to visit the Guggenheim Museum, didn't you?'

Lara nodded, surprised he'd remembered her saying that the other night at a function.

'I can take the afternoon off—we'll go after lunch.'

Lara felt a dangerous fluttering in her belly and said, 'Oh, it's okay...you don't have to. I can go by myself—'

'Don't you want me to come with you?'

Lara could feel her face grow hot. This teasing, re-laxed Ciro was so reminiscent of how he'd been before that it was painful. 'Of course I'd love to see it with you.'

Ciro stood up. *'Va bene.* I've a few calls to make—we'll leave in an hour.'

Lara watched him leave, striding off the terrace back into the house. She took a deep breath—anything to try and get oxygen to her brain and keep herself from imagining impossible things.

Like the fact that Ciro might actually be learning to like her again...

The following day Ciro watched Lara play on the lawn with the puppy from the window in his study. She was wearing shorts and her long slim legs had taken on a light golden glow. She wore a silk cropped top and he could see tantalising slivers of her belly when it rode up as she moved.

He might have cursed her for trying to tempt him, but he knew she wasn't even aware that he'd come home early. *Home early.* Since when had he started to come home early? Or work from home? Or take afternoons off to go to a museum? The only person who'd ever had that effect on him was on her back, laughing as the puppy climbed all over her, yapping excitedly.

There was a bone-deep sense of satisfaction in his body from night after night of mind-blowing sex. He'd stopped sending Lara back to her own bed. She effectively shared his room now—something he'd never done with another woman, far too wary of inviting an intimacy that would be misread, or taken advantage of.

And they'd spent hours wandering around the Guggenheim the day before. It had been one of the most pleasant afternoons Ciro could remember in a long time.

As he looked at Lara now he had to acknowledge that his desire for her wasn't waning. Far from it. It seemed to be intensifying. But if he stuck to his agreement with her they'd be divorcing—at the earliest in only a few months. That thought sent something not unlike panic into his gut.

So far she'd fulfilled her side of the marriage, and introduced him to people who would never have welcomed him into their sphere before. He had a list of new deals to consider. Invitations to events and places he'd never been allowed access to before. All because of her.

But in truth, he found it hard to focus on that when she filled his vision and he spent most days reliving the night before and anticipating the night ahead.

She was not what he'd expected. More like the Lara he'd known first. And if this was an elaborate act, then what was the point? He couldn't figure it out, but something wasn't matching up…

At that moment his phone rang and he answered it impatiently, only half listening as he watched Lara throwing a ball for the puppy.

He turned away from the view, though, after his solicitor had finished speaking. 'Repeat what you just said.'

'I said that we know who was behind the kidnapping, Ciro, and I don't think you're going to like what you hear.'

* * *

The sun was throwing long shadows on the grass by the time Lara picked up Hero and went back inside the house. All was quiet except for the dull hum of Manhattan traffic outside.

But then she heard a sound coming from the main reception room, and put Hero down in her bed before investigating. She walked in to find Ciro throwing back a shot of alcohol. Predictably, her heart rate increased.

'I didn't know you were home.'

Her heart fluttered at the thought that maybe he'd come back early to take her on another excursion. But when he turned around she had to stifle a gasp. He was pale, and she realised he was pale with fury, because his eyes were burning.

'What is it? What's wrong?'

Ciro put the empty glass back on the tray with exaggerated care and then he looked back at Lara. She had only the faintest prickling sense of foreboding before he said, 'So, when were you going to tell me that you and your uncle were behind the kidnap plot?'

Lara's insides turned to ice. 'How do you know about that?'

'I've been investigating the kidnap since it happened. I kept hitting dead ends until now. Is it true?'

Lara felt sick. She nodded her head slowly.

Not exactly, but... 'Yes. My uncle planned it. He didn't want us to marry.'

Ciro's lip curled. 'And so he came up with a lurid plan to have us kidnapped? Or was that your contribution?'

Lara shook her head. She felt as if she was drowning, and moved sluggishly over to a chair where she sat down. 'I didn't know anything about it...not until after.'

Ciro looked at Lara. He couldn't believe it. Couldn't believe that after everything he'd been through with this woman she had done it again. The emotion he felt transcended anger. He was icy cold with it. Far worse than heat and rage.

He could feel the livid line of his scar. The phantom throbbing of his little finger. He wanted to go over and haul Lara up to stand. She looked pathetically, unbelievably shocked.

'I want to know everything. *Now*.'

He saw her swallow. She was so pale he almost felt the sting of his conscience but he ruthlessly pushed it down. This woman was the worst kind of chameleon. And potentially a criminal.

'I was forced to marry Henry Winterborne. By my uncle.'

Ciro shook his head. 'That's ridiculous.'

'I wish it was. My uncle was obsessed with status and lineage. There was no way he was going to allow me to marry you. But it went much further than that.'

Ciro said nothing. He saw Lara clasp her hands together and in that moment had a flashback to how her hands had felt on his buttocks only hours before, squeezing him, huskily begging him for more.

He gritted out, 'Keep going.'

'My uncle was in debt. Serious debt. Millions and millions of pounds. He'd run through his fortune— and my trust fund. I was his only hope of saving his reputation and clearing the debt. He'd had us followed from the moment I mentioned you to him. He knew we were serious.'

Ciro said nothing so Lara continued.

'He knew that I was sheltered…not experienced. He was fairly certain we hadn't…'

Remarkably, colour stained her cheeks, and it made Ciro feel so many conflicting things that he decided to focus on the anger.

'Save your blushes, *cara*. This really is the most intriguing story.'

Lara's mouth tightened for a moment, but then she said, 'He sold me—like a slave girl at an auction. To Henry Winterborne, the highest bidder.'

Ciro struggled to take this in. It was such a far-fetched story. He decided to see how far Lara would go towards hanging herself and pretending she was an innocent player. 'When are you claiming that you knew about this?'

'I didn't know until after the kidnapping. That's when he told me. And that's when he told me he would kill you if I pursued the relationship.'

'So you came to the hospital to convince me you'd never wanted to marry me in order to *save* me? *Cara*, that is the most romantic thing I've heard in my whole life.'

Something occurred to Ciro then, and he went very still.

Then he said, 'I told you that story in Sicily...about my great-grandmother. About how she couldn't marry the man she wanted, how he was threatened. You appropriated it as your own... You didn't even have the creativity to come up with something original. You make me—'

Lara shot up from the chair. 'It's true—I swear. That's just a coincidence. It all happened exactly like I said.'

Ciro forced down his anger. Forced himself to stay civil just for a little longer. 'So why didn't you tell me this when you had the chance at the hospital? We were alone—no one to hear you tell me the gory details.'

He held up his hand when she opened her mouth.

'I'll tell you why, shall I? Because even though you might not have liked the idea of marrying an old man, it was still preferable to marrying a man of no lineage except a dubious one, hmm?'

She shook her head. 'No. I would never have wanted to marry that man—not in a million years. He disgusted me.'

'So why didn't you leave him? He was in a wheelchair—he could hardly run after you.'

He saw Lara flinch minutely at that and he crushed the spark of emotion when he thought of her being threatened. For all he knew that was an elaborate fabrication.

'My uncle was alive until three months before Henry Winterborne died. The whole time he held the threat of doing you harm over my head. I had nothing—no money and nowhere to go. I felt guilty because I had put Henry in a wheelchair. And then, after he had the stroke, it was clear he was dying, so I felt even less able to try and leave.'

Ciro snorted. 'No money? The man was a millionaire.'

Lara avoided his eye. 'After the accident…he was angry. He gave me nothing.'

Ciro's fury increased—she was manipulating him again with this wildly elaborate tale. He wasn't even sure to what end, but he felt sure it couldn't be as simple as she was making out. And he'd had enough.

Ciro's voice was low and lethal. 'I don't know why you're doing this, Lara, but it serves no purpose.'

Lara could see the total rejection of what she'd said on Ciro's face…hear it in his voice. It was exactly as she'd feared. Worse. She could also see the torment of those dark memories in the lines etched into his face.

She'd witnessed his horrific nightmares. Instinctively she reached out towards him. 'Ciro, I'm so sorry. I never meant for any of this to happen—'

He lifted his hand to stop her words. '*Basta.* Enough. My investigative team haven't ruled out your involvement with your uncle. You *do* know you could be prosecuted for this?'

She went pale again—white as parchment. 'Ciro, please, you have to listen to me… I knew nothing. I was as much a victim as you were. I loved you so much… I was terrified of what my uncle might do. I had no choice.'

Ciro's expression turned to one of disgust. 'You *loved* me? You go too far, Lara.' He continued, 'If what you say is true—and I'll verify that myself—how do you explain not telling me all this when we met again?'

She swallowed. 'I was afraid you wouldn't believe me—and apparently I was right.'

Ciro's expression got even darker. 'Not good enough. The truth is that you colluded with your uncle in sending me a message to stay away from you. You could have just *told* me you didn't want to marry me—you didn't have to go to such dramatic lengths.'

Lara realised that further defence would be futile. She said, 'Do you remember I asked you if you loved me, that day in the hospital?'

A flash of irritation crossed Ciro's face. 'What does that have to do with anything?'

'I did want to tell you everything. In spite of my uncle's threats…in spite of the kidnapping… I believed that somehow you'd be able to fight him. But when I knew you didn't feel the same for me as I felt for you, I believed there was no point in risking your life.'

He looked at her for such a long moment that Lara almost believed for a second that she might have got through—but then he said in a toneless voice, 'I've heard enough, Lara. Enough to last a lifetime. This marriage is over—we're done. I want you to leave today. Right now. I'll organise getting you on a flight back to the UK. If you leave with no fuss I'll consider not pressing charges. To be perfectly frank you're not worth the legal hassle or the headlines. Now, get out of my sight.'

A numbness was spreading from Lara's heart outwards to every extremity. She moved jerkily away from Ciro, towards the door. When she got there she stopped and turned around. Ciro was staring at her with such disgust on his face that she almost balked.

She grabbed the door knob to try and stay standing. 'I love you, Ciro. I always have. I did what I thought was best for you and it almost killed me. The last two years have been purgatory. I won't apologise for loving you, whether you choose to believe me or not. And I'm sorry I had to lie to you.'

She left then, before he could say anything caustic. He didn't love her. He'd never loved her, and this was the final lethal blow.

It all happened with military precision. Staff came and helped her to pack, but she insisted on taking just a small case with the belongings she'd arrived with. A car was waiting to take her to JFK, and she was on-board a flight within a few hours.

She'd had to leave Hero behind, as the dog didn't have documentation, and Lara hadn't seen Ciro before she left, so she wasn't even sure he'd still been there. But one thing was certain. She'd never see him again.

* * *

The following evening Ciro sat in the back of his car as it inched its way down Fifth Avenue towards Central Park and his house. His heart was beating a little too fast and he had to modulate his breathing. It was at times like this that he felt most claustrophobic—when he cursed the kidnappers for doing what they had to him, so that no matter how strong he was mentally he still felt a residue of fear that clung to him like a toxic tentacle whenever he was in a small confined space.

He hated it that he couldn't just ease his sense of claustrophobia by jumping out of the car to walk, because he'd spark a massive security alert.

The thought occurred to him that when Lara had been in the back of the car with him he hadn't noticed the claustrophobia as much. He'd been too distracted by her. He scowled at that.

Since the revelations of yesterday, and Lara's departure, he'd been existing in a kind of fog. He couldn't recollect what he'd done today, exactly. The puppy had barked pitifully that morning and Ciro had let her out into the garden, where she'd sniffed around disconsolately in between directing accusatory looks his way.

For a man who was used to thinking clearly he was beyond irritated that he was still thinking of her.

Whether or not it was true that she hadn't colluded with her uncle, she'd *known* about the kidnapping the day she'd come to him at the hospital. He would never forget the blasé way she'd dropped her bombshell that day. When he'd been lying there, beaten and battered. *Because of her!* She'd had her chance and she'd said nothing.

Last night had been the first night he'd spent alone in his bed in weeks. He'd had the nightmare again—except this time he hadn't woken to the cooling touch of Lara's hand or her tempting body. He'd woken sweating, tangled in the sheets, his voice hoarse from shouting. And this time the dream had been slightly different— it had been one moment, repeated over and over. The moment they'd ripped Lara out of his arms and opened the van door to dump her outside.

Her voice drifted into his head then: *'Do you remember I asked you if you loved me?'* He did, actually. He shifted in his seat now, feeling uncomfortable. He did recall it, and he also recalled the feeling of panic that had gripped him.

Love.

He remembered thinking of his father and his slavish devotion to his unfaithful wife, how it had disgusted him. If that was love then, no, he didn't feel that. But there had been something almost desperate on Lara's face and so he'd made some platitude.

What about the terror you felt when she was taken from you by the kidnappers? In that moment you thought you loved her.

Ciro shifted uncomfortably again. He'd always put that surge of emotion down to the extreme circumstances.

His staff had informed him that her flight had left on time yesterday. She'd be back in the UK now. She could be anywhere. For the first time in two years he didn't have tabs on her.

Before the car had even come to a standstill outside his house Ciro got out, not liking the panicky feeling in his gut. He went inside, dropping his things, and the puppy sped across the tiled floor towards him, yapping. It was quickly followed by the housekeeper, apologising profusely. Ciro picked Hero up and waved away the apology.

Feeling restless, he climbed the stairs to the bedrooms. He stood outside Lara's door for a long moment, and then an image of his father came into his head and he scowled and pushed the door open.

It had been tidied, and the bed remade. It was as if she'd never been there. But he could still smell her scent in the air. Lemon and roses.

He put the puppy down on the bed, where she promptly curled up and went to sleep.

Ciro went to the dressing room and opened the doors, expecting to find it empty. But it was full of clothes. He frowned. Everything he'd bought her was there. As was her jewellery. Neatly lined up on velvet pouches under glass display cases.

He went and picked up the phone in the room and rang down to the housekeeper. 'What did Lar— Mrs Sant'Angelo take with her when she left?'

He listened for a moment and then hung up, sitting down on the bed. She'd taken one suitcase. And he knew which one. The one she'd come with. The battered one.

The puppy crept towards him and got into his lap. Ciro stroked her absently. After a while he stood up, taking her with him. He left her with the housekeeper in the kitchen.

Still feeling restless, Ciro went into the reception room. It was filled with priceless paintings and *objets d'art*... Persian rugs. It could be a museum it was so still and stuffy.

When he'd bought this property he'd felt as if he'd reached a pinnacle. One of the many he'd set himself. Then, when he'd proposed to Lara, he'd imagined her here as his wife and hostess. Charming people with her natural warmth and compassion.

Giving you access to a higher level of society, reminded a voice.

A crystal decanter glinted at him from the drinks tray nearby. It seemed to mock him for thinking he'd had it all worked out. For believing that he'd had his fill of Lara. That he was done with her. For believing that all this excess around him actually meant anything.

The tightness in Ciro's chest intensified, and with an inarticulate surge of rage he grabbed the decanter and threw it at the massive stone fireplace, where it smashed into a million pieces.

He heard footsteps running, and for some inexplicable reason he thought it might be—

But when he turned around it was just a shocked-looking staff member.

'Is everything okay, Mr Sant'Angelo?'

He felt ragged. Undone. Empty.

'Everything is fine.'

But he knew it wasn't.

'Two pints of bitter, love!'

Lara forced a smile. 'Coming up.'

After-work drinks on a warm Indian summer evening in London meant packed pubs with people spilling out onto the pavements. Laughing, joking. Delighted that the end of the week had come and they had two days off stretching ahead.

Lara didn't have two days off. At weekends she worked in a small Italian restaurant, near where she was living at a hostel in Kentish Town. But she refused to feel sorry for herself as she went outside with the two pints and collected money and dirty glasses.

A man leaned towards her. 'You're far too pretty to be working here, love. Let me take you out of this cesspit and we'll run away.'

His friends guffawed loudly, but ridiculously Lara couldn't even force a fake laugh. She felt tears sting her eyes. Which was pathetic. She was lucky to have found two jobs. She was earning her own money for the first time in her life. She was finally free… If only that freedom didn't feel so heavy.

She never thought about…*him*. She couldn't. Not if she wanted to keep it together.

'Hey, gorgeous! A pint and a white wine, please!'

Lara looked up at the flushed face of a city boy and forced herself to smile. 'Coming up.'

CHAPTER NINE

A WEEK LATER Ciro was back in London. He was at a black tie event in Buckingham Palace. Lesser members of the royal family mingled with the guests, and he'd just had a long conversation with a man who was in direct line to the throne of England. And it hadn't just been an idle conversation—it had been about business. Ciro's business.

He looked around. This was literally the inner sanctum—the most exclusive group of people on the planet. And he, Ciro Sant'Angelo, a man descended from pirates and Mafiosi, was standing among them. Accepted. Respected. *Finally*.

So why wasn't he feeling more satisfied?

Because he'd just had a call from his solicitor to say that Lara had finally been in touch about going forward with divorce proceedings and had given him a PO box address. She'd told his solicitor that she had no interest in taking the money due to her in the event of their divorce and had named a charity for it to be sent to, if they insisted.

Ciro's charity—Face Forward.

And other things had come to light too—discomfiting things. He'd found the credit card he'd given her on the desk in his study in New York. And her engagement ring and wedding ring, which were both worth a small fortune.

There had been a note.

I'll pay back what I owe.

On inspection, there had been a sum of just a few hundred dollars owing on the card. A laughable amount to someone like Ciro.

She'd also said that once Hero had her papers in order she would appreciate being reunited with the dog. And a parcel had arrived for her. When Ciro had opened it, it had contained a wedding dress. Clearly from the eighties. It wasn't even new.

Nothing made sense.

He had to acknowledge uncomfortably that the Lara who had appeared in his hospital room that day...the unrecognisable Lara...he'd never seen her again. Just flashes at the beginning. If she really was some rich bitch who had only been concerned with status and wealth, then wouldn't she have fleeced him for all he was worth?

Wouldn't she be here right now? Her elegant blonde head shining like a jewel amongst the dross, dressed in a silky evening gown as she hunted for a new husband?

A feeling of clammy desperation stole over Ciro. Maybe she was still playing him. Maybe she *was* here. He looked around, heart thumping, almost expecting to see her blonde head, hear her low, seductive laugh...

'Who are you looking for, Sant'Angelo? Your wife? Have you mislaid her?'

Ciro looked to his right and down into the florid features of a man whose name he'd forgotten and whom he had never liked on previous acquaintance.

'No,' he said tightly. 'She's not here.'

Where the hell is she?

'Pity,' said the man, leaning in a little. 'She's a rare jewel. But I doubt she's *that* rare any more...' He winked. 'If you get what I mean... After all, she's been married twice now. Winterborne got the best of her, lucky sod. If I'd had more money at the time maybe it would have been me.'

Ciro looked at the man with an awful kind of cold horror sinking into his blood. 'What on earth are you talking about?'

The man looked up at him and suddenly appeared uncomfortable. 'Ah... I thought you knew... The auction, of course. I mean, obviously it wasn't a *real* auction. Just something between a few of Thomas Templeton's friends. Girls like Lara are few and far between these days. Innocent. Pure...'

Lara's voice was in Ciro's head. *'He sold me like a slave girl at an auction. To Henry Winterborne, the highest bidder.'*

The man slapped him on the shoulder. 'All right there, Sant'Angelo? You've gone very pale.'

Ciro felt sick to his stomach. 'How many men were involved?' he managed to get out.

Blissfully unaware of the volcano building inside Ciro, the man looked around and said conspiratorially, 'There's always a market for girls like her. With the right breeding. Especially virgins. It's a rare commodity these days, you know.'

Ciro didn't stop to think. His right hand swung back and his fist connected with the fleshy part of the man's face, sending him windmilling backwards into the crowd, where he collided with a waiter holding a tray of glasses, and a woman, who shrieked just before he landed in a heavy heap on the ground.

Instantly security men were beside Ciro, taking his arms in their hands. He briefly caught the eye of the member of the royal family he'd been talking to and saw disdain spreading over his aristocratic features. Everyone was staring at him. Shocked. And then they started whispering as Ciro was led out.

And he didn't give a damn.

For the first time in his life, he didn't give a damn.

It was another hot, muggy evening in the bar and Lara's feet were aching. But at least she wasn't wearing heels any more. She was wiping down the counter under the bar when she heard it.

'Lara.'

She stopped. She'd dreamed about him nearly every night. Was she hallucinating now?

She kept cleaning.

'Lara.'

She looked up and her heart jumped into her throat. *Ciro.* Standing head and shoulders above everyone else around him at the bar.

'Oi, mate—if you're going to take up space at the bar, put in an order for us too, will ya?'

A group of young guys behind Ciro sniggered. He ignored them.

Lara gripped the cloth. 'What are you doing here?'

'Can we talk?'

She noticed that he looked drawn. Dishevelled. 'Is something wrong? Has something happened?'

He shook his head. 'Everything is fine…but we need to talk.'

It was the familiar bossy tone that reassured her in the end—and also told her that this was real, not a fantasy. She was aware of her grumpy boss hovering... aware that no drinks were being served.

Lara sent her boss a reassuring glance and said to Ciro, 'I can't just leave. Sit down and I'll bring you a beer. You'll have to wait until my shift ends.'

'How long is that?'

'Three hours.'

She ignored his look of affront and handed him a pint of bitter, willing him to disappear. Eventually he turned away when she started serving the people behind him.

It was the most excruciating three hours Lara had experienced. With every move she made she was aware of Ciro's eyes burning into her from where he was sitting in a corner. She was surprised she didn't drop every glass, fumble every order.

But finally the pub was empty and she stood in front of Ciro in beer-spattered jeans and T-shirt, a cardigan over her arm and her bag across her body. She felt exhausted, but also energised.

'Where do you want to talk?'

Ciro stood up. 'Do you live near here?'

Lara walked with him out of the pub. She saw Ciro's security team nearby, and his car and driver. She thought of the hostel she called home.

'I don't think you'd like where I'm living. There's a late-night café near here that should still be open.'

'We could go to the townhouse.'

Lara immediately shook her head. *That* London was a million miles from her life now. 'No.'

'Fine—where's this café?'

Lara led him around the corner and into the friendly

café. They were given a booth at the back. Ciro commanded attention and special treatment even here.

Lara ordered tea; Ciro coffee.

When the drinks were delivered, Lara said, 'So what do you want to talk about?'

For a second Ciro looked comically nonplussed, and then he said, 'You left no forwarding address.'

Lara stifled the hurt of recalling that moment in New York. 'You kicked me out, Ciro. I didn't think my forwarding address was high on your list of priorities. I contacted your solicitor with my details.'

'A PO box. What even *is* that?'

Anger surged. If he'd just come here to harangue her because she wasn't following divorce etiquette properly... 'I'm living in a hostel, Ciro. I don't know where I'll be in a month's time. That's why I have a PO box.'

Now he looked horrified. 'A *hostel*?'

Lara nodded. 'It's perfectly clean and habitable.'

Ciro had gone pale under his tan. Lara refused to let it move her.

He put a parcel on the table and said, 'This arrived for you. I opened it. Why did you buy a wedding dress, Lara?'

Lara pulled the package towards her, lifting out the familiar dress. Her mother's wedding dress. She'd tracked it down online and it had only been a couple of hundred dollars to buy it back. Emotion surged in her chest. *She had it back.*

She fought to keep her composure. 'It was my mother's wedding dress. I sold it once.' Tears blurred her vision but she blinked them away, saying as briskly as she could, 'Thank you. I'll pay you back.'

'Why did you sell your mother's dress in the first place?'

Lara avoided looking at him in case he saw how much this dress meant to her. When she felt composed enough, she looked at Ciro. 'I needed the money. After Henry Winterborne got injured I was useless to him. He made me work for him—for free, of course. He sacked his housekeeper. I put up with it because my uncle was still alive and he continued to hold the threat of hurting you over my head. I think he was scared I'd go to you, ask for help. Or that I'd try to warn you. I fantasised about doing that so many times.' Lara touched the package. 'I'd hoped to wear this dress when I married you… it was a connection to my mother. A piece of the past.'

'But you sold it?'

Lara looked at him again. 'The housekeeper who had worked for Henry Winterborne…we'd become friendly. After losing her job she was in dire straits. Her husband had lost his job and was ill… She couldn't find work. I couldn't do much, but I sold this dress and some of my other clothes. Some jewellery. I tried to help her. I felt responsible.'

'Why on earth did you feel responsible?'

Ciro sounded almost angry. Lara avoided his eye. 'If I hadn't injured Henry Winterborne—'

Ciro cut her off. '*Dio*, Lara. The man would have raped you if he could. It wasn't your fault.'

Lara felt a flutter in her chest. *Dangerous*. She looked at Ciro. 'Why are you here?'

'You don't want anything? From the divorce?'

She shook her head, stifling the disappointment. He'd only tracked her down because he needed to discuss this. He probably didn't believe her.

'It was never about money for me. Ever. Not the first time around. Not now.'

Ciro pulled out a tabloid newspaper and handed it to Lara. He said, 'I presume you haven't seen this?'

She looked down and gasped. On the front page there was a picture of Ciro in handcuffs, being put into a police car. His knuckles were bleeding and he looked grimmer than she'd ever seen him. The headline read: *Sant'Angelo Brawls in Palace Amongst Royalty!*

She took in the few words underneath.

You can take the man out of the Mafia...

Lara looked at him, shocked. 'What happened?'

Ciro said, 'I met a man. He was one of the men at the select little auction run by your uncle. One of the men who—' He stopped.

Lara finished for him, feeling sick. 'One of the men who might have become my husband?'

Ciro nodded.

He flexed his hand and Lara reached for it, turning it over to see his bruised knuckles. She said quietly, 'Thank you, but you did't have to do that. You must hate the press attention.'

Ciro flipped his hand so he held hers. 'I don't care about any of that. Finally I've got it through my thick skull that it doesn't matter. Respect and acceptance come from living with integrity and honesty. I can't do more than that and I'm done trying.'

Lara was almost too scared to breathe for a moment. She looked at Ciro and saw a blazing light in his eyes. Something she'd never seen before. A different kind of pride. It made her emotions bubble up again.

'You've never needed to. You tower above men like my uncle and Henry Winterborne. You always have.

But I can understand your father and his father's desire for acceptance. They deserved better.'

Ciro huffed a laugh. He still held Lara's hand. 'Did they? They had blood on their hands, Lara. We all did, by association—although we've come a long way since those times. I'll never be fully accepted into that world, but what I've realised is that money and commerce talk more than social acceptance. That's all that matters in growing a business and a reputation.'

His scar stood out against his olive skin and Lara's emotions finally got the better of her. Ciro would never have had to come to this painful realisation if not for her.

'I'm so sorry, Ciro. If we hadn't met…if I hadn't fallen in love with you…my uncle never would have—' She stopped, biting her lip to stem the tears threatening to flow down her cheeks.

His grip on her hand tightened. 'You have nothing to be sorry for, Lara. *Nothing.* From the moment we met again you confounded me. I expected the woman who had appeared in my hospital room that day, but I got *you*. The Lara I remembered. Except I couldn't trust it. You. I was afraid to after you hurt me so badly.'

Lara chest seized. '*Hurt…?* But you didn't have any feelings for me.'

Ciro huffed out a sound halfway between a laugh and a groan, his hand still tight on hers. 'I didn't know *what* I was feeling. All I knew was that when you asked me if I loved you I panicked. All I could think of was my father, and his toxic obsessive love of my mother. I knew it wasn't that I felt. But I couldn't deny that I felt obsessive about you, and suddenly I was terrified that I was just like my father—that I would lose myself over a woman and make a fool of myself like he had.'

Before Lara could fully absorb this, or what it meant, Ciro asked her a question.

'Why did you agree to marry me this time?'

She swallowed her emotions. 'I felt so guilty for what had happened to you. I owed you. After everything that had happened…'

Ciro took his hand from hers, his expression changing. 'You felt obliged…' He grimaced. 'And why wouldn't you? I *told* you that you owed me.'

He looked at her and she saw pain in his eyes. The pride was gone.

'You had nowhere to go. No money. You felt guilty already. I left you no choice.'

Lara shook her head. 'Of course I had a choice. I could have walked away… I could have told you everything that day and let the chips fall where they may. But I didn't.'

'Why didn't you?'

She kept looking at him, even though it was hard. 'Because you were back in my life. I didn't tell you because I'd convinced myself I owed it to you. I was afraid that if I told you everything you'd despise me even more than you already did.' She took a deep breath. 'Even though I denied it to myself I still loved you, I would have done anything to be with you—even let you take your revenge out on me.'

Ciro looked shell-shocked. 'What you went through… for two years… When I think of that man and what he could have done to you if you hadn't been brave enough to fight him off…' He stood up abruptly and stalked out of the café.

Shocked, Lara sat there for a moment, before throwing down some cash and grabbing the wedding dress. He was outside on the empty street, a fist up to his mouth. When she got close he turned away from her, but not before she'd seen the agony on his face. Moisture on his cheeks.

'Ciro—'

His voice was thick. 'Don't look at me. I can't bear it, Lara. To know what you went through because I was too much of a coward to own up to my feelings...'

Lara went and hugged him from behind, resting her head against his back. The parcel fell by her feet, unnoticed.

Eventually he turned around and she sucked in a breath at the ravaged look on his face.

'How can you ever forgive me?'

A weight lodged in her gut. She'd never expected to see this: Ciro feeling guilty. *She* was the guilty one.

She reached up and wiped away the moisture on his face, her heart aching, because she knew that even though Ciro might have feelings for her it wasn't love, and she would have to walk away again.

'It was my fault—' she said.

He shook his head. '*No.* Never say that again. It was your uncle. Lara, I've had him investigated. You have no idea how corrupt he was. What he did to you was the tip of the iceberg. He was involved in fraud, and in trafficking women in and out of the UK.'

Lara's hands dropped. 'My God...'

'Lara... I'm so sorry.'

She was unable to speak. She'd never expected the cruel irony of Ciro feeling guilty. Saying sorry.

He took her hand. 'This isn't a conversation for here. Come with me to the townhouse—please?'

Lara knew that she should pull back. She'd heard all she needed to. Ciro was right. It wasn't her fault. Or his. They'd both been used as pawns. But she couldn't pull away—not just yet. Soon she'd have a lifetime to try and forget him.

'Okay.'

Ciro picked up the wedding dress and led her over to his car, where she got into the back. When he got in on the other side, he surprised her by pulling her into his arms, enfolding her close. She closed her eyes and guiltily revelled in his strength. It wouldn't last. He just felt guilty. But she'd take it while she could.

Amazingly, she fell asleep, with Ciro's heartbeat thudding against her cheek. She was only vaguely aware of the car stopping, of Ciro lifting her out and carrying her. There was another familiar voice. And then she was being put down on a soft surface and a warm blanket was being pulled over her.

She struggled to wake up but Ciro's commanding voice said, 'No, go to sleep, Lara. You need to rest.'

When Lara woke the next morning it was early. Just after dawn. It took a minute for her to realise that she wasn't in her disinfectant-scented room at the hostel. She was in a luxurious bed.

Ciro's townhouse.

She sat up and looked down, grimacing. She was still dressed in her T-shirt and jeans. A faint smell of beer and fried food wafted up. She got up and went into the bathroom, stripping off and stepping under the shower.

As the water sluiced down over her body she finally allowed herself to remember the previous cataclysmic evening. The outpouring of emotion. The pain on Ciro's face.

The fact that he didn't love her but that he was sorry.

Lara hugged herself under the water for a long moment, willing back the emotion. She had to hold it in until she left this place. Then she could grieve. *Finally.*

When Lara stepped out of the shower she felt lighter, in spite of the heaviness in her heart. Cleansed. At peace. She had something she could hold to her and cherish, no matter what happened with Ciro.

Because, in spite of the catharsis of the truth finally being revealed, and what he'd said about his priorities, she knew him too well. She knew he would have had time now to assess what had happened, and that he must be mortified by how much he'd revealed. Not to mention the public humiliation of being arrested at a party in Buckingham Palace.

He wouldn't thank her for that when he realised the full extent of the repercussions. He'd worked too hard not to mind.

She pulled on a towelling robe from the back of the door and made her way downstairs to the utility room with her clothes, intending to wash and dry them.

When she was on her way back up she heard a noise in the kitchen and went in. Ciro was there, in jeans and a shirt, sipping a cup of coffee. He turned to face her and she felt shy. Ridiculously.

'I'm sorry about that—falling asleep. I must have been more tired than I thought.'

Ciro looked stern. 'I'm not surprised…working two jobs.'

Lara's mouth fell open. 'How did you know?'

'I tracked you down a few days ago. My investigators told me.'

Lara tried not to sound defensive. 'I need the money.'

Ciro changed the subject. 'Coffee?'

Lara nodded. 'Please.'

She tried to gauge his mood but it was hard. He

wasn't exhibiting any sign of the emotion of last night and her worst fears seemed to be coming true. He was regretting having said anything.

He handed her a cup. 'Let's talk upstairs.'

'We really don't have to. You must be busy. And I have to get to work at the restaurant—'

He stopped her. 'You're not working there again.'

'Ciro, I can't just—'

'Come upstairs with me. Please.'

Lara followed him, trying not to give in to the anger and panic that Ciro was riding roughshod over her life all over again.

He led her into one of the informal living rooms, with soft slouchy sofas and chairs. She took a chair and Ciro walked to the window. She tried not to let her gaze drop to where the material of his snug jeans hugged his buttocks so lovingly.

She took a fortifying sip of coffee and put down her cup. 'As soon as my clothes are dry I'll get out of your hair. I know you mean well, but I really can't afford to lose that job—'

Ciro whirled around, the first crack in his calm façade showing. 'I said you are *not* going back there, Lara. *Dio.*' He put down his own cup and shoved his hands deep in his jeans pockets, as if afraid he might do something bad with them.

Lara was stunned into silence. She saw a muscle beating in his jaw.

'This house is your house, Lara. You have somewhere to live. You don't need to work to put a roof over your head. Ever again.'

She looked at him. Totally confused. 'You're giving me your house?'

'I mean, it's *ours*. My home is your home.'

She shook her head. 'I don't… What are you saying, Ciro?'

He came over and sat down. Stood up. Sat down again. Suddenly she could see the emotion on his face.

'I'm saying that I want us to stay married, Lara. But after everything you've been through… I know you deserve your independence. You've had people—*men*—telling you what to do since you lost your family, and I don't want to just be another man running your life.'

Lara's heart constricted. 'You don't want me to go?'

He shook his head, kneeling down beside her. '*No*. I *don't* want you to leave. *Ever*. But I also don't want you to feel obliged to stay because you feel like you owe me, or because of guilt. I love you, Lara, but I don't want you to feel trapped.'

The world stopped on its axis. 'You…what?'

Ciro frowned. 'I love you… I told you yesterday…'

Lara shook her head. 'No. I'm pretty sure I would have remembered that piece of information. You were upset…feeling guilty… You mentioned *feelings*. But you never mentioned love.'

Ciro took her hand. 'Well, I do love you. I've loved you since the moment I laid eyes on you in that street in Florence. I just didn't know what it was. You were the first woman to get under my skin without even trying, Lara. The first woman I spent a whole night with in my bed. When I proposed to you it was because you were the first woman who made me want more. Who made me hate the cynicism I'd been brought up with.'

Ciro went pale.

'When those kidnappers ripped you out of my arms that day…that's when I knew… But even afterwards I told myself that it couldn't be *love*. I would never be so foolish, such a slave to my emotions—not like my father.'

Lara saw it on his face. Pure emotion. She put a hand to her mouth to stifle a sound of pure joy mixed with shock.

But Ciro took her hand down. 'Please believe me, Lara. I love you more than life itself. Without you the world didn't make sense. I never truly believed you were that person you'd turned into in the hospital, but it was easier to believe that than admit you'd broken my heart.'

Lara touched his face, his scar. Tears blurred her vision. 'Oh, my love...my darling. I'm so sorry.'

He caught her face in his hands. He looked fierce. 'Never say sorry again. *Never.*'

She nodded. 'I love you...so much.'

Ciro shook his head. 'I'm almost scared to believe... We've been through so much—I've put you through so much...'

Lara put a finger to his mouth, stopping his words. 'Don't *you* ever say that again. Neither of us were to blame. We got caught up in events outside our control. I love you, my darling, and that's all you have to believe.'

She bent forward and kissed him. A sweet chaste kiss. Then she pulled back and said shakily, 'Even if you had told me you loved me, and we'd stood up to my uncle, I dread to think what might have happened. He was crazy, Ciro. I was his only hope of redemption and he was capable of anything.'

Ciro was grim. 'Maybe—but he put us through two years of hell.' He said then, 'Do you know why I really bought this house?'

She shook her head, marvelling at how full her heart could feel.

'I kept tabs on you for those two years...hoping for

God knows what to happen. I knew where you lived and I bought this house sight unseen. I think I had nefarious plans to seduce you away from Henry Winterborne. It would have proved that you had no morals, but more importantly it would have brought you back to me. I had no qualms about playing dirty to get you back.'

Lara smiled a shaky smile. 'You have no idea how many nights I dreamed of you coming to rescue me. But then I'd see photos of you, out and about, getting on with your life, with other women…'

The pain of that still made her gut churn. She looked away.

Ciro caught her chin and turned her back to face him. 'I didn't take one of those women into my bed. I couldn't. The thought of you—it consumed me. You ruined me for anyone else. *Ever.*'

Lara couldn't hold back. She flung her arms around Ciro and he caught her. Lifted her up and sat down on the sofa, settling her across his lap. Cradling her.

Lara clutched at his shirt. 'We've wasted so much time…'

He caught her chin again, tipping it up. 'No. We start again now. No more regrets, okay?'

Lara nodded, humbled by Ciro's capacity to forgive and move on.

He sat up then, and put her beside him. Then he got off the sofa and down on one knee in front of her.

'Ciro…'

He drew a box out of his jeans pocket. A familiar velvet box. Her heart tripped. He opened it and she saw her engagement ring and wedding ring.

Ciro suddenly looked anxious. 'Maybe I should have bought new ones.'

Lara touched them reverently. 'No, I love them.'

He took the rings out of the box and looked at her. 'Lara Sant'Angelo, will you please stay my wife—for the rest of our lives?'

She nodded, and got out a choked, 'Yes.'

When the rings were back on her finger, where they belonged, she said, 'I wondered why you hadn't thrown the engagement ring away...'

Ciro looked deep into her eyes and said huskily, 'Maybe because I was already dreaming of this moment.'

He kissed her then, so deeply that he touched her heart and mended all the broken shards back together.

Much later, when they were lying in bed, sated and at peace, Lara said, 'I think maybe that's why I tracked down my mother's wedding dress when I had the chance. Maybe I was hoping for a second chance.'

Ciro caught her hand and her rings sparkled. He kissed her there and she looked at him, caught in those dark eyes that held so much love.

'Second chances and new beginnings.'

'Yes, my love, for ever.'

EPILOGUE

A month later...

DUSK WAS MELTING into night as Lara walked to the entrance of the small chapel in the grounds of the *palazzo* in Sicily. Apparently it was a tradition, marrying at night. She didn't really care.

Lighted torches had guided her from the *palazzo* to the chapel and to Isabella, who was her bridesmaid. The young girl's eyes were suspiciously shiny as she fussed over Lara at the entrance, where flowers festooned the doorway, making the air heavy with a million scents.

Hero danced around their feet, looking up at Lara adoringly. She was attached to Isabella's wrist with a ribbon and had a velvet cushion tied to her collar, upon which was tied a gold wedding band inlaid with sapphires. A new wedding ring to celebrate this renewal of their vows.

'Your dress is so beautiful.'

'Thank you,' said Lara.

She hadn't been allowed to look at herself in a mirror with the dress on—apparently another Sicilian tradition. But she'd had her mother's dress adjusted slightly so that it fitted her perfectly.

It was classically simple and sweetly bohemian, with its high neck and ruffled bodice. She wore her hair down and a garland of flowers adorned her head. No veil. She didn't need to hide any more—from anything.

Isabella pressed a simple bouquet of local flowers into her hands and then stepped in front of her to start her walk down the aisle.

Roberto, her twin brother, was acting as groomsman to Ciro. And Lazaro was there too—Ciro's best friend. His eyes had been suspiciously shiny earlier, when they'd had an informal pre-ceremony lunch.

He'd taken Lara's hands and said, 'I'm sorry for doubting you.'

Lara had shaken her head and said, 'No need to apologise. I'm glad you were there for him.'

Lazaro had grimaced. 'He wasn't a pretty sight the day you got married the first time. I had to peel him off the floor of a bar—'

'Filling my wife's head with stories again, Lazaro?'

Lara had smiled and put her hand over Ciro's, where his arm had wrapped around her waist, leaning back against him and revelling in his solid strength and love. He'd told her about how he'd gone out and got blind drunk the day of her wedding to Henry Winterborne.

She knew everything. And so did he. No more secrets.

Now she hesitated for a moment on the threshold of the small chapel. Hovering between the past and present. Ciro hadn't turned to look at her walk down the aisle at their first wedding ceremony, but even as that thought formed in her head he turned around now.

And even though she hadn't been allowed to look at herself in her wedding dress, she didn't need to. She could see herself reflected in his eyes as she walked towards him and she'd never felt more beautiful or more desired.

Or more loved.

She was home. At last.

Hours later, after the revelry had finally died down and Ciro had picked her up to carry her to their suite amidst much catcalling and cheering, Lara stood facing out to where the dawn was breaking on a new day on the horizon.

Ciro was behind her, undoing each tiny button on the dress—undressing his bride to make love to her, kissing each sliver of exposed skin.

Lara's eyes filled with tears. She whispered, 'I dreamt of this moment but I never dared to believe it might come true. I was so scared to love again after losing my family.'

Ciro's hands stopped and he turned her around to face him. He wiped her tears away. 'It's not a dream... it's real. Because you were brave enough to trust.'

Lara smiled through her tears. 'Because you made me fall for you.'

Ciro smiled smugly. 'That too.'

Then his smile faded and he put a hand to her belly between them. 'And we can have more too, if you trust me.'

She whispered, 'A family...'

He nodded. 'I wouldn't want this with anyone else. Only you.'

'Me too.'

'Let's start now. This morning.'

Lara reached up and put her arms around his neck, pressing her mouth to his before saying emotionally, 'Yes, please.'

* * *

Nine months later, in a hospital in Palermo, Ciro and Lara welcomed a baby son—Carlo—and their family was complete.

At least until Margarita arrived a couple of years later.

And then Stefano.

Then it was complete.

* * * * *

PRINCE'S VIRGIN IN VENICE

TRISH MOREY

To magical Venezia,
floating city of love and romance.

CHAPTER ONE

PRINCE VITTORIO D'MARBURG of Andachstein was fed up. Bored. Even in Venice at the height of carnival season, even on his way to the most exclusive party of the festival, still the Playboy Prince couldn't ignore the overwhelming sense of frustration that permeated his skin and drilled straight down into his bones.

Or maybe it was just the icy pricks from the February pea soup fog needling his skin that were turning his thoughts from carnival to cynical. It was a fog that turned the magical city invisible, precisely when the *calles* and narrow bridges were more crowded than ever with waves of costumed partygoers surging to and fro, competing for the available space—brightly garbed men and women for whom the fog failed to dampen the air of excitement and the energy that accompanied Carnevale.

It was if the floating city had been let off a leash and, fog or no, it was going to party.

Vittorio cut a swathe through the endless tide of carnival-goers, his cloak swirling in his wake, his mood blackening with every step.

The thronging crowds somehow parted and made way for him. He didn't think too much about it. Maybe it was his warrior costume—a coat of mail and blue leather dressed with chain and gold braid—or maybe it was his battle-ready demeanour. Either way, it was as if they could read the hostility in his eyes as he headed towards the most exclusive party of the night.

And they could all see his eyes. Vittorio had given up playing with disguises when he was a child. There'd been no point. Everyone had always known it was him behind the mask.

Before the ancient well in the square that housed the Palazzo de Marigaldi, Vittorio's long strides slowed. Ordinarily he would have been relieved to reach his destination and escape the exuberant crowds—*should* have been relieved—except for the fact that his father had all too gleefully shared the news in his latest call, just minutes earlier, that the Contessa Sirena Della Corte, daughter of one of his oldest friends, was opportunely going to be in attendance.

Vittorio snorted—just as he'd done when his father had told him.

Opportunely.

He doubted it.

Opportunistically would no doubt be a better word. The woman was a human viper draped in designer artistry, lying in wait for a royal title—which marriage to him would bestow upon her. And his father, despite Vittorio's blanket protests, had encouraged her to pursue her desperate ambition.

Little wonder Vittorio was in no hurry to get there.

Little wonder that, despite the assurances he'd made to his old friend Marcello that nothing would stop him attending his party tonight, Vittorio's enthusiasm had been on the wane ever since his father's call had come through.

Dio.

He'd come to Venice thinking the famous carnival would offer an escape from the stultifying atmosphere of the palace and the endless demands of the aging Prince Guglielmo, but it seemed they had stalked him here—along with the Contessa Sirena.

His father's choice for his next bride.

But after the experience of his first doomed marriage Vittorio wasn't about to be dictated to again—not when it came to the woman who would share his marriage bed.

The crowds were thickening, party deadlines were calling, and their excitement was at odds with his own dark thoughts. He was a man out of place, out of time. He was a man who had the world at his feet, and destiny snapping at his heels. He was a man who wanted to be able to make his own choices, but he was cursed with the heritage of his birth and his need to satisfy others before he could entertain his own needs.

He all but turned to walk away—from his destiny as much as from the party. He wasn't in the mood for going another few rounds with Sirena—wasn't in the mood for her blatant attempts at seduction, the pouting, and the affected hurt when her all too obvious charms went ignored.

Except there was no question of his not going. Marcello was his oldest friend and Vittorio had promised him he would be there. Sirena would just have to keep on pouting.

But curse his father for encouraging the woman.

Something caught his eye. A flash of colour amongst the crowd, a static burst of vermilion amidst the moving parade of costumes and finery, a glimpse of a knee, down low, and a hint of an upturned angular jaw up high—like snatches of a portrait in oils when all around were hazy watercolours.

His eyes narrowed as he willed the surging crowd to part. Catching a glance of a dark waterfall of wavy hair over one shoulder when the crowd obliged, he saw the woman turn her masked face up to the bridge, moving her head frantically with every passing costume, scanning, searching through the short veil of black lace that masked the top half of her face.

She looked lost. Alone. A tourist, most likely, fallen victim to Venice's tangle of streets and canals.

He looked away. It wasn't his problem. He had somewhere to be, after all. And yet still his eyes scoured the square. Nobody looked as if they had lost someone and were searching for her. Nobody looked anywhere close to claiming her.

He glanced back, seeking her between richly decorated masks topped with elaborate wigs and feathers, their wearers resplendent in costumes that spoke of centuries long past, when men wore fitted breeches and women wore gowns with tight bodices spilling their plump white breasts. For a moment he couldn't find her, and thought her gone, until a group of Harlequins with jester hats ringing with bells passed. And then he saw her raise one hand to her painted mouth before seeming to sag before him.

He watched as she thumbed off the mask and shook her hair back on a sigh—the long hair that curled over one shoulder. She swept it back with one hand, and her cloak slipped down to reveal one bare shoulder and a satin gown riding low over one breast, before she shivered and hurriedly tucked herself back under the cover of the cloak.

She was lost.

Alone.

With the kind of innocent beauty and vulnerability that tugged at him.

And suddenly Vittorio didn't feel so bored any more.

CHAPTER TWO

LOST IN VENICE. Panic pumped loud and hard through Rosa Ciavarro's veins as she squeezed herself out of the flow of costumed crowds pouring over the bridge and found a rare patch of space by the side of the canal, trying to catch her breath and calm her racing heart. But nothing could calm her desperate eyes.

She peered through the lace of her veil, searching for a sign that would tell her where she was, but when she managed to make out the name of the square it meant nothing and offered no clue as to where she was. Scanning the passing crowds for any hint of recognition proved just as useless. It was pointless. Impossible to tell who was who when everyone was in costume.

Meanwhile the crowds continued to surge over the bridge: Harlequins and Columbinas, vampires and zombies. And why not zombies, when in the space of a few minutes her highly anticipated night had teetered over the edge from magical into nightmarish?

Panic settled into glum resignation as she turned her head up to the inky sky swirling with fog and clutched her own arms, sighing out a long breath of frustration that merely added more mist to the swirling fog. It was futile, and it was time she gave up searching and faced the truth.

She'd crossed too many bridges and turned too many corners in a vain attempt to catch up with her friends, and there was no chance they'd ever find each other now.

It was the last night of Carnevale, and the only party she'd been able to afford to go to, and instead she was lost and alone at the base of a fog-bound bridge somewhere in Venice.

Pointless.

Rosa pulled her thin cloak more tightly around her shoulders. *Dio*, it was cold. She stamped her feet against the stones of the pavement to warm her legs, wishing she'd had the sense to make herself something warmer than this flimsy gown with its bare shoulders and high-low hem. Something that better suited the season. Preferably something worn over thermals and lined with fur.

'You'll be dancing all night,' Chiara had protested when Rosa had suggested she dress for the winter weather. 'Take it from me, you'll roast if you wear anything more.'

But Rosa wasn't roasting now. The damp air wound cold fingers around her ankles and up her shins, seeking and sucking out what body warmth it could find. She was so very cold! And for the first time in too many years to remember she felt tears prick at the corners of her eyes.

She sniffed. She wasn't the type to cry. She'd grown up with three older brothers who would mercilessly tease her if she did. As a child, she'd stoically endured any number of bumps and scratches, skinned knees and grazed elbows when she'd insisted on accompanying them on their adventures.

She hadn't cried when her brothers had taught her to ride a bike that was too large for her, letting her go fast on a rocky road until she'd crashed into an ancient fig tree. She hadn't cried when they'd helped her climb that same tree and then all clambered down and run away, leaving her to pick her own tentative way down. She'd fallen the last few feet to the dusty ground, collecting more scratches and bumps. All wounds she'd endured without a whimper.

But she'd never before been separated from her friends

and lost in the labyrinthine *calles* of Venice on the biggest party night of the year, without her ticket or any way to contact them. Surely even her brothers would understand if she shed a tear or two of frustration now?

Especially if they knew the hideous amount she'd spent on her ticket!

She closed her eyes and pulled her cloak tighter around her, feeling the icy bite of winter working its way into her bones as resignation gave way to remorse. She'd had such high hopes for tonight. A rare night off in the midst of Carnevale. A chance to pretend she *wasn't* just another hotel worker, cleaning up after the holidaymakers who poured into the city. A chance to be part of the celebrations instead of merely watching from the sidelines.

But so much money!

Such a waste!

Laughter rang out from the bridge, echoing in the foggy air above the lapping canal—laughter that could well be directed at her. Because there was nobody to blame for being in this predicament but herself.

It had seemed such a good idea when Chiara had offered to carry her phone and her ticket. After all, they were going to the same party. And it *had* been a good idea—right up until a host of angels sprouting ridiculously fat white wings had surged towards them across a narrow bridge and she'd been separated from her friends and forced backwards. By the time she'd managed to shoulder her way between the feathered wings and get back to the bridge Chiara and her friends had been swallowed up in the fog and the crowds and were nowhere in sight.

She'd raced across the bridge and along the crowded paths as best she could, trying to catch up, colliding with people wearing headdresses constructed from shells, or jester hats strung with bells, or ball gowns nearly the width of the narrow streets. But she was relatively new to Venice,

and unsure of the way, and she'd crossed so many bridges—
too many—that even if Chiara turned back how would she
even know where to find her? She could have taken any
number of wrong turns.

Useless.

She might as well go home to the tiny basement apartment she shared with Chiara—wherever that was. Surely
even if it took her all night she would stumble across it
eventually. With a final sigh, she reefed the mask from her
face. She didn't need a lace veil over her eyes to make her
job any more difficult. She didn't need a mask tonight, period. There would be no party for her tonight.

Her cloak slipped as she pushed her hair back, inadver-
tently exposing one shoulder to the frigid air. She shivered
as she grappled with the slippery cloth and tucked herself
back under what flimsy protection it offered against the
cold.

She was bracing herself to fight her way back over the
bridge and retrace her steps when she saw him. A man
standing by the well in the centre of the square. A man in
a costume of blue trimmed with gold. A tall man, broad-
shouldered, with the bearing of a warrior.

A man who was staring right at her.

Electricity zapped a jagged line down her spine.

No. Not possible. She darted a look over her shoulder—
because why should he be looking at *her*? But there was
nothing behind her but the canal and a crumbling wall beyond.

She swallowed as she turned back, raising her eyes just
enough to see that he was now walking purposefully towards her, and the crowd was almost scattering around him.
Even across the gloom of the lamp-lit square the intent in
his eyes sent adrenaline spiking in her blood.

Fight versus flight? There was no question of her response. She knew that whoever he was, and whatever he

was thinking, she'd stayed there too long. And he was still moving, long strides bridging the distance between them, and still her feet refused to budge. She was anchored to the spot, when instead she should be pushing bodily into the bottleneck of people at the bridge and letting the crowd swallow her up and carry her away.

Much too soon he was before her, a man mountain of leather tunic and braid and chain, his shoulder-length hair loose around a face that spoke of power. A high brow above a broad nose and a jawline framed with steel and rendered in concrete, all hard lines and planes. And eyes of the most startling blue. Cobalt. No, he was no mere warrior. He must be a warlord. A god. He could be either.

Her mouth went dry as she looked up at him, but maybe that was just the heat that seemed to radiate from his body on this cold, foggy evening.

'Can I help you?' he said, in a voice as deep as he was tall.

He spoke in English, although with an accent that suggested he was not. Her heart was hammering in her chest, and her tongue seemed to have lost the ability to form words in any language.

He angled his head, his dark eyes narrowing. *'Vous-êtes perdu?'* he tried, speaking in French this time.

Her French was patchier than her English, so she didn't bother trying to respond in either. *'No parlo Francese,'* she said, sounding breathless even to her own ears—but how could she not sound breathless, standing before a man whose very presence seemed to suck the oxygen out of the misty air?

'You're Italian?' he said, in her own language this time.

'Si.' She swallowed, the action kicking up her chin. She tried to pretend it was a show of confidence, just like the challenge she did her best to infuse into her voice. 'Why were you watching me?'

'I was curious.'

She swallowed. She'd seen those women standing alone and waiting on the side of the road, and she had one idea why he might be curious about a woman standing by herself in a square.

She looked down at her gown, at the stockinged legs visible beneath the hem of her skirt. She knew she was supposed to look like a courtesan, but... 'This is a costume. I'm not—you know.'

One side of his mouth lifted—the slightest rearrangement of the hard angles and planes of his face that turned his lips into an almost-smile, a change so dramatic that it took her completely by surprise.

'This is Carnevale. Nobody is who they seem tonight.'

'And who are you?'

'My name is Vittorio. And you are...?'

'Rosa.'

'Rosa,' he said, with the slightest inclination of his head.

It was all she could do not to sway at the way her name sounded in his rich, deep voice. It was the cold, she told herself, the slap of water against the side of the canal and the whisper of the fog against her skin, nothing more.

'It is a pleasure to meet you.'

He held out one hand and she regarded it warily. It was a big hand, with buckles cuffing sleeves that looked as if they would burst open if he clenched so much as a muscle.

'I promise it doesn't bite,' he said.

She looked up to see that the curve of his lips had moved up a notch and there was a glimmer of warmth in his impossibly blue eyes. And she didn't mind that he seemed to be laughing at her, because the action had worked some kind of miracle on his face, giving a glimpse of the man beneath the warrior. So he was mortal after all...not some god conjured up by the shifting fog.

Almost reluctantly she put her hand in his, then felt his

fingers curl around her hers and heat bloom in her hand. It was a delicious heat that curled seductively into her bloodstream and stirred a response low down in her belly, a feeling so unexpected, so unfamiliar, that it sent alarm bells clanging in her brain.

'I have to go,' she said, pulling her hand from his, feeling the loss of his body heat as if it had been suctioned from her flesh.

'Where do you have to go?'

She looked over her shoulder at the bridge. The crowds were thinning now, most people having arrived at their destinations, and only latecomers were still rushing. If she set off now, at least she'd have a chance of getting herself warm.

'I'm supposed to be somewhere. A party.'

'Do you know where this party is?'

'I'll find it,' she said, with a conviction she didn't feel.

Because she had no idea where she was or where the party was, and because even if she did by some miracle manage to find the party there was the slight matter of an entry ticket no longer in her possession.

'You haven't a clue where it is or how to get there.'

She looked back at him, ready to snap a denial, but his eyes had joined with his lips and there was no mistaking that he'd know she was lying.

She pulled her cloak tighter around her and kicked up her chin. 'What's it to you?'

'Nothing. It's not a crime. Some would say that in Venice getting lost is compulsory.'

She bit her tongue as she shivered under her cloak.

Maybe if you hadn't dropped more money than you could spare on a ticket, and maybe if you had a phone with working GPS, you wouldn't mind getting lost in Venice.

'You're cold,' he said, and before she could deny it or

protest he had undone the chain at his neck and swung his cloak around her shoulders.

Her first instinct was to protest. New to city life she might be, but in spite of what he'd said she wasn't naïve enough to believe that this man's offer of help came without strings. But his cloak was heavy and deliciously warm, the leather supple and infused with a masculine scent. The scent of *him*. She breathed it in, relishing the blend of leather and man, rich and spiced, and her protest died on her lips. It was so good to feel snug.

'Grazie,' she said, warmth enveloping her, spreading to legs that felt as if they'd been chilled for ever. Just for a minute she would take this warmth, use it to defrost her blood and re-energise her deflated body and soul, and then she'd insist she was fine, give his cloak back and try to find her way home.

'Is there someone you can call?'

'I don't have my phone.' She looked down at the mask in her hands, feeling stupid.

'Can I call someone for you?' he asked, pulling a phone from a pouch on his belt.

For a moment Rosa felt a glimmer of hope. But only for a moment. Because Chiara's phone number was logged in her phone's memory, but not in her own. She shook her head, the tiny faint hope snuffed out. Her Carnevale was over before it had even begun.

'I don't know the number. It's programmed into my phone, but…'

He dropped the phone back in its pouch. 'You don't know where this party is?'

Suddenly she was tired. Worn out by the rollercoaster of emotions, weary of questions that exposed how unprepared and foolish she'd been. This stranger might be trying to help, and he might be right when he assumed she didn't know where the party was—he *was* right—but she didn't need a post-mortem. She just wanted to go back to her apartment and her bed, pull the covers over her head and forget this night had ever happened.

'Look, thanks for your help. But don't you have somewhere to be?'

'I do.'

She cocked an eyebrow at him in challenge. 'Well, then?'

A gondola slipped almost silently along the canal behind her. Fog swirled around and between them. The woman must be freezing, the way she was so inadequately dressed. Her arms tightly bunched the paper-thin wrap around her quaking shoulders, but still she wanted to pretend that everything was all right and that she didn't need help.

'Come with me,' he said.

It was impulse that had him uttering the words, but once they were out he realised they made all kinds of sense. She was lost, all alone in Venice, and she was beautiful—even more beautiful than he'd first thought when she'd peeled off her mask. Her brandy-coloured eyes were large and cat-like in her high-cheekboned face, her painted curved lips like an invitation. He remembered the sight of her naked shoulder under the cloak, the cheap satin of the bodice cupping her breast, and a random thought amused him.

Sirena would hate her.

And wasn't that sufficient reason by itself?

Those cat-like eyes opened wide. *'Scusa?'*

'Come with me,' he said again. The seeds of a plan were already germinating—a plan that would benefit them both.

'You don't have to say that. You've already been too kind.'

'It's not about being kind. You would be doing me a favour.'

'How is that possible? We'd never met until a few moments ago. How can I possibly do you any favour?'

He held out his forearm to her, the leather of his sleeve creaking. 'Call it serendipity, if you prefer. Because I too have a costume ball to attend and I don't have a partner for the evening. So if you would do me the honour of accompanying me?'

She laughed a little, then shook her head. 'I've already told you—this is a costume. I wasn't waiting to be picked up.'

'I'm not trying to pick you up. I'm asking you to be my guest for the evening. But it is up to you, Rosa. Clearly you planned on going to a party tonight.'

He eased the mask from where she held it between the fingers clutching his cloak over her breasts and turned it slowly in his hands. She had no choice but to let it go. It was either let him take it or let go of the cloak.

'Why should you miss out on the biggest night of Carnevale,' he said, watching the way her eyes followed his hands as he thumbed the lace of her veil, 'just because you became separated from your friends?'

He could tell she was tempted—could all but taste her excitement at being handed a lifeline to an evening she'd all but given up on, even while questions and misgivings swirled in the depths of her eyes.

He smiled. He might have started this evening in a foul mood, and he knew that would have been reflected in his features, but he knew how to smile when it got him something he wanted. Knew how to turn on the charm when the need arose—whether he was involved in negotiations with an antagonistic foreign diplomat or romancing a woman he desired in his bed.

'Serendipity,' he repeated. 'A happy chance—for both of us. And the bonus is you'll get to wear my cloak a while longer.'

Her eyes lifted to meet his—long-lashed eyes, shy eyes, filled with uncertainty and nerves. Again, he was struck by her air of vulnerability. She was a very different animal from the women he usually met. An image of Sirena floated unbidden into his mind's eye—self-assured, self-centred Sirena, who wouldn't look vulnerable if she was alone in six feet of water and staring down a hungry shark. A very different animal indeed.

'It is very warm,' she said, 'thank you.'

'Is that a yes?'

She took a deep breath, her teeth troubling her bottom lip while a battle went on inside her, then gave a decisive nod, adding her own tentative smile in response. 'Why not?'

'Why not indeed?'

He didn't waste any time ushering her across the bridge and through the twisted *calles* towards the private entrance of the *palazzo* gardens, his mood considerably lighter than it had been earlier in the evening.

Because suddenly a night he hadn't been looking forward to had taken on an entirely different sheen. Not just because he was going to give Sirena a surprise and pay her back for the one she had orchestrated for him. But because he had a beautiful woman on his arm in one of the most beautiful cities in the world and the night was young.

And who knew where it would end?

CHAPTER THREE

ROSA'S HEART WAS tripping over itself as the gorgeous man placed her hand around the leather of his sleeve and cut a path through the crowds, and her feet struggled to keep up with his long strides.

Vittorio, he'd told her his name was, but that didn't make him any less a stranger. And he was leading her to a costume ball somewhere, or so he'd said. But she had no more detail than that. And she had nobody and nothing to blame for being here but a spark of impulse that had made her abandon every cautionary lesson she'd grown up with and provoked her into doing something so far out of her comfort zone she wondered if she'd ever find a way back.

'Why not?' she'd said in response to his invitation, in spite of the fact she could think of any number of reasons.

She'd never in her twenty-four years done anything as impetuous—or as reckless. Her brothers would no doubt add *stupid* to the description.

And yet, uncertainty and even stupidity aside, her night had turned another corner. One that had tiny bubbles of excitement fizzing in her blood.

Anticipation.

'It's not far,' he said, 'Are you still cold?'

'No.'

Quite the contrary. His cloak was like a shield against the weather, and his arm under hers felt solid and real. If anything, she was exhilarated, as though she'd embarked upon a mystery tour, or an adventure with an unknown destination. So many unknowns, and this man was at the top of the list.

She glanced up at him as he forged on with long strides through the narrow *calle*. He seemed eager to get where he was going now, almost as if he'd wasted too much time talking to her in the square and was making up for lost time. They passed a lamp that cast light and shadow on his profile, turning it into a moving feast of features—the strong lines of his jaw and nose, his high brow and dark eyes, and all surrounded by a thick mane of black hair.

'It's not far now,' he said, looking down at her.

For a moment—a second—his cobalt eyes met hers and snagged, and the bubbles in her blood spun and fizzed some more, and a warm glow stirred deep in her belly.

She stumbled and he caught her, not letting her fall, and the moment was gone, but even as she whispered her breathless thanks she resolved not to spend too much time staring into this man's eyes. At least not while she was walking.

'This way,' he said, steering her left down a narrow path away from the busy *calle*. Here, the ancient wall of a *palazzo* disappeared into the fog on one side, a high brick wall on the other, and with each step deeper along the dark path the sounds of the city behind became more and more muffled by the fog, until every cautionary tale she'd ever heard came back to mock her and the only sound she could hear was her own thudding heartbeat.

No, not the only sound, because their footsteps echoed in the narrow side alley and there also came the slap of water, the reflection of pale light on the shifting surface of the path ahead. But, no, that would mean—

And that was when she realised that the path ended in a dark recess with only the canal beyond.

A dead end.

Adrenaline spiked in her blood as anticipation morphed into fear. She'd come down this dark path willingly, with a man of whom she knew nothing apart from his name. If it even *was* his name.

'Vittorio,' she said, her steps dragging as she tried to pull her hand from where he had tucked it into his elbow. 'I think maybe I've changed my mind...'

'*Scusi?*'

He stopped and spun towards her, and in the gloomy light his shadowed face and flashing eyes took on a frightening dimension. In this moment he could be a demon. A monster.

Her mouth went dry. She didn't want to stay to find out which. 'I should go home.'

She was struggling with the fastening of his cloak, even as she backed away, her fingers tangling with the clasp to free herself and give it back before she fled.

Already she could hear her brothers berating her, asking her why she'd agreed to go with someone she didn't know in the first place, telling her what a fool she'd been—and they'd be right. She would never live down the shame. She would regret for ever her one attempt at impetuosity.

'Rosa?'

A door swung open in the recess behind Vittorio, opening up to a fantasy world beyond. Lights twinkled in trees. A doorman looked to see who was outside and bowed his head when he spotted them waiting.

'Rosa?' Vittorio said again. 'We're here—at the *palazzo*.'

She blinked. Beyond the doorman there was a path between some trees and at the end of it a fountain, where water rose and fell to some unseen beat. 'At the ball?'

'Yes,' he said, and in the low light she could see the curve of his lips, as if he'd worked out why she'd suddenly felt the urge to flee. 'Or do you feel the need to remind me once again that you are just wearing a costume?'

Rosa had never been more grateful for the fog as she swallowed back a tide of embarrassment.

Dio, what must he think of me? First he finds me lost and helpless, and then I panic like I'm expecting him to attack me.

Chiara was right—she needed to toughen up. She wasn't in the village any more. She didn't have her father or her brothers to protect her. She needed to wise up and look after herself.

She attempted a smile in return. 'No. I'm so sorry—'

'No,' he said, offering her his arm again. '*I'm* sorry. Most people take a motorboat to the front entrance. I needed the exercise but walking made me late, so I was rushing. I should have warned you that we would be taking the side entrance.'

Her latest burst of adrenaline leeched out of her and she found an answering smile as she took his arm and let him lead her into a garden lit with tiny lights that magically turned a line of trees into carriages pulled by horses towards the *palazzo* beyond.

And as they entered this magical world she wondered… She'd been told to expect heavy security and bag searches at the ball, but this doorman had ushered them in without so much as blinking.

'What kind of ball is this?' she asked. 'Why are there no tickets and no bag searches?'

'A private function, by invitation only.'

She looked up at him. 'Are you sure it's all right for me to come, in that case?'

'I invited you, didn't I?'

They stopped just shy of the fountain, halfway across the garden by the soaring side wall of the *palazzo*, so she could take in the gardens and their magical lighting. To the left, a low wall topped with an ornate railing bordered the garden. The canal lay beyond, she guessed, though it was near impossible to make out anything through the fog, and the buildings opposite were no more than shifting apparitions in the mist.

The mist blurred the tops of the trees and turned the lights of those distant buildings into mere smudges, giving the garden a mystical air. To Rosa, it was almost as if Venice had shrunk to this one fairy-tale garden. The damp air was cold against her face, but she was deliciously warm under Vittorio's cloak and in no hurry to go inside. For inside there would be more guests—more strangers—and doubtless there would be friendships and connections between them and she would be the outsider. For now it was enough to deal with this one stranger.

More than enough when she thought about the way he looked at her—as if he was seeing inside her, reaching into a place where lurked her deepest fears and desires. For they both existed with this man. He seemed to scrape the surface of her nerve-endings away so everything she felt was raw. Primal. Exciting.

'What is this place?' she asked, watching the play of water spouting from the fat fish at the base of the three-tiered fountain. 'Who owns it?'

'It belongs to a friend of mine. Marcello's ancestors were *doges* of Venice and very rich. The *palazzo* dates back to the sixteenth century.'

'His family were rulers of Venice?'

'Some. Yes.'

'How do you even *know* someone like that?'

He paused, gave a shrug of his shoulders. 'My father and his go back a long way.'

'Why? Did your father work for him?'

He took a little time before he dipped his head to the side. 'Something like that.'

She nodded, understanding. 'I get that. My father services the mayor's cars in Zecce—the village in Puglia where I come from. He gets invited to the Christmas party every year. We used to get invited too, when we were children.'

'We?'

'My three older brothers and me. They're all married now, with their own families.'

She looked around at the gardens strung with lights and thought about the new nephew or niece who would be welcomed into the world in the next few weeks, and the money she'd wasted on her ticket for the ball tonight—money she could have used to pay for a visit home, along with a special gift for the new baby, and still have had change left over. She sighed at the waste.

'I paid one hundred euros for my ticket to the ball. That's one hundred euros down the drain.'

One eyebrow arched. 'That much?'

'I know. It's ridiculously expensive, and ours was one of the cheapest balls, so you're lucky to get invited to parties in a place like this for free. You can pay a lot more than I did, though. Hundreds more.'

She swallowed. She was babbling. She knew she was babbling. But something about this man's looming presence in the fog made her want to put more of herself into it and even up the score. He was so tall, so broad across the shoulders, his features so powerful. Everything about him spoke of power.

Because he hadn't said a word in the space she'd left, she felt compelled to continue. 'And then you have to have a costume, of course.'

'Of course.'

'Although I made my costume myself, I still had to buy the material.'

'Is that what you do, Rosa?' he asked as they resumed their walk towards the *palazzo*. 'Are you a designer?'

She laughed. 'Hardly. I'm not even a proper seamstress.

I clean rooms at the Palazzo d'Velatte, a small hotel in the Dorsoduro *sestiere*. Do you know it?'

He shook his head.

'It's much smaller than this, but very grand.'

Steps led up to a pair of ancient wooden doors that swung open before them, as if whoever was inside had been anticipating their arrival.

She looked up at him. 'Do you ever get used to visiting your friend in such a grand place?'

He just smiled and said, 'Venice is quite special. It takes a little getting used to.'

Rosa looked up at the massive doors, at the light spilling from the interior, and took a deep breath. 'It's taking me a *lot* of getting used to.'

And then they entered the *palazzo*'s reception room and Rosa's eyes really popped. She'd thought the hotel where she worked was grand! Marketed as a one-time *palazzo*, and now a so-called boutique hotel, she'd thought it the epitome of style, capturing the faded elegance of times gone by.

It was true that the rooms were more spacious than she'd ever encountered, and the ceilings impossibly high—not to mention a pain to clean. But the building seemed to have an air of neglect about it, as if it was sinking in on itself. The doors caught and snagged on the tiled floors, never quite fitting into the doorframes, and there were complaints from guests every other day that things didn't quite work right.

Elegant decay, she'd put it down to—until the day she'd taken out the rubbish to the waiting boat and witnessed a chunk of wall falling into the canal. She figured there was not much that was elegant about a wall crumbling piece by piece into the canal.

But here, in this place, she was confronted by a real *palazzo*—lavishly decorated from floor to soaring ceiling with rich frescoes and gilded reliefs, and impeccably furnished with what must be priceless antiques. From somewhere high above came the sounds of a string quartet, drifting down the spectacular staircase. And now she could see the hotel where she worked for what it really was. Faded…tired. A mere whisper of what it had been trying to emulate.

Another doorman stepped forward with a nod, and relieved Rosa of both Vittorio's leather cloak and her own wrap underneath.

'It's so beautiful,' she said, wide-eyed as she took it all in, rubbing her bare arms under the light of a Murano glass chandelier high above that was lit with at least one hundred globes.

'Are you cold?' he asked, watching her, his eyes raking over her, taking in her fitted bodice and the skirt with the weather-inappropriate hem.

'No.'

Not cold. Her goosebumps had nothing to do with the temperature. Rather, without her cloak and the gloom outside to keep her hidden from his gaze, she felt suddenly exposed. Crazy. She'd been so delighted with the way the design of the gown had turned out, so proud of her efforts after all the late nights she'd spent sewing, and she'd been eager to wear it tonight.

'You look so sexy,' Chiara had said, clapping her hands as Rosa performed a twirl for her. 'You'll have every man at the ball lining up to dance with you.'

She had *felt* sexy, and a little bit more wicked than she was used to—or at least she had felt that way then. But right now she had to resist the urge to tug up the bodice of her gown, where it hugged the curve of her breasts, and tug down the front of the skirt.

In a place such as this, where elegance and class oozed from the frescoes and antique glass chandeliers, bouncing light off myriad marble and gilded surfaces, she felt like a cheap bauble. Tacky. Like the fake glass trinkets that some of the shops passed off as Venetian glass when it had been made in some rip-off factory half a world away.

She wondered if Vittorio was suddenly regretting his rash impulse to invite her. Could he see how out of place she was?

Yes, she was supposed to be dressed as a courtesan, but she wished right now that she'd chosen a more expensive fabric or a subtler colour. Something with class that wasn't so brash and obvious. Something that contained at least a modicum of decency. Surely he had to see that she didn't belong here in the midst of all this luxury and opulence?

Except he wasn't looking at her with derision. Didn't look at her as if she was out of place. Instead she saw something else in his eyes. A spark. A flame. *Heat.*

And whatever it was low down in her belly that had flickered into life this night suddenly squeezed tight.

'You say you made your costume yourself?' he asked.

If she wasn't wrong, his voice had gone down an octave.

'Yes.'

'Very talented. There is just one thing missing.'

'What do you mean?'

But he already had his hands at her head. Her mask, she realised. She'd forgotten all about it. And now he smoothed it down over her hair, adjusting the crown so that it was centred before straightening the lace of her veil over her eyes.

She didn't move a muscle to try to stop him and do it herself. She didn't want to stop him. Because all the while the gentle brush of his fingers against her skin and the smoothing of his hands on her hair set off a chain reaction of tingles under her scalp and skin, hypnotising her into inaction.

'There,' he said, removing his hands from her head. She had to stop herself from swaying after them. 'Perfection.'

'Vittorio!'

A masculine voice rang out from the top of the stairs, saving her from having to find a response when she had none.

'You're here!'

'Marcello!' Vittorio answered, his voice booming in the space. 'I promised you I'd be here, did I not?'

'With you,' the man said, jogging down the wide marble steps two by two, 'who can tell?'

He was dressed as a Harlequin, in colours of black and gold, and the leather of his shoes slapped on the marble stairs as he descended. He and Vittorio embraced—a man hug, a back-slap—before drawing apart.

'Vittorio,' the Harlequin said, 'it is good to see you.'

'And you,' Vittorio replied.

'And you've brought someone, I see,' he said, whipping off the mask over his eyes, his mouth curving into a smile as he held out one hand and bowed generously. 'Welcome, fair stranger. My name is Marcello Donato.'

The man was impossibly handsome. *Impossibly.* Olive-skinned, with dark eyes and brows, a sexy slash of a mouth and high cheekbones over which any number of supermodels would go to war with each other. But it was the warmth of his smile that made Rosa instinctively like the man.

'My name is Rosa.'

She took his hand and he drew her close and kissed both her cheeks.

'I'm right in thinking we've never met, aren't I?' he said as he released her. 'I'd be sure to remember if we had.'

'I've only just met Rosa myself,' Vittorio said, before she could answer. 'She lost her party in the fog. I thought it unfair that she missed out on the biggest night of Carnevale.'

Marcello nodded. 'That would be an injustice of massive proportions. Welcome, Rosa, I'm glad you found Vittorio.' He stepped back and regarded them critically. 'You

make a good couple—the mad warrior protecting the run-
away Princess.'

Vittorio snorted beside her.

'What's so funny?' she said.

'Marcello is known for his flights of fancy.'

'What can I say?' He beamed. 'I'm a romantic. Unlike
this hard-hearted creature beside me, whom you managed
to stumble upon.'

She filed the information away for future reference.
The words had been said in jest, but she wondered if there
wasn't an element of truth in them. 'So, tell me,' she said,
'what is this Princess hiding from?'

'That's easy,' he said. 'An evil serpent. But don't worry.
Vittorio will protect you. There's not a serpent in the land
that's a match for Vittorio.'

Something passed between the two men's eyes. A look.
An understanding.

'What am I missing?' she asked, her eyes darting from
one to the other.

'The fun,' Marcello said, pulling his mask back on. 'Everyone is upstairs on the second *piano nobile*. Come.'

Marcello was warm and welcoming, and nobody seemed
to have any issues with the way she was dressed. Rosa
began to relax. She'd been worrying about nothing.

Together they ascended the staircase to the *piano nobile*,
where the principal reception rooms of the *palazzo* were
housed one level above the waters of the canal. With its
soaring ceilings, and rock crystal chandelier, Rosa could see
that this level was even more breath-taking, more opulent,
than the last. And the *pièce de résistance* was the impossibly ornate windows that spread generously across one wall.

'Is there a view?' she asked, tempted to look anyway. 'I
mean, when it isn't foggy?'

'You'll have to come back,' Marcello said, ignoring the
crowded reception rooms either side, filled with partygoers,

and the music of Vivaldi coming from the string quartet, and walking to the windows before them. 'On a clear day you can see the Rialto Bridge to the right.'

Rosa peered through the fog, trying to make sense of the smudges of light. But if the Rialto Bridge was to the right... 'You're on the Grand Canal!'

Marcello shrugged and smiled. 'Not that you can tell today. But Venice wearing its shroud of fog is still a sight to behold, so enjoy. And now please excuse me while I find you some drinks.'

'We're in San Polo,' she said to Vittorio.

The hotel where she worked was in the Dorsoduro *sestiere*, the ball she was supposed to be attending was in the northern district of Cannaregio. Somehow she'd ended up lost between them and within a whisker of the sinuous Grand Canal, which would have hinted at her location if only she'd found it.

A smudge of light passed slowly by—a *vaporetto* or a motorboat carefully navigating the fog-shrouded waterway—and Rosa's thoughts chugged with it. Vittorio had been kind, asking her to accompany him, but strictly speaking she wasn't lost any more.

She turned to him. 'I know where I am now.'

'Does that matter?'

'I mean, I'm not lost. At least, I can find my way home from here.'

He turned to her, putting his big hands on her shoulders as he looked down at her. 'Are you looking for yet another reason to escape?'

A wry smile kicked up one side of his mouth. He was laughing at her again, and she found she didn't mind—not when seeing his smile made her feel as if she was capturing something rare and true.

'I'm not—'

He cocked an eyebrow. 'Why are you so desperate to run away from me?'

He was wrong. She wasn't desperate to run away from him. Oh, sure, there'd been that moment when she'd panicked, at the end of the path outside the side gate, but she knew better now. Vittorio was no warrior or warlord, no demon or monster. He was a man, warm and real and powerful…a man who made her blood zing.

Except the warm weight of his hands on her shoulders and the probing questions in his eyes vanquished reasoned argument. There was only strength and heat and fear that it would be Vittorio who might change his mind. And then he'd take his hands away. And then she'd miss that contact and the heat and the zing and the pure exhilaration of being in his company.

A tiny worm of a thought squeezed its way through the connections in her brain. *Wasn't that reason enough to run?*

She was out of her depth with a man like him—a man who was clearly older and more worldly-wise, who moved in circles with people who owned entire *palazzos* and whose ancestors were amongst the *doges* of Venice. A man who made her feel stirrings in her belly, fizzing in her blood— things she wasn't used to feeling.

Nothing in the village—not a teenage crush on her maths teacher nor a dalliance with Antonio from the next village, who'd worked a few months in her father's workshop, had prepared her for meeting someone like Vittorio. She felt inadequate. Underdone.

She was dressed as a courtesan, a seductress, a temptress. But that was such a lie. She swallowed. She could hardly admit that, though.

'You invited me to this party tonight because I was lost and you felt sorry for me, because I was upset and was going to miss my own party.'

He snorted. 'I don't do things because I feel sorry for

people. I do things because I want to. I invited you to this party because I wanted to. And because I wanted you to be with me.' His hands squeezed her shoulders. 'So now, instead of trying to find all the reasons you shouldn't be here, how about you enjoy all the reasons you should?'

What could she say to that? 'In that case, it very much seems that I am stuck with you.'

'You are,' he said, with a smile that warmed her to her bones. 'At least for as long as this night lasts.'

'A toast.' Marcello said, arriving back with three glasses of Aperol spritz. He handed them each a glass. 'To Carnevale,' he said, raising his glass in a toast.

'To Carnevale,' said Rosa.

'To Carnevale,' echoed Vittorio, lifting his glass in Rosa's direction, 'And to the Venetian fog that delivered us Rosa.'

And if the words he uttered in his deep voice were not enough, the way Vittorio's piercing blue eyes looked at her above his glass made her blush all the way down to her toes. In that moment Rosa knew that this night would never last long enough, and that whatever else happened she would remember this night for ever.

She was skittish—so skittish. She was like a colt, untrained and unrehearsed, or a kitten, jumping at shadows and imaginary enemies. And it wasn't an act. He was good at spotting an ingénue, a pretender. He was used to women who played games and who made themselves out to be something they were not.

Just for a moment Vittorio wondered if he was doing the right thing, pitting her against Sirena. Maybe he should release her from her obvious unease and awkwardness and let her go back to her own world, if that was what she really wanted, back to what was, no doubt, the drudgery of her work and the worry of losing the paltry sum of one hundred euros.

Except Vittorio was selfish enough not to want to let her go.

He saw the way her eyes widened at every new discovery, at every exquisite Murano glass lamp, every frescoed wall or gilded mirror that stretched almost to the ceiling.

She was like a breath of fresh air in Vittorio's life. Unsophisticated and not pretending otherwise. She was a refreshing change when he had been feeling so jaded.

And she was a beautiful woman in a gown that fitted like a glove and make him ache to peel it off.

Why should he let her go?

CHAPTER FOUR

IT WASN'T A party or even a ball. It was like being part of a fairy-tale.

Rosa ascended the wide staircase to the second level above the water—yet another floor with soaring ceilings and exquisite antiques and furnishings. The music from the string quartet was louder here, richer, its sweet notes filling the gaps between the sound of laughter and high-spirited conversation coming from the party rooms either side of the staircase.

And the costumes! A brightly coloured peacock strutted by as they reached the top, all feathers and flashes of brilliant colour, and Rosa couldn't help but laugh in sheer wonderment as a couple with ice-white masks wearing elaborate gowns and suits of the deepest purple nodded regally as they strolled past arm in arm.

Rosa felt herself swept away into a different world of riches and costumes—a sumptuous world of fantasy—and only half wished that the man who had rescued her from the foggy *calles* wasn't quite so popular, because then she could keep him all to herself.

Everyone seemed to recognise Vittorio and to want to throw out an exchange or a greeting. He was like a magnet to both men and women alike, but he always introduced her to them, including her in the conversation.

And, while her presence at his side wasn't questioned, she wondered what she might see if everyone wasn't wearing masks. Would the women's eyes be following Vittorio's every move because he was so compelling? Would they be looking at her in envy?

If she were in their place she would.

And suddenly the music and the costumes and the amazing sumptuousness of the *palazzo* bled into a heady mix that made her head spin. She was part of a Venice she'd never seen and had only ever imagined.

Suddenly there was a shriek of delight from the other wing, and a commotion as someone made their way through the crowds into the room.

'Vittorio!' a woman cried, bursting through the party-goers. 'I just heard you were here. Where have you been hiding all this time?'

But not just any woman.

Cleopatra.

Her sleek black bob was adorned with golden beads, the circlet at her forehead topped with an asp. Like Vittorio, she hadn't bothered with a mask. Her eyes were kohled, their lids painted turquoise-blue, and her dress was simply amazing. Cut low—*really* low—over the smooth globes of her breasts, it was constructed entirely of beads in gold and bronze and silver, its short skirt just strings of the shiny beads that shifted and flashed skin with her every movement.

It wasn't so much a dress, Rosa thought as she took a step back to make room for the woman to reach up and kiss Vittorio on both cheeks, as an invitation. It showed the wearer's body off to perfection.

Cleopatra left her face close to his. 'Everyone has been waiting hours for you,' she chided, before she stood back to take in what he was wearing.

Or maybe to give him another chance to see her spectacular costume.

She held her hands out wide. 'But must you always look so dramatic? It's supposed to be a costume party.'

'I'm wearing a costume.'

'If you say so—but can't you for once dress out of character?'

'Sirena,' he said, ignoring her question as he reached for Rosa's hand, pulling her back into his orbit. 'I'd like you to meet a friend of mine. Rosa, this is Sirena, the daughter of one of my father's oldest friends.'

'Oh,' she said, with a knowing laugh, 'I'm *far* more than that.'

And then, for the first time, Sirena seemed to notice that there was someone standing next to Vittorio. She turned her head and looked Rosa up and down, letting her eyes tell Rosa what she thought about his 'friend'.

'Ciao,' she said, her voice deadpan, and Rosa couldn't be certain that she was saying hello as opposed to giving her a dismissal.

She immediately turned back to Vittorio, angling her back towards Rosa.

Definitely a dismissal.

'Vittorio, come with me—all our friends are in the other room.'

'I'm here with Rosa.'

'With who? Oh…'

She gave Rosa another look up and down, her eyes evaluating her as if she was a rival for Vittorio's affections. Ridiculous. She'd only just met the man tonight. But she wasn't mistaken. There was clear animosity in the woman's eyes.

'And what do you think of Vittorio's outfit…? What was your name again?'

'Rosa,' Vittorio growled. 'Her name is Rosa. It's not that difficult.'

'Of course it's not.' Sirena gave a lilting laugh as she

turned to the woman whose name she couldn't remember
and smiled. 'What do you think of Vittorio's outfit? Don't
you think it's a bit over the top?'

'I like it,' she said. 'I like the blue of the leather. It
matches his eyes.'

'It's not just blue, though, is it?' Sirena said dismissively.
'It's more like *royal* blue—isn't it, Vittorio?'

'That's enough, Sirena.'

'Well, I would have said it was *royal* blue.'

'Enough, I said.'

The woman pouted and stretched herself catlike along
the brocade chaise longue behind her, the beads of her skirt
falling in a liquid slide to reveal the tops of her long, slender legs—legs that ended in sandals with straps that wound
their way enticingly around her ankles.

The woman made an exquisite Cleopatra. But then, she
was so exquisitely beautiful the real Cleopatra would no
doubt have wanted to scratch out her eyes.

'It's all right, Vittorio, despite our difference in opinion
Rosa and I are going to be good friends.' She smiled regally
at Rosa. 'I like *your* costume,' she said.

For the space of one millisecond Rosa thought the
woman was warming to her, wanted so much to believe
she meant what she'd said. Rosa had spent many midnight
hours perched over her mother's old sewing machine, bat-
tling with the slippery material and trying to get the seams
and the fit just right. But then she saw the snigger barely
contained beneath the smile and realised the woman hadn't
been handing out a compliment.

'Rosa made it herself—didn't you, Rosa?'

'I did.'

Cleopatra's perfectly threaded eyebrows shot up. 'How...
enterprising.'

Vittorio's presence beside her lent Rosa a strength she
hadn't known she had, reminding her of what her broth-

ers had always told her—not to be cowed by bullies but to
stand up to them.

Her brothers were right, but it was a lot easier to take
their advice when she had a man like Vittorio standing
beside her.

Rosa simply smiled, not wanting to show what she really thought. 'Thank you. Your costume is lovely too. Did
you make it yourself?'

The other woman stared at her as if she had three heads.
'Of course I didn't make it myself.'

'A shame,' Rosa said. 'If you had you might have noticed that there's a loose thread…'

She reached a hand out to the imaginary thread and the
woman bolted upright and onto her sandalled feet, a whole
lot less elegantly than she had reclined, no doubt imagining one tug of Rosa's hand unleashing a waterfall of glass
beads across the Persian carpet.

'This gown is an Emilio Ferraro creation. Of *course*
there's no loose thread.'

'Oh, I'm sorry. I must have been mistaken.'

Sirena sniffed, jerked her eyes from Rosa's and placed
a possessive hand on Vittorio's chest. 'Come and see our
friends when you're free. You won't *believe* what they're
wearing. I'll be waiting for you.'

And with a swish of her beaded hair and skirt she was
gone.

'That,' said Vittorio, 'was Sirena.'

'Cyclone Sirena, you mean,' Rosa said, watching the
woman spinning out of the room as quickly as she'd come
in, leaving a trail of devastation in her wake.

She heard a snort and looked up to see Vittorio smiling
down at her. It was a real smile that warmed her bone-deep,
so different from one of Sirena's ice-cold glares.

'You handled that very well.'

'And you thought I wouldn't?' she said. 'My brothers

taught me to stand up to bullies.' She didn't mention that it was Vittorio's presence that had given her the courage to heed her brothers' advice.

'Good advice,' he said, nodding. 'If she finds that thread you saw she'll bust the balls of her precious Emilio.'

Rosa returned his smile with one of her own. 'There was no thread.'

And Vittorio laughed—a rich bellow that was laced with approval and that made a tide of happiness well up inside her.

'Thank you,' he said, his arm going around her shoulders as he leaned down to kiss her cheek. 'For the best belly laugh I've had in a long time.'

It wasn't really a kiss. Mouth to cheek…a brush of a whiskered jaw…a momentary meeting of lips and skin— probably the same kind of kiss he might bestow upon a great-aunt. Even his arm was gone from her shoulder in an instant. Yet to Rosa it felt far more momentous.

It was the single most exciting moment in her life since she'd arrived in Venice.

Chiara had told her that magical things could happen at Carnevale. She'd told her a whole lot of things and Rosa hadn't believed her. She'd suspected it was just part of Chiara's sales technique, in order to persuade Rosa to part with so much money and go along to the ball with her.

But maybe her friend had been right. Rosa had been kissed by a man. She couldn't wait to tell her friend.

'You're blushing,' said Vittorio, his head at an angle as he looked down at her.

She felt her blush deepen and dropped her head. 'Yes, it's silly, I know.'

He put his hand to her chin and lifted her face to his. 'No,' he said. 'It's delightful. It's been a long time since I saw a woman blush.'

She blinked up at him, her skin tingling where his fingers lingered.

Oh, boy.

Talk about a distraction… She'd wanted to ask him more about Sirena, but the woman had faded into insignificance. Now all she could think about was Vittorio and the way he made her feel.

'Come, come!' said Marcello, clapping his hands as he walked into the room to gather everyone. 'The entertainment downstairs is about to begin. You don't want to miss it.'

Downstairs, the entire level of the *piano nobile* had been divided into performance areas, with stages and dramatic velvet drapes, and they spent the next hour wandering between the rooms to see the spectacle of gymnasts and jugglers and opera singers, and aerobatic performers who spun on ropes in the air. Then it was the turn of the clowns, and Rosa was soon almost doubled up with laughter at their antics.

She found herself thinking about Chiara and wondering how her night was going. They'd treated themselves to the cheapest tickets to the cheapest Carnevale ball they could find—and that only gave admission to the dancing segment of the evening. They hadn't been able to afford the price for the dinner and entertainment that came first. But surely even that entertainment would be no match for this.

And then Vittorio took her hand in his and she stopped thinking about Chiara, because her heart gave a little lurch that switched off her brain.

She looked sideways up at him to find him watching her, the cobalt of his eyes a shade deeper, his sensual slash of mouth curled up at the ends.

He gave the slightest squeeze of her hand before he let her go, and she turned her eyes back to the entertainment. But suddenly she wasn't laughing any more. Her chest felt too tight, her blood was buzzing, and she was imagining all kinds of impossible things.

Unimaginable things.

Chiara had said that magical things could happen at Carnevale.

Rosa had been a fool not to believe her.

She could *feel* the magic. It was in the air all around her. It was in the gilded frames and lush silks and crystal chandeliers. It was in the exquisite *trompe l'oeils* that adorned the walls with views of gardens that had only ever existed in the artist's eyes. And magic was pulsing alongside her, in leather of blue and gold, in a man with a presence she couldn't ignore—a man who had the ability to shake the very foundations of her world with just one look from his cobalt blue eyes.

Chiara had said she might meet the man of her dreams tonight. A man who had the power to tempt her to give up her most cherished possession.

She hadn't believed that either.

It would have to be a special kind of man for her to want to take such a momentous step. A *very* special kind of man.

Vittorio?

Her heart squeezed so tightly that she had to suck in a breath to ease the constriction.

Impossible. Life didn't work that way.

But what if Chiara had been right?

And what if Vittorio was the one?

She glanced up to sneak another look at him and found him already gazing down at her, his midnight hair framing the quizzical expression on his strong face.

His heart-stoppingly beautiful, strong face.

And she thought it would be madness not to find out.

Sirena either had spies everywhere, or she had a knack for knowing when Rosa had left his side for five minutes. The entertainment was finished but, while the party wouldn't wind down until dawn, Vittorio had other plans. Plans that didn't include Sirena, no matter how hard she tried to join in.

'This is supposed to be a *party*,' Sirena sulked conspiratorially to Marcello when she cornered him standing at the top of the stairs, where Vittorio was waiting for Rosa so they could say their goodbyes. 'A party for *friends*. An *exclusive* party. But did you see that woman Vittorio dragged along?'

'Her name is Rosa.'

Sirena took no notice. 'Did you see what she was wearing, Marcello? It was appalling.'

'Nobody's listening, Sirena,' Vittorio said dismissively.

'Rosa seems very nice,' said Marcello. 'And I like her costume.'

Vittorio nodded. 'She *is* nice. *Very* nice.' He thought about the way she'd pulled that ruse with the loose thread and smiled. 'Clever, too.'

Sirena pouted, her hand on Marcello's arm, pleading. 'She wasn't even invited.'

'*I* invited her.'

'You know what I mean. Someone like her wouldn't normally be allowed anywhere near here.'

'Sirena, give it up.' Vittorio turned away, searching for Rosa. The sooner he got her away from here—away from Sirena—the better.

'That's our Vittorio for you,' Marcello said, trying to hose down the antagonism between his guests, playing his life-long role of peacemaker to perfection. 'Always bringing home the strays. Birds fallen from their nests. Abandoned puppies. It made no difference. Vittorio, do you remember that bag of kittens we found snagged on the side of the river that day? *Dio*, how long ago was that? Twenty years?'

Vittorio grunted, hoping that Rosa was nowhere within earshot, because he didn't want her overhearing any of this.

He did remember that day. Marcello had been visiting. They'd wandered far and wide beyond the castle walls that day—much further than Vittorio had been permitted to roam. They'd both been about ten years old, and filled with the curiosity and compulsion of young boys to explore their world.

They'd been wading in the stream, chasing the silvery flashes of fish in the shallows, when they'd heard the pitiful cries. By the time they'd found the bag and pulled it from the stream all but one of the kittens had perished, and the plaintive mewls of the lone survivor had been heartrending. Vittorio had tucked the tiny shivering creature into his shirt and hurried back to the castle.

'So now you're saving sweet young things who get themselves lost in the streets of Venice? Quite the hero you've turned out to be,' said Sirena.

'It's lucky Vittorio was in the right place at the right time,' Marcello said, still doing his utmost to pour oil on troubled waters. 'Rosa would have had a dreary night by herself otherwise.'

Sirena bristled, ignoring Marcello's peacekeeping efforts. 'And does your father know you've found another stray?'

Vittorio sighed. *Where the hell was Rosa?* 'What's who I bring to a party got to do with my father?'

'Only that the three of us might finally settle our differences and work out a timeline for uniting our two families. That's what was supposed to happen tonight. That's what was intended.'

'Intended by whom? By your father and mine? By you? Because it certainly wasn't intended by me—tonight or any other night.'

He turned away. Where *was* she?

'Oh, Vittorio…' he heard Sirena say behind his back, and he recognised the change in her voice as she switched on the charm offensive. He heard the slither of beads and when he turned back he saw that she'd dropped Marcello's arm and edged herself closer to him. She placed one hand on his chest and snaked it around his neck. 'Do you *have* to play so hard to get? You know we're made for each other. And while I admit it's been fun at times, playing this game of cat and mouse, it gets so tiring…always keeping up the charade.'

Vittorio put his hand over her forearm and sighed. 'You're right, Sirena. It *is* tiring,' he said. 'I think it has gone on long enough.'

'You see?' she said, her smile widening. 'I knew you'd think it was time we worked this out. We have to start making plans. Marcello will be your best man, surely?'

She didn't let her eyes shift from her target as Marcello, knowing it should be the groom who asked him, muttered an anxious, 'I'd be honoured, of course.'

'We'll have to have the wedding in the cathedral in Andachstein, of course,' Sirena said, as if Marcello hadn't uttered a word, 'and in spring. It's so beautiful in Andachstein in spring. But where should we honeymoon? We *have* to start planning, Vittorio. It's so exciting.'

Her nails were raking the skin at the back of his neck, but if the woman thought she was stroking his senses into compliance she was very much mistaken.

He put his hand over her forearm, pulling her hand away before he dropped it unceremoniously into what little space there was between them.

'No, Sirena. What I meant was that this farce has gone on long enough. Can you for once accept that whatever our fathers might have schemed, whatever they promised you, and whatever fantasy you've been nurturing in your mind, it's never going to happen. That is my promise to you.'

'But Vittorio,' she said, once again reaching out for him, with a note of hysteria in her voice this time. 'You can't be serious. You can't mean that.'

'How many times do I have to tell you before you accept the truth?'

'The truth is you're a playboy—everyone knows that. But you have to settle down some time.'

'Maybe I do,' he conceded, and it was the only concession he was prepared to make. 'But when I settle down it won't be with you.'

She spun away in a clatter of beads. 'You bastard!' She turned her regal chin over one shoulder and glared at him, the rage in her eyes all hellfire and ice. 'Go back and slum it with your little village slut, then. See if I care.'

Finally the real Sirena had emerged. He sighed. What kind of man would want to hitch himself to *that*, no matter the packaging? 'What you care or don't care about is not my concern, Sirena. But, for the record, that's exactly what I plan to do.'

Watching Sirena storm off, her sandalled feet slapping hard on the marble floor, was one of the most satisfying yet exhausting moments of Vittorio's life. Maybe she had finally got it through her head that there was never going to be a marriage between them. *Dio*, he was sick of this world of arranged marriages and false emotions.

But right now he had more pressing needs. He needed to find Rosa. He'd been wrong to bring her here. He'd exposed her to the best and the worst aspects of his life. And he'd exposed her to the worst of himself, using her as cannon fodder to make a point to a woman he had no intention of marrying.

What had he been thinking, inviting her here tonight? She deserved to be treated better than the way he had treated her. She'd been out of her depth—he'd known that from the start. She'd been overawed by the wealth and sumptuousness of this world she'd been given a glimpse of and yet she had handled herself supremely well, dealing with Sirena's antagonism with a courage he hadn't anticipated.

He slapped Marcello on the back in acknowledgement of what he'd attempted and told him he'd be back soon.

He didn't want to contemplate the carnage if Sirena found Rosa before he did. He'd never forgive himself. He was already feeling ill at ease for taking advantage of Rosa's circumstances the way he had. Serendipity, he'd called it. *Serendipity nothing.* He'd been out-and-out opportunistic. He'd charged Sirena with that same crime, and yet he was guilty of the charge himself. When he'd found Rosa he'd seen a decoy—a buffer for Sirena's insistent attention.

He should just take Rosa home, back to her dingy hotel and her humdrum life. Maybe she would be relieved to be back in her own world. Maybe she would see it as an escape. She should.

He wandered from room to room, brushing aside the calls to him to stop and talk.

He knew he should take her home. Except part of him didn't want to let her go—not just yet. His final words to Sirena hadn't been all bluff. Not when he thought about Rosa's upturned face looking into his. He remembered the change in her expression, her laughter drying up, her lips slightly parted. He remembered the hitch in her breath and the sudden rise of her chest.

He'd seen the way she'd gazed up into his eyes.

Rosa had been the best part of his evening.

He hated it that it had to end. And he had enough experience of the female to know that she didn't want it to end just yet either.

Eventually he found Rosa, surrounded by a group of guests he recognised—members of Sirena's retinue, simpering men and women who were her 'rent-a-court', always sitting around waiting on her every word, waiting for a rare treat to be dispensed. Now they were formed around Rosa like some kind of Praetorian Guard, looking at Rosa as if *she* was the treat.

Sirena's work, no doubt. It had her fingerprints all over it.

'Here you are,' he said, barely able to keep the snarl from his voice as he surveyed the smug-looking group. 'I've been looking everywhere for you.'

She didn't look pleased to see him. Her eyes didn't meet his with relief, or with the delight he would have preferred. The brandy in her eyes was un-warmed. Non-committal. Even her body language had changed, her movements stiff and formal.

'I've been making some new friends,' she said.

He glanced around at the six of them, all dressed the same—or rather, *un*dressed the same. The men were bare-chested, wearing white kilts, blue and white striped head-dresses and wide gold armbands. The women had the addition of a golden bralette.

Cleopatra's so-called friends. More like a guard of hon-our. And he knew that, like Sirena, they were capable of tearing an unsuspecting person to pieces. He wasn't the only one who would be able to see her lack of sophistication and absence of guile. Rosa was like the first bright flare of a matchstick in a darkened room. She was all vulnerability in a world of weary cynicism.

'I'm sorry to disappoint your new *friends*,' he lied, eye-balling each and every one of their heavily kohled eyes, 'but we're leaving. I'm taking you home.'

Rosa's chin kicked up. 'What if I'm not ready to go home? I know where I am now. I can find my own way.'

'We can take you,' one of her new friends offered, with a lean and hungry smile.

'Yes,' said another, his lips drawing hyena-like over his

teeth as he took one of her hands. 'Stay a little longer, Rosa. We'll see that you get home.'

'It's up to you,' Vittorio told her.

There was no hiding the growl in his voice even as he had to force himself to back off—because if she didn't want him he could hardly drag her out of here, no matter that his inner caveman was insisting he simply throw her over his shoulder and leave. She was a grown-up, with a mind of her own, and if she was foolish enough to choose them over her it would be on her own head.

But still the idea sat uneasily with him.

She looked from the group to Vittorio and he saw the indecision in her eyes, the brittle wall of resistance she'd erected around herself waver. And, like that moment by the bridge, when he'd seen her shoulders slump as she recognised the hopelessness of her situation, he could tell the moment she made a decision.

'No,' she said to the group with a smile of apology. 'Thank you for your kind offer. But it's late and I have to work tomorrow.'

Vittorio grunted his approval while they pleaded with her to reconsider. So she'd witnessed what was in their eyes and decided he was the lesser of two evils? At least she had *that* much sense.

But it occurred to him that he might have to rethink his plans for the evening. Things had changed in the balance between them. He'd thought she was learning to trust him, losing her skittishness, but something had happened in the time she'd been out of his sight. Something that had fractured the tentative bond that had been developing between them.

It was too bad, but it was hardly the end of the world.

Tomorrow he would return to Andachstein, a tiny coastal principality nestled between Italy and Slovenia. He had duties there. There was a film festival gala to attend and a new hospital wing to be opened, along with school visits to make—all part of his royal duties as heir. So he'd see Rosa safely home now, and then he'd head back to the family *palazzo*—the legacy of a match between the daughter of a Venetian aristocrat and one of Andachstein's ancestral princes.

No doubt his father would be waiting for the news he'd been wanting to hear for years. He was not going to be happy to hear there was none.

'I'll be fine now,' she said, once they were out of the room. 'I'll find my own way home.'

'I don't think so.'

'Listen, Vittorio—'

'No. *You* listen. If you think I'm going to let you loose in the fog-bound *calles* at this time of the morning, after half the city's been partying all night, you've got another think coming. That lot upstairs aren't the only ones who'd take advantage of a lone woman feeling her way home in the fog.'

She swallowed, and he saw the kick of her throat even as her eyes flashed defiantly. He could tell she saw the sense in his words, even if she didn't want to.

'So I'm still stuck with you, then,' she said.

'So it would seem.'

She turned her head away in resignation and they descended the staircase in silence, together but apart, the earlier warmth they'd shared having dissipated.

His mood blackened with every step, returning him to that dark place he'd been earlier in the evening. It didn't help that Rosa had lost the air of wonderment she'd arrived with. It didn't help that she couldn't find him a smile and that he had been relegated to mere chaperone—one that she was only putting up with under sufferance. It raised his hackles.

'I'm sorry,' he said, maybe a little more brusquely than

he'd have preferred, but then, he wasn't in the mood for pleasantries. 'Perhaps I shouldn't have brought you here. I shouldn't have invited you.'

'Why shouldn't you have invited me?' she asked. 'Because I don't belong? Because I'm no better than a little village slut for you to slum it with?'

'You heard. How much did you hear?'

'I heard enough.'

Vittorio wanted to slam his head against the nearest wall. As if it wasn't enough that Sirena had subjected her to those poisoned barbs face to face, Rosa had heard what Sirena had said behind her back.

'I didn't call you that.'

'I didn't hear you deny it,' she said, but she didn't sound angry, as she had every right to. She sounded…disappointed.

He could have explained that there would have been no point, that it wasn't what *he* thought of her and that Sirena would have taken no notice, but she was right. He hadn't made any attempt to deny or correct it.

Dio. What a mess.

They collected their cloaks in silence, and only three words were playing over and over in Rosa's mind.

Little village slut.

Stone-faced, Vittorio covered her shoulders with first her own cloak and then his cursed scented leather cloak. She hated the fact that it smelt so good now, and tried to slip away from beneath it.

'I don't need that.'

But he persisted, like a father whose patience with his recalcitrant toddler was all but used up. 'Yes, you do,' he insisted, and he turned her towards him and did up the fancy clasp she'd had trouble undoing before.

She looked everywhere but at him. And the moment he

released her she turned away from his touch and his stony features, wishing she could so easily turn away from the warmth of his cloak and the promise it had given her.

Instead, the evening had finished up a huge disappointment. It had been a rollercoaster of emotions from the start, from excitement to panic to despair to hope. Or a kind of hope. But now she could see that that hope had been like those strings of beads in the glamorous Sirena's skirt, and that one pulled thread would have seen it fall apart and skitter away into a million irreconcilable parts.

And now there was just the end to be negotiated.

She took a deep breath. She'd had a night out. A fantasy night such as she could never have expected or afforded. She'd had an experience with which to reassure Chiara, when her friend apologised profusely about losing her in the crowds without her phone or ticket, as she expected she would.

And she'd had a glimmer of something special. Of a man who looked like a warrior, a man who'd been chivalrous and generous enough to include her in his world, a man who simultaneously excited and frightened her, a man who made her insides curl when he looked at her as if she was something special.

At least she imagined that was what he'd been thinking.

She sighed. Soon she would be back home in the tiny basement apartment she shared with Chiara and this night would be just a memory.

Little village slut.

The words kept on circling in Rosa's mind. It was true, she did come from a small village in the heel of Italy. A dot of a town, to be sure. But that was where the truth ended. And it was so unfair.

'They're only words,' her brothers had told her when she'd been bullied at school. *'Words can't wound you.'*

She'd wanted to believe her brothers. Maybe she had

for a time—except perhaps now, because the man she'd thought he was, the man she'd built up in her mind, had turned out to be somebody else. The man who had been a stranger to her, the man she'd thought was something else entirely, was a stranger still.

'Where are we going?' she asked, when Vittorio led her down the steps into the garden.

'We're going home by motorboat,' he said, as he steered her to the big wooden doors that were opened for them onto the Grand Canal.

Rosa shivered as the damp air surged in. She'd forgotten how very cold the fog was—although that didn't make her want to be any more grateful for Vittorio's cloak or want to tell him that he'd been right. She wouldn't give him the satisfaction.

A few steps below them a motorboat sat rocking on the lapping waters of the canal. Fog still clung low, swirling in the air and rendering the glow of lights to ghostly smudges.

'Palazzo D'Marburg,' he told the driver, handing her into the boat before bundling her into the covered interior.

The motor chugged into life once they were seated, and the boat pulled away slowly into the canal, still moving slowly when it cleared the dock. It was so painfully slow that Rosa wished they had walked after all. The journey home would take for ever at this rate, and the interior of the cabin was already too small for the both of them. Too intimate. Vittorio took up too much of the space and sucked up the remaining oxygen in the cabin. Was it any wonder she was breathless?

And meanwhile the man opposite her had turned to stone, his expression grim, his body language saying he was a man whose patience had worn thin and who was stoically waiting to be rid of her. Or a man who was sulking because she wasn't falling victim to his charms any more.

Well, she was waiting too—to be free of this warrior whose charms had long since expired.

Maybe she should have stayed at the party. She'd been meeting people and having fun, hadn't she? Okay, so she hadn't liked the way a couple of them had looked at her enough to want them to take her home, but at least she'd been able to breathe there, and her heart hadn't tripped over itself like it did every time this man so much as looked at her.

She would have been perfectly all right if she'd stayed. And Marcello would have looked after her if he'd thought she was in any danger. Vittorio was such a drama queen.

He chose that moment to shift in his seat, his big knee brushing against her leg, and she bristled in response. What *was* it about the man? He couldn't move without making her notice. He took up so much space. He had such presence. He made her feel small. Insignificant.

She sucked in air and, and as if it wasn't bad enough that she had to put up with the scent of him, even the air now tasted of him.

Suddenly it was all too much—the fog and the rocking and the cursed muffled silence. It was like being entombed with one of those Chinese stone warriors from the Terracotta Army she'd seen on display at a museum in Rome on a school visit. And she wasn't ready to be entombed.

She launched herself at the door that led to the small rear deck.

'It's too cold out there,' he growled.

'I don't care!' she flung back at him, shoving her way through the door.

She had no choice. She had to get outside. She had to escape.

The cold air hit her skin like a slap in the face, but at least the air outside didn't taste of Vittorio and smell like Vittorio, and it wasn't filled with the bulk of him. Finally she could breathe again. She gulped in great lungsful of it, letting it cleanse her senses even as she huddled her arms around her chest.

Of course he followed her, as she'd known he would, standing beside her silently like a sentinel. She didn't have to turn her head to know he was there. She could sense his presence. Feel his heat. Cursed man.

The motorboat chugged and rocked its way slowly along the canal. It was other-worldly. The sounds and sights of the city had vanished. Items appeared suddenly out of the fog—a lamp on a post, another motorboat edging its way cautiously by—and then just as quickly were swallowed up again.

And he was the most other worldly part of it all.

A fantasy gone wrong.

She searched through the fog, suddenly frantic, trying to find a reference point so that she could tell how long this trip would last. But there was nothing. Not a hint of where they were. No clue to how long she would be forced to endure this torture.

Nothing but silence. Tension. And her utter disappointment with how this evening had ended when it had started out with such excitement. Such promise.

Like a rubber band stretched too far, she snapped. 'Why did you ask me to come with you tonight?'

Slowly, almost as slowly as the boat they were travelling on, he turned his head towards her. His expression told her nothing and his face was a mask of stone.

'Because you were lost and alone. Because I thought I could help.'

She scoffed. 'I think we both know that's not true, Vittorio. I don't want that line you spun me about chivalry and concern for my happiness and well-being and not wanting me to miss out on the last night of Carnevale. I want the real reason.'

He was silent for a few seconds, but Rosa wasn't going to give him time to make something else up.

She gathered the strength to ask the question that had been plaguing her ever since that woman dressed as Cleopatra had burst onto the scene. 'Who is Sirena to you?' she demanded. 'What claim does she hold over you?'

'None. Sirena is nothing to me.'

Rosa gave a very unladylike snort, and if it made her sound like the country girl she was, instead of some pampered city girl with polished manners, she didn't give a damn. 'You expect me to believe that when I witnessed her draped all over you like a limpet.'

'That meant nothing,' he said. 'Whatever Sirena likes to think.'

She shook her head. 'She thinks you're going to marry her!'

He looked shocked.

'I was there,' she said. 'I heard what she said.'

He took a deep breath and sighed, long and hard. 'My father wants me married. It would suit him if I married his friend's daughter. That is all.'

'That's *all*?' She laughed into the mist, her breath turning to fog. 'What I don't understand is why I had to get dragged into your mess. Did you know she'd be at the ball tonight?'

'I'd had word.'

Finally something that made sense. She gave a long sigh of her own. 'So there we have it,' she said, nodding her head as she looked out into the mist and the pieces of the puzzle fell into place. 'You invited me to come with you to make her jealous.'

'No! It was never to make her jealous.'

'Then what? To run interference? To make a point? Was it sport you had in mind? Is *that* what asking me to go with you was all about?'

He said nothing—which told her everything she needed to know.

She heard his deep breath in, felt him shift as he ran his hand through his untamed hair.

'You were lost.'

'One of your strays?'

He sniffed. 'Maybe. And I thought I could help you—and you could help me—at the same time.'

She shook her head 'Bottom line, Vittorio, you used me.' Even as she said the words tiny tears squeezed from her eyes. She'd had such high hopes for this night. He'd made her think all kinds of things. That she mattered. That he cared. That she wanted…

'Rosa…'

'No,' she said, turning further away, because he didn't care, and the disappointment of the evening was weighing heavily down on her, crushing her.

'Rosa.' His hands were on her shoulders. 'I'm sorry.'

'And that's supposed to make it better? That's supposed to make it all right?'

She hated it that her voice sounded so quaky, that she sounded so needy, when she'd thought that growing up with three brothers had toughened her up for anything. She hated it that she could feel the warm puff of his breath on her hair. She hated it that his hands were on her shoulders and it wasn't enough. She hated herself because she wanted more.

'No, it's not all right. I hurt you.'

She sniffed as he turned her with his big hands, but she didn't resist. Didn't resist when he drew her against his body and wrapped his arms around her. Didn't object when she felt him dip his head and kiss her hair.

'Can you forgive me?'

It felt so warm, being cradled against his big body. So firm. So hard. And the drumbeat of his heart added another note to the lullaby chugging of the engine, made the movement of the boat beneath their feet like the rocking of a cradle.

'I'm sorry that I hurt you,' he said. 'I knew Sirena would be angry. The only reason I said I should never have invited you was because I'd anticipated Sirena's reaction. I knew she'd be furious and she didn't disappoint. To subject you to that was unthinkable. You didn't deserve that.'

She should pull away. Her tears had passed and she should put distance between them, she knew. He'd treated her shamefully and she should want nothing more to do with him, apology or no. Why should she forgive him?

But she remembered the way he'd looked at her during the entertainment. She remembered the warmth of his hand, that shared moment when it had seemed the world was made of magic. His body felt so good next to hers. So very warm. And that was a kind of magic too. Was it wrong to want the magic to last just a little bit longer?

He stroked her back and she felt the crushing disappointment of the evening ebb slowly away. 'It was a good party,' she said. It was a concession of sorts. Because it *had* been an experience. She had so much to tell Chiara in the morning. 'I enjoyed it. Most of it.'

He squeezed his arms and she felt the press of his lips to her hair again, and she knew she wasn't drawing away from him any time soon.

'That's good. I'm sorry that Sirena had to spoil it for you.' A moment later he added, 'No, I'm sorry *I* had to spoil it for you.'

Rosa thought about how the woman had looked in her costume, her limbs so long, her skin so smooth and perfect. The woman had made Rosa feel so ordinary. So drab and inconsequential. The woman would have made the real Cleopatra feel inconsequential.

'She's very beautiful, isn't she?'

He sighed and placed his chin on her head. 'Beauty is an empty vessel,' he said, his deep voice a bare whisper over the chug of the motor. 'It needs something to fill it. Something meaningful and worthwhile to flesh it out and make it whole.'

She was struck by his whispered words. 'Where did you hear that?'

'Something my mother once said.'

'She sounds very wise.'

'She could be, at times.' A pause. A sigh. 'She's dead now.'

'I'm sorry.'

'Thank you, but it's not your fault.'

'I understand. But my mother is gone too. She was diagnosed with leukaemia. She died three years ago. There's not a day goes by that I don't think about her…that I don't miss her.'

He shook his head. 'And now it's my turn to say I'm sorry, and your turn to say it's not my fault.'

She laughed a little at his words, then stopped. The sound was so unexpected when her thoughts had been tuned to disappointment. 'The language of death. It's so complicated.'

He loosened one arm and lifted his hand to her face, touching her gently with the knuckle of one finger. He was so gentle that she barely felt the brush of his skin against hers, and yet his touch sent bone-deep tremors through her. Made her want to lean into his hand.

Then he took her chin and lifted her face to his. 'Maybe instead we should talk the language of the living.'

Her breath hitched in her throat. His hand was warm against her skin, his face filling her vision. She swallowed. 'I think I'd prefer that.'

His eyes were dark blue against the foggy night and the force of them pulled her towards him.

Or maybe it was just the motion of the boat drawing their

faces together. Or perhaps the fog muted every word, rendering every breath more intimate than it would otherwise have been. Because suddenly his mouth was hovering mere millimetres over hers, then even closer, his warm breath mingling with her pale puffs of air, and then his lips met hers and her world tilted on its axis.

He had soft lips. In a face that looked as if it had been chiselled from stone she hadn't expected that. Nor tenderness, surprising in its sweetness. But there was warmth and heat and the feel of his long-fingered hands through her hair. The combination was lethal.

Time stood still. The chugging of the engine disappeared under the *whump-whump* of her own heartbeat in her ears. The world was reduced to this boat, to this one man and one woman and the magic swirling like the fog around them. She sighed into him, melting as his mouth moved over hers, parting her lips so that she could taste him, and his kiss deepened, his tongue tracing the line of her teeth, duelling with hers.

He tasted of coffee and liqueur, leather and man, and underneath was another layer which was heat and strength and desire, and she wanted more.

This was a kiss—not a mere peck on the cheek like he'd given her earlier. This was a kiss that spun her senses out of control, a kiss that melted her bones and short-circuited her brain.

When finally they drew apart her knees were trembling and her breathing was ragged, as though she'd run a sprint.

'Rosa…' he whispered in her hair. His breathing was coming fast too, and she could see that he had also been affected by their kiss. 'I'm so sorry.'

'You're sorry that you kissed me?'

He made a sound, like a laugh. 'Oh, no. I'm not sorry for that. Not sorry at all.'

'That's good,' she said, still clinging to him, afraid that

if she let go he might take his arms away and her legs wouldn't have the strength to hold her up. 'I think...' she started. 'I think that I forgive you.'

'You do?'

'But only on one condition.'

'Name it.'

'Only if you kiss me again.'

He growled.

To Rosa it sounded like a cry of triumph, of victory, as he swept her up in his arms and twirled her around so that her feet left the deck. At any other time she would have been fearful of falling out of the vessel, but not now. With Vittorio's strong arms around her she felt that nothing could go wrong. And when he put her down his big hands were cupping her face.

'I dreamed about this,' he said.

She was breathless all over again. 'You dreamed about kissing me?'

'More. I dreamed about spending the rest of the night with you.'

She gasped. There was no way she could prevent it. It was as involuntary as the flip of her stomach and the sudden clench of muscles between her thighs she'd never realised existed.

'But that's up to you. Let's see about my earning your forgiveness first.'

His mouth descended once more. She felt the tickle of his falling hair around her face, the graze of his whiskered cheeks and the exquisite, unexpected softness of his lips as his mouth met hers.

He took it slowly. He nibbled and suckled at her lips, teased her tongue with his and beckoned hers into the heated cavern of his mouth; he reassured the rest of her body that it wasn't missing out by sending his hands underneath the cloaks and sweeping them in arcs from her shoulders to the curve of her behind, and if forgiveness could truly be earned in a kiss he was earning a lifetime's worth.

But the kiss didn't end there. He changed gear, ratcheting up from gentle and considerate to plundering. Demanding. And she gave herself up to passion and to a heat such as she'd never known. She was burning up from the inside out.

Tiny details assumed major status. The precise angle of his mouth over hers, the puff of his breath on her cheek, the creak of leather as his arms moved around her. Tiny things, insignificant in themselves, and yet all part of something major, something momentous. Her breasts were straining tight inside her bodice, her nipples ached, and all she knew, with the tiny part of her brain that was still functioning, was that she never wanted these feelings to end.

Was it magic? Or merely lust?

She didn't care.

What did it matter when it felt this good?

By the time his head drew back she was lost to it. They could have fallen into the dark and frigid waters of the canal and she would have noticed nothing—not even the steam that would have come from their union.

'Make love to me, Rosa.' His breathing was rushed and ragged, his voice no more than a rasp on the night air. 'Spend the night with me.'

A spike of fear made its presence known—an age-old fear that she'd carried with her all her womanly life—and despite her earlier fantasies about the magic of the night that fear reared its head.

Sure, she wasn't completely naïve. She knew how things were supposed to work. But what did she really know of the intimacy of the bedroom? What if she couldn't? What if she did something wrong? What if it hurt? What if she made a fool of herself?

But those fears were no match for the arousal that spiralled up from within and surrounded her. Like a suit of armour, it protected her from her fears. There were still curling tendrils of doubt, but they were all but blunted, making room for anticipation and heady excitement, because this night would be a night like no other.

And somehow she knew she couldn't be in better hands.

She sucked in a breath while he waited for her answer, needing the cold night air to cool her while it could. 'I'd like that,' she said, and he gave a low growl of approval in his throat.

He took a moment to yell instructions to the driver and she had a sense of the boat changing direction as he turned her face up to his for another kiss.

Maybe it was just lust, Rosa thought as he pulled her against his mouth.

But there was magic happening tonight too.

Pure magic.

CHAPTER FIVE

FROM THE FIRST moment their eyes had met Rosa had recognised that there was something about this man, something magnetic that had drawn her towards him, something
commanding. But something that scared her, too. There
was an edge to him, as though if she ventured too close
she might fall.

And yet she'd agreed to spend the night with him.

But now, stepping from the deck of the motorboat and
into a building, she felt a further sense of unease. Because
it wasn't any ordinary building.

'What is this place?' she asked as he led her by the hand
towards a flight of stairs. It was not a hotel, as she'd been
expecting. And it was no humble apartment. 'Is this your
home?'

'What? Here in Venice? No,' he said dismissively. 'It's
a private residence. I just get to stay here occasionally.'

He shrugged, as if having access in any capacity to a
palazzo on the Grand Canal was nothing special.

Rosa looked around. Maybe this *palazzo* didn't quite
rival Marcello's in grandeur, but it was still very definitely
a *palazzo*, and it was filled with treasures of Murano glass,
sculptures, chandeliers and gilt everything.

'So where *do* you live?' she asked, her heels tapping on
the marble staircase.

'North of here. Near the border with Slovenia.'

'Near Trieste?'

He turned to her and smiled. 'Do you always ask this many questions when you're nervous.'

'I'm not nervous,' she lied on a lilting laugh.

But a few moments later he opened the door to a bedroom and her heart all but jumped out of her chest with nerves.

He dimmed the lights, but there was no dimming the vision that met her eyes, because across the room was a wide bed—impossibly wide. She swallowed. There was only one place this could end, and she wanted it, but still...

'Would you like something to drink?' he offered, already stripping away her armour of cloaks, peeling away her courage at the same time. 'Prosecco or another spritz?'

She shook her head. She didn't need more alcohol, or anything with bubbles. There was already too much fizzing going on in her blood.

'Then water.'

He pulled a bottle of water from a cabinet and poured them both a glass. She accepted it, more to give herself something to do with her hands rather than because her throat was suddenly desert-dry.

She was still contemplating that bed. She knew what the act entailed, but why was there no guidebook for the prelude? *Dio*, she really hoped she didn't mess this up.

She heard the soft tap of his glass being put down on a cabinet behind her, and then a sound that could only be the unbuckling of his leather trousers and a long zipper being undone. She clutched her glass with both hands.

Help!

'Rosa...' he said as he gently took her arm and turned her towards him.

He was bare-chested, dressed only in the leather of his costume pants. Her hungry eyes could not help but drink in the muscular perfection of his shoulders, his chest and his sculpted abdomen. She'd thought him perfect wrapped in leather of blue and gold, but now, dressed only in a pair of leather trousers slung low over his hips, he looked even more magnificent.

Breathtaking. Heart stopping.

Terrifying.

He smiled, then eased the glass from her tangled fingers and put it aside. 'Now,' he said, as he put his hands to her neck and eased her hair back over her shoulders. 'Where were we?'

Her mind was a blank. She had no idea what he was talking about, let alone how to answer.

But his warm hands answered his question for her, meeting at the nape of her neck and drawing her closer to him. Closer to his intense blue eyes. Closer to his parted, waiting lips.

She felt the heat of his mouth, the warmth of his hands at the back of her head, holding her to him. She felt the heat of his body even before he drew her still closer and her breasts met the hard wall of his chest as he deepened the kiss.

Her breasts ached for release. Her nipples were pressing hard against a suddenly too tight bodice as her blood swirled drunkenly around her veins. Her legs felt boneless and she had to put her hands to his chest to steady herself. But once they were there steadying herself against his body was the lesser priority. She needed to feel him, to drink in the texture of his sculpted body, to see if he felt as good as he looked.

And he did. He was magnificent, his body a landscape of contrasts. Hard muscles. Smooth skin. Wiry tangle of chest hair. Firm nub of nipples. But the realisation only ramped up both her desire and her nervousness.

'You're trembling…' He breathed rather than said the words as his lips worked the soft folds and ridges of her ears, his breath fanning like a musical breeze against her skin. 'Are you cold?'

Anything but. She was alight with fire, flames were burning her up from within, breathing life into the coals that already glowed hot deep down in the pit of her belly.

'No…' she whispered on a gasp of oxygen, and that tiny, one-syllable word was all she was capable of before his mouth once against captured hers and she was sucked back into the vortex of his kiss.

Was it possible to spin any more out of control?

Yes, she realised when she felt his fingers tug on the pull of her zip. Clever fingers to find such a well-disguised invisible zip, but even the knowledge that he was a man used to finding his way into women's clothing couldn't stop another rushing tide of heat as her dress loosened around her and threatened to fall away.

And, then like the burst of cool air that swirled into the exposed space at her back, a surge of panic saw her hands fold over her breasts. She wasn't wearing a bra and there would be nothing between them…

It was too late, and she realised how unsophisticated it must make her look, but all she could do was clutch her dress to her all the harder.

'So shy,' he said with a smile. 'Anyone would think…'

She turned her head away, but not before he'd seen the truth she tried to hide skittering across her eyes and the heated blush flooding her skin.

'No…' he said, and when she dared look back she saw disbelief mixed with something that looked like horror in his eyes. 'But you *can't* be a virgin. How old are you?'

'I'm sorry,' she said, wanting to run away. 'I didn't realise virginity came with a use-by date.'

He let her go and stepped away. Ran a hand through his hair. A *virgin*! Why the hell hadn't he picked up on it? She'd been like a startled doe trapped in the headlights from the start—flighty and nervous and blushing like a schoolgirl.

And desperate to point out that she was no courtesan. All the clues had been there and yet he'd been too blind to see what had been staring him in the face.

He turned and she was still standing there, holding her dress to her breasts like a shield. 'Rosa,' he said, 'why didn't you tell me? You should have told me.'

'When should I have done that, exactly? When you found me lost in the square and you asked my name? Or when you were kissing me on the motorboat and asked me to make love to you? When would have been the best time to slip my lack of sexual expertise casually into the conversation?'

She had a point. But a *virgin*?

He shook his head. Virgins were trouble. They had expectations. It wasn't a sacrifice most made lightly—parting with the known and the safe for the unknown. They took the act of love as an act of sharing and a promise of commitment. They had hopes and dreams he had no way of fulfilling.

'Look—' he said, shaking his head.

'I'm sorry,' she said cutting him off. 'You asked me to spend the night with you.' The end of her tongue found her lips. 'I said yes. So why should this make a difference?'

'It's your first time,' he replied. 'You don't want to waste it on a one-night stand. And that's all it will be, Rosa. That's all it can ever be—one night. I can't offer you any more than that.'

'I just want to finish what you started. I don't want any more than that.'

No? That was what they all said, and then afterwards would come the tears.

'Rosa—'

'Please,' she said. 'I really want to. I'm just a bit nervous, that's all.'

She took a deep breath, then took her hands away from

her dress and let it crumple to the floor, standing naked before him but for her panties.

Breath hissed through his teeth. *Dio*, but she was beautiful. Curvy, with dark-tipped breasts and a narrow waist that begged a man to run his hands down the sides, to drink them in, to feel for himself the exquisite flare of her hips.

An erection he thought had been banished by her revelation kicked back into life with a vengeance.

'Are you sure about this?' he asked, taking a step closer. Because she needed to be certain.

'I'm sure,' she said. 'What do you want me to do?'

'Oh, Rosa,' he said as he swung her into his arms, 'Your first time—all I want you to do is feel and enjoy.'

He laid her on the bed and sat beside her, held her face in his hands and kissed her gently on the mouth.

She was so nervous, her skin alive to sensation and his every touch like a brand, but he stilled her with his kiss. Soothed her.

'Don't be afraid,' he said, as if he could see inside her.

She smiled tremulously up at him and he kissed her again before dipping his mouth lower, kissing her throat, her collarbones, her shoulders, then kissing first one peaked nipple and then the other.

'So beautiful,' he said, and returned to her mouth, his kiss deeper, giving and taking more.

Her hands moved of their own volition, wanting to feel, to explore. His muscles bunched and shifted under her hands, and every touch, every texture, fed into her need, adding to the mix bubbling in the cauldron inside her.

She'd thought it would be quick, that it would be over soon. But he took his time exploring her body with his hot mouth and his clever fingers, until every nerve-ending in her body felt as if it was about to explode. When he drew down her underwear and touched a hand to her mound, one finger sliding between her slick folds, she almost did. Then and only then he stood and peeled down his leather trousers.

His erection sprang free and she gasped, feeling a momentary spike of panic. He was too big…there was no way… But then he was back, kissing her, and she could feel him hard against her belly, and she knew she wanted him inside her—whatever it took.

Still he didn't rush. Her body was burning up with need. She was panting with it, desperate, searching for relief, when he reached for a packet on the bedside table. He ripped it open and knelt above her, sliding protection down his long length. So long…

And then he was there, nudging at her entrance and sending those acutely sensitive nerve-endings into a frenzy. He kissed her deeply, opening her to him, his tongue plundering as he raised one of her legs over his hip and plunged into her.

Stars exploded behind her eyes. Stars that sent shimmering fragments whirling around the delicious feeling of fullness at her core.

He held himself still, his words coming in heady gasps. 'Are you all right?'

She remembered how to breathe, drawing in a ragged breath. 'I'm good,' she managed.

He started to move, to withdraw, and she missed him already. Newly found muscles clamped down, trying to hold on to him, and just when she thought he was lost to her he was back, and she was better than good.

He picked up the rhythm and in the friction he generated she found her stars again, this time strewn on the surface of the sea, wave after wave of shimmering sensation building inside her with every thrust. She was tossed higher and higher, faster and faster, until with one final plunge the star-filled waves crashed over her and washed her bonelessly to the shore.

She came back from the delicious place he'd sent her to slowly. Reluctantly. She wondered why the world in front of her eyes seemed so much the same as it had been before when everything had irrevocably shifted.

She'd expected to feel different. Regretful. Maybe even a little sad.

Instead, she felt…*good.*

Vittorio lay breathing hard next to her, his body hot, his skin slick with sweat. He lifted his head and kissed her cheek. 'Did I hurt you? Are you okay?'

She smiled and shook her head. There'd been a momentary flash of pain, but it had been lost in a shower storm of stars.

She kissed him back. 'Thank you. That was nice.'

His eyebrows shot up. *'Nice?'* he growled as he rolled out of bed to pad to the bathroom.

She grinned and scooted up the bed, slipping under the covers to hide her naked body. It was insane, after what they'd just done, but with him gone she felt exposed again.

'Very nice?'

She heard him chuckle and then he returned, sliding into the bed alongside her.

'Oh,' she said, unsure of the protocol. 'Should I go home now?'

'I promised you one night,' he said, settling her into the crook of his shoulder so he could dip his head to kiss her again. 'We might as well make the most of it.'

It was later, much later, and Vittorio's body was humming its way down from another crescendo. Rosa's fingernails were idly stroking his chest, and she asked, 'What happened to the kitten you rescued?'

He'd been so lulled by the rhythmic strokes of her fingernails, making swirls in the hair on his chest, that he almost missed the question.

'What?'

'The one you pulled from the bag in the stream.'

'You heard that?'

'I was nearly at the stairs when I saw Sirena was talking to you and Marcello. What happened to it? Did you keep it?'

'I took it to the housekeeper.'

He thought back. There would have been no point taking it to his father. His father would have told him that he was his mother's son and therefore weak—too weak to be the heir to the throne.

'My father would have told me to show some backbone for once in my life and throw the wretched thing back where I'd found it.'

But Maria had cried when she'd heard his story and she'd taken it and cuddled it before setting about finding it some bread to soak in milk.

'She kept it in the kitchen to keep down the mice.'

The thick medieval castle walls had shifted so often over the centuries, and been renovated so many times, it was impossible to plug all the tiny hidey holes. He'd often arrived in the kitchen to find Maria breathless as she chased after another mouse with her straw broom across the flagstones.

'You had your own housekeeper?'

'Que?' Too late he realised he'd almost given too much away, but this woman had a way of breaking down his defences. Of disarming him. 'Oh. After my mother died…'

'Of course,' she said, filling in the blanks as she understood them, relieving him of the need to finish while the circles of her fingers grew larger, sweeping lower over his abs. 'Somebody had to look after you both.'

'Somebody had to,' he agreed, lulled by the caress of her nails on his skin.

Maria had looked after them, along with a *castello* full of staff and courtiers and advisers. For a moment he felt guilty that he couldn't tell her, and that once again he was keeping secrets from her. But it wouldn't be the same if she knew. It would change things. It always did. It was better to leave it the way she understood it to be—that he was a friend of someone whose family had once been something important in Venice.

'Your father sounds very controlling. I mean, not just the kitten, but expecting you to marry who he chooses.'

He gave a low snort. 'That's one word for it. But I've been married. It ended badly.'

'Oh, I didn't know. I'm sorry.'

'It's not your fault,' he said, and she chuckled as both of them remembered their earlier conversation.

'Some families are like that, though, aren't they?' she said. 'Expecting to stage-manage their children's lives, maybe even wanting them to live the life they couldn't.'

He nodded, feeling the caress of her fingertips like a balm to his soul. 'What about your family, Rosa?' He smiled apologetically. 'Your *papà*, I mean. What's he like?'

'Wonderful. He's the one who urged me to leave home and find work somewhere else. I was happy at home— it was nice taking care of the house for everyone after Mamma died—but one by one my brothers married and left home, and eventually there was just my *papà* and me. He told me that if I didn't leave home and the village I'd never see anything of the world, and I'd be stuck looking after him when he got old.'

Her hand stopped and her head lifted.

'I don't think I should be talking about my father right now.'

He patted her shoulder. 'My fault,' he said, wondering why he had asked. He didn't need to know anything more about Rosa than what she'd brought to this bed. He didn't need to know about her family. He didn't want to hear it. 'Let's talk about something else.'

'Talk?' she said, her fingertips back in action and growing bolder, her nails raking circles around his navel, swooping in and out. Teasing. Taunting.

His loins stirred. 'You've got a better idea?' he asked, his voice laced with a gravel edge.

Her fingertips edged lower, gliding over his tip. Her courage was growing by the minute. She'd always been a quick learner.

'Could we, do you think…? Just once more?'

Could we? He was suddenly harder than the question was to answer. But he had to remember she was new at this. Brave, curious, but inexperienced.

'You're not too sore?'

She shook her head, her fingers encircling him. Stroking him.

'Right now I'd like you to make love to me again,' she said. 'I can be sore tomorrow.'

CHAPTER SIX

VITTORIO WOKE TO watery sunlight slipping through the gaps in the heavy brocade drapes, a supreme sense of satisfaction and a goodly measure of anticipation. But sunlight…? So the fog had lifted.

He rolled over on his back and reached out an arm, searching for the source of his satisfaction and the reason for his anticipation, only to find the other side of the bed empty and the sheets cold.

What the…?

He rose up on his elbows. 'Rosa?' he called into the gloom, his eyes scanning the room, searching for any evidence of her.

But the chair where he'd flung her dress after he'd peeled it off was empty and the rug where he'd placed her shoes after he'd slipped them off was bare. There was only his rapidly discarded leather trousers littering the floor.

'Rosa!' he called, louder this time, swiping back the covers to pad barefoot across the carpet to the bathroom. But that room was dark and empty too.

She was gone.

He headed back to the bedroom, sat on the side of the bed and picked up his watch from the side table. Almost noon. *Dio*, what time had they got to sleep? The last thing he could remember thinking was that he would shut his eyes for ten minutes to recover—and then he didn't remember thinking anything at all.

He put his head in his hands and thought back. She'd said something about working today. He'd wondered at the time if it had just been an excuse to escape the party, but she'd told him she was a cleaner in a three-star hotel. Maybe she *did* have to work. Which meant… What godawful time must she have left?

He stood up on a sigh and headed back to the bathroom, swiping open the nearest curtains on the way. Milky light spilled into the room, banishing the gloom, while outside, if Venice had a hangover it didn't show.

Venice was getting on with being Venice. *Vaporettos* and gondolas alike were ferrying tourists backwards and forwards, rubbish barges filled with last night's garbage were skulking out of the way as a water ambulance screamed along the canal.

He had to get back to Andachstein.

Even so, he thought as he looked at his face in the bathroom mirror, his hands stroking his rough jaw, it was disappointing that she'd cut and run before he could make love to her one last time.

He stepped under the rain-shower spray, sighing in approval as he turned his face into the hot water and felt it cascade down his body. Just because he was in a fifteenth-century *palazzo* it didn't mean he had to go without modern plumbing.

He smiled to himself. A virgin. Rosa had started out so shy and timid and then turned to liquid mercury in his arms, as sinuous as the canal that weaved its way outside his windows. One spark and she'd sizzled with sensuality, turning an otherwise dark night into a blaze of heat and passion.

He'd been honest—at least as far as commitment went. He'd laid all his cards on the table. One night and one night only, and definitely no chance of for ever. So it was probably for the best that she'd already gone. It avoided any of those awkward post-coital conversations when last night's warnings tended to get somehow twisted by the act of intercourse, when words took on a different meaning from how they'd been intended and first understood.

How many times had he heard the same old arguments? *'But that was before you made love to me...'* and *'I thought you cared about me...'*

At least she'd saved them both that anguish.

He roughly towelled himself off and dropped his towel on the floor as he headed for the dressing room. A virgin. How about that? It had been a long time since he'd encountered a virgin. He didn't tend to move in the same circles as teenagers or gauche twenty-somethings.

She'd made him laugh. And she'd been perfectly right. It wasn't as if virginity self-destructed if you didn't use it up. It was just that most people he knew seemed to have found a way to dispense with it before they'd abandoned their teens.

He had his underwear and trousers on, and had just pulled a white shirt from a hanger, was reefing it over his shoulders, when he saw it. A glint of something gold amidst the tangle of linen and coverlets on the bed. His eyes narrowed. A trick of the watery light?

He moved closer as he buttoned his shirt. No. There was definitely something there. Something small.

He reached down and picked it up and realised what it was as the pearl swung free on the ring that attached it to a golden stud. One of Rosa's earrings.

She'd left it here.

On purpose?

The moment the thought popped into his mind he discarded it. He was far too world-weary. While plenty of women he'd met would, Rosa wouldn't play games like that. She wasn't the type.

It looked old. She would be sure to miss it.

He should return it. There were no excuses. He knew where she worked.

He should give it to the housekeeper and have it delivered. Rosa would have it back in a matter of hours.

He should return it.

He twirled the delicate earring in his fingers, held it to his nose as if by doing so he could conjure up her scent.

He should return it.

His fingers closed around it where it lay in his palm and he slipped it into his trouser pocket.

He would return it.

Later.

CHAPTER SEVEN

'WHERE DID YOU get to?' Chiara cried, bolting upright in bed and turning on her bedside lamp the second Rosa walked into the tiny basement flat the girls shared. 'I've been worried sick about you.'

'I got lost,' Rosa said, checking the time on the alarm clock glowing red. Four-thirty a.m.

She unzipped her gown and let it slip down her body for the second time that night, shivering at the memory of the first. She would have time for an hour's sleep if she put her head down on her pillow right now.

Sleep? After what she'd experienced tonight? She might be kidding herself about that. But at least she'd have an hour to savour the memories.

'I'm really sorry I suggested carrying your phone for you,' Chiara said, watching her prepare for bed. 'I feel so bad for ruining your night.'

'Don't worry about it. How was the ball?'

'So much fun,' she said, and her face lit up before she could think better of it. 'I tried to find you. We searched and searched and I called the hotel in case you'd come back, but nobody had seen you. I didn't expect to be home before you.'

'It's okay. Forget it.'

'So where were you?'

'I met someone,' Rosa said, sliding between the sheets. 'He invited me to a party he was going to.'

'He? A man? You went to a party with a stranger?' Chiara was all agog. She swung her legs out of bed and sat up. *'You?'*

Rosa didn't take offence at her friend's surprise. She knew what she meant.

'What was he like?'

'Oh, Chiara…' Rosa sighed, propping herself up on her elbow, head resting on her hand. 'You should have seen him. He was tall, and strong, and… I wouldn't call him really handsome—but powerful-looking. With the most amazing blue eyes I've ever seen.'

'What was his name?'

'Vittorio.' Even now the sound of it on her tongue was delicious.

'And he asked you to go to a party with him?'

She smiled. *'Si.'*

'Why?'

Rosa shrugged. This part could do with a bit of airbrushing of the truth. She plucked at some imaginary fluff on her sheet. 'He felt sorry for me that I was missing my costume ball after I'd spent so much money on a ticket.'

'And there *was* a party, I hope?'

'Oh, yes. In this amazing *palazzo* right on the Grand Canal. It even had a second *piano nobile*—can you imagine? The party was on the second level and the first level was set up with the entertainment. They had music and jugglers and opera singers, and even gymnasts performing on ropes. It was amazing. And you should have seen the costumes, Chiara! *Amazing.*' Rosa punched her pillow and settled down. 'Can you turn off the light? We have to get up soon.'

'And you were at this party all night, then?'

'Uh-huh. Turn off the light.'

'And then you came home?'

'I'm tired,' Rosa said, hugging her precious secret to

her, not willing to share just yet. She might tell Chiara one day about what had really happened. Maybe. 'And we've got to be up in less than an hour.'

Chiara sniffed and extinguished the light, clearly recognising the sense in Rosa's words and the fact she was not going to hear any more tonight.

'All right, have it your way. But I want all the details tomorrow!'

'Goodnight,' said Rosa noncommittally, snuggling into her pillow, and only then noticing the press of her earring stud into her flesh. In her rush to get to bed she'd forgotten to take her earrings off. She removed the offending article and reached for the one on the other side—only to find it gone.

She sat up, switching on the lamp.

'What now?' said Chiara grumpily. 'I thought you wanted to go to sleep?'

'I can't find one of my earrings.' Her eyes searched the floor around the bed. She got out and shook her dress, in case she'd dislodged it when she'd pulled the gown over her head. But of course it wasn't there, because she hadn't done that at all.

'Go to bed.'

'They were my grandmother's,' she said. 'A gift from my grandfather on their wedding day.' And, apart from her mother's sewing machine, they were the only thing of real value she had.

'Go to bed!' Chiara repeated grumpily. 'Look for it tomorrow.'

'But—'

'Turn off the light!'

Rosa did a quick sweep with her hands of her bedding and her pillow before she complied and climbed back into bed. She switched off the light and settled back down.

Where could it be? She'd been wearing them both at Vittorio's. She remembered seeing them when she'd looked in the mirror in the bathroom. But that had been before...

Dio. But at least if it was there someone might find it—a cleaner or a housekeeper—and she might be able to get it back. Better that than thinking it had fallen out on her way home somewhere along the twisty *calles.*

Either way, if she couldn't find it here she'd go looking after her shift tomorrow—*today.*

One night only.

She thought about Vittorio's warning that one night was all there would be, that it wasn't an affair and he didn't do for ever. If he was at home she wouldn't pester him. She wouldn't ask for him. She just wanted her earring back, if it had been found. And if he learned she had visited he'd understand why she'd had to come back. She was sure he would.

So she'd retrace her steps to his *palazzo,* and if she didn't find it on the way she'd knock on the door. There was no harm in asking, surely?

Rosa was almost overcome with exhaustion by the time she finished her shift. She'd been exhausted before she'd started, though for an entirely different reason, but by the end of the shift it was pure drudgery weighing her down. It seemed every visitor had hung around until the end of Carnevale and then checked out today, which had meant changeovers in almost every room.

By the time she was finished all she wanted to do was collapse in a heap in her bed. Except that wouldn't get her pearl earring back, so she changed into jeans and a jacket and headed out into the tortuous *calles* of Venice once again, trying to retrace her steps.

It was no wonder she took a wrong turn once or twice—she was so busy looking at the ground in front of her—but eventually she found it: the gate where she'd made her escape that morning from Vittorio's *palazzo*. She rang the buzzer and waited. And waited.

She rang the buzzer again.

Eventually the door opened to reveal a stern-looking middle-aged woman. 'This is a private residence. We're not open to visitors.'

'No,' Rosa said, before the woman could shut the door as abruptly as she'd opened it. 'I was here last night. I lost an earring.'

The woman shook her head. 'I think you have the wrong residence.' She started closing the gate again.

'I was with Vittorio,' Rosa said. 'I don't want to bother him, but it was my grandmother's earring, given to her on her wedding day. I think I may have lost it here, and if I could get it back...'

The woman sniffed as she opened the gate a fraction more, looking Rosa up and down as if finding her story hard to believe and yet not impossible. 'Vittorio is no longer here. I don't know when he'll be back. He's not in Venice very often.'

'I didn't come to see Vittorio,' said Rosa. 'It's my grandmother's earring I'm looking for. That's all. I promise.'

The woman sighed. 'Then I'm sorry. I can't help you, I'm afraid. I cleaned that room myself. Nothing was found.'

And she eased the door shut in Rosa's face.

It could have been worse, Rosa thought, heading home, still checking the ground in case her earring had come loose during the evening and fallen out on the way home. The housekeeper might have practically slammed the door in her face but at least she'd listened to her. At least she knew she hadn't lost it there.

'I'm sorry, Nonna,' she said as she got closer to home and there was still no sight of the missing earring. 'I'm sorry I didn't take better care of it for you.'

The streets had no answer.

It was gone.

She'd thought she'd got off scot-free, but maybe this was the price she had to pay, Rosa rationalised as she dragged herself back to the hotel and her tiny basement flat and home to bed. For nothing came without a cost. She knew that.

Maybe one lost earring was the price she had to pay for one night of sin.

And the worst part of it was her night with Vittorio had been so special, so once-in-a-lifetime, she almost felt the loss of one of her grandmother's earrings was worth it.

CHAPTER EIGHT

THE SUMMONS FROM his father's secretary came within five minutes of Vittorio's arrival back at the *castello*. Vittorio snorted as he settled back into his rooms. Some things never changed. His father had never once come to *him*, let alone met him at the castle doors when he'd returned from being away. Not when he'd come home as a child on holiday from boarding school in Switzerland. Not when he'd come home after three years of college in Boston.

Although there was something to be said for knowing how a person worked. You knew exactly how to press their hot buttons.

'At last,' his father said when Vittorio arrived thirty minutes after the summons.

On the Guglielmo Richter Scale, as Vittorio had termed it as a boy, his father seemed to be in good spirits, and he wondered if he shouldn't have taken longer to accede to his father's request.

'I've been waiting for news. I thought you might have had the decency to let me know before now, but now that you're finally here tell me everything.' Prince Guglielmo clearly enunciated his demands as he wandered from one side of his office to the other. In his blue double-breasted jacket, and with one hand tucked behind his back, he looked as if he was inspecting the guard.

Through the vast windows behind him Vittorio could see down to the glorious sweep of Andachstein coast that separated Italy from Slovenia, and the swarm of white yachts that lay at anchor in the protected harbour while their occupants entertained themselves in the casinos, clubs and restaurants that lined the white sand beaches. Even at the tail end of winter they came in their droves—the rich and famous, the billionaires and their mistresses, the actors and actresses. The only difference was that in summertime it would be a sea of white and there wouldn't be a spare berth anywhere.

His father stopped pacing.

'Well? Have you set a date?' the older Prince prompted. 'Can we alert the press, the public? I need to get Enrico on to it immediately, before the news leaks from other sources.'

Other sources. Clearly his father didn't trust Sirena to keep a secret. If there had been one to keep. But he didn't say that. Instead he frowned and said, 'Have I set a date…?' He was being deliberately obtuse, playing the game.

His father snorted, impatience winning over civility, edging him higher up the Guglielmo Richter Scale. 'You and the Contessa Sirena, of course. Who else?' He fixed his son with a gimlet stare. 'Have you agreed a date?'

Vittorio picked up a paperweight from his father's desk—a crystal dragon, symbol of the principality—and tossed it casually from one hand to the other. He saw his father's eyes follow the object that he'd been forbidden to touch as a child. He half expected him to snap now, tell him to put it down in case he dropped it, as he had then. But his father said nothing and Vittorio sighed. It was time to put his father out of his misery.

He put the paperweight down and leant with both hands against the desk, wanting no distractions when he delivered his message. 'There is no date. There will be no marriage. At least not between Sirena and me.'

'*What?*'

His father's voice boomed so loud in the cavernous room that Vittorio swore the windows rattled.

'When are you going to take your responsibilities seriously?'

'There's no rush.'

'There *is* a rush! It was all supposed to be organised. You two were supposed to come to an agreement. All you had to do was set a date and it seems you can't even be trusted to do that.'

'Actually, I have an idea,' Vittorio suggested. 'If you're so desperate to welcome Sirena into the family business, why don't you marry her yourself?'

His father spluttered and banged his fist on the desk. 'You damned well know this isn't about the Contessa. This is about providing Andachstein with an heir. Without a prince there can be no principality. Andachstein will be swallowed up into the realm of Italy.' He looked his son up and down with disdain. 'You might like to think you're invincible, my son, but you won't last for ever, you know.'

'Look, Father,' he said with a sigh. 'It will happen. I will marry again. But don't expect that I'm going to fall in with your plans just because it's what you want. And don't make such a big deal out of it.'

'I'm *dying*!' Guglielmo blurted, his face beetroot-red.

The son who had grown up with a father who had always used drama to bend the people around him to his will said, 'We're all dying, Father.'

'Insolence!'

'I'm thirty-two years old. I'm not a child, even if I am your son. So if you've got something to tell me then simply tell me.'

'Heart problems.' His father spat out the words.

Heart problems? But that would mean... Vittorio bit back on the obvious retort while his father waved his hands around, looking for words.

'Something to do with the valves,' his father said, 'I forget the name. So fix it, I told the doctors. Replace them. And they told me that while one of them was operable the other was more problematic. They say it is fifty-fifty that I would survive the operation. Without it they say I most likely have less than a year to live.'

Guglielmo collapsed into the chair behind his desk, suddenly weary, and Vittorio noticed that he looked more like an eighty-year-old, rather than the sixty he was supposed to be.

'I've decided to take my chance on life,' he said, 'rather than on some cold operating table.' He turned to his son. 'But I want you married before I die, whatever happens.'

'Dio,' Vittorio said, with the shock of realisation reverberating through his body. 'You're actually serious.'

'Of course I'm serious!' he said. 'And I have a son who won't face up to his responsibilities and do what his duty demands of him.'

Vittorio's hands fisted at his sides. Dying or no, his father was not getting away with that one. 'I faced up to my responsibilities once before. Don't you remember? And look how that turned out!'

His father waved his arguments aside. 'Valentina was weak. She was a bad choice.'

'She was *your* choice,' Vittorio snarled.

His father had decided on the match before the two had even been introduced. The first time they'd met Vittorio had been smitten. She'd seemed like a bright and beautiful butterfly and he'd fallen instantly and irrevocably in love with her. And he'd believed her when she told him that she loved him.

But she had been young and impressionable, and he'd been too foolish to see what was in front of his face. That the family helicopter pilot she'd insisted move with her to the *castello* at Andachstein, so that she could continue her flying lessons, was teaching her a whole lot more than how to handle a helicopter…

He would never forgive himself for not talking her out of leaving with her lover after he'd confronted her with the knowledge that they'd been seen together. He'd been too gutted. Too devastated. He'd loved her so much and she'd betrayed him, and so he'd let her run distraught to her pilot and escape, tears streaming down her face.

He'd never been sure who had been at the controls when they'd hit the powerlines that had ended their lives.

'*Dio*, Father, don't you understand why I don't want you to have anything to do with choosing another bride for me?'

It was as much about getting out from under his father's thumb as it was about the fact that he'd sworn never to be such a fool again. Never to trust a woman's lies. Never to let his heart control his decisions.

His father mumbled something under his breath. Something mostly incoherent. But Vittorio was sure he heard the word *ungrateful* in the mix.

'Well,' he said, 'something has to be done and I don't have long to wait. I'm giving you three months.'

'What?'

'Three months should be perfectly adequate. Find your own bride, if you must, but you're getting married in the Andachstein Cathedral in three months and that's my final word. I'll have Enrico make a list of the best candidates.'

His father couldn't be serious. But then, Vittorio had thought he was joking about dying. *Heart problems. A year to live.* If it were true, Vittorio would be the new Prince of Andachstein, not just the heir apparent.

The ground shifted under his feet. Longevity ran through the line of Andachstein Princes—the last had died at ninety-seven. The youngest ever to die had been seventy-eight. He'd imagined his father, in these modern medicine times, had at least another twenty years to run down on his body clock.

'No,' Vittorio said, and his father's head jerked up, as if Vittorio was rejecting his demand out of hand. 'Not Enrico,' he said. His father's secretary had just as poor judgement for who would make a good wife as his father did. 'I'll get Marcello to help me.'

His father cocked one wiry eyebrow. 'She needs to be the right kind of woman,' he said. 'With the right family connections.'

'Of course.'

'Not to mention good breeding stock.'

Vittorio almost raised a smile. He wasn't entirely sure how he was supposed to assess that, but he simply said, 'Next you'll be insisting she's a virgin.'

The older man looked over at him. 'I may be dying, but I'm not stupid. The search will be difficult enough without making it impossible.'

This time Vittorio did smile. There was no way he wasn't trying before buying.

His father nodded, taking his son's smile as agreement, seemingly satisfied with how the meeting had gone. 'You have three months. Don't let me down. I would very much like to meet the next Princess of Andachstein before I die.' His voice cracked on the final word and he put his head down and gave a dismissive wave of his hand. 'Now, leave me.'

Vittorio nodded, and left his father at his desk, and as he walked down the long corridor that led from his father's official rooms to his own apartment he wondered about the glint that he'd seen in his father's eyes.

Tears?

It hardly seemed possible. He'd never seen his father cry. Not when they'd been sitting at the bedside of his wife of thirty years and she'd given up her last breath and slipped silently away. Not even when they'd interred her in the family crypt and the hound she had loved for twelve years had howled uncontrollably and mournfully at their feet, as if he knew he'd just lost his best friend. Every other mourner except his father had lost it right then.

But tears would mean that his father was almost human.

Was that what knowing you were going to die—having an end date rather than a vague statistic—did to you? Made you confront your own mortality? Made you human?

His father.

Dying.

It was an impossible concept to grasp.

He'd always been closer to his mother. She'd never been warm, exactly—he'd felt far more welcome in the kitchen than in his mother's salon—but she'd been the one who'd held the two men in her life together, and when she'd died the yawning chasm between father and son had widened. And that had been before Valentina had died and the gulf and the resentment between them had grown still wider.

Vittorio was in no hurry to get married again. His experience of marriage was no fond memory. And his parents…? They were hardly shining lights for the institution. No, he was in no hurry.

But he *was* heir to the throne of Andachstein. A position he might be forced to take up long before he had ever imagined. And it *was* his duty to sire an heir.

And, when it all came down to it, Guglielmo was still his father—the only father he'd ever had. So, despite their differences over the years, didn't he owe him something?

Vittorio's footsteps echoed in the old stone stairwell that led up to his apartments the back way. There was a flashier terrazzo-tiled staircase that went the front way, but he preferred the feel of the stone under his feet, the stone steps that held the grooves of the feet of his ancestors and their servants. Ever since he was a child he'd liked stepping into those grooves and wondering how many footsteps it would take to make a dent in the stone. He liked to think he was doing his bit by contributing his own footfall.

Every few steps there was a long narrow window that offered glimpses of the tree-covered hills behind the coast and the city. Once used by archers against marauding invaders, now they were glassed in against the weather. He stopped at one near the top and gazed out over the countryside, not really seeing, just thinking.

Maybe it was time. He was thirty-two and he was tired. Tired of the Sirenas of this world hunting for a title. Tired of the life he was leading.

There had to be something else.

Something more.

It couldn't be too hard to find himself a wife once he set his mind to it, surely? It shouldn't take long to vet the candidates. It wasn't as if he had to go through the motions of falling in love with the woman first.

He'd been in love with Valentina and what a disaster that had turned out to be. But then, was it any wonder? Look at his role models. He wasn't sure his father had ever loved his mother. They'd had separate suites as far back as Vittorio could remember. He'd never once witnessed a display of affection between them.

When it came down to it, it was a miracle he even existed...

CHAPTER NINE

HE CAME OUT of the fog in blue leather trimmed with gold, his long cape swirling in his wake. He emerged tall and broad and powerful, his cobalt eyes zeroing in on her, as if he'd sensed her presence through the mist.

He strode purposefully towards her, stopping bare inches away, so close that she could feel the heat of his body coming at her in waves…so close that she was sure his intense eyes would bore into hers and see inside her very soul.

'Rosa…' he said, in a deep voice that threatened to melt her bones.

'Vittorio,' she said, breathless and trembling, 'you came for me.'

'I had no choice,' he said, and he opened his arms for her.

She stepped into the space he had created just for her and felt his arms ensnare her in his heat and strength as he dipped his head to hers.

Her lips met his. She sighed into his mouth and gave herself up to the delicious heat of his mouth. His tongue. His taste. She felt herself swung into his arms, as if she were weightless, and then time slipped and they were in bed, and he was poised over her, and his name was on her lips as he drove into her…

'Rosa!'

The voice was wrong. It didn't fit. It was in the way.

She tried to ignore it. Tried desperately to hang on to what was happening even as the vision wobbled at the edges.

'Stop mooning,' someone said.

Someone who sounded like Chiara.

But what would she be doing at Vittorio's *palazzo*?

'It's time to get up!'

Rosa blinked into wakefulness, feeling a soul-crushing devastation. Feeling cheated. She'd thought Vittorio had come back for her, but it had been nothing but yet another pointless and cruel dream.

'All right,' she said, blinking, getting herself out of bed. 'I'm coming.'

'Forget about him,' Chiara said, brushing her hair.

'Forget about who?'

'Vittorio, of course. He must have been something special for you to dream about him all the time.'

'Who says I was dreaming about him?'

Chiara raised her eyebrows. 'Why else would you call out his name? You've really got it bad.'

Rosa kicked up her chin as she headed for the bathroom. 'I don't know what you're talking about. It was a dream, that's all.'

'When are you going to tell me what happened that night?'

'I told you what happened.'

Chiara just laughed. 'Hurry up,' she said. 'Or you'll be late for work.'

Rosa stepped under the shower spray. How could she share the events of that night with Chiara and convey the magic of the evening without cheapening it? No. She held the secret of what had happened that night like a precious jewel, still too new and too special to share with anyone.

She didn't have stars in her eyes. She wasn't stupid. She knew that despite the dreams that plagued her nights she'd never see Vittorio again. Not that the knowledge stopped her looking out for him every time she ventured anywhere near the Grand Canal. She'd hear a deep voice or see a broad pair of shoulders up ahead and for a split second she'd be hurtled back to that night and think she'd found him again. But the voice always belonged to someone else, and the man with broad shoulders would turn and the likeness would end there.

She didn't mind. He'd told her how it would be. She didn't expect to see him ever again.

He'd just been so wonderful that night. So tender and gentle, so generous in his willingness and desire to ensure her pleasure, so generous in the knowledge he'd shared.

She knew about lovemaking now. She knew what she liked in bed and how to pleasure a man. She had Vittorio to thank for introducing her to the ways of the bedroom.

She didn't really mind that she would never see him again.

She just had a horrible feeling he had ruined her for any other man.

'So this is the list Enrico gave you?'

Marcello looked up and down the three-page printout listing the eligible noblewomen his father's secretary had assembled who might just be persuaded to take on Vittorio and the title of Princess of Andachstein. There was a photograph of each woman alongside her name, together with a sketchy bio giving height, age and weight.

Vittorio snorted. 'I see Enrico's covered all the important details.'

'A veritable smorgasbord of aristocratic talent,' Marcello said drily 'But one thing worries me.'

'What's that?'

'You've only got three months until the date of the wedding. Does that give you enough time to sleep with them all?'

The would-be groom crossed his legs at the ankles and smirked. Now that he'd made up his mind to fall in with his father's crazy plan and find himself a wife—a princess for Andachstein—he found he liked the idea more and more. An arranged marriage, a convenient marriage—but this time without foolishly falling in love. All he had to do was produce an heir. If the marriage itself floundered after that, so be it. It would be nobody's fault. Nobody would be hurt. It was perfect. Failsafe.

Besides, he was growing tired of his lifestyle. Tired of fighting his destiny. But he wasn't interested in searching for a wife by any other means. So he'd had Enrico clear the appointments that could be cleared, undertaken those that couldn't be avoided, and now, within the space of a week, was sitting in one of the reception rooms in Marcello's *palazzo*.

'Did you see who's at the top of the list?'

Marcello cocked an eyebrow. 'I did notice that. Maybe your father ascribes to the view that it's better the devil you know?'

Vittorio laughed. '*He* might. But I'm not that much of a masochist.' He sat up, forearms on knees, hands clasped. 'So what do you think?'

Marcello flicked between the pages, exhaling long and loud as he shook his head. 'Well, it's not the list *I* would have given you.'

'In what way?'

'Doormats, one and all.'

Vittorio leaned forward and snatched the pages out of his friend's hands. 'They can't all be doormats?'

Marcello nodded. 'Every last one of them.'

'Apart from Sirena, you mean.'

'Well, apart from her, clearly. Otherwise that's a carefully curated list of "women who won't."'

Vittorio frowned. 'Won't what?'

Marcello shrugged. 'Argue. Object. Have an opinion on anything or speak their own mind.'

Vittorio gazed at the list more enthusiastically. 'Sounds exactly like what I want!'

'Ah, Vittorio,' Marcello said, shaking his head. 'Some of us know that you're not entirely the bad boy Prince that you like to make out. But you're no walkover either. You'd be bored with any one of these before she'd made it halfway down the aisle. By the time she did you would have plucked a woman from the choir who showed a bit more spirit.'

'All right,' said Vittorio, thrusting the papers onto the nearby coffee table. 'What have *you* got for me?'

'Ah,' said Marcello, a man in his moment. 'Three of the best.' He pushed a folder across the table and flipped open the cover to reveal candidate number one. 'Katerina Volvosky. Former ice-skating supremo, now an international rights lawyer working with the UN. She comes with good, if not royal lineage. Her father is a former ambassador to the USA. Her mother is a doctor—a burns specialist.'

Vittorio nodded. She was attractive, and looked intelligent. 'She definitely looks like she wouldn't be afraid to voice an opinion. What makes you think she'd want to get married?'

'She's just been dumped by her long-term boyfriend, she's thirty-five, and her body clock's ticking. She'd have time for an heir and a spare at the very least. I think, given the right inducement, she could be persuaded to marry you.'

'Huh. As if anyone would need an inducement to marry me.'

Marcello snorted. 'You just go right on believing that, Vittorio.' He turned the page. 'Potential bride number two—Emilija Kozciesko, former animal activist turned environmentalist, a woman with a passion for protecting the Mediterranean in particular. Her mother was president of Ursubilia for ten years, her father is a concert pianist who put his career aside to support his wife's political aspirations. And—get this—she speaks eight languages.'

Vittorio looked at the picture. She was beautiful too, but with a feistiness in her features that said she would fight tooth and nail for what she believed in. No doormat there. She was standing on the bow of a boat, looking out to sea, with the wind catching her long hair. Dark hair that reminded him of something. *Someone*. He dug his hand deeper into his pocket.

'And her body clock?'

'No issues. She's twenty-eight, but she's a rebel who recognises that it's easier to agitate when you're attached to a title.'

Vittorio held out one hand. 'Pass me that list of doormats again.'

'Hah!' Marcello said, sweeping them out of reach. 'Be serious. Now, option number three…' He flipped the page to a photograph of a stunning blonde with Nordic good looks. 'Inga Svenson. Shipping heiress whose family has fallen on hard times. Former model, B-grade actress and now children's ambassador. She's also fluent in French, Italian, English…along with all the Scandinavian languages, of course.'

Vittorio was impressed. 'And she hasn't found a husband yet because…?'

'She was engaged to be married when the family business imploded. She got unceremoniously dumped and the fiancé promptly found himself another heiress.' Marcello eyed his friend. 'She's vulnerable, and I know how you like to rescue vulnerable things.'

Vittorio's fingers squeezed tight.

'What's that in your hand?' asked Marcello.

'What?' Vittorio looked down to see Rosa's earring in his fingers. He hadn't even realised he'd been playing with it. 'Oh, just a trinket,' he said, putting it back in his trouser pocket.

Marcello looked at him levelly. 'A trinket that you keep

in your pocket? Have you taken to collecting souvenirs, Vittorio? Because if you have that could be a precursor to something entirely more sinister.'

Vittorio snorted and leaned forward in his chair. 'You make me laugh, my friend.'

He lined up the three photographs next to each other and pushed away the middle one—Emilija, with the dark hair that reminded him of someone.

'Right, how do you propose we do this?'

CHAPTER TEN

'ROSA!' CHIARA YELLED, thumping her roommate on the chest with a pillow. 'Get out of bed. You'll be late.'

'Ow, that stung,' Rosa said, rubbing her sore chest as she struggled to come to. Her head felt full, as if it had somehow absorbed her pillow in the night. But Chiara was right—she needed to get up. Rosa was usually the first of the two to get ready, but lately that was changing, and Chiara was already dressed in her uniform and tying her hair back.

Rosa swung her legs over the side of the bed and pushed herself upright—and immediately wished she hadn't. She put her hand to her mouth. Whatever had been on that pizza last night must have disagreed with her.

'God, you look awful,' Chiara said, watching her. 'What's wrong with you?'

'I don't feel—'

She didn't get any further. A wave of heat welled up inside her and Rosa bolted for their tiny bathroom, where she collapsed boneless while her stomach rebelled against the world.

'You really are sick,' said Chiara, handing her a wet hand towel once the heaving spasms had passed, leaving Rosa breathless and almost too weak to wipe her heated face.

'Must have been the pizza,' Rosa said, gasping, pressing her face into the towel.

'We shared the pizza. It can't be that.'

'You feel okay?'

'I'm fine. And I had all the wine, because you said you didn't like how it smelt, so if anyone should feel sick it's me.'

'So if it wasn't that pizza, and it couldn't have been the wine, what else can it be?' Rosa struggled to her feet and splashed more cold water on the towel, wiped her neck and throat. 'Please let it not be the flu. I can't afford to take time off.'

She put her hands on the sink and leaned against them, waiting for her body to calm. She took a breath and looked up, and caught sight of her roommate's scowling expression in the mirror over the sink.

'What?'

'You felt queasy yesterday at breakfast too.'

She shook her head, pushing herself away from the sink. She really needed to get moving. 'The coffee was too strong. I felt fine all day after that.'

'You love your coffee.'

Not yesterday, Rosa hadn't. One whiff and she'd turned her head away.

She threw off her nightgown and pulled her uniform from the hanger on the single clothes rail the girls shared. 'An aberration,' she said.

Chiara watched her clamber into the button-up dress. 'Only...if you think about it...it's about six weeks since Carnevale.'

'So?' Rosa looked around. 'Where are my shoes? Have you seen my shoes?' she asked, only to see the heels poking out from under her bed, where she always left them.

'Six weeks since you got lost and said you met someone. A man...' She let that sink in before she asked, 'When was your last period, Rosa?'

Rosa lifted her head, her expression deadpan as she

thought back, counting the weeks, finding they didn't add up. 'Come on, Chiara. Now you're frightening me.'

'Aha!' Chiara said. 'And why would you be frightened? Unless there's something you're not telling me.'

'Stop it,' she said, pushing past her to go back into the bathroom.

She looked at her face in the mirror. She needed to slap on some make-up and do something to fix the weird pallor of her skin…hide the dark shadows under her eyes. She couldn't be pregnant. She just couldn't.

'You had sex with him, didn't you?' Chiara said. 'This stranger who took you to a party.'

'You make it sound shabby,' Rosa protested. 'It wasn't like that.'

'Aha! Then you *did* sleep with him!'

'Okay, so I did. What of it?'

Chiara clapped her hands, her eyes alight at the admission. 'And you never said a word.'

'I don't know why you're so excited,' Rosa said.

'Sorry,' Chiara said, looking suitably penitent. 'I'm just happy for you. Was it good?'

'Chiara!'

'All right. All right. But you could be pregnant, then?'

'I can't be pregnant.' She fiddled in her make-up bag, searching. She was absolutely ruling out being pregnant. 'He used contraception.'

'Condoms aren't one hundred per cent reliable,' Chiara said. 'And you're not on the pill, are you?'

'Of course I'm not!'

Chiara rolled her eyes, but had the good sense not to say anything about that. 'Do your breasts feel tender?'

Rosa's hand stalled on the mascara wand that she'd just started wielding over her lashes. She flicked her eyes to Chiara's, remembering the pillow she'd been walloped in the chest with. *How did she know?*

'Maybe it's just a twenty-four-hour bug? I don't know. But until I know for sure I'm not going to panic about it.'

Like hell. Just the thought of being pregnant made her feel sick with fear.

'I'll get a test from the pharmacy at lunch,' Chiara offered. 'You need to do it as soon as you can.'

Rosa shook her head. 'Don't waste your money.' *Please, God, let it be a waste of money.* 'Anyway, if anyone is going to be buying a test it should be me.'

'No. You'll put it off because you don't want to know, just in case you are. But you need to know one way or the other, and the sooner the better. Because if you are pregnant you need to start thinking about your options.' Then her roommate smiled and gave her a quick hug. 'Now, are you sure you're feeling well enough to go to work?'

The only good thing about that morning was that an entire tour group had checked out and the hotel was down two cleaners who had the flu. She didn't have time to panic, she told herself, exhausted after the third room-clean and changeover. She operated on autopilot, not letting herself think about anything beyond linen and towels and scooping away all the used bottles of cheap toiletries and replenishing them with new.

Because if she didn't think, she couldn't panic. And if she didn't panic, then she wouldn't work herself up over something that was probably nothing.

Though why would her period be late…?

Stress. Overwork. Money worries. That would probably do it. It wasn't as if she was in denial…she was just considering the other options. Making sense of it.

By the time her lunch break rolled around Rosa wanted to tell Chiara to forget it. She was feeling much better than she had in the morning. But Chiara had already slipped away to the *farmacia* and was having none of it.

She tugged Rosa into their tiny basement flat and then their tiny bathroom, passed her the box, and said, 'Do it.'

Rosa looked at the packet, read the instructions. 'It says to do it first thing in the morning.'

'Rosa,' her friend growled, pointing at the toilet behind her shoulder. 'Go.'

She did as she was ordered this time, but she grumbled all the way from the opening of the box, through the peeing on the stick to the waiting.

There was no point. She couldn't be pregnant. It was a waste of money and she'd be delighted to tell Chiara when the test showed up as negative.

Except it didn't.

She swallowed. Looked at the instructions again in case she'd read them wrongly. Looked back at the stick. She had never been more grateful that she was sitting down.

Chiara banged on the door. 'Well, what's happening? What does it say?'

Rosa washed her hands, splashing a little water on her face for good measure. She lifted her heated face to the mirror. She didn't look any different. A little paler than usual, maybe, and her eyes a little wide with shell shock.

She didn't *feel* any different. Shouldn't she feel different? Shouldn't she know? But pregnant... A baby... She was going to be a mother.

Rosa swallowed and looked down at the hand she'd curled low over her abdomen. And she realised the price for one night of sin wasn't just the loss of one of her grandmother's earrings.

The price was much, much higher.

'Come on!' cried Chiara impatiently from outside the door. 'What's going on?'

Rosa took a deep breath and opened the door, holding up the stick. 'Apparently I'm pregnant.'

And she let Chiara's arms enfold her.

* * *

'But if I'm pregnant,' Rosa said, sitting on her bed and nursing the cup of sweet tea that Chiara had made for her. 'Doesn't Vittorio have a right to know? Don't I have a responsibility to tell him?'

'There's no "if" about it. You're pregnant,' Chiara said. 'And why do you think he'd want to know?'

'Because he's the father?'

'Have you seen this man since?'

'No. Not since that night.'

'Did he give you his phone number? Anything else so you could contact him?'

'No. Only his first name.' Rosa shook her head. 'He said it was only for one night.'

Chiara sat back and slapped her hands on her legs. 'That says it all, right there. He's married.'

'No!'

'Face it, Rosa. A man picks you up and makes love to you and tells you that it's one night only—what do you *think* that means? His wife is probably about to give birth to their fourth *bambino* and didn't feel like going out that night. Do you really think he'll want to know he's got another one on the way?'

'No. He's not like that!'

'How do you know? You knew him for all of ten minutes, and that was most likely spent with him working out the fastest way to get inside your pants.'

'Stop it! It wasn't like that!'

'All right. But seeing as you haven't told me what it *was* like, what am I supposed to think?'

Rosa flicked her eyes up to her friend. 'Vittorio said his father wants him to get married.' Hadn't that been why Sirena was pursuing him? So that she would be the next Mrs... Mrs... She didn't know what. He'd never told her what his surname was.

She swallowed. So that she couldn't find him?

'Right. And he does what his father tells him, does he? How old was he? Twelve?'

'Chiara!'

'Well, who does what their father demands when they're all grown up?'

'So he has a demanding father? I don't know.'

Chiara gave an exasperated sigh. 'Clearly.' Then she sat down next to Rosa on the bed and put an arm around her shoulders. 'But you know, you might as well forget about him. You've got more pressing things to worry about now.' She gave her shoulders a squeeze. 'Like what you're going to do about this pregnancy.'

'What do you mean, what I'm going to do about it? I'm pregnant, aren't I? What *can* I do?'

'Oh, *cara*,' her roommate said softly. 'You must know it's not the only way you have to go. There are things you can do. You don't need a child now—how are you going to provide for it?'

'But it's a *baby*, Chiara. I'm having a baby.'

'It's not *technically* a baby yet, though, is it?'

'But it will grow.'

'I'm not saying you shouldn't do it, all I'm saying is having the child is not your only option. You need to think about all your options, Rosa, and what is best for you.'

'And the baby?' Rosa sniffed, her hand already wrapped protectively over the belly under which it lay. 'What about what's best for the baby?'

'I can't answer that,' said Chiara, 'but I can honestly say that there are plenty of children living in dreadful circumstances who would probably have preferred not to have been born at all.' She smoothed the hair from Rosa's brow. 'All I'm saying is think about it, okay? Don't assume that you're trapped and that you have no choices. You have choices. They might not be easy, but they're there.'

CHAPTER ELEVEN

'WHAT THE HELL'S wrong with you, Vittorio?' Marcello said. 'You're not taking this seriously. How do you expect to find yourself a bride to marry by the date your father decreed if you won't ask one?'

Vittorio sighed, hands in pockets, and turned away from the big windows overlooking the Grand Canal. More than halfway through the three months his father had decreed and he was back in Venice—although the intention had been to bring either Katerina or Inga to Venice with him and formally propose.

It was a business decision first and foremost, sure, but Marcello had suggested that no woman was going to say no in such a romantic setting, even if the wedding itself would have to take place in the cathedral in Andachstein.

The worst of it was that he didn't understand it himself. He'd decided to comply with his father's demands. He'd decided to follow his destiny. He'd decided it was a good thing. Perfect. Failsafe. And yet…

'For God's sake Vittorio, what are you thinking?'

'Nothing.'

Marcello sighed theatrically. 'Tell me something I don't know. Now, let's take this from the top. Katerina Volvosky. What do you think of her?'

'She seems nice,' he conceded. They'd been twice to the opera, and had flown to Paris in the royal jet for dinner one night.

'*Nice,*' said Marcello, deadpan. 'Right. How about Inga?'

Vittorio nodded. Together they'd gone ballooning in Turkey, with a side visit to Petra in Jordan. 'Yes, she's nice too.'

'And you can't decide between these two...' he made apostrophes in the air with his fingers '...*"nice"* women?'

'No,' Vittorio said on a shrug. And they *were* nice women. Lovely women, both. 'There's nothing wrong with either of them,' Vittorio said. 'They'd both be fine.' They were intelligent, passionate about their interests and attractive. 'They'd both be an asset to Andachstein.'

'So let's take it back to basics, shall we? Let's make it really, really easy for you.'

Vittorio turned back to look out at the shifting traffic on the canal, his fingers toying with the earring in his trouser pocket. 'I wish you would.'

Because he wasn't finding any of it easy as his eyes sought out the direction of the hotel where Rosa worked. What would she be doing right now? Would she be on her lunch break? Did she even *get* a lunch break?

'Which woman is better in bed?'

'What?' Vittorio spun around.

'Which one—Katerina or Inga—do you like better in bed?'

Vittorio's eyebrows shot up, answering the question with another. He shrugged. 'I don't know.'

'They're both as good as each other?'

Vittorio turned back to the view. 'I haven't slept with them.'

Marcello blinked. Slowly. 'You haven't slept with them? *You?*' He pressed the knuckle of one finger into the bridge of his nose. 'Vittorio,' he said, looking up, 'don't mind me asking this, but are you all right? Health-wise, I mean? Is there something you're not telling me?'

Vittorio shook his head. 'Never better.'

Marcello looked as if he didn't believe him. What was his problem? The women were nice enough, certainly, and they'd given him enough cues to let him know that they wouldn't say no if he did ask. It was just that when it came down to it he hadn't felt like taking them to bed.

'Okay,' said a weary-sounding Marcello. 'Then all I can suggest to sort this out is to flip a coin.' He held out his hand. 'Have you got one on you?'

'No,' he said, turning back to the canal and looking in the direction of the Dorsodura *sestiere*, where her hotel was situated. But he did have an earring.

'Is there something out there?' asked Marcello, coming closer to see for himself. 'Something that I'm missing?'

'No,' Vittorio said.

Not something. Someone. He'd always intended to return Rosa's earring and, given that he was back in Venice, there was no time like the present.

Serendipity.

'I have to go,' he said, already heading for the stairs.

'But, Vittorio, you need to make a decision—'

'Later,' he said. *'Ciao.'*

Vittorio strode purposefully through the narrow streets of Venice. He wasn't wearing leather today, nor even a swirling cloak, and yet people still moved out of his way when they saw him coming, flattening themselves against the walls of the *calles* or ducking into shop and café doorways.

He barely noticed. He was a man on a mission and he was too busy working out how long it had been since he'd seen her to care. Carnevale… Six weeks ago? Seven? Did she still work at the same hotel? Was she still in Venice or had she moved on? Or gone home to her tiny village in Puglia?

The sooner he got to the hotel, the sooner he'd find out. Eventually he found it—a shabby-looking hotel, tucked away in the corner of a square with a tiny canal running down one side. The entire side of the wall looked as if it was leaning into it.

He marched through the entry doors that announced it as Palazzo d'Velatte into a tiny foyer and saw heads swivel towards him. He marched towards a thin man sporting a backwards horseshoe of hair and standing behind a tiny counter. He wouldn't swear on a stack of bibles, but he was sure he saw the man swallow.

'Are you checking in?' he asked, craning his neck so high there was no missing the Adam's apple in his throat, bobbing up and down.

'No. I'm looking for someone who works here. A woman.'

'Erm…' The man offered a simpering smile. 'We don't offer that kind of service.'

'She's a cleaner. Her name is Rosa. Does she still work here?'

'I'm not sure I can divulge that—'

Vittorio leaned over the reception desk. 'Does. She. Still. Work. Here?'

The man's eyes bugged. 'Well, yes, but…' His eyes darted to his watch. 'She won't finish her shift for another two hours.'

'So she's working today? In this hotel?'

'Well, yes…'

Vittorio smiled—although it was probably more of a baring of his teeth, because he noticed he didn't get one in return. 'Then I'll find her myself.'

He looked around the tiny foyer, spied a likely set of stairs and set off.

'Wait!' the man called. 'You can't do that.'

'Watch me,' he said, taking the steps three at a time.

There were only three levels. It shouldn't take long.

On the first level he found nothing.

On the second level he found a cleaner backing out of a room and towing a vacuum cleaner behind her.

'Rosa?' he asked.

The woman looked up. She was a pretty woman, with bright eyes and dark curly hair tied back in a ponytail behind her head, but definitely not Rosa.

Her eyes narrowed when she saw him. She straightened, looking him up and down, frankly assessing. 'You're looking for Rosa?'

'Do you know where I can find her?'

'Your name wouldn't be Vittorio, by any chance?'

'What if it is?' he said.

Her eyes widened in appreciation before they flicked upwards. 'In that case, she's working the floor above.'

It was the worst day of her life. She'd started the morning throwing up and now, after confronting the room of some guests who had clearly thought last night was party night, only to lose the 'party' they'd consumed all over the bathroom, she kept right on heaving while she cleaned up the mess and cleared away the soiled towels. They were empty retches, because there was nothing in her stomach to bring up, but that didn't stop her retching all the same.

But she could hardly beg off work, because she needed this job and she didn't need anyone knowing she was pregnant. Not until she'd worked out what to do.

Dio, she felt so drained.

She replaced all the towels in the now clean bathroom with fresh ones and then caught sight of her reflection in the bathroom mirror as she swung around. She was shocked at what she saw. She looked like a ghost of herself. Her dull, lifeless eyes were too big for her head, and her hair stuck together in tendrils around her face after her temperature had spiked during each pointless yet violent round of dry heaving.

She needed to take a moment to get herself straightened up before anyone saw her like this.

'Rosa!' someone called in a booming deep voice, and a shudder went down her spine and sent the muscles clenching between her thighs.

She knew that voice. She'd heard it in her dreams at night. She'd imagined hearing it a hundred times a day in the crowded *calles* and the market stalls along the busy canals. She'd looked around, searching for the source, but it had never been him, of course.

'Rosa!' she heard—even closer.

Her heart thudded loudly in her chest. She wasn't imagining it this time. She peeked out of the bathroom to see a bear of a man entering the room. So tall and broad, with his mane of hair brushed back from his face, his carved features fixed into a frown.

'Vittorio…' she whispered, before her insides twisted on a rush of heat and sent her lurching once more for the pan.

There was nothing to lose. Nothing to give up but the strength in her bones and any shred of self-respect she'd ever had as she gagged where she'd flopped, huddled on the floor. But for him to see her this way was beyond cruel.

And yet he was by her side in an instant, pressing a damp towel to her heated forehead, his big hand on her back, as if lending her strength. As if he were saying, *I'm here*.

Gradually the churning eased, the spasms passed. She had the strength to lean back, to take the dampened towel from his hands and press it to her face. *Dio*, how could she let him see her ghastly face?

'What are you doing here?' she said, between gasps.

'What's wrong with you?' he replied, ignoring her question. 'You're ill.'

'No,' she said, trying to struggle to her feet.

She was confused. She still had rooms to clean, and Vittorio was here, and she didn't understand any of it.

When she turned, Chiara was there at the door to the room, silently watching.

'Are you going to tell him?' she said.

'Tell me what?' he said, looking from one woman to the other, but she could see by the dawning realisation on his face that he was already working it out for himself.

She looked up into a face that spoke of power and strength and everything she lacked in this moment, and told him. 'I'm so sorry, Vittorio, but I'm pregnant.'

He roared. A cry of anguish or triumph she couldn't be sure. But before she could decide she was swept up into his strong arms and cradled against his chest. She could have protested. She was hardly an invalid. She could walk. But instead of protesting she simply breathed him in, The scent was as she remembered. Masculine. Evocative. It was all she could do not to melt into the *whump-thump* of his heart in his chest.

'Where is her room?' she heard him say.

Followed by Chiara's voice. 'I'll show you.'

'I have to finish my shift,' she said weakly.

'No, you don't.'

He laid her down on her bed. Reverently. Gently. As if she were a fragile piece of glass blown by a master craftsman rather than made of flesh and blood.

'Leave us,' he told Chiara, and the usually bossy but now boggle-eyed Chiara didn't bother trying to argue with him and meekly withdrew.

He sat down beside her and smoothed the damp hair from Rosa's brow. 'It's mine?' he asked.

'What do you think?' she snapped, through a throat that felt raw from throwing up.

He smiled at that, although she didn't understand why. There was nothing funny that she could see about any of this.

He looked around at the tiny windowless room that contained two beds—cots, really—a small chest of drawers that doubled as a bedside table with a lamp between them, and a hanging rack filled with an assortment of clothes.

'This is where you live?'

She nodded, her strength returning enough that she could scoot herself upright with her back to the wall. 'With Chiara.'

'The two of you?' he asked, clearly aghast. 'Here? Barely above the water level?'

'It's not that bad. It's cheap for Venice. Chiara said it only floods at king tides, and not very often.'

He shook his head and swore softly under his breath. 'Have you seen a doctor?'

'Not yet,' she said. 'I was still—'

'Working out what to do about it?'

He'd stiffened as he said it and she noticed an edge to his voice. A harsh edge. Judgmental?

She swallowed. 'I was still coming to terms with it. I only found out a couple of days ago.'

He pulled out his phone, thumbing through it. 'When were you going to tell me?'

Rosa closed her eyes. Maybe this was another of her dreams. Maybe the hormones running through her bloodstream had turned her a little bit mad and she'd conjured Vittorio up—a combination of thin air and wishful thinking.

'Well?'

She opened her eyes, half surprised that he was still there. 'Chiara said you wouldn't want to know. That you probably had a wife and four *bambini* tucked away somewhere.'

'Why would you believe that when you were there that night? You heard what Sirena said. You knew my father wanted me to marry her. Why listen to Chiara?'

'Because you told me "one night and one night only."
That you didn't do for ever. It made as much sense as your
father wanting you to marry his friend's daughter.'

This time he swore out loud.

'You mean you *don't* have a wife and children somewhere?'

He smiled down at her, and then whoever he was calling
picked up. 'Elena, I need some help,' he said, and issued a
list of demands. 'We're going to get you seen to,' he said.
'My housekeeper is organising it. She knows everyone in
Venice. And meanwhile we're going out.'

She shook her head. 'I should get back to work. I've been
away too long already.'

'You're not going back to work today. If I have anything
to do with it you're never going to clean another room in
your life.'

'What?'

'Are you all right to walk now?'

She nodded. She felt a million times stronger than she
had before, but she was still confused. Nothing he said
made sense. The fact he was even here made no sense.

'Good. Then get changed,' he said, gently pressing his
lips to her forehead. 'I'm taking you out.'

'Where to?'

'First of all I'm taking you somewhere you can get a decent meal. You need feeding up. And then we're going to
sit down for a talk.'

He took her to a restaurant tucked away in an alleyway behind the Rialto Bridge, where the tables were dressed in
red and white checked tablecloths. Clearly they were off
the tourist trail, in a restaurant that catered to locals, because instead of the multitude of languages she was used
to hearing in the hotel and the *calles* the predominant language was Italian.

There they lunched on the best *spaghetti alle vongole* Rosa had ever tasted—but then, she wasn't just hungry by then, she was ravenous. The pasta with tiny clams filled a void inside her, and her once rebellious stomach welcomed every mouthful. Relished it.

Not even the presence of this man opposite could stop her. He seemed to heighten her appetite along with her senses. Maybe it was because he was content just to eat his own pasta as he watched her eat hers, watching approvingly every mouthful she consumed.

But there was something going on behind those cobalt blue eyes, she could see. Something that went beyond ensuring that she ate well. Something calculating. Unnerving.

'What have you been doing the last few weeks?' she asked between mouthfuls, wanting to break the tension, to see if she could encourage him to say what was on his mind.

'This and that,' he said, giving nothing away. 'What about you?'

'Same. Work, mostly. I was planning to take a few days off and go home. Rudi, one of my brothers, and his wife Estella are due to welcome their second child soon. But that was before I found out—well, you know.'

'Why wouldn't you still go home?'

She shook her head, halting her loaded fork halfway between bowl and mouth. 'I don't know that I can face my father or my family right now. I don't think my head's in the right place.'

'Will they even be able to tell so early?'

'It's not that. It's because I feel like I've let them down. Papà wanted me to live and see the world—he wouldn't have encouraged me to leave the village otherwise. But I don't think he was expecting this to happen. Not to me. Not so soon.'

'Would he be angry?'

'No. Not exactly. Probably just—disappointed.' She put her fork down and looked up at him. 'And isn't that worse?'

Vittorio didn't know. He had a father who specialised in anger. He'd got so used to disappointing his father over the years it was no longer a deterrent. If it ever had been. It had become more like a blood sport between them rather than a familial relationship.

Rosa finished off the last of her pasta and leaned back in her seat. 'That was amazing. Thank you.'

'Good,' he said. 'And now we need to talk.'

'I'm ready,' she said.

But he shook his head, looking at the tables full of diners clustered around them—tables full of diners who all spoke Italian and who might overhear. 'Not here.'

She had to hand it to Vittorio—if you had to sit down to have a talk you could find a worse venue than floating down the Grand Canal. She'd raised her eyebrows when he'd stopped at the gondola stand, but he'd merely shrugged and said, 'When in Venice...' and handed her into the gently rocking vessel.

He was doing it again—sweeping her out of her world and into his—but this time there was no panic. No fear. Because it was broad daylight and she knew enough about him to trust him. Besides, it was his child that she carried in her womb. His seed that had taken root.

Once they were seated on the golden bench the gondolier set off, sweeping his oar rhythmically behind them in the time-honoured way, sending the long, sleek vessel effortlessly skimming over the surface of the canal.

All these months she'd been in Venice and never once had she taken a gondola ride. It was something for the tourists, and hideously expensive in her eyes, but here on the water you gained a different perspective. It was seeing

Venice as it was meant to be seen, from the watery streets that made up its roadmap.

For a while they were content to take in the views and point out the sights as they slid under the magnificent white Rialto Bridge, with its eleven arches, crowded with tourists looking down at the passing traffic, looking down at them with envy.

And if Venice in the fog had been atmospheric and mystical, under the pale blue skies of spring it turned magical. It was as if the city had been reborn and emerged fresh and renewed from under its winter coat.

The colours of the buildings popped. Red brickwork stained with salt, pastel pink and terracotta, Tuscan yellows and even shades of blue trimmed with white competed for attention as they stood shoulder to shoulder above the slick green-grey waters of the canal.

And at its heart were the waterways they traversed, the canals alive with *vaporetto* and motorboats and gondolas all fighting for space. For a few minutes they were just two more tourists, enjoying the sights and sounds.

And there, with Vittorio smiling at her, she couldn't imagine a place she'd rather be—not even at home in her village, with her *papà* and her brothers and their families nearby. It was magical. And the most magical thing about it was that Vittorio was actually here, bursting into her life as suddenly as he had on that cold, fog-bound night of Carnevale.

It was no wonder that she'd missed him. No wonder that she'd dreamed of him. He was tall and broad and powerful. He was larger than life. He was—*more*. More than anything she'd ever experienced before. And he made her feel more alive than she'd ever felt.

At one stage she was smiling up at the bridge they were about to pass under when she turned and saw the he was taking a photograph of her. She tried to protest. 'I would have made more of an effort,' she said, pulling her hair away from her face.

'You look beautiful,' he said, and her heart felt as if it would bursting.

And still the question that he had not yet answered hung between them.

'Why did you come today?' she asked. 'I never expected to see you again.'

'I came with one purpose. But now you have given me another.'

Her brow furrowed with confusion. 'I don't understand…'

He took her hand in his. 'I wanted to see you, even if briefly. And seeing you again has reminded me. We were good together, Rosa.'

Sensation skittered down her spine. She blinked. She hadn't known what to expect, but certainly not that. 'It's good to see you.'

More than good. She'd dreamed about him. Had replayed every moment of their lovemaking until she could run it on a loop in her head, and the experience was still as exciting as it had been the first time.

He smiled as he pressed her hand to his lips. 'What are you going to do?'

Back to that. She looked at the buildings, glorious relics of centuries gone by and still defying the logic that said buildings must be built on solid ground.

She turned back to him. 'What can I do? I have so few options. But I want to do what's best for the baby.'

He nodded and squeezed the hand he still held.

'Marry me.'

The words were gone before she could grasp and process them, lost on the lapping waters and the hustle and bustle and sounds of the busy canal. She couldn't have heard right.

'*Scuzi?*'

'Marry me. Our child will have a mother and a father and you'll have no need to feel ashamed when you go home. And you'll never have to clean another hotel bathroom in your life.'

She laughed. 'Don't be ridiculous, Vittorio. I don't expect a proposal. That's crazy.'

'Rosa, I mean it.'

She looked up into his face and the fervent look in his blue, blue eyes stopped her in her tracks. 'You're actually serious?'

'Of course I'm serious.'

'But it's so sudden. You can't make a decision like that so quickly.'

'I already have.'

'But *I* can't!'

The idea was ridiculous. There were all kinds of reasons why it made no sense. They barely knew each other. And it was so early in her pregnancy—anything could happen, and then they'd be stuck together, and one or both of them would resent it for ever.

The gondola slipped slowly down the sinuous canal and the richly decorated *palazzos* drifted by, at odds with the turmoil going on in Rosa's mind.

She'd always wanted to marry for love. She wanted what her mother and father had shared before her mother had been cruelly wrenched from them by her disease: a deep, abiding love, the kind of love that took death to break it apart.

She knew that it was no idle dream, no fantasy that she aspired to, that she wished for herself. She'd witnessed it first-hand, initially with her grandparents and then with her parents, and she wanted it for herself. More than that, she believed she deserved it.

So this—Vittorio's bizarre offer—wasn't how it was supposed to be. This was all wrong. She was pregnant by a man she'd met only once before and now he was asking her to marry him because of the baby she was carrying.

It was so not how she'd imagined a proposal to be.

It would be crazy to say yes.

Even if a part of her was tempted.

She gasped in a breath as she numbly watched the passing parade. How many nights had she lain awake, when all was silent aside from Chiara's soft breathing, and thought about that night? Replaying the events, the emotions, the heart-stopping pleasures of the flesh he'd revealed to her? He'd taught her so much. Had given her so much.

For how many nights had she dreamed he would come for her?

And here he was.

And if a city could defy logic and be built atop the sea then maybe what he said could make some kind of sense too. He'd come for her today. Despite saying they'd never see each other again.

He'd tilted her world off its axis in just one night. If he could do that, then maybe it wasn't so impossible. Maybe they had what it took to make a marriage work?

She turned back to him. 'Did you come here today to ask me to marry you?' she asked.

'No,' he said, slipping his hand into his trouser pocket. 'Otherwise I would have come prepared with a ring to offer you. But I do have this…'

And there, in the palm of his hand, lay her grandmother's gold and pearl earring.

Her hand went to her mouth as her heart skipped a beat. She could scarcely believe it. She reached down to touch it, still not believing it was real, curling her fingers around the precious item, still warm from being tucked away next to Vittorio's body.

'This is the reason I came today. I found it nestled on your pillow after you had gone.'

She looked up at him. 'But I went to your *palazzo*. Your housekeeper said nothing had been found.'

'She didn't know. I intended to return it before now.'

'I thought I'd lost it for ever.'

'I meant to have Elena package it up and send it to you. But then, if I had…'

She looked up at him as electricity zipped down her spine. 'You might never have found out about the baby.'

He smiled down at her. 'Serendipity,' he said.

And she curled the hand holding the earring close to her chest, tears of gratitude, of relief, of joy, pricking at her eyes.

'Or maybe fate, or even destiny.'

Or magic, she thought as he pulled her into his kiss. *Don't forget magic.*

It was like coming home, her lips meeting his, their warm breath intermingling, the taste of him in her mouth. And she wondered if a day that had started so badly, so desolate and without hope, could get any better.

He drew back as the gondolier drew his vessel into a private dock outside a *palazzo*. And even though it had been foggy the one night he'd brought her here she would have recognised it in a heartbeat.

Vittorio's *palazzo*.

He was on his feet and had leapt onto the deck like a natural before he handed her out of the vessel. He slipped the gondolier some notes and then collected her arm to lead her inside.

'There's one more thing I need to tell you. One more reason you need to agree to marry me.'

CHAPTER TWELVE

'Now I *KNOW* this is some kind of joke.' Rosa burst from the chair she'd been settled in, needing to pace the room in long, frantic strides. 'You can't do this to me, Vittorio. You can't ask me to marry you—can't try to convince me to marry you with your kisses and your sweet talking about destiny and fate—and then drop a bombshell by telling me you're a prince. The Prince of Andachstein, no less!'

'Rosa, calm down.'

'How do you expect me to calm down? How did you think I'd react? That I would bow and scrape and be grateful that I've been offered this royal condescension? Am I supposed to be humbled? Or intimidated? Or both?'

'Rosa, listen!'

'No. I don't want to listen. I'm going home.'

She turned towards the doors—gilt-framed doors, elaborately carved with tigers and elephants, just one more treasure in a *palazzo* dripping with treasures of Murano glass and crystal chandeliers and rich velvet-upholstered antiques.

And it wasn't as if she hadn't noticed the insane luxury of this *palazzo* before. How had she accepted his explanation that it was simply somewhere he stayed without realising that he must have connections to the rich and famous—or that he must be one of them? Had she been so blinded by lust at that stage that she hadn't cared to notice? That she hadn't been able to see what was in front of her face?

She sniffed. 'Don't bother showing me out. I found the way myself once before. I can find my way home.'

'What? Home to your squalid basement apartment and your hand-to-mouth cleaning job? Home to throwing up every morning while you clean up somebody else's mess? Why would you want to go back to that life when I can offer you so much more?'

She spun on her heel. 'Because it's *my* life, Vittorio,' she said, her hands over her chest. 'It might be hard, and it might involve cleaning up the filth and garbage of other peoples' lives, but it's the life I choose to lead because that's the life I know. That's the world I belong to—not yours.'

'And you think, therefore, that that's the only life you deserve? You sell yourself short, Rosa. I would never have expected that.'

'I thought you belonged to my world too. At least that you were closer to my world. When you took me to the party that night you made me think that you were on the fringes of Marcello's world. "He's descended from the *doges* of Venice," you told me. I asked you how you knew such people. "Friends," you said. Your father and his were friends. Just friends. You let me think your father worked for him, and yet your father sits on the throne of Andachstein. Were you laughing at me when I told you I understood? When I told you about my father working for the mayor of our small village? Because you should have been. You sure made a fool out of me.'

'No! You constructed your own story. You believed what you wanted to believe.'

'You could have told me then how wrong I was. But you didn't make one effort to correct me.'

'How was I supposed to tell you? If I'd told you I was a

prince in that square would you have believed me? Would you have come with me?'

'Of course not!'

'You see?'

'No! You could have told me you were a prince when we were in the garden before the party.'

'And would you have believed me then?'

She wavered. *Probably not.* But still… 'Look, we slept together. But you can't be serious. You can't expect me to marry you.'

'Rosa,' he said, 'what are afraid of?'

'I'm not afraid.'

'Aren't you? Weren't you ready to say yes to me before, when you thought I was just a man?'

'Well, maybe…'

'Then what's changed? Unless you're afraid that you're not good enough to be a princess? Is that what you're telling me? That you don't deserve it?'

'You should have told me.'

'Did you tell me you were a virgin? Before you were in my bedroom, having already agreed to make love?'

'Maybe not—but it's not like that puts us on an even footing. After all, you're *still* a prince.'

He didn't need her to spell it out. What he needed was for her to agree to marry him.

'Why are you so angry with me? You wanted me to make love to you that night.'

'Yes. I wanted you to make love to me. *You.* Vittorio. The man I met that night. Not the Prince of some random principality I've barely heard of. I wasn't there for *him*.'

'Does it matter? I'm still the same person.'

'Of course it matters! You're next in line to the throne of Andachstein. Royalty. I'm a girl from a tiny village in the heel of Italy. Don't you think there's something of a power imbalance there?'

'I do. But there's another one that we have to deal with. Because you're the one who holds all the cards.'

'I don't see how. Like I said, you're still a prince, whatever I decide.'

'But you're the one carrying the heir.'

She blinked. 'But if we don't—if I don't—'

'There's no escaping it,' he said. 'You can't just sidestep being the mother to the heir of a throne.'

She kicked up her chin. 'It might be a girl. Surely a girl can't be the heir to the throne in a principality steeped in antiquity? Surely the throne can't go to an accidental princess?'

'That's why I'm taking you to a clinic, so that we can find out.' He looked at his watch. 'It's time we were leaving.'

'I didn't say I was going to marry you even if it is a boy.'

'And you didn't rule it out. Let's go.'

'But it's too early to tell,' she said.

'No,' he said. 'It's not.

Rosa could scarcely believe it—that a blood test that took only a few moments could deliver them the sex of their unborn child at such an early stage. But the doctor taking the sample of her blood had assured her it was correct.

'This test is not commercially available yet, but it is accurate in determining the sex of an unborn baby with up to ninety-five percent certainty.'

'What if it's one of the five per cent?' she said while they sat quietly together afterwards. 'What if it is a girl?'

'I'll take that risk. Meanwhile, you carry my son and the heir to the throne of Andachstein. You can say no to marrying me. You can walk away from this marriage if you choose. But in doing so, know that you are denying our child his rightful destiny.'

'You would put that load on my shoulders?'

'The load is already there. It is up to you what you decide to do with it.'

She turned away, her mind reeling. The pregnancy. The arrival of Vittorio. Finding out he was a prince. A proposal of marriage.

It was like being bombarded from every side with no respite. There was no time to take anything in. No time to process anything. And yet she had to make a decision that would impact her entire life—and that of their unborn child.

She swallowed. 'And if I agree to marry you?'

'Then our son will be brought up to assume his rightful place in Andachstein, with all the rights, privileges and responsibilities that go with it.'

She thought about the tiny basement flat that would never do to bring up a child in. She thought about her home in Zecce, a tiny dot of a dusty village in Puglia, where their child would grow up happy—she would make sure of that—but in no way in wealth or the lap of luxury. And she thought about this *palazzo* that would be part of his heritage, and no doubt much more besides.

Would it be fair to deprive their son of all that because his father had neglected to inform her that he was a prince?

And the biggest question of them all. What about love? Where did love factor in? He'd said nothing of love.

'What about love?' she asked, her throat so dry she had to force the words out.

'We'll both love our son,' he said.

She squeezed her eyes shut. So that was how it was. She'd read far too much into his sudden arrival, his kind attention, his comfort and his care. She'd read far too much into a romantic gondola ride and the fact that he'd wanted to see her again to return her grandmother's earring, as if it meant something.

But it had been an accident that he'd turned up. A twist of fate. He hadn't come for her at all—he was simply returning a piece of jewellery. And now the only reason he wanted her to stay was because she was having his baby. The child of a prince.

'You're using me,' she said.

'No.'

'Yes! You used me before and now you're using me again. But this time because I'm carrying your child.'

'It's not like that.'

'Isn't it? Then what would you call it? Blackmail? A world of spun gold for my child if I agree to marry you? Otherwise he lives the life of a peasant?'

'Think of the child. It's the best thing for the child. The fair thing.'

She spun away. She didn't want to hear it. Because part of her knew he was right. How could she say no and deprive their child of its birthright?

But this was not how her dreams had looked. Vittorio had come for her, yes, but not the way she'd imagined. Not for love. And now her dreams were turned to dust, and her hopes of love with them.

She couldn't help but wonder whether he had loved his first wife. A stab of jealousy pierced her heart. Or perhaps this was just how royal families did things—even in the twenty-first century—cold, loveless, contractual marriages.

How could she live without love? It was the foundation stone of her very existence. But then, how could she live without Vittorio? Without his touch? With just her dreams to sustain her, to mock her, when she could have the real thing even in the absence of love.

How could she wake up from those dreams to a sense of devastating loss and know that things could have been different if only she hadn't been so headstrong? So proud?

'Think of the child,' he'd said.

And she was. But she was thinking about herself too. Thinking about parting from this man one last time after he'd found her again, and how much harder this time would be when it didn't have to be this way.

In the end, when it came down to it, he wasn't offering her a choice at all.

'All right,' she whispered, feeling her life spiralling out of control. 'I'll marry you.'

But not without conditions.

CHAPTER THIRTEEN

MARCELLO ANSWERED VITTORIO'S call on the third ring. 'I was wondering when I was going to hear from you again,' Marcello said. 'Have you come to your senses and made a decision yet?'

'You'll be delighted to know I have.'

'So who's the lucky lady? Katerina or Inga?'

'Neither.'

'What kind of game are you playing now?' Marcello sounded as if he was at the end of his tether. 'You know—'

'I know. I have to marry someone. So I am. I'm marrying Rosa.'

There was a pause at the end of the line. 'You don't mean—the woman from that night at Carnevale? The one you brought to the party?'

'The very same.'

Marcello snorted. 'Well, it's good you've made a decision, but how is your father going to react to that news?'

'It's other news that might just swing it. She's pregnant, Marcello, and—get this—she's having a boy.'

'You sly dog. You've been seeing her, then. That explains why your heart wasn't seriously in the hunt for a bride.'

'No, I haven't seen her since Carnevale. Not until today.'

'Ah,' said Marcello. 'She must have made quite an impression on you, in that case. I'm beginning to see why you might have been off your game. If you'd told me you were besotted with the woman it would have saved everyone a lot of time and effort.'

Vittorio growled. 'Stop talking rubbish, Marcello!'

'When are you going to tell your father?'

'As soon as Rosa's father agrees to the marriage.'

There was a pause at the end of the line. 'You—Prince Vittorio of Andachstein—are going to ask a woman's father for permission to marry her? After you've already taken certain liberties with his daughter, evidenced by the fact that she's pregnant with your child?'

Vittorio wished his friend wouldn't make such a big deal out of every single thing. 'Rosa's giving up a lot. She wants to do at least this part the old-fashioned way. We're travelling to Puglia this weekend.'

'And you have agreed?'

'Rosa insisted I meet her family and ask his permission or no wedding.'

'I like this woman more and more,' Marcello declared, chuckling down the phone line. 'I'm so glad to know you're not getting yourself a doormat. But, Vittorio, have you thought about what you're going to do if her father says no?'

'*Ciao,*' Vittorio said, putting his phone down on the coffee table.

Rosa's father wasn't going to say no. He couldn't.

As for not getting a doormat—he was well aware of that. He'd seen the way she'd stood up to Sirena that night, refusing to be cowed. He'd seen the way she'd stood up to him, insisting that she wasn't going to give up her job and move into the *palazzo* until such time as her father had given permission and the wedding was confirmed to proceed.

He shook his head as he looked around him at the luxurious fittings and furniture of the *palazzo*, all with a view of the Grand Canal. Why she would want to stay in that job and live in her dingy room when she could have all this, he didn't know. But it seemed important to her, and he figured she might as well enjoy what freedom she had now.

Soon enough she would be married to him and she'd find herself bound up in palace protocol and demands that she had no say in. She might as well enjoy her independence now.

He shook his head. No doormat there. With Rosa he was getting the whole package. A woman who could light up his nights, to please him—and who had already proved herself a breeder, to please his father.

What could be better than that?

Unless it was the child. A son.

His son.

It was something he'd yearned for once. Something he'd waited for with every passing month of his marriage. He'd expected it to happen quickly. After all, nothing else had been a problem. He'd been served up a bride he'd fallen madly in love with. All he'd needed was the news that he would become a father and the royal line of Andachstein would live on, his destiny fulfilled.

It had all seemed so easy in those bright, halcyon days. Except his wait had been fruitless. And then he'd discovered the reason why, and his world had turned sour and rancid, with bitterness usurping hope.

This child was like a reclaimed dream. A second chance. But he wouldn't make the same mistake again. He was taking no chances if this marriage didn't work out. He wasn't about to risk losing himself in the process.

There were some places he wouldn't go again.

Love was one of them.

CHAPTER FOURTEEN

IT WAS A two-hour drive from Bari Airport to Zucca. First along the straight highway that crossed the ankle of Italy, before turning on to narrower and yet narrower roads that meandered past stone walls and olive groves through the undulating countryside.

The sprinkle of towns and villages here seemed mostly deserted, except for the odd herd of goats and the brightly coloured pots of geraniums and the bougainvillea clambering over crumbling walls. Here and there an old man in a chair outside his house would lift a lazy hand as they passed.

Summer felt closer here, in this far southern region of Italy. The sky was clear blue, the air was clean and warm, and the late April sun held the promise of hot, airless summer days.

Along the route Rosa told Vittorio about her family. There was her father, Roberto, her three brothers, Rudi, Guido and Fabio, and their wives, Estella, Luna and Gabriella. There were three *bambini* between them now, with the addition of Rudi and Estella's second child, born just a week ago. The first granddaughter had been a cause of much excitement, and had been named Maria Rosa after her late grandmother and her aunt.

Vittorio tried to pay attention and take it all in, but it was hard when his gut was roiling. Oddly, he was never afraid to meet his own father, to put up with his disappointment and even his anger, but he was nervous about meeting Roberto. Rosa's father was an unknown quantity, and he suspected that the man wasn't about to be dazzled by his title.

'They're all going to be so excited to learn there's going to be another cousin soon.'

'You don't think it's too early to tell them about the baby?' Vittorio asked.

Rosa wasn't showing yet—not in a way anybody else would notice. Surely only he would appreciate the extra fullness to her breasts and what it meant.

'If we're going to get married because I'm having your baby,' she said, 'why should we pretend otherwise?'

He looked across at her in the passenger seat. There was a strange note to her voice, as if it was fraying around the edges and she was straining to hold it together.

'Are you tired?' he said. They had made an early start to make it to Zucca by lunchtime, and with the flight and then the undulating road he wouldn't be surprised if she was feeling a little motion sick.

'I'm fine,' she said, looking out of her window.

'Is everything all right?'

She sighed, still keeping her head turned away. 'Everything's fine.'

He grunted. Clearly something was wrong, but he wasn't about to argue the point. He'd given her plenty of opportunity to say if anything was bothering her.

They didn't speak for the final ten minutes of their journey, and when they pulled up outside the stone walls of her family home they didn't have to announce their arrival. Their vehicle had obviously been heard, because a swarm of people piled out of the house, their faces beaming, their arms outstretched.

Rosa just about bounded from the car, casting off her strange glumness like a cloak, laughing and squealing as she was gathered into the warm embrace of her family. The realisation that he was somehow the cause of her mood ratcheted up his own grumpiness.

He leaned against the car, his arms crossed, watching the reunion. Such a foreign, unknown thing—like an object he had to study to work out the very shape and texture of it.

So this was family?

Everyone seemed to be speaking at once, voices piling up one over another, men and women, and the two older babies were being passed around so that Rosa could hug them and cluck over them and remark on how much they'd grown. And there was Rosa, in the midst of the celebrations, hugging and laughing and happy. Everyone was happy.

In the background, with his hands on his hips as he watched on, stood the man who had to be her father. He wasn't as tall as his three sons, but he stood broad-shouldered and rosy-cheeked and proud as he waited for a chance to welcome his daughter home.

'Papà!' he heard her squeal when she saw him, and then they were in each other's arms and everyone was crying and whooping and back-slapping some more.

And then, as if Vittorio were an afterthought, Rosa said something and all heads swivelled towards him. In their gazes he saw interest and suspicion, curiosity and mistrust—until Rosa came back and claimed his hand and pulled him into the fray, introducing him to them all.

It was because he was with her that they welcomed him, he had no doubt. And even if they didn't trust him they welcomed him as Rosa's friend, and not as the heir to the throne of a tiny principality that had been irrelevant to their family until now. He knew who mattered here and it wasn't him, and he felt the power imbalance that she'd pointed out as existing between them tilt markedly the other way.

In Venice she was alone. Vulnerable.

But here she was surrounded by her family, like a guard all around her, and *he* was the outsider, the one who had to prove himself.

They sat down under a vine-covered pergola at a table already spread with platters of antipasto and cheeses and crusty loaves of bread, all sprinkled with dappled light. Rosa handed out gifts for the babies. Gifts she'd made. Sailor suits for the boys and a lacy gown she'd made for the tiny Maria Rosa. Everyone praised Rosa's needlework—gifts she'd made herself on her mother's beloved old sewing machine and all the more special for it.

'Tell us about Andachstein,' Rudi said, pouring ruby-red Puglia wine into glasses.

And Vittorio found himself telling them all about the principality—a gift of the far corner of his lands by an ancient monarch, bestowed upon a knight in return for faithful service. He told them about the *castello*, set high on the hilltop above the sparkling harbour far below. He told them of the landscape, of the rugged wooded hills and the pathways lined with thyme and rosemary that scented the air.

They all listened with rapt attention while they ate and drank wine. Rosa's beautiful eyes were the widest, and she looked both excited and afraid. He realised he'd never spoken to her of the place where she would one day live.

He squeezed her hand to reassure her and the conversation moved on.

The three wives were about to prepare the next course when the sound of a baby crying came from inside the house.

'I'll come and help with lunch,' said Rosa.

'No, you stay,' said Estella, 'I need you here. Wait.'

She was back a few minutes later, dropping a bundle on Rosa's lap. 'Say hello to your auntie Rosa, Maria.'

Rosa's eyes lit up as she took the tiny bundle. 'Oh, Estella, she's beautiful. Look at those big eyes…and such long hair!' The child blinked up at her, her rosebud mouth still moving, tiny hands crossed over her chest.

Vittorio watched as Rosa cradled the child in her arms. Not a two-year-old this time, and not an eleven-month-old like he'd seen her hold before, already halfway to childhood. This was practically a newborn.

And he was struck by the beauty of the tableau.

Something shifted inside him at that moment. It shifted the tiniest of fractions, and yet it was so momentous that for a few moments his throat choked shut.

In a few months Rosa would be holding their child. And if she could look so beautiful, so beatific, holding somebody else's child, how much more rapturous would she look when she was holding theirs?

Everything she did told him that he was doing the right thing. She would be the perfect mother.

'You are so lucky to go to the city and meet your handsome man,' said Luna, generously ladling pasta into bowls that got passed from hand to hand around the table. 'You would never have found anyone as good-looking as Vittorio in the village.'

'Hey,' said Guido, looking aggrieved. 'What's that supposed to mean?'

'Exactly what it sounds like,' said Fabio, rolling his eyes. 'Apparently all the hot guys are in the cities.'

'No,' Rudi said, the voice of authority. 'Luna means all the good men are already taken, don't you, Luna?'

'Is that what you meant, Luna?' laughed Gabriella, clearly not convinced.

Estella laughed too. 'I could have sworn you meant something else entirely.'

'These women,' Rudi said, shaking his head. 'They are something else.' He pointed a finger at their guest in warning. 'Vittorio,' he said, 'don't expect Rosa is going to be any different. And don't, whatever you do, think that she's going to be a pushover. These women, they have a mind of their own.'

'Rudi!' Rosa scolded.

Vittorio just looked sideways at Rosa and smiled. 'I'll keep that in mind.'

Rosa's father wasn't old—not in years anyway—but the creases in his leathered face and the oil stains on his hands spoke of a man who had not just worked but rather had laboured his entire life. A man who had suffered the devastating loss of his wife but who had carried on, welcoming the new generation of Ciavarros one by one.

'Come,' he said to Vittorio after the family had sated themselves on the feast the women had prepared. 'We need to have a talk, man to man.'

Rosa squeezed Vittorio's hand as he rose to follow Roberto. He was inordinately grateful for the gesture. It was ridiculous, but he hadn't felt this nervous since he was a child, starting boarding school in Switzerland as a seven-year-old, when he'd felt as if he'd gone to a different world, with new languages to grapple with and comprehend, and older boys who'd seen a man-child and decided to take him down a peg or two before he was too big and he got the upper hand.

They left the family under the vine-covered pergola and Roberto led him to a patio on the other side of the house via the big kitchen, where he pulled a bottle and two shot glasses from a shelf.

Both men settled themselves down and Roberto poured a hefty slug into each glass, handing Vittorio one.

'To Rosa,' he said, and the pair clinked glasses.

The older man threw his down his gullet. Vittorio followed suit, and felt the liquor set fire to his throat and burn all the way down.

He set his glass on the table without feeling he'd disgraced himself, only to see Rosa's father top the glasses up.

'And to you, Vittorio,' he said, and downed the second glass.

Vittorio swallowed the fiery liquor down, feeling it burst into flames in his belly.

'It's good, no?' said Roberto. 'I make it myself.'

'Very good,' Vittorio agreed, thankful that his voice box still worked.

He was even more thankful to see the stopper placed back in the bottle.

'I hear you want to marry my daughter.'

'I've asked her, it's true.'

'She also tells me that she is carrying your child.'

Vittorio was catapulted right back to school again—to a summons to the headmaster's office for punching a boy who had been picking on a junior grader. He'd got the *don't think just because you're a prince* speech then, and he half expected to hear it again now.

'Also true.'

The other man nodded and sighed. 'Maria—my wife— was very beautiful. Rosa has her eyes.'

'They're beautiful eyes. The colour of warmed cognac,' Vittorio said.

'Yes,' said Roberto with a wide smile that smacked of approval. 'That's it. I used to tell Maria that I could get drunk just by looking into her eyes.' His eyes brightened. 'She would tell me, "Go and drink your grappa if you want to get drunk. I have work to do."' He laughed a little, then sniffed, ending on a sigh. 'There is a lot of Maria in Rosa. I can promise you, you will never be bored.'

'I know that.'

'But Rosa says that while she wants what's best for the *bambino*, she is not sure.'

His words were like a wet slap about the face.

'It's so sudden,' Vittorio said, 'and there's a lot Rosa will need to take on. It's not a normal marriage, in many respects.'

Roberto nodded. 'True. But then, what *is* a normal marriage? When it comes down to it, every marriage is a game of give and take, of compromise and of bending when one least wants to bend.'

And breaking, Vittorio thought. Sometimes marriages just broke you into pieces.

'Did Rosa tell you I was married once before?'

'*Si,*' he said, with a nod of his head. 'She says you are a widower.'

'It wasn't a good marriage and it didn't end well,' Vittorio said, studying his feet.

'You see,' Roberto said. 'We are not so different. You might be a prince, but we are both widowers, after all. We both know loss.'

'I guess we do,' he said.

'You know,' Roberto said, leaning back in his chair, 'when a man marries a woman for life, and he has a good marriage, and he only gets thirty years, that is nowhere near enough.' He shook his head. 'I am sorry that you haven't found this satisfaction—yet.'

He leaned forward, removing the stopper from the bottle again. He poured two more slugs before he put the stopper back, raised his glass.

'Here is to the marriage of you and Rosa,' he said. 'May it be a good one from the very beginning. And may it be a long one, filled with love.' He nodded, and said, 'I give you my blessing,' before downing the shot.

The liquor stuck in Vittorio's throat and burned. Or maybe it was her father's words as he'd blessed the union.

Love...

All Vittorio wanted from this marriage was the heir Rosa

was carrying. A spare would guarantee the principality's survival. Having Rosa in his bed would be a bonus.

But love?

Surely her father could see that this was a convenient marriage? That love didn't factor into it? Surely he wasn't that unworldly?

But what was he to say in the face of the man's reminiscences about his own loving marriage and his wishes for them to be happy? He could hardly tell Roberto that he would never let himself love his daughter, not when he had been embraced so warmly into the family. That was between him and Rosa.

The man had given his approval. Vittorio swallowed down on the burning in his throat. It didn't feel altogether comfortable, but wasn't Roberto's blessing the thing he'd come for?

The announcement was made. Roberto had given his blessing and the entire family would go to Andachstein for the wedding. Cheers ensued, but a ruddy-cheeked Roberto quelled them, because he had even more news to share— the secret Rosa had shared with him—that in a few months they would be welcoming a new baby into the family, his new grandson.

Bottles of Prosecco appeared from nowhere and corks popped. Toasts were made, backs were slapped, cheeks were kissed, and Vittorio found himself hugged by everybody, men and women, multiple times. His acceptance into the family was now beyond dispute.

The one person who didn't seem to want to hug him was the one he wanted to the most. Rosa had let him quickly kiss her on the lips as everyone had toasted the couple, before she'd swooped upon one of her nephews and sat down, hiding herself beneath him. She knew what she was doing.

She was using the child as a human shield. What he didn't understand was why.

He stood in a circle of men and watched her with the child, making a fuss of it, talking with her sisters-in-law and avoiding his eye. It was killing him. It had been so many weeks since he'd taken her to bed that magical night, and having her back in his life, being so close, was an exercise in frustration.

He burned for her. He wanted nothing more than to bury himself in her sweet depths.

But she'd refused to move into the *palazzo* with him. She'd refused to sleep with him. Not until everything was settled, she'd said.

He watched her laughing. Her hair was down today, curling over her shoulders, dancing in the light spring breeze, and her eyes were warm like cognac heated by a flame.

Well, everything was settled. Her father had given his approval of their marriage. The wedding would go ahead. Andachstein would have its heir.

And tonight he would hold Rosa and make love to her again.

The celebrations were on the wane by late afternoon, and one by one the brothers drifted off to their own homes with their families and sleepy babies. Roberto was sitting in an armchair, quietly snoring, when Rosa said she was tired and was going to turn in.

At last, thought Vittorio.

They collected their overnight bags from the car, and Vittorio felt his anticipation rising with every step back into the house. Rosa was wearing a dress splashed with big bright flowers today, with a full skirt, and a cardigan over her shoulders. He wasn't sure whether he was going to be able to wait to get the dress off before he rucked up her skirt and took her.

'I hope my family wasn't too much for you today,' she said.

'No,' he said as he followed her through the house, his hands itching to hold her, to glide over her skin, smooth as satin. 'You have a good family. Noisy, but good.'

She laughed a little over her shoulder. 'Definitely noisy.' And then she opened a door. 'Here's where you're sleeping tonight.'

He stepped into the room, confused. He looked around. There was one single bed surrounded by girlie things. A basket of dolls in one corner. Pictures of Rosa growing up. Artwork that she must have done as a child on the walls and a poster of a boy band she must have once followed.

'This is your old room?'

'It's the most comfortable single bed there is. It's yours tonight.'

He tried to pull her into his arms. 'But where are *you* sleeping? I thought that tonight we could celebrate our engagement.'

She laughed again and slipped out of his reach.

'Won't you stay with me?' he invited.

She shook her head. Her beautiful face was lit by a sliver of moonlight through the curtain, and he was reminded of liquid mercury and silver, fluid and impossible to contain.

'I can't make love to you under my father's roof.'

'He's asleep. He won't know.'

'*I'll* know,' she said, shaking her head, smiling softly.

He reached for her again, knowing he could change her mind if only she would let him kiss her. He knew she would melt in his arms. But she backed off to the door, all quicksilver and evasion.

'Then when?' he said, a cold bucket of resignation pouring down over him. 'When can we make love again?'

'Our wedding night, of course,' she said.

'What? But that's weeks away.' Three or four. Too many to contemplate.

'Then it will be all the more special for waiting.'

'Rosa,' he said, pleading now, raking one hand through his hair.

'No,' she said. 'You're getting what you want. Let me have this.'

'But do you know how long it's been?'

She smiled a sad, soft smile. 'I know how long it's been for me.' She blew him a kiss. 'Goodnight.'

Vittorio was alone. All alone in a single bed dressed with her sheets and her pillows and surrounded by her childhood things. All of which made it impossible to sleep. Impossible to relax.

It was like being tortured. Being so close to her, surrounded by her, but unable to touch her. It would be better to be sleeping under a tree somewhere far away.

With a groan, he gave up on sleep and got out of bed, snapping on the light. He moved to a big old chest of drawers and looked at the photos on top—photos of Rosa growing up.

There was one of her with a gap-toothed smile and pigtails at school. Even then her eyes had been beyond beautiful. Another showed her flanked by her brothers, all on bikes. Rosa had been a young teenager then, wearing shorts and a checked shirt, and there was a view of coastal cliffs and sea behind her. A family holiday by the sea. Another one had been taken of her between her mother and father.

Vittorio picked it up. Roberto was right. Rosa looked like a younger version of Maria. He touched a finger to her cheek and growled softly in the night. Soon she would be his. Soon there would be no more room for playing this game of look-but-don't-touch. Soon they would share a bed and much, much more.

And he thought of what Rosa's father had said to him, *'You will never be bored.'*

He believed him.

But, *Dio*, meanwhile he burned.

CHAPTER FIFTEEN

VITTORIO DIDN'T HAVE time to visit Andachstein and deliver the news to his father personally, but he was selfish enough not to want to miss his reaction when he heard the details of his marriage. He had Enrico set his father up to expect a video call the evening they returned to Venice.

At the appointed time Vittorio called, and a few moments later his father appeared on his screen, waving away his secretary. 'Yes, yes, I can manage this now, Enrico.'

Vittorio smiled. 'I've got news, Father.'

Guglielmo grunted as he turned his attention to the screen, and Vittorio could see his patience was already wearing thin.

'There's only one piece of news I'm interested in hearing, so this had better be good.'

'Then you're in luck. I'm getting married.'

'Huh,' he snorted. 'About time. I was hoping I might finally hear something once I had Enrico draw up that list. Who is it, then? Or have you finally managed to sort out your differences with the Contessa.'

'I'm not marrying Sirena.' The words were more satisfying than he'd expected. Far more satisfying.

'No?' The old Prince rubbed his jaw. 'I'm not sure how Sebastiano is going to take that.'

His father's surprise quickly turned to resignation, as Vittorio had suspected it would. Prince Guglielmo's friend's disappointment was not his most pressing concern. Getting his son married and producing heirs was. Just who provided those heirs was incidental.

'Then who is the lucky woman?'

'Her name is Rosa Ciavarro.'

His father frowned. 'I don't recall seeing anyone on Enrico's list by the name of Ciavarro.'

'She wasn't on Enrico's list. Her family come from the village of Zecce in the south of Italy.'

'A village, you say? Then who is her father?'

'Roberto Ciavarro.'

His father shook his head and looked even more perplexed. Vittorio smiled. He could enjoy letting his father fruitlessly search for connections, but then again there would also be a great deal of satisfaction in revealing the truth.

'I believe he runs the local gas station and motor vehicle repair shop. I hear his speciality is servicing Piaggio Apes.'

Colour flooded his father's cheeks, but to his credit he didn't blow. He was used to being baited by his son.

Vittorio let the news sink in for a second, before he offered, 'Apes are those three-wheel trucks that zip down the narrow laneways carrying produce to market.'

'I know what they are!' his father growled, and his son could almost feel the old man's temperature escalate. 'Don't treat me like an idiot.'

The old man looked upwards to the ceiling, almost as if he was hoping for divine intervention. When that didn't come, he sighed. 'So tell me,' he said, with the air of someone who couldn't be shocked any more than he already had been, 'what does this Rosa do?'

'She works in a hotel in Venice.'

His father swallowed, looking pained. 'Dare I ask in what capacity?'

'She's a maid. A cleaner.'

Closed eyes met that response, along with lips pressed

together tightly before they parted enough to say, 'A peasant. You want to marry a peasant. Is this some kind of joke?'

Vittorio knew that he'd well and truly blown that part of his brief. His bride was supposed to be the right kind of woman—someone eligible, from their own social strata, and preferably from the list Enrico had drawn up.

'Because I can tell you it's not funny from where I'm sitting. Can't you for once be serious about your responsibilities?'

Vittorio bristled. 'I've never been more serious about anything, Father. I'm going to marry Rosa.'

His father threw up his hands. 'What on earth for? I suppose you're going to get stars in your eyes and tell me you love the girl.'

'Of course I don't love her. When did this family ever marry for love?'

Guglielmo snorted. It was an agreement of sorts. An acknowledgement of the root cause of all that had been wrong with Vittorio's family. The age-old resentment that lay festering in Vittorio's gut sent up curling tendrils of bitterness. When had love ever come into anything this family did?

'Then why?'

'Because she's pregnant.'

His father shrugged, waving one hand in the air. 'Is that all? It happens. One might say with someone of your ilk it's an occupational hazard. You have the morals of a common alley cat, after all.'

'Perhaps, given my title, not quite so common.'

'Might as well be.' The aging Prince sniffed. 'Anyway, a mere pregnancy still doesn't mean you have to marry the wench. An heir is no good to us if it turns out to be a g—'

'She's having a boy.'

For the first time Vittorio saw his father pause and show just the slightest modicum of interest. The older man's eyes narrowed as he wheeled back, his gimlet eyes focused hard on his screen as he stroked his beard again. 'You're sure of that?'

'That's what the blood test results said.'

His father sighed and rested his head on his hand. 'But still…a commoner. A peasant, no less.'

'This is the twenty-first century, Father—think about it. The press will lap it up. It's a fairy-tale romance: the Prince and the maid…the ordinary girl who becomes a princess. And a royal baby as the icing on the cake. It's got newspapers and women's magazines across the world written all over it. And when has Andachstein ever had such good press coverage? Think what it will do for our economy. Our hotels and casinos will be filled to overflowing.'

'They're already filled in summer.'

'We'll build more, and those will be full in winter too.'

His father continued to trouble his neat white triangle of a beard, his expression conflicted, before his chin suddenly went up, jerking his beard out of his fingers. 'Do you have a picture of this girl?'

Vittorio pulled out his phone, finding the picture of Rosa he hadn't been able to resist taking that day on the gondola—the one with her dark eyes lit up and her cupid's-bow lips smiling, the wind scattering tendrils of her dark hair across her face. It was a picture that showed Rosa in all her unguarded beauty, raw and innocent—though he knew that she wasn't as innocent as she appeared.

He'd seen to that.

He held it to the screen, saw his father's eyes narrowing as he surveyed the photo, his fingers now more contemplative on his neat beard, and breathed a sigh of relief, knowing that she'd just passed one almighty test. Clearly his father agreed that Rosa would at least pass muster as a princess.

'She'll need instruction,' his father decreed. 'In grooming and, no doubt, in deportment. And she'll need education on the history of the principality and her future role and duties within it.'

Vittorio nodded as he pocketed the phone. 'She'll get it.'

'She's got a lot to catch up on before she can be let loose in public.'

'I said, she'll get it.'

'See that she does. I mean...' his father sighed before continuing '...a simple girl, plucked from a village...'

'Did I *say* she was simple?'

His father paused. 'You're right. She managed to get herself pregnant by a prince, didn't she?'

It was Vittorio's turn to shake his head. 'Father, for the record, she had no idea I was a prince. And she didn't get herself pregnant. *I* got her pregnant.'

Guglielmo waved his hand in the air dismissively. 'Yes, yes, a technicality. But it happened, and it proves she's a breeder. At least that takes care of who you're going to marry.'

Vittorio couldn't prevent the smile that followed his dinosaur of a father's words. 'Was that congratulations, Father? Because I can almost believe you consented to this marriage.'

The old Prince sniffed as he looked away from the screen and started shuffling his papers.

'I agree to this marriage,' he said, without looking up. 'Given that it is the only option I am apparently going to be presented with. But that does not mean I have to celebrate it.' He looked back at the screen, a look of confusion on his face, and then he yelled over his shoulder. 'Enrico! How do I turn this cursed contraption off?'

CHAPTER SIXTEEN

Rosa was almost looking forward to the next few weeks of wedding planning. She'd called Chiara while Vittorio was speaking with his father and given her the news, asking her to be her bridesmaid. She imagined they'd spend evenings together in their apartment, poring over bridal designs. She even entertained tentative plans to sew her own gown. There was enough time, if she could settle on a design and find the right fabric. And if her mother couldn't be there in person, Rosa felt, then at least her sewing machine could provide the magical means of sewing Rosa's wedding gown together.

But it seemed things didn't operate that way when you were going to marry a prince.

Vittorio returned from his call, looking smug and well satisfied, and announced that her time was up. He was moving her into the *palazzo* the very next day, in preparation for the wedding and her move to Andachstein.

Rosa dug her heels in. 'I don't see why.'

'There's every reason why. Because you're now my fiancée, and I can't guarantee your safety while you stay in that basement hovel you call a home.'

'Safety?' she said, really wishing her voice hadn't squeaked.

'You're going to be a princess, Rosa. As soon as the official announcement is made you're going to have people lining up wanting a piece of you. Reporters, the paparazzi, even conmen. All sorts of hangers-on.'

Maybe he was laying it on thick, but he hadn't been in a very good mood lately, and she had a lot to do with that.

'I've tolerated your obstinacy long enough. I can't protect you while you live in the basement of a hotel, where anyone and everyone can just walk in unchallenged. You'll be safer here.'

'I don't call it obstinacy. I call it independence.'

'Call it what you like. It's coming to an end. You're moving into the *palazzo*.'

'What about Chiara?' Rosa said, because there was no way she wanted to be in the sprawling *palazzo* alone with Vittorio but for a sprinkling of staff. It wasn't as if she had super powers. There was no way she was going to be able to stick to her guns and resist him until the wedding without help.

'If it means you'll do what I ask,' he conceded grumpily, 'then Chiara can come too.'

'I didn't think you were *asking*.' She sniffed. 'It sounded more like an order to me.'

He cursed under his breath. *Dio*, a man needed the patience of Job. But then, hadn't her father and brothers warned him?

'Okay,' he said, 'that's the first thing.'

'There's more?'

'I've organised sketches from some of the best designers to be delivered, so you can work out who you'd like to design and create your gown.'

'What if I want to make it myself?'

'Come on, Chiara—this isn't some cheap knock-off you'll be wearing when you walk down the aisle. This is going to be televised all over Europe and possibly the world. Do you want that kind of pressure?'

'I don't make cheap knock-offs.'

He held up his hands. 'Fine. Only I don't think you're going to have much free time in the next few weeks anyway.'

'Why?' she asked, her arms crossed against her chest. 'When you've already made me give up my job?'

'Because Enrico—my father's secretary—is preparing several volumes for you to study on the history, constitution and governance of Andachstein.'

'That sounds like bags of fun.'

'You'll need to be familiar with it all by the time you're required to attend and speak at official functions.'

'What functions?' She hadn't spoken in public since she'd been at school, and even in front of her school friends she'd been a bundle of nerves.

'Lots of them. The people have missed having a princess. My mother was patron of the children's hospital and at least a dozen other charitable organisations besides. You'll be expected to fill that role.'

She kicked up her chin. 'So I agree to marry you and I lose my life.'

'It's not all bad, Rosa,' he said, gritting his teeth. 'You gain me.'

'Huh,' she said, and turned away.

It wasn't an easy thing to do. She'd fallen a little bit in love with him that magical night of Carnevale and nothing had changed that. Not the fact that he'd disappeared for six weeks, because he'd been honest about that. And not the fact that he'd quietly neglected to inform her that he was a prince until it was too late and she'd already discovered she was pregnant.

Because she hadn't fallen a little bit in love with a prince. She'd fallen for the man. Vittorio. And lately he reminded her more and more of how he'd been that night. There was an edge to him, magnetic and powerful, bordering on dangerous, and the knowledge that she'd put it there by defying him was exciting. Intoxicating.

She didn't need an aphrodisiac. She still dreamed of him at night, still replayed their love scenes, every touch and every sound. She still longed to make love to him again and again.

But she wanted all of him this time. She didn't just want his lust. She wanted his affection. More than that, she yearned for his love.

Come the wedding, she would be bound to him. They would be man and wife under the sight of God and she would take her place in the marital bed. And she would enjoy it.

But for now the only thing she had control of, the only ace she had up her sleeve, was her resolve to keep Vittorio at arm's length. So he might look beyond the sex and see the woman she was.

If Vittorio had thought having Rosa residing in the *palazzo* might weaken her resolve and make her more accessible and more amenable to his affections, and if he'd thought he might pay her a little nocturnal visit, he had another think coming.

Rosa and Chiara were moving in amidst a whirl of excitement—mostly on Chiara's part. She was running up and down the stairs, shrieking at just about everything. But that wasn't the worst of it. He'd thought the move was taking longer than he'd expected, and he'd gone to see what was happening, and found his staff carrying beds around.

'What the hell is going on?' he bellowed as he watched them grappling with an ancient four-poster bed.

'Calm down,' snapped Rosa. 'There's no need to shout.'

'Just answer my question.'

She shrugged on a grin. 'We're simply moving this bed into my room.'

'You've already got a bed in your room.'

'But there isn't a bed for Chiara.'

'She has an entire bedroom at her disposal.'

'Oh, but Vittorio,' she said, 'we *like* sharing a room. How else are we going to talk late into the night?'

'You could always phone each other,' he said.

She laughed. 'That would be silly when we're in the same building.' She smiled up at him. 'Don't worry,' she said. 'It's only until the wedding.'

And she leaned up to press the lightest of kisses to his lips. A touch. A tease. A peck. And nowhere near enough. He tried to catch her and pull her close, but she'd whirled away, quicksilver in motion, before he could get hold of her.

He grumped back to his suite.

Only until the wedding.

He wanted her. He burned with wanting her. But what irked him more was that he could not help but admire her.

'Not a doormat,' Marcello had said.

Not a chance.

She was like a wily negotiator, the way she made her quiet demands. And there was no budging her. She would not be swayed. But she was definitely tempted. Otherwise why would she move Chiara into her room? She didn't trust herself and Chiara was her wall.

It was infuriating. She was defending the terms of their agreement like a tigress defending its cub.

He smiled a little at that. Whatever kind of father he turned out to be, he knew Rosa would make a good mother. He'd seen her holding her tiny niece and nephews. He'd seen the way she doted on them. And maybe, just maybe, she would help him be the kind of father he wished he'd had.

He sighed as he went to his room and rummaged through his closet for gym clothes. He could last. It seemed he had no choice but to burn off some energy in more conventional ways. But, hell, a man could burst with wanting her.

CHAPTER SEVENTEEN

ROSA RUBBED THE bridge of her nose and sighed as she studied the dusty tome in the library.

'What's wrong?' asked Chiara, who was lying on a chaise longue nearby and reading a bridal magazine.

'The constitution of Andachstein. It's the most boring thing I've ever read in my life. I'm never going to get through all these volumes. No wonder Vittorio said I wouldn't have enough time to make my own gown.'

'Hey,' Chiara said, flicking through the pages, 'Vittorio wants you to have a designer gown, and I say go for it. There's only a few weeks until the wedding. You'd be crazy to try and rush it yourself when a designer would have an entire team of seamstresses at their disposal. You can always make something else for the wedding. A garter for your leg, or Vittorio's bow tie.' She looked up suddenly. 'Do princes even wear bow ties to their own weddings?'

'Who knows?' said Rosa, turning back to her tome. 'Don't they usually wear medals or a sash?'

Chiara shrugged next to her, and for a while there was silence but for the flicking of pages—Chiara's magazine pages, because it was taking for ever for Rosa to make her way through even one of the pages in her turgid tome. She sighed again.

Chiara looked up. 'Tell you what. How about we take a look at some of those sketches from the designers Vittorio organised? You've barely looked at them and you don't have long to make a decision.'

'Yeah…' Rosa said, rubbing her forehead with her hand. She had barely looked at them because she'd had her heart set on designing and making her own gown, but time was slipping by and there was so much to do. So much to read. 'Maybe you're right.'

'Great,' said Chiara, jumping up. 'You could do with a break. I'll go get them. Be right back.'

Rosa sat back in her chair and closed her eyes. Her head ached with the effort of trying to make sense of the medieval mumbo jumbo she was reading. How was she ever supposed to get a handle on it all?

'Rosa?'

She opened her eyes with a start to see Vittorio standing in the wide doorway.

'Are you all right?'

Her heart skipped in her chest as he strode towards her purposefully, like a powerful cat, all grace and barely leashed power. In a soft winter-white sweater that hugged his sculpted chest and fitted black trousers he looked amazing, and her hands ached to reach out and trace the skinscape of his body through the luxurious wool.

'I'm fine,' she said.

But her skin was tingling, and she was feeling strangely vulnerable. It was the first time they'd been alone together since she'd moved into the *palazzo*. The first time she hadn't had Chiara's presence to shield her and give her the confidence to pretend to be unmoved and light-hearted.

There was no pretending to be unmoved now. Her mouth had gone dry.

'Then what is the problem?'

You, she wanted to say. She looked around him. *Where was Chiara?*

'These damned books,' she said. 'They're so boring. I can't be expected to read them all.'

'You don't like the history of Andachstein?'

'I don't see a lot to interest me so far, no.'

He smiled and looked around too, and she knew he was checking for Chiara. His smile widened when he didn't find her.

'Then maybe you are starting in the wrong place. Andachstein has a rich and fascinating history.' He rounded the desk. 'Perhaps I can show you.'

'It's okay,' she said, even as he leaned over her and examined the volumes on the desk. She felt his heat wrap around her, caress her like a breeze stirring a crop of grain, sparking her sensitive nerve-endings, coaxing her nipples into hard peaks.

'Have you read about the lace industry? That would interest you, surely?'

'Andachstein has a lace industry?'

He nodded and plucked one volume from the collection on the desk and opened it to a particular page. 'Here,' he said, pointing to where there were some photographs of various patterns of lace, some delicately shell-like, others resembling flowers. 'The then Princess Rienna wanted to open schools to girls. She invited a group of nuns to move from Bruges to Andachstein and start a school. They brought with them their lace-making skills and passed them on to the girls and women of the principality.'

Rosa tried to ignore his presence at her shoulder and concentrate on his words, but she could feel the puff of his breath in her hair and against her skin and it was all she could do not to turn her face to his.

'She sounds,' she said, trying to stop her voice sounding tremulous, 'very forward-thinking.'

'She was. She wanted to do something to repay Andachstein for saving her life and she saw this as a way.'

This time her head did turn to his—just a little. Her gaze caught the strength of his jaw, the curve of his lips and strong nose, and she looked away again, feeling dizzy. Breathless. She hadn't been this close to Vittorio for so long, and the masculine scent of him was like a drug.

Her eyes were fixed on the pages in front of her, her hands flat on the desk lest they move of their own volition towards him. *Where the hell was Chiara?*

'How was she saved by Andachstein?'

'Rienna was a Celtic princess, taken prisoner on a pirate ship bound for Constantinople. Various accounts say she had eyes the colour of sapphires. She'd been kidnapped from her home and intended as a gift for the Sultan, destined to join his harem as one of his concubines. There was a storm and the pirate ship got blown off course into Andachstein waters, where a naval vessel attacked the ship and freed the Princess. The girl's father was so grateful he offered her to the then Prince, whose own wife had died in childbirth, along with their stillborn son, one year earlier. Princess Rienna went on to bear him eight children, and her intensely blue eyes have been passed down through the generations ever since.'

This time Rosa did turn her head—all the way. She looked up at his cobalt eyes, entranced by the story of pirates and Celtic princesses and times long gone. 'Will our son have those same eyes?'

He turned those eyes down at her, and she felt her insides quiver.

'If he is my son.'

'You know he is your son.'

'I do,' he said, and his eyes were so intense that her breath hitched and she wasn't sure for a moment whether he was answering the same question. She knew that if he asked her in this moment if she wanted to make love to him she would utter those same two words.

His lips were closer. How had that happened when she hadn't taken her eyes from him? His lips were only a breath from hers now, the time that separated them no more than a heartbeat.

She was going to kiss him. There was nothing surer, no matter the bargain they'd made or the terms he'd agreed to. *Her* terms—except they didn't seem to matter now.

All that mattered was that Vittorio was here now.

'I found them!' Chiara breezed into the room and stopped dead.

Beside her Rosa was almost certain she heard Vittorio growl.

'Sorry, am I interrupting something?'

Rosa sprang up from her chair. 'No. Vittorio was just filling me in on some of Andachstein's history. Weren't you, Vittorio?'

'Something like that,' he said, pushing himself upright.

'Chiara and I are going to look at those sketches and choose a designer,' Rosa said, talking too fast but unable to stop herself. 'You were right, of course, I will never have time to make something myself.'

'In that case,' said Vittorio, looking from one woman to the other, 'I will leave you to it.'

And he departed.

'What was that about?' asked Chiara.

'Nothing,' said Rosa, both grateful and annoyed at Chiara's sudden reappearance. 'Show me the designs.'

Chiara looked as if she didn't believe her, but then her excitement returned. 'I think I've found the perfect gown. There are others too, but what do you think?'

Rosa took the sketch. It was an off-the-shoulder gown with a fitted bodice, three-quarter sleeves and a back finished with a row of tiny pearl buttons that dropped much lower. There was a long train and a cathedral veil trimmed in lace. Swatches of the suggested fabric—a white Shantung silk—and a sample of the veil were attached.

There were no embellishments apart from the row of tiny buttons at the back. Nothing fancy. Nothing fussy. Just sleek, unfettered design.

Rosa felt a zing of excitement. 'It's beautiful.'

Chiara grinned. 'It would look magic on you. You'll only be three months pregnant by then, and you shouldn't be showing, but even if you are it will be hidden by the cut of the skirt.'

Rosa quickly flipped through the pages to see the other designs. She stopped at one—a gown made entirely of lace. Andachstein lace. Her thumb fingered the swatches while she was thinking.

'You'd rather have a gown made in lace?' Chiara said.

Rosa smiled. 'No, but it's given me an idea.'

CHAPTER EIGHTEEN

ANDACHSTEIN'S CATHEDRAL WAS a grand affair on the headland overlooking the harbour, with origins that harked back to Roman times. The cathedral had been built and ruined and rebuilt over the ages, until the existing building had been erected from the ruins some time in the fourteenth century and extended half a dozen times since.

A testament to the architect's love and knowledge of arches, the cathedral boasted a long central aisle and a Gothic rose window at one end, with a golden domed nave at the other. Stained-glass windows had been added over the centuries.

Rosa knew all this as she stood at the entrance, her father by her side and Chiara behind her, to straighten her train and stop her veil blowing away. Vittorio had brought her here for a rehearsal, and she'd been stunned then by the magnificence and history of the place. The tiny chapel in the village where she'd grown up, where they'd said goodbye to her mother, seemed like a dot in a dusty landscape in comparison.

And now, with the music from the pipe organ sweeping out of the interior, rising to the moment where she would have to enter the cathedral, Rosa had a moment of self-doubt.

What was she doing here?

She'd been thrust into this position because of one passionate night that had been meant to be the end. She was marrying a man whose child she carried. They were about to exchange vows declaring that they would love and cherish each other, that they would forsake all others.

But did Vittorio love her? Would he ever love her enough to forsake all others? She wanted so much what her mother and father had shared. She wanted it all. Marriage, family, and love at the heart of it.

What if it never happened?

What if Vittorio never loved her?

She wouldn't be able to bear it.

She'd wither slowly from the inside out.

Her father must have noticed her shallow breathing. He patted the hand tucked under his arm.

'All right?' he asked, his forehead creased into a frown, concern lining his eyes.

She took a deep breath and found a weak smile to reassure him. Of course she was. She had to be. She thought of her unborn child, of the things she would be denying him if she turned her back on all this now, and she couldn't do it. Not just to satisfy her own personal needs and longings.

She smiled up at her father again. 'Bridal jitters,' she said. 'I'm fine.'

He kissed her then, and told her, 'You look beautiful today. No father could be prouder.'

Rosa gave a tremulous smile. How could she not look beautiful today? Her gown was divine. She'd decided on a simple sleek design, similar to the one in the sketch Chiara had shown her, and together with the designer had decided on a champagne-coloured silk. A long veil edged with Andachstein lace was held in place with a tiara that had belonged to Vittorio's mother and boasted a magnificent Brazilian topaz.

The whole ensemble was so utterly perfect she was glad she'd been talked out of trying to make a dress herself. Besides, it had given her time to tackle some other projects.

'My only regret is that your mother isn't here to witness this moment.' Her father gave a sad, soft smile, his eyes glazed. 'She would be so proud, and I know she is smiling down on you like the sun is today.'

'Don't make me cry,' Rosa pleaded, dabbing at her eyes.

And then there was no time for tears as the music shifted up a notch.

'There's our cue,' her father said as a footman gave him a signal. 'Are you ready?'

Rosa sucked in a breath, smiled weakly and nodded. 'Ready,' she said.

The sun through the stained-glass windows drenched the waiting congregation in puddles of coloured light. Dust motes glowed like sparks of gold in the vast space above. Either side of her were wall-to-wall smiles. But she didn't have eyes for any of it.

For there at the front, waiting for her, stood Vittorio, tall and proud. Her breath caught in her throat. Because, outfitted in the black dress uniform of the Andachstein Guard, trimmed with gold braid and buttons, once again he looked just as he had that first night—more like a warrior, or a warlord, or even a god, than any mere mortal.

He watched her approach...didn't take his eyes off her as she took every slow step down the aisle. He was smiling a little, she noticed as they grew closer, just enough to soften the hard angles and planes of his warrior face, and in his eyes she saw approval and satisfaction, desire and maybe even a little wonderment.

But was there room in them for a little love? She wanted with all her heart to see love there.

At the last moment she noticed her family, all smiles as they passed, and there was Prince Guglielmo watching too, wearing his perpetual frown and as beady-eyed as ever.

She drew level with her groom and he offered her his arm, his amazing blue eyes searching her face.

Beautiful, he mouthed, and her heart gave a little kick that had her trembling.

Tonight she would lie with this man in the marital bed. Tonight they would consummate this unlikely marriage and be as one. All this time Vittorio had thought *he* was the one missing out, the one hard done by, but he had no idea of the sacrifice she'd made in not giving in to her desires. She wanted to be back in his arms more than he knew. She'd longed for this night, this intimacy, this connection. But she was afraid of it too, and of what it might mean.

She'd told Vittorio that she was worried that this marriage would mean losing her independence. But tonight she knew she was in danger of losing herself.

The ceremony began. The priest spoke his solemn words, music soared at intervals, and a choir filled with what sounded like angels turned hymns into the sweetest sounds she had ever heard.

Rosa felt as if she was standing outside herself, watching on. How could it be her, Rosa Ciavarro, from a tiny village in the south of Italy, standing there marrying a prince? It was unbelievable. Surreal.

When they exchanged their vows it was Vittorio who sounded confident and assured in the soaring space, whose voice didn't waver. It was Vittorio who looked her in the eye and made her want to believe that some part of this was not just an act of convenience, going through the motions, that some part of it was real.

And then they were pronounced husband and wife, and their lips met in a kiss that had her doubting again. Because it was more businesslike than affectionate. Sealing the deal.

He walked her down the aisle a married woman—a princess—and she felt numb. Shell-shocked.

In a touch of unexpected informality the guests spilled out of the cathedral behind them, full of congratulations and good wishes for the newlyweds. She found herself separated from Vittorio as they were tugged in different directions, but even that didn't matter because everyone was so happy.

Until a woman latched on to her arm. 'I suppose I should congratulate you,' she said.

Rosa turned. There was no mistaking the vampish woman, even though Cleopatra had turned honey-blonde since she'd last seen her. 'Thank you, Contessa.'

'I'll let you into a little secret, though,' the woman whispered as she air-kissed Rosa's cheeks. 'He'll never love you. His lot are incapable of it.' She smiled as she stepped back. 'So you might as well lose those stars in your eyes right now.'

Rosa gasped, too stunned to speak. Was she that obvious? Was she so transparent that everyone could see the longing to be loved written plain on her face?

And then her brothers and their wives and children were swarming around her and she was surrounded by joy and love in abundance, and she almost felt greedy that she wanted more when she already had more than some people had in a lifetime.

'Where's my wife?' she heard a booming voice say over the crowd.

My wife.

A zing of electricity sent shockwaves down her spine. Possession. It was there in his words, there in his tone.

Nothing to do with love. It was all about lust, and anticipation for the evening ahead. She knew because the time had come and she felt it too.

And then the crowd parted and Vittorio was there, larger than life. His jewel-coloured eyes lit up when he saw her. 'Ah, there you are, my Princess. We have a state reception to get to,' he said. 'But first—'

He swept her up in his arms and kissed her, to the cheers of the crowd. Not like the kiss he'd given her in the cathedral—that one had been warm but brief. Sweet. Official, even. This was a kiss that spoke of barely restrained passion, of desire that was about to be taken off the leash. A kiss that left her breathless and weak-kneed and pulsing in places that knew how Vittorio could make them feel and wanted it as much as she did.

Maybe tonight she should just let herself be possessed. Maybe tonight should be all about desire. About slaking mutual need and lust.

And tomorrow, and all the tomorrows to come, maybe then she could worry about love.

The party was still raging, the orchestra still playing and wedding guests still dancing, when Vittorio approached Rosa and growled softly in her ear, 'It's time.'

Rosa had been enjoying herself, having found ten minutes to be with her family. She'd smiled when Chiara had taken to the dance floor yet again with Marcello. Marvelled when Prince Guglielmo had accompanied Sirena to the floor for a waltz. But mostly she'd just enjoyed being in the company of her family again. Soon they'd have to return to Zecce and she'd miss them.

But now Vittorio was telling her it was time. She trembled. His breath was warm against her skin, his own scent flavoured with the cognac he'd had with coffee. It was a powerful combination. Addictive.

Her heart was thumping in her chest as they made their exit and he walked her down the long passageway, their footsteps ringing out on the stone floor, the sounds of the reception given up to silence.

She didn't talk.

There were no words. And even if there had been, her throat was too tight.

He didn't talk.

He didn't rush. His steps were measured. Unhurried.

It was nerve-racking.

Excruciating.

A flight of stairs took them to the next level and then into his apartments. By the time he opened the door to his softly lit suite her nerves were stretched to breaking point. She knew her things had been moved into his suite while the formalities took place today, but this was the first time she'd seen his room. As she took it in, the dark wood furniture, the big leather sofas and the wide expanse of the massive four-poster bed, one word immediately sprang to mind.

Masculine.

He closed the solid door behind them with an equally solid *thunk*. She jumped at the sound.

'Nervous, my Princess?' he said, close behind her.

She'd dispensed with her veil before the reception, and now there was nothing between the puff of his breath and the nape of her neck. So close that she could feel his heat.

'It's been a long day,' she said.

She would have taken a step away, but his hands were already at her shoulders, and his lips—she gasped—his lips were pressed to that place where his breath had touched. Warmth suffused her flesh and threatened to turn her bones to jelly.

'Did I tell you,' he whispered, his thumbs stroking the bare skin of her back, 'how beautiful you look today?'

She nodded. He had—though not in so many words. And he'd made her believe it.

She'd expected he'd turn her then, and pull her into his kiss, but instead his thumbs traced a line down the V at her back, his touch sparking fires under her skin.

'And I love this dress,' he said, his fingers reaching the point where the row of tiny buttons began. 'But now it's time to do something I've been itching to do all evening.'

She felt his fingers settle on the top button. His long fingers on his big hands. She wanted to protest—he would never manage to undo the tiny buttons, she would have to call for a maid to help.

But she felt the first button give. His lips pressed to the other side of her neck and she felt the brush of his hair against her skin and breathed him in. She would have turned herself then, to kiss him, to replay that wondrous deep kiss he'd given her after they were married, but he wouldn't let her, and his surprisingly nimble fingers were still working away at the buttons.

But, as with his measured steps, he didn't rush. He took his own sweet time, pressing his lips to the skin of her exposed back as his fingers moved still lower, until he reached the small of her back, where the touch of his fingers tripped a secret cord that pulled tight inside her so that her muscles clenched. His hands were nowhere near her breasts, but she felt them swell, her nipples turning to bullets.

The gown was loosening around her. 'You don't have to do them all,' she said, surprised to hear how husky her voice sounded.

He chuckled softly against her skin and the sensation reverberated through her flesh and down to her bones.

'You sound impatient, my Princess.'

If she wasn't mistaken, his voice had gone down an octave.

'Surely you don't want me to hurry the most special night of your life?'

She was, and she did,—but she wasn't about to admit that.

She was at fever pitch when she felt the last button give. She felt his hands slide down inside her dress to cup her cheeks, and then sweep up her sides to cup her breasts. Breath caught in her throat. *At last!*

Then, and only then, he turned her and lifted her face to meet his. Lips met lips. Mouth slanted across mouth. Breath intermingled. And it was like returning to a fantasy place where her every dream came true.

She groaned, protesting into their kiss as he angled her away, but only to ease her arms from the sleeves and let the gown fall in a pool at her feet.

'*Dio...*' he said, looking down at her, taking in the tiny scraps of delicate lace that barely covered her breasts and the tiny triangle that concealed the V at the apex of her thighs. Thigh-high lace-topped stockings completed her underwear. 'What are you doing to me? All day long and you were as good as naked under that gown.'

Rosa felt empowered. 'Do you like them? I made them myself.' She could see by the flare and the heat in his eyes what his answer would be before she asked the question.

'Like them?' he said, his fingers tracing the intricate gold patterns in the lace.

'It's lace made by the Andachstein Lace-Makers' Guild. I ordered it especially.'

He lifted his eyes to hers. 'Did they have any idea what you planned to do with their lace?'

He sounded as if he had a lump in his throat that it was difficult to talk past. She smiled. 'Do you think they'd mind?'

'I'm not sure, but I've got a pretty good idea you've just committed an offence against the moral fabric of Andachstein society.'

'You'd charge me?'

'No, but only on one condition.'

'Which is?'

'You let me take them off.'

She smiled, hope creeping into her heart. 'I thought you'd never ask.'

He gave a roar of triumph and swept her into his arms, placing her reverently on the bed before shedding his dress uniform. Shoes and other garments were going everywhere, until he stood naked before her, proud and erect. She gasped. Her memories had failed her. Her dreams hadn't done him justice. The man was magnificent.

And now he leaned over her, kissing her lips, his big hands in her hair, cupping her cheek, following the curve of her shoulders and seeking the clasp for her bra, finding it.

He slid the fabric away and drew back. Air hissed through his teeth before he dipped his head again and drew one nipple into his hot mouth. So hot. Her back arched as he suckled, sending spears of pleasure straight to her core, and then again when he turned his attentions to her other breast.

'So beautiful,' he said, before he scooped his hands lower, over the curve of her abdomen and the flare of her hips.

She was panting when he dipped his head and pressed his lips over the place where their unborn child lay. So gentle. So tender. She wanted more. Needed more.

But he bypassed the heated place that screamed out for his attention, and moved straight to her ankles, sliding off first one high-heeled shoe and then the other, before kissing his way up her calf and then her inner thigh, until she was molten and pulsing with need.

'Vittorio!' she cried.

'I know,' he said, his hands curled into the sides of the scrap of lace that was all that separated them. 'I feel it too,' he said, and slowly drew them down her legs.

She was burning up before he slipped a hand between her thighs and coaxed them apart. She was on fire before he slipped one finger between her lips and brushed past that tight nub of nerve-endings, inciting it to fever-pitch.

'So hot,' he said on a groan.

'Vittorio!'

'I know,' he said again, soothing her as he knelt between her legs, his big hands palming her body, her breasts, her arms, her belly, her legs, as if he couldn't get enough of the feel of her. He poised himself over her, kissed her deep and hard, devouring her like a starving man who had been served up a feast.

She welcomed him at her entrance. Cried out with the contact, with the agony and the ecstasy of it, with the frustration and the promise. Cried out again when he surged into her, filling her, pausing before he withdrew and surged in again. This was skin against skin, his skin against hers in the most intimate of contacts, and it was pure magic.

She was already on the brink, already close, when he dipped his mouth and tugged on one peaked nipple. A shooting star flashed behind her eyes, one star that became two, and then another, until her world hurtled through the path of a meteor shower and everything was light and fire and the brilliance of feeling.

She was still spinning back down to earth, still finding her place back in the world and feeling warm and delicious when she said it.

It wasn't her fault—not entirely—but she was lulled by Vittorio's big body next to hers, his strong arms still around her, their legs interwoven, and they seemed the most natural words in the world to well up inside her at that moment.

She pressed her lips to his magnificent chest, felt the squeeze of his arm at her shoulders. *'I love you.'*

She felt him stiffen. Felt every muscle in his body tense. Felt him pull away.

'Vittorio…?'

'No,' he said, his body stiff as he rolled away. 'Don't say that. I didn't ask you to say that.'

Only then did she realise that she'd spoken out loud the words branding her heart.

'Why? What's wrong? I know it's too soon. But it's how I feel.' She reached out a hand to his shoulder, feeling as if she was losing him. 'I can't help how I feel.'

He sprang from the bed. 'Did I ask you to love me?

Don't love me,' he said. 'Never love me. Because I can't love you back.'

'Vittorio—'

'Don't you remember? I was a bastard to you at Carnevale. I used you.'

'What? That's all in the past. We're beyond that. Why are you dragging it out now?'

'Because you need to remember the kind of person I am. I don't love people, Rosa.'

'But now... Surely now that we're married—'

'You *know* why I married you. If you hadn't been pregnant we wouldn't be married now. It's got nothing to do with love.'

His words stung. So what if he was speaking the truth? It was his attitude that slashed at her soul. 'But it could. What is to stop me loving you and you loving me? It's normal. It's natural.'

'Not in my world!' he yelled. 'Do you think I can simply flick a switch? So don't love me. Don't ever tell me you love me. And don't expect anything of me. It's not going to happen.'

'You just made love to me—'

'It was *sex*, Rosa. Just sex! That's all it was. It's time you understood that. That's all it can ever be.'

He stormed out of the room through a side door that slammed heavily in his wake. She heard water running. A shower. And she sensed he wouldn't be back to share her bed tonight.

She sat shell-shocked in the bed, perilously close to tears, her wedding night reduced to ashes, her hopes and dreams in tatters. But she refused to let loose the tears. She took great gulps of air until the urge to cry was suppressed, even as Sirena's words came back to haunt her.

'He'll never love you. His lot aren't capable of it.'

What was Vittorio so afraid of? He'd acted as if it was

a curse. A horrid affliction for which there was no cure and death the only release. But there was nothing to fear from love.

And he was wrong, she knew it. He *could* love. A man who had grown up from a boy who would rescue a drowning kitten. A man who rescued strays and the vulnerable. This was not a man devoid of love.

He just didn't know how to show it.

Or maybe he just didn't know how to show it to *her*. Maybe he'd loved his first wife so much that he'd never got over her death.

Rosa was too afraid to ask. That wasn't a conversation she wanted to have on their wedding night.

The new bride sniffed, a new resolution forming in her mind. She knew how to sew. She was good at stitching pieces of fabric together and making something good, something worthwhile. So she would take the tattered shreds of her hopes and dreams and stitch them back together.

Because, despite what Vittorio had told her to do, there was no way she was giving up on her hopes and dreams just yet.

CHAPTER NINETEEN

THE NEW PRINCESS of Andachstein threw herself into her role. She visited the local primary schools and read the children storybooks and every child was entranced. She gave speeches at colleges into which she incorporated her newfound knowledge of the history and the proud heritage of Andachstein.

Wherever she appeared with Vittorio they were mobbed by cheering crowds waving the Andachstein flag. And when the first pictures of her baby bump were snapped and flashed to the world by the media, satisfaction levels regarding the principality went through the roof.

And if Vittorio himself wasn't entirely happy with how things were proceeding, Prince Guglielmo was beside himself. 'You got yourself a gem there, Vittorio,' he said during their weekly meeting. 'An absolute gem.'

Vittorio couldn't disagree. Rosa was proving perfect in the role. She was proving perfect in his bed. This night of their wedding had been an aberration. She'd made no unwanted transgressions since. But then, how could she when she said nothing at all? Sure, she was passionate enough, but they made love without a word from her. It was as if she was there in body, but not in soul.

But wasn't that what he wanted?

'What is the Princess up to today?' his father asked, dragging him out of his misery.

For the first time Vittorio noticed that his father looked a little better. A little younger than he had before. It couldn't all be down to the recent haircut he'd clearly had.

Vittorio leaned one hip against the desk and tossed the crystal paperweight from one hand to the other. It spoke volumes for his father's lighter mood that he barely blinked at Vittorio's audacity. He sighed.

'She's at a meeting of the Lace-Makers Guild. She's asked to become their patron. Apparently the women were delighted to have a patron who is herself a seamstress.'

The old man nodded his approval. 'Her first solo appointment? Impressive. We're not working her too hard, are we?'

'I don't think so.'

But maybe that was the problem, Vittorio mused, looking out of the window at the harbour below. Maybe she was just tired.

He shook his head and turned back to his father. 'Rosa seems to be loving it. And the baby is growing well. Rosa just had her twenty-week scan. All is looking good.'

'Good! So we're still expecting a boy?'

Vittorio smiled. 'That is now beyond doubt.' He'd seen the unmistakable evidence on the screen himself.

The old Prince grunted. 'Excellent.' And then he sighed and walked to stand in front of one of the big picture windows, his hands clasped behind his back. 'Late November, then...' he said, his voice reflective.

'That's what they say.'

'My doctors say there is a new technique. Still risky, but less so.'

For a moment Vittorio searched for this thread in the conversation, and then his father spun around and said, 'I'm thinking I would like to see my grandson growing up. I'm thinking I should tell the doctors to go ahead with my surgery.'

'But still risky?' Vittorio queried.

'Eighty per cent chance of success, they tell me. That sounds better than one hundred per cent chance of death if I don't have it, wouldn't you say?'

Vittorio left his father in unusually high spirits. The chance offered by surgery, he guessed. That would do it.

But then he saw Sirena walking towards him. 'Contessa,' he said.

She smiled. She was dressed in what he'd heard was called a 'tea dress', all big floral skirts and a tribute to the fifties, right down to the gloves, hat and strappy shoes.

'*Buongiorno*, Vittorio,' she said, stopping to kiss him on both cheeks. 'I hope married life agrees with you.'

'What are you doing here, Contessa?' he asked, sidestepping the question. He'd hoped that now he was married she would set her sights on some other target.

'I have an appointment with Guglielmo.'

'With my father?'

'Well, not really an appointment, as such. We're having a picnic down by the lake. It's such a beautiful day for a picnic, don't you think?' She raised her eyebrows and gave a flutter of her gloved hand. 'I'd better go. He's waiting for me.'

And with a click-clack of her heels she was gone, and Vittorio was left thinking, maybe she already had.

Rosa had enjoyed her first solo appointment. She'd been right to tell Vittorio she could handle this one herself.

The women of the Lace-Makers' Guild had made her so welcome. They'd given her an amazing display of their craft—flashing hands shifting threaded bobbins and pins—and she'd been dazzled by their skills. They'd even given her a lesson in lace-making, and watched patiently while she'd attempted to follow the pattern before declaring that she was much better at using their lace in her sewing projects than creating it. Then they'd all laughed and shared late-morning tea together.

Then they'd presented her with two gifts. One a lace shawl for their baby. So fine and beautiful, with a pattern of doves cleverly tatted through it. And the second a pair of pillowcases for the royal bed. Exquisitely made, they must have taken weeks and weeks to create.

She'd promised them that they would be cherished, even if she couldn't think about her marriage bed without a tinge of sadness. It had been weeks since their marriage—weeks during which she'd said not a word during their lovemaking. Weeks during which she wasn't even sure Vittorio had noticed.

A group of children were waiting with their teachers outside the Lace-Makers' Guild, pre-schoolers from the nearby kindergarten, huddled under a shady tree, out of the hot July sun. All she wanted to do was be out of the hot sun too, and inside the air-conditioned comfort of her waiting car, being whisked back to the cool confines of the *castello* high above the town, where the summer heat didn't seem to penetrate.

But the children were waiting for her, and she wasn't about to disappoint them. She knelt down to their level just as a delivery van trundled slowly past, pulling to a stop a few houses up the street. Rosa took no notice of the man who jumped out with a parcel under his arm—she was already talking to the children.

A little boy presented her with a posy of flowers.

A little girl in a wheelchair was wheeled forward to ask a question.

'Can I be a princess when I grow up?' she asked shyly.

Rosa took her small hand in hers, and said, 'You can be anything you want.'

The little girl threw her arms around Rosa's neck and hugged her tight. And Rosa thought that it wasn't so bad, being a princess, even if your husband didn't think he could love you.

Someone shouted something up the road. There was a murmur of concerned voices, and then more shouting, but she was still disentangling herself from the girl's arms when she heard her driver call, 'Your Highness! Watch out!'

Children started shrieking. 'Run this way!' she heard one teacher call.

She turned her head to see her driver lunging for her. But there was something that would beat him. The delivery truck, bearing down on them, with a man futilely chasing after it.

Fight or flight? There was no question.

She pushed the wheelchair as hard as she could and flung herself after it.

CHAPTER TWENTY

VITTORIO WAS FURIOUS by the time he got to the hospital. Furious with himself. He should never have agreed to let Rosa go by herself today. And he was furious with everyone who might have had a part in this.

But most of all he was furious because of all the things he could have said to her and never had. All the things he *should* have said to her. And all the cruel things he'd said to her because he had been so desperate to protect himself.

'What happened?' he demanded of her driver as he marched along the disinfectant-smelling corridor in the hospital. 'I want to know everything that happened and in detail. And then I want to know *how* it happened.'

It was all the chauffeur could do to keep up with him, let alone give him a detailed account of all that had transpired.

'The delivery vehicle is being checked over now,' the man said. 'But it looks like brake failure.'

'On a damned hill, of all places,' Vittorio said, seething, 'and right above where Rosa was standing.'

'The Princess was kneeling down,' said the driver, 'talking to a child in a wheelchair. The child was hugging her. The Princess didn't know what was happening until too late.'

A doctor strode towards them. 'Prince Vittorio, I'm Dr Belosci. I'm looking after the Princess. I'll take you to her. We're prepping her for Theatre now.'

Fear slid down Vittorio's spine.

He dismissed the driver, waiting for him to be out of earshot. 'Is it the baby?' Nobody had told him there was a problem with the baby—but then nobody had mentioned Theatre either.

'No. Didn't they tell you? The baby's fine. It's Her Highness's ankle. A tree took the brunt of the crash, but a tyre snapped free with the force of the collision and caught her on the ankle.'

Breath whooshed out of Vittorio's lungs. 'She's going to be all right, then?'

'They're both going to be fine. Just as soon as we can get that ankle set. Come and see her, and then I'll show you the X-rays.'

The baby was all right, his heartbeat sound and strong. Someone had come and told her that the little girl in the wheelchair had got a bump on the head but was fine. It couldn't be better.

Rosa hugged her baby bump while she drifted in and out of dreamland. She'd told them she didn't want a fuss, that she would be just as happy back in her own bed in the *castello*, but they'd insisted, telling her she was to be attached to a drip and that she needed an operation on her ankle.

And then she'd remembered the pain as she'd waited for the ambulance and thought maybe it was better to be here in hospital after all. At least it was quiet here.

She heard voices coming down the corridor. Loud voices. No—one loud voice and one quieter. No guessing which one was Vittorio's.

She put one hand to her head. *Dio*, why had they had to tell him? Couldn't they have waited until after the operation? The baby was fine. It wasn't as if he wanted to see *her*.

The door to her room creaked open. 'Rosa?' he said.

She turned her head away. 'The baby's fine, Vittorio. Didn't they tell you?'

'Yes, they told me.'

'So, thanks for coming, but don't feel you need to stay. I'm in good hands here.'

'Rosa, I came to see *you*.'

She laughed. Maybe it was the drugs in her drip, or maybe she was just fed up with being silent, but she wasn't going to stay silent any more. 'Nice one, Vittorio, but I don't think so.'

'Rosa—'

She snapped her head around. 'What are you still doing here? Staying long enough to convince the staff we're madly in love, like you pretended to be at our wedding? Well, I don't read the tabloids—and even if I did that fantasy died a death on our wedding night, thanks to you. So I don't need you to stay, Vittorio. I don't *want* you to stay.'

But he didn't leave. Infuriatingly, he sat down in the visitor's chair beside the bed.

'For once and for all, the baby is fine. I'm sure someone here will let you know the moment that changes. Can you please go?'

She heard him sigh, and was about to snap at him again when he said, 'I didn't come here because of the baby.'

'Liar,' she said, but she was curious enough to hear what else he had to say.

'All right. I was worried about the baby. But I came because you'd been hurt and I was worried about you. Because today I realised something that has been staring me in the face for almost as long as we've been together.'

Her heart slammed into her chest wall. She barely dared to breathe waiting for him to continue. 'What did you realise?' she said when he wouldn't tell her.

'That I care for you, Rosa. I just didn't want to admit it because I was afraid you might leave me. When I heard about the accident today I thought I might lose you without ever telling you…'

'But why were you afraid I'd leave you?'

'Because my first wife did. Because she told me she loved me and she lied. Because she betrayed me, and I was scared it might happen again.'

'You thought I might *betray* you?'

He laughed. 'I know. It seems ridiculous. But I had to protect myself somehow. Not loving you—not admitting it—seemed the best way.'

She blinked up at him, wondering if he was really there, wondering if the drugs were giving her hallucinations and spinning stories that she wanted to hear. 'So what are you admitting?'

He took her free hand. 'I love you, Rosa. I'm sorry I made you sad. I'm sorry I ruined our wedding night. If I could make it up to you I would, a thousand times over.'

Tears pricked Rosa's eyes. 'Only one thousand?'

He smiled down at her and pressed his lips to hers before he said. 'Every night of our marriage. How does that sound instead?'

She smiled tremulously up at him. 'Much better. I love you so much, Vittorio.'

He gave a smile of wonderment then, as if he was exploring the new territory of these words and finding it to be everything he wanted and more. 'I love you, Rosa.'

They kissed just as the doctor bustled in.

'I'm so sorry to interrupt,' he said. 'Theatre is ready.'

'Don't be,' Vittorio said, smiling down at Rosa. 'We've got the rest of our lives to finish this.'

EPILOGUE

PRINCE GUGLIELMO ROBERTO D'MARBURG of Andachstein was born late one November morning, with a shock of black hair, a healthy set of lungs and weighing in at a very healthy four kilograms.

Measurements had been taken, paperwork completed, and the nursing staff had left now that the formalities were complete. Finally it was time for the new family to be left alone to bond.

Rosa relaxed into the pillows on the bed, her baby cradled in her arms, and leaned down to drink in his new baby breaths. 'He's so beautiful,' she said, her heart already swollen in size to accommodate this new love.

The baby yawned then, cracking open his eyes. 'Look,' she said. 'Blue eyes like sapphires. He's like a mini you.'

Vittorio sat by her side, one hand stroking his wife's still damp hair, the other under the arm holding their child, totally entranced.

'You were amazing,' he said to her. 'So strong.'

She shrugged, the pain of childbirth gone now that she was holding her reward. 'That's what women do. All around the world every day. It's not that special.'

'It's a miracle,' he said. 'Today I witnessed a miracle, performed by the woman I love.'

She smiled over at him. Things had been so different since her accident. Something had shifted in her warrior's hard and cynical heart, and the word he'd been most afraid to use and to hear was now a word she heard several times a day. And it would never grow old.

'Thank you,' she said. 'I love you, Vittorio.'

He lifted the closest of her hands and kissed it gently. 'And I love *you*. For this child you have given me. For just being you. But most of all I love you for loving me.'

Tears sprang from her eyes. Tears of joy.

'I made you cry,' he said, touching the pads of his forefingers to her eyes to wipe away the dampness.'

'Only because I'm so happy.'

'Then never stop crying,' he said, smiling. 'Thank you for rescuing me, Rosa. That day I found you lost by the bridge in Venice... I look back at that moment and I see...'

'Serendipity?' she offered.

'No,' he said. 'It was magic. Pure magic.'

And he leaned over and kissed the woman he loved.

* * * * *

COMING SOON!

We really hope you enjoyed reading this book. If you're looking for more romance, be sure to head to the shops when new books are available on

Thursday 8th August

To see which titles are coming soon, please visit

millsandboon.co.uk/nextmonth

MILLS & BOON

Coming next month

HIS CINDERELLA'S ONE-NIGHT HEIR
Lynne Graham

'So...er...the job?' Belle prompted tautly.

'The job would be a little unusual but completely above board,' he assured her and then, as though suddenly recollecting his manners, he moved closer to extend a lean hand. 'My name is Dante Lucarelli.'

'Yes.' Belle barely touched the tips of his fingers. 'The bartender identified you before you'd been seated for five minutes. He's a business student.'

'Tell me about yourself,' he urged.

'There's not a lot relevant to tell,' Belle retorted uncomfortably, wishing he would just get to the point instead of keeping her in ignorance. 'I'm twenty-two. I left school at sixteen with a bundle of GCSEs and I haven't had any educational input since then. I'd like to change that when I get back to London. These days you need training and qualifications to make a decent life.'

'If you know that why did you skip that opportunity until now?'

'I never *had* the opportunity,' Belle countered wryly, settling down on the concrete bench beneath the trees. 'My grandmother died and then my grandfather fell ill and needed looking after. After they were both gone, I took a job here, which was basically housekeeping but which turned into full-time caring as well.'

Dante lounged back against a tree trunk, all lithe, lean power and thrumming masculinity. He was as relaxed as she was tense. 'Is caring for older people what you want to do going forward?'

Belle stiffened. 'No, definitely not. I think professional caring's a job you need a vocation for and I don't have that.'

'Fair enough,' Dante murmured, increasingly surprised by her cool, unapologetic self-containment because at the very least he had expected bubbly encouragement and flirtation from her. In his experience women came onto him whether they thought they had a chance with him or not, but Belle wasn't making the smallest effort in that direction. 'You may not have a vocation for the job I'm about to offer you either, but it *would* eventually get you back to the UK and I would *pay* you handsomely to do it.'

Belle twisted round to get a better view of him, wishing he would step out of the shadows so that she could see him better. 'Tell me about it…'

'I need a woman prepared to pretend that she's my live-in girlfriend. Faking the part would be *all* that was required from you,' Dante assured her with calm emphasis. 'The job would only last for a couple of weeks and then you would be free to pursue your own plans with the cash I give you. It would be a win-win proposition for both of us.'

Belle was rarely deprived of speech, but the shock of the nature of his job offer was sufficient to glue her tongue to the roof of her mouth because such an exotic possibility wouldn't have crossed her mind in her wildest dreams. 'But…er…you don't even know me,' she protested weakly when she could find her voice again.

'Why would I need to know you? Steve vouches for your trustworthiness. It's a job, a role if you want to call it that. It's casual and temporary but also financially rewarding,' he completed smoothly.

'But pretending to be someone's girlfriend would mean knowing stuff about each other, that sort of thing,' Belle protested in a rush. 'And we're complete strangers.'

Continue reading
HIS CINDERELLA'S ONE-NIGHT HEIR
Lynne Graham

Available next month
www.millsandboon.co.uk

MILLS & BOON
MODERN
Power and Passion

Prepare to be swept off your feet by sophisticated, sexy and seductive heroes, in some of the world's most glamourous and romantic locations, where power and passion collide.

Eight Modern stories published every month, find them all at:

millsandboon.co.uk/Modern

LET'S TALK
Romance

For exclusive extracts, competitions
and special offers, find us online:

facebook.com/millsandboon

@MillsandBoon

@MillsandBoonUK

Get in touch on 01413 063232

For all the latest titles coming soon, visit
millsandboon.co.uk/nextmonth

MILLS & BOON

THE HEART OF ROMANCE

A ROMANCE FOR EVERY KIND OF READER

MODERN

Prepare to be swept off your feet by sophisticated, sexy and seductive heroes, in some of the world's most glamourous and romantic locations, where power and passion collide.
8 stories per month.

HISTORICAL

Escape with historical heroes from time gone by. Whether your passion is for wicked Regency Rakes, muscled Vikings or rugged Highlanders, awaken the romance of the past.
6 stories per month.

MEDICAL

Set your pulse racing with dedicated, delectable doctors in the high-pressure world of medicine, where emotions run high and passion, comfort and love are the best medicine.
6 stories per month.

True Love

Celebrate true love with tender stories of heartfelt romance, from the rush of falling in love to the joy a new baby can bring, and a focus on the emotional heart of a relationship.
8 stories per month.

Desire

Indulge in secrets and scandal, intense drama and plenty of sizzling hot action with powerful and passionate heroes who have it all: wealth, status, good looks…everything but the right woman.
6 stories per month.

HEROES

Experience all the excitement of a gripping thriller, with an intense romance at its heart. Resourceful, true-to-life women and strong, fearless men face danger and desire - a killer combination!
8 stories per month.

DARE

Sensual love stories featuring smart, sassy heroines you'd want as a best friend, and compelling intense heroes who are worthy of them.
4 stories per month.

To see which titles are coming soon, please visit

millsandboon.co.uk/nextmonth

JOIN US ON SOCIAL MEDIA!

Stay up to date with our latest releases, author
news and gossip, special offers and discounts, and
all the behind-the-scenes action
from Mills & Boon...

 millsandboon

 millsandboonuk

 millsandboon

It might just be true love...